The Garden
of
Lost and Found

Harriet Evans

REVIEW

First published in Great Britain in 2019 by
HEADLINE REVIEW
An imprint of HEADLINE PUBLISHING GROUP

2

Cataloguing in Publication Data is available from the British Library

ISBN 978 1 4722 6192 2 (Hardback)
ISBN 978 1 4722 5104 6 (Trade Paperback)

Typeset in Garamond MT Std by Palimpsest Book Production Limited,
Falkirk, Stirlingshire

Printed and bound in Great Britain by Clays Ltd, Elcograf S.p.A.

Headline's policy is to use papers that are natural, renewable and recyclable
products and made from wood grown in sustainable forests. The logging and
manufacturing processes are expected to conform to the environmental
regulations of the country of origin.

HEADLINE PUBLISHING GROUP
An Hachette UK Company
Carmelite House
50 Victoria Embankment
London EC4Y 0DZ

www.headline.co.uk
www.hachette.co.uk

For my Martha

'The future is yet unwritten; the past is burnt and gone'
Inscription on the plaque of The Garden of Lost and Found
Sir Edward Horner, 1900

The children who played in the garden:

Helena & Charlotte Myrtle

Helena's daughter Lydia Dysart Horner

Her children Eliza, John & Stella Horner

Stella's son Michael Horner

His daughter Juliet Horner

Her children Beatrice, Isla & Sandro Taylor

Prologue

I

June 1918

For the rest of her life, after it happened, she would wonder if she could have stopped it. If she'd checked on Ned earlier – he had been *so* peculiar since their return from London – if she had understood what her husband really intended to do when he spent every last penny they had buying back *The Garden of Lost and Found*, if she'd not been sitting at her desk staring into space, remembering, if she'd *noticed* more, could she have stopped it? But by the time Lydia Dysart Horner reached her husband's studio, it was too late to save perhaps the most famous – certainly the most beloved – painting in the world from the flames.

It was June. Liddy had been in the drawing room, the french windows open to the garden which was then at its most lovely, the perfume of jasmine, rose and lavender hanging faint in the air. Periodically, as she sifted listlessly through the ever-present pile of unpaid bills, she would inhale deeply, trying to catch the scent of the flowers over the smell of musty books and carpets, gas lamps and Zipporah's cooking: a leg of mutton, studded with rosemary. Liddy had cut the rosemary that morning, and she had also dug up the new potatoes herself, smooth gold nuggets in the black soil. She had picked the flowers for the table: heavy roses, lilac, geums, in shades of violet, dusky-pink, dark red, all from her garden.

They had come to this house twenty-four years ago almost to the day, one bright hopeful June afternoon when the willow wept in the stream beyond and the thrusting young green oak, which now towered over the house, was still a sapling. The countryside was at the height of its glory and they were weary and sick with travel. Ned had handed his young wife – *they were both so young*, no more than children really – out of the cart, and then carried her down the drive. She had sprained her ankle back at their old cottage – the dear Gate House, how long since she had thought of it! – and it was never quite right afterwards, not even now. Liddy could recall still how, as she was borne by Ned towards the threshold, she could feel the uneasy sensation of wanting to attend to her hair – the great coil falling down about her shoulders after the jolting of the cart on the uneven road – but his hands gripped her tight, his face shiny with exertion and with the furious conviction which drove him in everything, which killed him in the end.

'Liddy – listen! There are nightingales in the trees, I've heard them at night. I've heard the songs they sing.'

The tall, strange house welcomed you in but would not really ever be owned by people, merely inhabited by them. It had been built in lichen-flecked golden Cotswold stone that stayed cool in summer and trapped the sunshine in winter. A Virginia creeper smothered the south side, lime-green in spring, raspberry-pink in autumn. Lacy white hydrangeas flourished beneath the study and dining room windows. There were owls around the door, squirrels above and, perched proudly atop the house, four stone nightingale finials on the roof.

They were on her doll's house too, and that is how she recognised where he had brought her.

The memories, you see. They caught in her throat, that time, all those times.

John's first steps, unsteady, determined, so tiny, so world-destroying, down the curved steps into the Wilderness, to find his sister singing her specially adapted song from *Mother Goose* that she used to sing him.

'John John, the painter's son, Stole a cake and away he rund.'

The frosted Christmas morning when Eliza crept out early and returned carrying trails of ivy and stiff sharp holly into the house, her face red with the cold.

The first time Mary came to stay, her sweet dark face at the door, tears in her eyes, and her honeyed low voice: 'I can feel Mama here,

Liddy – she's here, isn't she?' But it had been eighteen years now and she did not even know if Mary was alive or dead.

The time of the painting – that golden summer when she sat for hours. The children – fairies, dancing in the garden, as the light faded, wearing their bird wings and Ned mad to catch it all, trapping the memories and the love and setting it down on canvas . . .

The trundle of the bicycle that iron-cold morning bringing the telegram, the birds frozen dead on the branches. All dead. She had tipped the telegram boy. Quite calmly.

Liddy had dreams in which another woman sat at the desk, this desk, her hair piled up like Liddy's, and looked out down at the garden. This woman was not her, but she could never see her face.

It was hard to concentrate, that afternoon. The spring had been dreadfully cold and the sudden glory of summer that afternoon was especially welcome. Letting a butcher's bill fall from her fingers, Liddy sat in near-content, drowsily listening out for the nightingales, the sound of a droning bumblebee at the glass only adding to her soporific state.

Then she caught the smell. Faint at first, sweetly spiced, the smell of winter.

But the fires were never lit in the house after Whitsun, at her direction. Nor was the smell in the garden. Darling, the gardener knew better than to light a fire when the birds might be nesting. And some instinct, some past muscle memory of disaster, made her rise and push past the desk out on to the terrace, where the smell of roses mingled more strongly now with the other.

It was the smell of burning. A fire.

Liddy ran towards the Dovecote, the ancient banqueting house on the edge of the grounds that was Ned's studio. Already she could hear the crackle and spit of burning wood, then a splintering sound, and an unearthly, almost inhuman cry. She picked up her pace, the heels of her small silk shoes sinking into the soft earth, the heavy dusky-pink silk of her dress slick against her legs like water, and as she reached the small building and paused in the doorway she cried out, hands raised above her head.

Ned was standing in front of a leaping, greedy, orange fire. White sparks flew from the flames and he grabbed at them with his hands, clutching, waving, feet stamping on the ground.

'Gone!' he was shrieking, fingers manically plucking at the dazzling flashes of fire. 'Gone! Gone! Gone!' His voice, like a bird, high-pitched, screaming. 'Gone!'

'Ned!' Liddy cried, trying to make him hear her over the roar of the fire. 'Darling! Ned!' As she reached him, she grabbed his shoulders to turn him away from the flames but he pushed her roughly aside, with the strength of a madman.

'I'm going to do it,' he said, and he didn't look at her, but through her. As though she wasn't there. The apples in his cheeks shone red. 'I've made it vanish. A magic trick! It won't haunt us any more, Liddy! It can't hurt us!'

The heat made her face ache, but she stared, mouth agape. She knew what she would see even before she looked over.

The Garden of Lost and Found had been on an easel in his studio since Ned had bought it back, eight months ago. He kept it wrapped in brown paper fastened with string. This, she could see, had been undone, the seal broken, the paper roughly tied up again. She could see too the edges of the painting's gold frame peeking out. And as she watched, Ned picked the package up and hurled it on to the fire.

Liddy screamed, as though in pain – the frame caught alight instantly. She lunged for the fire, eyes fixed on the paper, the gold frame melting, buckling away into nothing, disappearing before her very eyes, but he pushed her back.

Her children, their dear curved backs, the exquisite concentration, the wings that glowed golden in the setting sun – he had caught them, caught them perfectly and now they were burning. She could see no trace of them at all, only the plaque: '*The Garden of Lost and Found*: Sir Edward Horner, R.A. 1900' and the inscription underneath, licked by the greedy, hateful flames.

The noise! How could she have known a fire could roar, and scream, like this?

She strained against him. 'Ned,' she sobbed. 'Darling, how could you?' She managed to drag him back a few steps, pressing her hand to his clammy forehead. He was icy, his eyes glassy. 'Oh dear God – why?'

'He won't come back again. I've burned him. He's gone away. She's gone away. The little birds have all gone away,' was all he would say.

Liddy drew his shaking body towards her. He was trembling, hardly aware of where he was. Fear plucked at her stomach, her throat.

'Darling, come into the house,' she said. 'You're not well.'

But he shoved her back. 'I am well. I am well.' He clasped her hands, as a thick, feathering black plume of smoke caused her to cough and her eyes to stream. 'Now we won't have to look at them again,' he said, quite clearly, one side of his face in shade, the other orange-pink, licked by the light of the fire. 'The fire has cleansed us. Now, Liddy, this too.'

He pushed her away, and reached for the little oil sketch of *The Garden of Lost and Found* that had always hung in the corner of the studio. With all her strength Liddy yanked it from him and turning, she pushed him out into the garden, setting the sketch down, then turned back to the fire. She grabbed all the clothes and rags she could, realising with increasing terror that the turpentine in them would send the studio up in seconds. Everything else in it would be gone, too. There was a carpet rolled up on the floor: she hauled it over the flames, its weight pulling her hands on to the fire and she felt the searing, white-hot pain of melting flesh, smelled the sizzling of her own skin and looked down in surprise to see her own hands, burning. With more presence of mind than she had ever known, and some act of preservation for a future she could not see, with one hand Lydia held her silk skirt away, with the other lifted one leg and stamped, heavily, down on the carpet, on the fire, as hard as she could.

Up at the house they had realised what was happening. She could hear the cries, echoing down to them. 'Fire at the Dovecote! Water! Bring water!'

She staggered out of the little building, eyes streaming. Blinking, she peered at her own hands, red and raw, and could not feel any

7

pain. Zipporah and little Nora appeared from the kitchen, racing towards her. Nora's apron fluttered out in the breeze from the fire as Zipporah threw a basin of water on to the flames licking at the edge of the carpet. Darling materialised from the tangled garden, pushing a wheelbarrow with a metal bath in it, spilling over with water, his ancient bow-legged frame steadying the wheelbarrow's progress.

'Mrs Horner! Madam!' Nora was pointing in horror at the ground behind Liddy. Ned had collapsed to the floor, quite white. He half opened his eyes and there was some reason in them then. He beckoned her, and as she crouched down beside him, he said, quietly, in his old voice:

'Liddy,' he said. 'I don't feel well, my bird. I don't feel well.'

He had been in the studio all that previous day, then out for a long walk most of the afternoon, not returning till evening, when they had dined with Lord and Lady Coote. He had barely said a word then, nor afterwards. He had been distracted, volatile: last night, he had come to her bed and taken her, the first time he had claimed her in many months, though she thought he barely knew who she was. That morning as she considered the passion of his late-night visit, how he cried as he reached his crisis, her heart ached for him, even though after all these years so much had happened to separate them. She knew he was at his lowest ebb, since John had been lost.

He had not been as close to John as Liddy, but it had seemed to affect him more than her. He was utterly diminished, these last few months. Sir Edward Horner was out of fashion; it was years now since the Royal Academy had hired guards and put up cordons to control the crowds around his paintings. He was popular but had grown staid, producing patriotic works of Empire. He was not the same Ned Horner who had set the art world alight, nearly thirty years ago now. And this business with buying the painting back . . .

She knew he had grown to hate what *The Garden of Lost and Found* had come to mean, how it was mocked by so many now as a symbol of late-Victorian sentimentality. There had even been a *Punch* cartoon about it. '*Edna! Edna! I insist you come away from that*

8

painting. We can't afford to launder any more handkerchiefs, do you hear?'
It ate away at him. Not at Liddy. Liddy could not be hurt any more.

Now she put his head on her lap. He murmured something.

'He's gone now,' he said. 'It was right, wasn't it?'

'What?'

But his eyes were fixed, unseeing. *I wish you'd tell me*, she whispered in his ear. *I love you. I will always love you. Don't leave me alone here. Tell me why you did it.*

But she was never to know. Ned never regained consciousness. He slipped away a week later, one of millions to die from the influenza which would ravage the country, the continent, the world. It killed more people than had died in the Great War. It killed ten in the village, dear Zipporah, Farmer Tolley, their neighbour at Walbrook Farm, Lady Coote and Lady Charlotte Coote, leaving old Lord Coote alone, his two sons having already fallen in the war. It killed Nurse Bryant, she was to discover, and so finally Liddy was free. But she was all alone.

The day after Ned died Liddy, her burnt hands wrapped tightly in gauze, had swept the stone floor of the Dovecote. The fire had left a dark grey-red stain upon the golden-grey flagstones. She did wonder whether to keep the ashes as some kind of memorial but instead she brushed them into a sheet and, standing on the steps that led down to the Wilderness she shook them out into the garden. They fell, showering the sloping tangle of colour far and wide, like black and grey snow in June, as Liddy stood and watched, turning the small brass plaque in her bandaged hand.

By some miracle the plaque had remained intact, all that survived of the most famous painting of the age. In the year after its first rapturous reception at the Summer Exhibition it had gone on tour: Paris, St Petersburg, Adelaide, Philadelphia. Millions around the world had queued up to see it, to stare hungrily at the sight of that beautiful English country garden in the late afternoon, the two children, one with those curious birds' wings, crouched at the top of the lichen-and-daisy-speckled steps, peering into the house, watching their mother writing.

The children were long gone. The painter was gone and the painting. Only the sketch, and Lydia herself, remained – and Nightingale House, nestled in a fold of the ancient English wold, fringed by trees where birds sang all day and owls at night.

When she was a child, always afraid, she had dreamed of her own home, hidden away where no one could find her. Where she could be safe. Then Ned had brought her here and for a few years everything had been perfect. Utterly perfect. As summer soared into the garden and then faded away again, the silken light of golden September giving itself to the mist and damp of autumn and the darkness of winter, the question that had haunted Liddy kept coming back to her. Do you pay for happiness like that? Perhaps, yes, perhaps you do.

II

Ham, Richmond, June 1893

Dalbeattie — my dear fellow —

Will you come and see Nightingale House with me? I have found the perfect home for us — a rectory — built c. 1800 and lived in by Liddy's mother as a child, there's a thing — now sorely dilapidated, no stairs, no windows, no cupboards and doors, a shell — but it is a fine place with large rooms & full of light — in the garden there is a banqueting house, a relic of the old original manor built in Elizabeth's time for the partaking of ices and sweetmeats after a stroll across the lawn (the lawn is now a wilderness) — such a curious thing, but I shall use it as my studio. Will you remodel the rest of the house as you wish, to make a home for us? For you understand what we need —

Somewhere I might work in peace without disturbance and the noise of town — the jabbers, the agents, the critics

A home for our child and children yet to come, a place with clean fresh air so little Liza's cough vanishes

A place for my sister-in-law — sweet Mary must be cared for, for the situation in Paris has become intolerable and she cannot continue to live with Pertwee — Our old friend is lost to himself and others, the drink holds him utterly in its grip, my dear fellow — Mary must be welcome to live with us, for as long as she wants.

'Build for yourself a house in Jerusalem and live there, and do not go out from there to any place' —

My dear late father was as you know not a great one for the Good Book — but he liked an aphorism, as do you, and this is apt . . . for finally it must be a place my Liddy can be free — she must escape London, she must leave the ghosts behind! They continue to persecute

11

her most cruelly. What those three children have suffered, at the hands of those who should have cared for them most of all! Daily I work to expunge the horror of what they did, though I begin to understand I shall never fully succeed. My poor darling bird. She loved her mother — to come here would do her so much good. Finally

— A home for our family that endures until the final nightingale is gone from the trees behind the house — oh it is a beautiful spot, most strange, mystical one might say — in the heart of forgotten countryside — I know not yet whether it is Oxfordshire or Gloucestershire or Worcestershire or another county entirely new! There is something in the air and the trees, something of seclusion, of magic — but I am running on. Do come soon Dalbeattie — we must see you, all of us — do build us the house, there's a good fellow — let us begin a new story, a glorious one!

Yours in chestnuts and chicken —
Horner

III

**Lost masterpiece rediscovered: sketch of
'World's Favourite Painting' goes on sale**

An extremely rare sketch of *The Garden of Lost and Found*,
the masterpiece destroyed by its creator, the Edwardian
painter Edward Horner, comes up for auction today. The
painting is a preparatory work in oils of the artist's two
children, Eliza and John, in the garden of the family's —
shire home, peeking into the house where a mysterious
figure – generally believed to be the artist's wife Lydia
Dysart Horner – sits writing at a table.

There are no other versions of the painting beyond a
handful of contemporary photographs, all of poor quality.
The Garden of Lost and Found has, therefore, acquired an
almost mythic status due to the fate of the artist's children
and the painting itself. It was a sensation at the time of its
unveiling, a work which the great art critic Thaddeus La
Touche called 'perhaps the most moving resspentation
of childhood and lost innocence yet committed to canvas'.
It toured the Commonwealth and Americas, at the end of
which it was said that it had been viewed by up to eight
million people.

It later fell out of favour when, along with his later more
jingoistic works, such as *The Lilac Hours* and *We Built
Nineveh*, the once seemingly infallible Horner was rejected

by the critics and public. Horner himself famously grew to loathe his most famous picture and bought it back from the art dealer Galveston at 5000 guineas, thus bankrupting himself. He died shortly afterwards in the first wave of the Spanish Flu epidemic.

By the time the painting was destroyed by its creator days before his death, its reputation had been somewhat restored, and over the years the mystery of *The Garden of Lost and Found* has grown until it is regarded as one of the great lost works of art. The sketch for the painting is in oils, on commercially primed canvas, and shows signs of pen and ink underneath the paint. It has been rapidly executed, crammed with detail and notes to be used on the final canvas, and is dazzling in its assured technique and use of Impressionism, as well as the language of classical structure for which Horner was so admired. One unexplained detail in the upper left hand corner is the addition of a gold streak, thought to be a shooting star, which is not shown in photographs of the original painting or the sketch. Experts cannot explain its presence, though Jan de Hooerts, ex-director of Tate Britain, has poured scorn upon the upcoming auction saying it had obviously been tampered with. 'Horner did not "do" streaks of gold. This is not his addition. The sketch has been compromised, rendering the circumstances of the whole sale murky.'

The work, measuring only 32cm x 25cm, is being sold by an anonymous collector who acquired it from the artist's late daughter, Stella Horner (born after her father's death). It is estimated to fetch between £400,000 and £500,000 at auction today. Juliet Horner, great-granddaughter of the artist, who is also the Victorian and Edwardian Painting expert at Dawnay's, said: 'For years *The Garden of Lost and*

Found was the most famous painting in the world. Millions queued up to see it wherever it was shown. Its loss is a tragedy and to this day we have no idea why Horner destroyed his greatest work. So to have discovered this astonishing preparatory sketch has been a lovely surprise for us all.'

The Guardian, 17 May 2014

Part One

Chapter One

May

May was Mum's favourite time of year! Because she said it was when the garden wasn't quite at full glory but had it all to come. The luxury of anticipated pleasure, she called it. She was wonderful like that. She died in May, Juliet, did you know? And on her gravestone I made them inscribe: May is the fairest month for it is when the nightingales sing. *That is what she always told me. They fly to Africa for winter – do you remember me telling you all this? I went to Morocco once, before the war, and saw tens of them singing away on minarets and flat roofs. So incongruous to me, in February, there among the palm trees, golden desert shimmering in the distance. They are such plain birds, but for their song.*

They come back to England in May. Only the male birds sing, though. The female chooses her mate based on the beauty of his song, did you know?

Early May is also when you should plant the final summer bulbs and the rhizomes. Plant dahlias, plant hundreds of 'em. The irises will be almost coming out now, please feed them. Prepare the soil. Pick out any dead things. When May comes, I am in the garden from early morning till dusk. My body aches and I can never quite get rid of the earth under my fingernails. But I am more alive then than at any other time.

One more thing, Juliet: this month the bluebells are in flower in the wood below the stream. Enjoy them, but never step into a circle of bluebells should you see one. It is bad luck. You will be visited by an evil fairy, who will curse you. That is what Mum said happened to the little one.

Remember: May is the fairest month.

'I don't want muesli. I want toast.'

'There isn't any toast, Isla, darling. Have some muesli. Oh sh— blimey, it's nearly eight! Hurry up, everyone.'

'But, Mum, I *hate* muesli. The dried-up fruit! Muesli makes me feel like I will *vomit*. You can't make me have it. I will *vomit*.'

'OK, have Weetabix then. Sandy, darling, don't do that. Don't chuck it on the floor. Matt, can you stop him chucking it on the – oh.'

'I *hate* Weetabix. Weetabix makes me—'

'Then have a banana. Bea, can you eat something, please?'

'Well, Mum, Miss Roberts says we shouldn't have fruit first thing, she says it's bad for our stomachs.'

'Miss Roberts is wrong. Matt! Can you stop him chucking the cereal on the floor, please.'

'Jesus, Juliet! I heard you. Don't shout at me.'

Juliet realised her shoulders were somewhere around her jawline. She took a deep breath, and stepped away from the table. 'I'm not shouting.' Her foot landed on a small toy bus, but she sidestepped it before it acted as a roller-skate, swivelling neatly and using both hands to clutch on to the back of her eldest daughter's chair. 'Jesu— Goodness!' she said. 'Good save! Did you see that?!'

No one answered but Isla, her younger daughter, looked up at her plaintively, holding out her empty IKEA plastic bowl. 'Please, mother, *please I hate muesli and I hate Weetabix please don't make me have them.*'

'Oh, give her some toast, for god's sake,' Matt said, irritably. He leaned back in his chair and flicked the radio over. 'Let's have some music. I hate Radio 4 in the mornings. Don't we, kids? It's like inviting awful old people with bad breath to sit right next to you and shout at you while you're eating breakfast.'

The children giggled, even Bea. Juliet took a deep breath. 'There isn't any toast.'

Matt looked up from his phone. 'Why not?'

'We ran out.'

'We should get some more today.' He shook an empty carton at her. 'And orange juice.'

'My need juice,' came Sandy's small voice in the corner. 'Juice, please. My need juice.'

We should book a summer holiday. We should organise a playdate with Olivia. We should call your mother in Rome. We shouldn't sleep with other people. We should do all those things.

'You could go to the shops, Matt. They actually sell food there, I've heard.'

'I've told you about ten times I've got a team-building day. Thanks for remembering.'

'Oh. I'll go food shopping in my lunch hour, if there's time after the auction . . .' Juliet turned the radio station over again.

'*And now it's time for "Thought for the Day" with the Reverend . . .*'

Matt looked up at her and she saw anger shoot across his face. 'Jesus, Juliet.'

She used to dread that look on his face, it had made her insides twist with anxious pain. Lately, she'd got used to it.

'My need *juice*,' Sandy said, slightly louder than before.

'I just want to keep it on in case they do the bit on the auction. Henry said he'd be on before eight o'clock.' Juliet leaned over him to stop Sandy throwing cereal at Bea, still slumped at the head of the table. 'Bea, darling, eat some cereal.'

Bea raised her sleek head and stared at her mother. Shadows, like purple thumbprints, were imprinted under her dark eyes.

'I'm not hungry, thanks,' she said simply, and looked back down at her phone again, her thin fingers tapping on the screen, which glowed in the gloom of the kitchen.

Juliet hated that phone. She still remembered this same sleek-haired little person swinging her legs so that they banged against the chairs, chattering about the chicks they were hatching in class, what they'd done in Woodwork Club, the latest on Molly's new puppy. 'Oh What a Beautiful Morning!' she'd sing, every morning, every evening. 'Oh! What a beautiful Mummy! I've got a beautiful Daddy! I've got a beautiful sister! Everything's going my way!'

Once, she alone had owned the key that unlocked her eldest child's mind, her heart, her mouth. Now, she wasn't even sure if there was a key. You are only as happy as your unhappiest child. Bea was unhappy, and therefore so was Juliet.

'Here, have a few bites, sweet girl.' She stroked her daughter's shining black hair, and felt her tense at her mother's touch. 'Just something to line your stomach, Bea. You've got PE today remember and—' She glanced down. 'Jesus. Who's Fin? Why's he texting you pictures of some girl in a bra?'

'Oh shut *up*, Mum. Just leave me the hell *alone*.' Bea got up suddenly, and pushed the chair away, knocking Juliet with the back of the wooden frame, and stalked out of the kitchen, glancing awkwardly at her mother, as if to make sure she hadn't really hurt her. That look was the part that actually hurt Juliet.

Isla looked down at her bowl and began eating her muesli.

'Well *somebody's* rather grumpy,' she said, *sotto voce*, but she kept looking sadly towards the door, the corners of her mouth comically turned down. Sandy, beside her, banged his cup on the table.

'My need *juice*.'

'You shouldn't go on at her like that,' said Matt, still looking at his phone.

'But she's – there's something wrong.'

'Boy trouble. It always is, with her.' Matt sipped his cappuccino.

'Oh,' said Juliet, feeling even more inadequate. 'Really?'

'Someone called Fin. I've seen her texting him.'

'When?'

He stood up. 'I have to go. I'm late back tonight by the way—' Juliet put her hand on his arm. 'Listen. Don't start that again. It's the team-building thing, OK? I wish it –'

'No. Sshhhh a second. This is it.'

'Today in central London a sketch is being sold,' John Humphrys began in his best avuncular, this-is-a-fun-item-now-and-beneath-me voice. *'A sketch no more than the size of a laptop is up for auction at midday. And it is expected to fetch a quarter of a million pounds. Yes, you heard that right, a sketch.'*

'Stop saying "sketch",' Matt muttered, and Juliet put her finger to her lips, urgently. She stood stock still, one hand on her chest. She wished she knew why any talk of it made her feel like she was hurtling down a rollercoaster ride. It was silly.

This sketch isn't any ordinary sketch though; it's for a painting that was once probably the most famous in the world. I'm joined now by Henry Cudlip, of Dawnay's auction house, who are handling the sale.'

'Which is handling,' Juliet muttered automatically.

'Is that your boss? The posh boy?' said Matt, momentarily interested. He swung Sandy out of his chair and gave him a kiss. 'Hey, little man,' he said, ruffling his fluffy golden hair, as the stentorian tones of Henry Cudlip boomed out, accompanied by a crackling static as though radio waves alone were not enough to contain him.

'Juice!' Sandy began to cry. *'Juice, mama, juice, juice!'*

'. . . No one knows why he destroyed The Garden of Lost and Found. *He wasn't in his right mind, that's all. He was ill. Funny fellow.'*

'But why was it such a popular painting?'

'John, I couldn't tell you.'

'Experts,' Matt said. 'Save us from experts.' Juliet smiled. She stood, arms folded, as close to the radio as she could.

'. . . undoubtedly struck a chord with the British public when it was painted . . . It was supposed to be the most moving painting in the world, that was its USP. Grown men would stand and weep in front of it. The artist's children, caught in a moment of innocence in his garden, like magical sprites . . . as you'll probably know, they both—'

'Mum, what happens if you put a marble up your bum?' Isla bellowed, from just opposite her.

'That's great, darling – shh a moment . . .'

'. . . dead years later,' Henry Cudlip was saying. *'It's really a meditation on childhood—'*

'Who was dead?' said Isla, instantly. 'Shut up, Sandy!'

'No one. Someone a long time ago. Nothing for you to worry about,' said Juliet, automatically, and she reached around to pat Sandy, who was lying on the floor, screaming *'JUICE!'* and banging his IKEA plastic cup on the ground.

'Why did they die?'

'*How awful. And I suppose what everyone will want to know is –* '

'Because their bodies wore out and they'd lived a good long life. Eat up, faster, darling—'

'*– are there any other sketches or images left of the original?*'

'*Alas no!*' Henry Cudlip sounded almost pleased. '*We have nothing else, which is why the discovery of this piece is so important.*'

'*Now we're also joined by Sam Hamilton, unveiled last week as the new director of the Fentiman Museum in Oxford, which has one of the most important collections of Victorian and Edwardian art in the country. Sam Hamilton, thank you—*'

'Oh no *way*,' Juliet hissed. 'God. *God!* Bloody Sam *Hamilton?* Classic man swanning in to – *ow! Shit! Shit!*' Her fingers were resting against the boiling hot kettle: she swore, sucking them and wincing, but did not move from her place beside the radio.

'*The Fentiman going to bid for this today then?*'

'*Hi, John, thanks for having me. No – it's a little out of our price range, I'm afraid, but we'd love to borrow it from whomever does acquire it. It's—*'

'Why do you hate that man?'

'I was at university with him,' said Juliet, forgetting to censure herself. 'He was Canadian. Jesus, that guy. Classic. He was a total social-climbing know-it-all. He only ever wore two T-shirts, one of Justine Frischmann, one of Pulp, and socks with Birkenstock sandals. And he dumped my friend.'

'I don't understand what any of that means, Mum.'

'Never mind. It's that he was really patronising and he dressed like a – but anyway! It's not nice to be mean, is it? I'm sure he's perfectly nice now . . .'

'What's dumped? Like what Adam did to Darcy in *Hollyoaks?*'

'Why are you watching *Hollyoaks?*'

'I've never heard you mention him,' said Matt.

'I haven't seen him for twenty years. He's a – well, he *would* be director of a museum and vying with Henry Cudlip to be on Radio 4. He's –' She shook her head. 'Sam Hamilton. Typical.'

'*Any lover of Victorian art would want to own it. Ned Horner is greatly underrated today because of the success and then loss of* The Garden of Lost and Found *and the accusations he sold out in later years . . . he was very bitter about it and so was his widow, Liddy Horner, the artist's wife. They were a remarkable couple, they met very young, in extraordinary circumstances—'*

Henry Cudlip interrupted. *'In fact, his great-granddaughter works at—'*

'Mum!' Bea called from upstairs.

'One minute, just one minute – Oh Sandy, do shh, darling.'

'Juliet Horner, she's one of our experts on Victorian art.'

'One of his descendants works for you?'

'At the moment, yes. We were always asking her if she had any other paintings in the attic she could bring out, haha.'

'That's me!' Juliet said, trying to sound excited, but Sandy was playing with half an onion that had somehow ended up on the floor and Matt apparently wasn't listening. Only Isla looked up, and said sweetly,

'Of course, Mummy!'

'But, no, this sketch was a total surprise to her – to all of us, when it was brought in by our anonymous seller.'

'Fascinating. Well, good luck today with it, Henry Cudlip, of Dawnay's auctioneers, selling that sketch . . . Now, it's two minutes to eight on Tuesday, May the seventeenth, and over to—'

'What did he mean about you working there "at the moment"?' Matt said.

'What?' Juliet started clearing up the breakfast things, the brown flecks of processed cereals already stuck fast to the different bowls.

'That guy, your boss. It was like you don't work there any more.'

Juliet shook her head. 'I don't think so.' But her heart was thumping so loudly in her chest she thought they must all be able to hear it.

'Can you get Sandy's shoes on, and Isla's teeth cleaned—' She was backing out of the cluttered kitchen, towards the stairs.

'I have to go, Juliet. You know that.'

Just this once! Could you just this once *clean Isla's teeth for her, you lazy –*

25

At the top of the narrow stairs Juliet took another deep breath, feeling rather light-headed, and knocked on Bea's bedroom door.

'Darling, you wanted me? I'm afraid it's time to go to school.'

Bea was on the floor next to the doll's house, sucking her thumb, curled up like a comma. She had covered herself in a thick woollen blanket. It had been on the sofa at Nightingale House, the very one Juliet used to wrap herself in when she was tired, or sad.

'I don't want to go.'

'I know you don't but it's the second-to-last day before half-term. Then we'll do fun things.'

'Fun things. Bullshit.'

'Don't swear.' She stroked her daughter's soft, smooth forehead, the baby hair around the temples, before Bea pushed her hand away. 'Bea, darling, could you just maybe tell me a little bit about what's wrong and then I can—'

'Nothing. Nothing's wrong.' Bea sat up and opened the front of the doll's house, and it swung open on the huge hinge that was made around the great chimney. Her nimble little fingers gathered up the figures inside. Carefully, she stood each one in the hallway: two children, their smooth wooden limbs still pliant after a hundred years, one in a tiny smocked dress and wings, worn silver fabric wrapped around rusting wire, the other in a billowing linen shirt and teal-coloured velvet knickerbockers that swamped his tiny figure.

The doll's house had been a gift to Juliet's great-grandmother Lydia Horner's mother, Helena. A local craftsman had been commissioned to build it for the vicar's children after they moved into the new manse, so the family story went. Thus it was at least a hundred and seventy-five years old and Grandi never had to tell Juliet to be careful whilst she was playing with it: Juliet understood. There had been other dolls; grown-ups, perhaps. She remembered some from when she was a child, but along with favourite teddies and hats and books, they had been lost.

Grandi had kept the doll's house in the Dovecote, where she rarely went. She hadn't ever liked playing with it as a child, she said.

It was Juliet and her best friend Ev who wasted hours with it, dragging it out on to the grass, making up worlds around it, having their characters survive extraordinary events: plague, fire, bankruptcy, betrayal – penny-novelette rubbish, Grandi used to call it as she tidied away the pieces, closing the great hinge of the chimney shut, chivvying them out of the Dovecote to wash their hands, eat their tea, or whatever tiresome activity grown-ups insisted upon at regular intervals . . .

Absent-mindedly, Juliet stroked the fish-scale pattern of the roof. She had gone up on the roof of the real Nightingale House when her grandmother was still alive – When? The terracotta-coral tiles periodically required replacing and when they did two specialist roofers were summoned at great expense from Tewkesbury. The first stage was that they'd spend several days erecting the scaffolding. It was a precarious affair, terrifyingly rickety. One of the roofers, Laurence, had been doing this since he was sixteen; *his* father, as a boy, had known the men who'd tiled the roof in Dalbeattie's own original pattern, layering the glazed tiles so that they seemed to shimmer in the sun. 'Weren't no roof left, whole place were a shell. He'd make 'em do her and redo her till it were right.'

One day they'd come back from lunch at the pub and asked Juliet if she wanted to come up on the roof with them. She wasn't afraid of anything then. It was the best house in the world – why wouldn't she want to see the roof?

She remembered climbing the shaking scaffolding, how it felt like clambering up a skeleton. Then she was standing up on the apex of the roof, staring out at the whole of the house and its land – at the two long beds they called the Wilderness that were in fact a cleverly planted riot of flowers with the thin path between them that led down to the apple and quince and mulberry trees, and thence to the little river that was the boundary of their land. To the left was the Dovecote, with the glass roof Ned had put in himself obscured by the spreading fig tree above it. And the roof of the house itself, moving and spreading underneath her like a creature, a broad-backed salamander. Below and to the right was her grandmother, working in the vegetable garden, blue-overall-clad back curved like a hoop. Mum and Dad, at some remove on the lawn to the right of the Wilderness, sitting reading on the rusting, striped deckchairs. The call of some woodpigeon in the trees behind her that divided the house from the church. Which summer was it? And she remembered then. 1981, the summer of the Royal Wedding. This had taken place the day before. She had watched the wedding with Ev.

And the door to memory, once opened, led her further down those paths – Juliet shivered suddenly. The old man who'd arrived, the shouting . . . Juliet remembered showing him the doll's house, there in the Dovecote.

She hadn't thought of it for years. The Royal Wedding, blasting from the TV and every radio in the house. Grandi absolutely furious, ordering the old man away, yelling at Mum and Dad. She and Ev hiding like little birds in the garden. The next day everything changed, and she and her parents left Nightingale House right after breakfast. Juliet had cried all the way home. She had thought, for the first time, then, that she should have lived with Grandi, and not with Mum and Dad. That she belonged to her, not them . . . She remembered breathing on the window and writing 'Nightingales' in the condensation, as she wept, the plastic seats of the rickety Renault sticking to her thighs. They'd done Paradise in R.E. the previous term at school: Juliet, sacrilegiously, always imagined Paradise being like the garden of Nightingale House.

But her children had never seen it, and she had not been there since Grandi died. What a funny day today was going to be. Juliet blinked, aware Bea was still methodically moving the figures in the house around. She put her hand on her daughter's, bringing herself back to the present.

'Is it Amy again? Do you want me to have a word with someone?'

'No. No, please don't. Don't say *anything*.' Bea shut the doll's house with a slam, and there came the sound of the figures inside clattering to the ground. She pressed her fingertips into her eye sockets. 'Don't, Mum, please don't.'

'I won't – darling, I won't. But if someone's being nasty to you—'

'She's not. I mean, sometimes . . .' She swallowed again. 'Promise me.'

'What about that boy Fin? Daddy said Fin was your friend too—'

One of the texts from Amy that she had managed to read the other day before Bea caught her had said:

Tell them about Fin, Baby Girl or I will! Tell them
what you've been up to with Fin! Lool

'No. Oh God. Just – please, Mum, I know you're trying to help but please just leave me alone. *Please*. I can sort it out by myself. I don't need you.' Bea stood up, and stalked out of the room.

Feeling sick, Juliet made her daughter's bed and put away her pyjamas, folding them up under the pillow and putting Bea's beloved old Mog toy carefully at the centre of the duvet. She kissed the worn old cat, whose fur was grey and bobbly, hoping some of the love she kissed into the toy would magically disperse out. *You are loved, so much, I don't know how to make it all better.* Though she was late, she could not stop herself from opening up the front of the doll's house again and propping the figures upright, so they were leaning against the shelves. Then, shutting the door and leaning on the sturdy chimney pots, she stood up and followed her daughter downstairs.

Matt, with a great show, said he didn't mind taking Sandy to nursery as it was on his way. Bea insisted on travelling to school by herself these days so it was just Isla whom Juliet dropped at the primary school along the road. Since Isla only partly trod in the dog mess that was always freshly plopped outside their door, and since Juliet managed to put her hands in her coat pocket before she heard the familiar sound of the stolen moped engine that presaged the youth with a line of spots exactly following his jawline about to swipe your phone from your grasp, and since they weren't the last to arrive as usual, she chalked the morning up now as a raging success.

'Perhaps today we will learn about Egyptians,' said Isla hopefully as they approached Cheddar Class. 'Where did Cleopatra *put* the snake that bit her, Mummy? Where did she actually *put* it?'

'I heard your name on the radio this morning, Juliet!' called Katty, a nice newish mum Juliet mentally categorised as Boden Tribe, outside the classroom. 'How exciting, today's the day, is it?'

'What's today?' demanded another mum, deftly tucking some stray hair under her headscarf. 'Oh, of course, your sale. I hope it makes millions. Remember I've always been a good friend to you. Always. Even when you went through that dungarees phase.'

'What makes millions?' said Isla, jumping up towards her mother. 'Have I got an apple in my book bag?'

'My sale that was on the radio this morning. No, I don't get anything, and, Zeina, you know that perfectly well, so it's immaterial to me whether it goes for a fiver or five million.'

'It won't go for five million, I assure you,' said one of the fathers, a heavy-set man in the City.

'Oh right,' said Juliet.

Zeina shook her head, mock outraged. 'I'm still here if you need a lawyer to say you're entitled to a cut of the proceeds as sole descendant. Whoever it is, selling it and coining it all in. Justice for Juliet!'

The other mums laughed. The City dad walked away, shaking his head, as if they were all a gaggle of silly women, not variously a lawyer, an expert in Victorian art, a doctor. Juliet saw his wife, a small, dark-eyed woman named Tess, bend down and kiss their daughter goodbye, and the look she gave him, rolling her eyes at her retreating husband's back.

Juliet kissed Isla's cheek. 'Bye, darling.'

Isla paused in the class doorway and turned. Her eyes shining in outrage, cheeks flushing, she said dramatically, 'It doesn't matter about my apple, Mummy, or that you forgot to answer me as ever or that you ignore me and only listen to Bea. I am a person too. Goodbye.'

'Oh – darling – it's just that Bea –' Juliet said, starting forward, but Andrea, the teaching assistant, said firmly:

'Thanks Mum! Don't worry!'

'What's the drama today, Juliet?' Tess said, in her low, clear voice.

'Oh, nothing,' said Juliet, uneasily. 'The sale was on the radio, and it's . . . you know! Just one of those mornings.'

Though to be honest it was one of those mornings every day.

Tess smoothed her hair back. 'Robert thinks it's a sham, the whole auction. Says the sketch isn't real.'

Juliet, not sure how to respond to this – *your husband voluntarily wears pinstripes two inches apart and once told me the Candy brothers were pretty decent people when you got to know them* – instead did the face she reserved for retired men in red trousers who turned up at Dawnay's with a murky landscape they'd researched extensively and were positive was a Constable: a serious nod and noncommittal 'Mmmm. Right. Mmm.'

'It's so romantic, isn't it?' said Katty, smiling at Juliet. 'I was reading about it in the paper. Do you remember it?'

'No. He burned it—'

'I mean the sketch. Your grandmother lived in that house, didn't she, do you remember the house? Was she one of the children in the picture? Oh, it's like Manderley, or something!'

Katty's eyes bulged slightly too much with excitement and Juliet wondered if she'd categorised her wrongly, and whether she should be moved from Boden Tribe to Hidden Weirdnesses Tribe, to which, distressingly, new members were added with alarming frequency.

'I remember the house very well, yes. The sketch was in her study when I was little. I don't remember what happened to it, you don't pay attention when you're little, do you? It must have been sold when she died.'

'Oh! Oh right! Do you have to do anything today?'

Juliet frowned. 'My boss wants me to have my photo taken with the sketch for the press. Because of the family connection. I've said no.'

'Why not, babe?' cried Dana (Jobless Through Choice Yogic Tribe). 'Oh, that's so sad if you won't.'

'I don't know.' Juliet shrugged. She could hear Henry Cudlip's voice in her head.

'One of his descendants works for you?'

'At the moment, yes.'

'It makes me feel a bit strange.' She added. She didn't say her office was on the ground floor and several times a day she would, almost involuntarily, creep out to stare at the picture, hung in Dawnay's opulent lobby, stare so hungrily at it her eyes were paper-dry afterwards. Trying to drink in details – of the golden house, the curved roof upon which her own feet had been planted, the children . . .

The little girl, Eliza was her name, with the silvery wings glinting in the sun. The way she was beginning to turn back to the viewer as if she knew she was being watched – did she know what would happen? Was that her expression in the final picture? And the glimpse inside the house, the octagonal study lined with books, the woman writing there, the centre of the home, her face obscured, loosened hair tumbling down her back – was that Liddy herself? The paper on the floor, the knocked-over candle – what did they mean, or was it simply the breeze from the open french windows? And the golden bolt shooting overhead in the sky, like a star, showering sparks on to the ground beside the house – no photograph showed this was in the final picture. Why hadn't he painted it in? Was it a comet, bringing bad luck? Was it simply an accident, some paint knocked on to the sketch and cunningly disguised – she knew he'd done it before, with *The First Year*, when Eliza, then a baby who had just learned to crawl, had plonked a hand covered in chrome yellow on to the corner of the almost-finished canvas. *It is much improved by her addition. I think she will be a painter*, he had written to Dalbeattie.

'Who lives there now?' Gemma (Lawyer/Runner Tribe) asked. Juliet blinked. The mums were all watching her intently.

'Oh, an old couple bought it after Grandi died. I haven't been back for years.'

Fourteen years. Bea had been a tiny baby. Juliet rubbed her eyes again, looking round, and then glanced at her watch. 'Right. I'd better go.'

She, Zeina, Katty, Dana and a few others murmured goodbyes and smiled. Zeina patted Juliet's arm and gave her a strange look. 'Listen, lovey, I hope it goes well today. Call me later, afterwards, OK?'

Juliet watched her friend hurry off, the brisk familiar motion as she swivelled her leather shoulder-bag-cum-briefcase behind her. She turned and walked down the fume-clogged road where the smell of freshly mown spring grass mingled with the constant smell of drains that plagued the corner of the road by the Heath.

As she headed for the Tube, her mind tiredly sifted through the morning thus far – Henry on the radio, the fact that today was the last day she'd be able to pop out and look at that little sketch whenever she wanted, Bea's face when she asked if Amy was still bullying her, the memory of her feet up on the roof, of the Royal Wedding, Isla's heartbreaking smile and cool, firm little hand in hers, Matt's fetid contempt for her, oozing out of him like a fecal smell, like the drains, that was what it was like, and last of all the steady warmth of Zeina's friendship that sometimes meant Juliet just wanted to lay her head on her shoulder and weep, and stay like that. But you didn't, you couldn't. Ridiculous to think like that. As Grandi used to say, you simply kept on going.

Chapter Two

Juliet loved auctions, always had. Grandi had a great weakness for bric-a-brac and unusual items, and once made Juliet, aged nine, carry a large glass case with a pair of stuffed ferrets in it back to Nightingale House while she forced her best friend, Frederic, to wrestle with a huge astrakhan coat in the broiling heat which had allegedly belonged to an officer in the Russian Imperial Army. This coat had fleas and afterwards Frederic (himself an antiques dealer in the village) refused to go with her to another sale.

As Juliet pushed open the doors into the auction room, she caught sight of Henry Cudlip, talking to Emma, his terrified assistant, who was hopping from one leg to another, like a gazelle in need of a pee. Identical posh and immaculate girls buzzed around them, positioning the chairs, the cups and jugs of water on the stand next to the auctioneer's block, the bid slips, the catalogues with precise efficiency. On the far side of the room was the bank of chairs, phones and headsets for those dealing with telephone bids: the all-important overseas buyers, that was where the money was these days.

There was a huge screen behind the auction block on to which was beamed

Dawnay's
17th May 2014
Sale of Victorian, Pre-Raphaelite & Edwardian Art

which was a vain attempt to pretend the other paintings, even now being hung on flocked screens on wheels by jovial porters, mattered in the slightest. Everyone knew there was only one painting on sale today. There, at the front of the great hall, bathed in clear spring sunshine from the cupola lightwell high above, so tiny, so unsuited to its ornate thick gold frame, hung the sketch of *The Garden of Lost and Found*. This different setting gave it, to Juliet, a new energy. The strokes were sure and true, the tension in the children's small bodies apparent. The different brushes – the stiff hog's-head which suggested the lichen on the wall, the softer sable brushes for the sky, the little details which you could see had been scratched in by the thumbnail Ned kept long for just such a purpose, and the delicacy of the different glazes and scumbling, adding depth to the steps and the house with its sitting room where the figure sat writing. Today, the gold star shooting from the sky in a graceful arc seemed to shimmer. Oh, what would the finished painting have been like, when this sketch was so close to perfection itself!

I'll miss you, little thing. I wish you were mine. Juliet frowned. She had recommended it be sold without its Rococo-esque frame, which had been taken from another painting of the exact dimensions and put on to this, another rather desperate ploy by Henry Cudlip and Dawnay's to drum up interest and market this sale of a sketch – a vibrant, technically dazzling work but a sketch nonetheless – into a four-ringed circus, as though this were the original on sale.

She suddenly wished she had brought her children in to the auction house to see it. Why hadn't it occurred to her to do so? It was their history, Ned Horner was their great-great-grandfather, and who knew where the painting would end up after today? In the study of an American billionaire with a fetish for Victorian and Edwardian children's paintings? In the new Louvre in Riyadh, visited only by rich people in haute couture? Or in a vault in Switzerland? For both Victorian and Edwardian art historians and collectors Ned Horner was divisive, she knew: either you liked his bolder, energetic, realistic earlier work or you liked his later 'sellout period', the ramped-up patriotism and sentimental soldiers, but the myth of *The Garden of Lost and Found* seemed to straddle both.

Looking around it was apparent what a big deal this sale had become: TV cameras, the journalists standing at the side, the anxious Dawnay's grandees huddled in the doorway of the boardroom, scrutinising the unfolding scene, and, of course, the busy young women. She had been one of them – never as glossy but still placed front and centre on a day like this, when she was thin, and had time to blow-dry her hair every day, and wore wrap dresses and proper suede slingbacks, instead of long Titian hair hastily pulled into a bun from which it kept escaping, a too-long fringe that tickled her eyelashes, a long flared silk skirt covered in a pattern of curling peacock feathers which she'd found in a charity shop and decided to rebrand as a vintage find, much to Zeina's amusement ('It's from the Sue Ryder shop down the road,' she took great pleasure in informing everyone every time Juliet answered mysteriously at drop-off, 'This? Oh, it's vintage') . . . She didn't care about her appearance, not now. She just wished it wasn't so obvious that at Dawnay's, at least, her appearance mattered, that she didn't go with the interiors.

Henry Cudlip was adjusting his cufflinks and smoothing back his hair. The heavy tweed jacket he always wore was too warm for this bright May day, its sea-green velvet collar soaked at the edge with perspiration. Juliet could hear him giving instructions in his loud, almost bubbling voice. As if he felt her eyes on her Henry looked up and, with a jerk of his head, beckoned her over.

'Well, this is your last chance, Juliet,' he said, rubbing his hands in what seemed to be a jovial manner. 'Are you sure?'

As Juliet nodded, smiling coolly at him, she realised she hadn't had time to brush her teeth that morning. She hesitated, running her tongue around her mouth in what she hoped was a surreptitious manner, then said:

'I'm sorry. I'll happily talk about the painting, but I won't stand next to it and pose for pictures.'

Henry kept rubbing his palms together, fingers pointed towards her, like he was imitating a shark. 'Lord Dawnay has asked me to convey to you just how much it would mean to the company if you did.'

'I'm the expert, Henry.' She could feel her temper unfurling like a dormant beast. 'You know I am. I should be conducting this auction. I should be talking about the paintings. Not because I'm Ned Horner's great-granddaughter but because it's my job. The clients know me, and I know the work –'

'All we ask for is a nice photo of you next to the sketch, Juliet,' he said, teeth bared in a wide smile, and she knew now he was furious. His pale round blue eyes fixed on hers. 'You must see it adds a note of personal interest to the story.' And he reached up. 'Here, like that,' he said, tugging her rose-gold hair out of its coil and down over one shoulder. The extraordinary thing was no one seemed to notice. 'There. Come on, Juliet—'

Though this wasn't the first time something like this had happened, Juliet was so astonished she didn't know what to say, both at the act and at the physical contact itself – no one, apart from Isla and Sandy, if they fell over or when she was wishing them goodnight, touched her any more. She said, 'Oh!' and took a step back into a lectern placed next to the painting in readiness for the auction. It wobbled. She watched it, as if in slow motion, fall against the grey baize of the stand upon which the painting was placed, sharply hitting the gold frame.

With a low scream Henry lunged forward, as the lectern's edge sliced away a curlicue of burnished wood, managing to push it to the side before the sharp corner landed on the thick paint itself, on the little figures in their tangled reverie. The painting was pushed up, off its hook, and clattered loudly to the floor.

An elderly elegant lady by the door turned, sharply. Juliet bent down to pick the painting up, thrilling to its touch, as Henry crouched over the frame, muttering in a low voice, 'Shit. Oh shit, shit. What the hell have you done, you bloody . . . Oh shit . . .'

The veneer of bohomie that coated him was gone, and he was exposed, wild-eyed, red-faced, foolish. Juliet set the lectern right again and moved it out of danger. She glanced around the room –

one journalist, and a man with closely cropped grey hair in the third row looked up, but the journalist was half diverted by her phone and didn't seem to have fully appreciated what had happened. The man, however, gave her a small, rather strange smile, his green eyes moving from her to the painting. Juliet returned his gaze then followed it, staring at this small perfect thing in her hands.

'This is your fault.' Henry picked up the piece of gold frame.

'I'm—' Juliet began, and then she stopped before she apologised. 'No, it's not my fault, Henry,' she said, surprising herself again. 'You touched me. You shouldn't have.'

Henry laughed. 'What the hell do you mean?' he said, as the tiny figure of Lady Dawnay materialised beside them.

'Dear God. What on *arth* is going *on*,' she said, in appalled tones.

'Nothing, Lady Dawnay—'

'Don't be ridiculous,' she snapped, clenching and opening her hands, old garnets and amethysts glinting as her bony fingers flexed. 'Good *Lord*, Henry, have you dimigid the painting?'

'No, no . . .' Henry smoothed back his hair. 'No, it's fine, absolutely fine – dear Lady Dawnay—'

'Den't call me "Dear". The frame is cricked. What on earth do you have to say for yourself, Hen?'

'I – I—' Henry sputtered, and hung his head.

'The frame isn't original,' Juliet said, quietly. Lady Dawnay turned slowly towards her, beadily appraising her. 'For what it's worth, I don't like it at all. It's wrong for the sketch.'

'Who are you?'

'I'm Juliet Horner. Victorian and Edwardian specialist, Lady Dawnay.'

'In that case,' said Lady Dawnay, 'may I ask you why on arth has it been used to frame this painting?'

'Well,' said Juliet, 'it was felt by some that the sketch required a traditional gold-leafed oak frame to best display it. But I disagreed. It's from Goldschmidt's gallery, it used to be on a small oil painting of Rome by Frederick Fortt with the same dimensions. The sketch of *The Garden of Lost and Found* wasn't ever framed. It was painted on to a stretcher. If you remove the stretcher, you can see the notes he was making, trying different colours and so on.' Very carefully, she gestured, with the bent knuckle of her little finger. 'The detail of the tangled bushes, the daisies on the steps – he's tested them all out in this corner, where the fabric is folded up. It's a valuable resource for decoding the final painting itself. If it was up to me it would be unframed, as it always used to be.'

'If it was up to you,' Henry said, 'there'd have been no frame on it to protect it and it's highly likely the picture would have been ruined beyond repair.'

'As you know quite well, Henry, that wasn't down to me,' said Juliet in a low voice. She stared at him, suddenly not caring.

She had been scared of him when he'd joined three years ago and told her he hated working mothers: 'Just joking, my dear, but their mind's not on the job.' She'd been scared of him when she'd told him she was pregnant and wanted to come back four days a week and to leave at four every day and he'd said he'd employ her for three days but she'd have to work four. And she'd been scared of him when he'd kissed her at the Christmas party six months earlier, a 'festive kiss' where he'd slid his fat, wet tongue into her mouth and said she had to shape up because since coming back from maternity leave with Sandro her breasts were fantastic but otherwise she was well below her game. She was scared, because he'd stare at her sometimes – and her hair in particular – and that fat tongue would dart between his plump lips. He treated her like a wounded animal, wobbly, pale, tired, confused, he the lithe younger male stalking her, tripping her up all the time. Even though she knew more than him, was better qualified than him and with far more experience, and he was only there because he was Lord Dawnay's godson and had gone to the right school.

Had Juliet known what life as a working mother would be like, watching as she and her friends were slowly, gently, suffocated in socks and bath toys covered in black crud and unanswered party invitations and plastic *Peppa Pig* magazine toys, would she have thought again? No, of course not, because life without the children was unthinkable, because of the mere fact of their existence. Before children she wouldn't have understood this new, dreary sexism that beset you when you became a mother, which had dragged her into a pit out of which she couldn't ever seem to climb, but she did know one thing, fourteen years on: she was tired of it all. Tired of it being her fault, of bringing up girls, of dealing with phones, and friendships, and the children's Italian granny buying Sandy T-shirts that said: '*Uomo di Casa*' – 'The Man of the House'. Tired of broken glass and spilled drinks and endless, non-stop fear. Of men who swore at you when the buggy blocked their way, of women who gave you side-eye when your child screamed without stopping in the supermarket check-out queue. She'd tried discussing this with her own mother once, but Elvie Horner had almost backed out of the room as her parents tended to when uncomfortable emotion was in play. And though every newspaper or website tried to persuade you otherwise, she knew one thing: it was nothing to do with how much she loved her children, but everything to do with being a mother.

Juliet pressed her thumb hard against the bridge of her nose, as Lady Dawnay looked at Henry Cudlip. 'Is she right about the frame? Does it metter? She's the expert, isn't she?'

'Yes,' said Henry, after a moment's pause, glancing down at the chip of gold-painted wood in his hand. 'We can remove the frame.'

'I would,' said Lady Dawnay. 'You'll have to work out how to explain this to the sale room but, as they say, that is very much your problem, not mine.' And she turned on her brown court heel and left.

'It's – it's really time to get started,' said Emma anxiously. 'Shall I open the main doors?'

Henry Cudlip twisted his signet ring round and round. 'Wait five minutes. Here. Take this.' He wrenched the picture from Juliet's hands. 'Graham can remove the frame. Now. *Now!*' he snapped, as Emma, eyes huge, grabbed the little painting and skittered away with it, as though she were carrying the Ark of the Covenant and running for the bus. 'Oh, Juliet,' added Henry.

'I'll want to see you afterwards. My office. Thank you.' And he turned his back on her.

Juliet realised then she couldn't bear to stay and see the painting being sold and so turned to look at it one more time as it was borne out of the room by the restorer. 'Goodbye,' she said to it under her breath, eyes fixed on the disappearing figure through the french windows, her straight back, her delicate profile.

So instead Juliet watched the sale on the internal live feed in her office and saw the little sketch go for £1.25 million to an unnamed bidder after a frenzied, ping-pong few minutes, Henry's eyes practically popping out of his head as he tried to keep up with each bid and counter-bid. Juliet knew from the pre-sale briefing that the buyer was probably Julius Irons, the Australian oil billionaire who collected late-nineteenth-century art – she had sold him pieces before. He was as close-fisted and dry as a bone, no apparent passion for any of the Millaises or Leightons or Alma-Tademas he'd snap up whenever they came on the market. Though it wasn't the most expensive piece of art of this type one could buy, this sketch was the great prize. Would he put it in his sitting room above the fire and gaze at it on cold winter nights, or donate it to the Tate, where it could sit alongside *Ophelia* and *April Love* and the other great works of the era? She doubted it. It would go into a vault. If it was the finished painting, it'd never be allowed to leave the country: an export ban would be slapped on it – but it was a sketch. Just a little sketch.

Juliet chewed her pencil. For the umpteenth time she wondered who was selling it. A small-time dealer from a small market town had brought it into the gallery, acting on behalf of an 'anonymous client'. The client was fanatical about not wanting to be identified and Juliet knew what that meant. Of course, the painting was kosher – it had been verified by three separate experts, Juliet not included: the characteristics of Horner's later work were all there. The fresh white paint background he used for extra brilliance, even on sketches, the freeform, dazzlingly confident brushwork, the ingenious structure that showed so much and yet left you wondering, and the figures – no one since Hogarth was as good at capturing personality and character, even here – you could tell the little girl was the leader of the two, her brother a willing accomplice.

Where had the sketch been all these years since Grandi's death? Dad had inherited two paintings from his mother, Juliet knew that much; he and Mum had retired to France on the proceeds. But the sketch wasn't one of them. When Grandi had died, Dad had come back from France, and he and her friend Frederic had cleared out the house. She wished she understood what had happened, now, but she had only recently returned to work, Bea had been ill, a viral infection and croup, nothing really serious but still terrifying, involving a midnight dash to hospital, all of that. By the time she'd resurfaced, two months later, Dad was back in France, the house had been sorted out and someone else was living there.

Juliet was left the doll's house. She didn't expect any more; she and her grandmother had fallen out a year before her death, and she had left, saying she'd never return, sobbing helplessly on Matt's shoulder in the lane above the house.

She remembered the delivery man who worked for Frederic arriving at the house himself one chilly autumnal evening not long after she and Matt had moved into Dulcie Street. He'd helped Juliet to carefully move it into baby Bea's room as she slept. The driver had cooed over her, and still she hadn't woken.

'That's a nice present for her when she wakes up,' he'd said, and he'd gone, though she'd tried to persuade him to have a cup of tea. 'No, I'm to get back to Godstow tonight, Mr Frederic wants me early tomorrow morning', and the thought of him, driving back along the M40, back towards Nightingale House, filled her with a desperate jealousy that took her by surprise. 'He says to tell you you're to stay in touch, my dear. Says to tell you you're to come and visit him.'

But she hadn't, of course; life got in the way and what was there now to take her back there? She thought of her life as a series of expanding ripples in a pond – feeding, clothing and supervising three children on a daily basis was at the centre, Frederic a rippling circle just too far out, vanishing into the calm of the outer edges. One day, she'd get in touch with him, drive down for lunch. Perhaps she and Matt, on their anniversary in a couple of months. If she made more of an effort. One day –

The door opened, suddenly, making Juliet jump. She glanced at the live feed and saw the screen was blank, then at the doorway and saw Henry Cudlip, hands pressed together, rubbing, pointing, shark-like again.

'So, Juliet.' He kicked the door shut behind him, leaned against it, then pushed himself away from it, slightly too hard. She stood up, as if to mirror him, then cursed herself for doing so. She should have sat still, arms folded, smirking as he reverberated from the door frame into the bookcase, rubbing his arm. She should have pointed out the sweat stains which had now reached the breast of his pink shirt. She should have –

'Listen, I need to talk to you.'

'Right.'

'This is serious, I'm afraid. I've spoken to Lord and Lady Dawnay to clear up the misunderstanding about this morning.'

All Juliet's bravado vanished, like air escaping a balloon. She couldn't bear to meet his eyes.

'There's been some reorganisation in the department. Now, it will probably come as no great surprise that unfortunately you and I have to have a little chat about the future, my dear. You'd better sit down.'

'Yes,' said Juliet, sinking back into her chair. 'I had, hadn't I.'

Chapter Three

Juliet kicked the dry leaves gathered at the steps of the church. Why were there still dead leaves in May? She quickened her pace, though her shoes hurt. Her throat was dry. She wanted to get home, out of sight. Her uncleaned teeth felt furry. She would clean them when she got home, clean them till her gums bled.

'A parting of the ways,' Henry had called it, as if it was a mutual decision. 'We've outgrown one another, haven't we? Very sad.'

'You're not sad,' she'd said, furiously. 'You're snookering me to get this past HR. You say you're restructuring the department and making my position redundant and then you offer me a terrible job at a vastly reduced pay grade and position so I can't possibly accept it—'

'You could, my dear. I wish you would.' Henry had looked at his nails. 'I've worked with the HR team for weeks to try to create an enticing package for you—'

'You know it's not enticing, Henry. It's insulting. You want me to take a pay cut and reduce my hours and report in to some new bod who's getting what's effectively my job only renamed. It's bollocks.' She had chuckled at Gemma, a mum at school, who had ranted for ages after exactly this had happened to her last year. 'Don't you think you're being a bit paranoid, G?' she'd asked her.

Remembering this now, walking through the empty park, Juliet glowed with shame.

'So you decline the offer?' Henry had asked her in a flat voice, his jowly cheeks rendering emotion hard to read.

Juliet had laughed, and raised her hands in outrage; she could feel anger, rising up inside her again.

'I'm not saying that. I'm saying this isn't fair. If I hadn't come to the rescue about that crack on that awful bloody frame it'd have been your job on the line.'

'This is my point, my dear.' Henry had leaned against the wall. 'You seem to be forgetting your job is appraising and selling Victorian and Edwardian art. Not commenting on framing choices, or buyers' choices.'

'What about *The Garden of Lost and Found*?' Juliet said suddenly. 'It is Irons who's bought it, isn't it?' Henry's eyes narrowed. 'He'll just put it in a vault in Geneva and let it appreciate. Doesn't that bother you, Henry? That the sketch for the greatest lost painting in British art will just gather metaphorical dust in some metal-lined basement for the rest of time?'

'It's. Their. Money.' Henry shook his head, smiling. 'You're late every day, you're disorganised, you rush at things full pelt, and you argue with me constantly. And I wouldn't mind, if you were good at your job. But clients don't like being told that they're not the right owners for a painting.' Juliet began to say something and he raised his hand, as though he were in an auction. 'You know what I'm referring to.'

'I only said that to the guy who wanted to put the Leighton in his bathroom because the humidity would have ruined it,' said Juliet, clenching her jaw tightly.

'That painting was worth fifteen million pounds. Sheikh Majid al-Qasimi was willing to pay twenty,' said Henry. 'Do you know how much commission that is? If he wants to he can use that Leighton to wipe his racehorses' arses—'

'It's a work of art!' Juliet had shouted. 'Don't you *care*?'

'I *care* about my salary.' Henry Cudlip was laughing. 'If he buys it, it becomes his, and it's up to him what he does with it. You cost us a vast amount of money that day. And many other days – Look. Maybe you need a reboot my dear. Work for a museum, or something. The Walker Art Gallery's hiring, did you know?'

'It's for an Education Demonstrator, Henry. It's getting groups of thirty six-year-olds to sit quietly while you tell them about a painting.'

'Oh well, if you don't want that, what about the Fentiman? I keep hearing Sam Hamilton's quite the young Turk. Looking at things differently. Maybe a new younger dynamic would be helpful –'

Juliet couldn't stand any more of this. 'Sam Hamilton's my age. I was at college with him.'

'Oh, really?' Henry looked surprised. 'Anyway, think about the offer, my – think about it.'

'My lawyer will be in touch after I've looked it over,' said Juliet and once again she thanked whoever it was she should thank that, many years ago now, Zeina had qualified in employment law. She had acted for her before, when Dawnay's had tried to move her pension over from final salary to some lesser scheme because due to her two maternity leaves they said she hadn't been in the office for long enough to qualify as continuous employment. Two letters from Zeina had done the trick.

Now she wondered what difference even Zeina could make. Dawnay's had closed ranks. The rich would carry on buying their works of art, and perhaps there was nothing to do but accept the laughable redundancy package they were offering and clear out. She didn't say that to Henry, of course. She simply smiled at him and stalked out, closing the door firmly behind her, striding out of the building and down the steps into the May sunshine.

An hour of aimless wandering later Juliet had reached St Marylebone Church. She stopped, looking up at the vast classical portico, traffic rushing past her. Ned and Liddy had married in that church. She had had a sketch Ned Horner had drawn of it, framed above her bed.

How funny, to walk past it today of all days. She'd never walked home before. She was never free in the middle of the day to go for walks. Lunchtime was for child admin, for chasing down the plumber, buying birthday presents or tights, doing Ocado orders. These young lounging people, sunning themselves in Regent's Park: she'd been like that, once, hadn't she? She'd caught sight of herself in a shop window once, when Isla was three or so and Sandy a tiny baby, and didn't recognise her reflection. Then with horror, she saw herself as she really was: cross, hot, large, ranty, weighed down with bags for life and nappy bags and scooters . . .

The scent of late-spring flowers was everywhere. Juliet slowed her pace. She tried not to think too much: it was like a sore tooth – if she bit down on it, she knew the pain would be immense. She told herself this was all for the best, even as fear swirled around inside her, making her feel sick. She had been unhappy at work for a while. Probably for years now, but it would never have occurred to her to leave: she didn't have the luxury of choice. Matt had set up his own marketing consultancy business three years ago, while she was pregnant with Sandy. It would eventually do well, but it was still small and everything was precarious. He worked much harder than she did, she did all the childcare, but she was still the main earner.

I have to be positive about this. Juliet turned her face towards the sun and closed her eyes. She would set up on her own, be a freelance appraiser, or expert, do some consulting for the V&A if they needed her, or the Tate . . . her friend Darryl did it now for the London College of Fashion and loads of other places, she'd find . . . *something.*

But no one's got money for freelancers. How do I convince them to use me? How will I explain I've been made redundant? She thought of the children, with a prickle of shame and sadness. How proud she'd always been of her job. And telling Matt: Juliet stumbled slightly. He would be so angry . . . then she stopped. He wouldn't be angry, he'd be pleased. And suddenly she was sitting on a bench by the entrance to the Open Air Theatre, tears streaming down her face for the truth was she knew why. Somehow, in some way, things had got so toxic between them that Juliet knew he'd be glad at her failure. Her husband.

So stupid to cry. Juliet pressed the heel of her palms into her eyes. Her grandmother was a big believer in 'one foot in front of the other'. When she'd been scared or worried about something Grandi would always say: keep on going. Just keep putting one foot in front of the other. But Juliet found she couldn't now: tears poured down her face. She sank on to a bench. *Oh, please stop it*, she implored herself. But it was like pleading with a child mid-tantrum: entirely to her alarm she found she couldn't stop it. For the first time in years, decades even, she didn't seem to be able to control herself at all.

Eventually, she could cry no more and, besides, she was aware of attracting odd looks. An old man even came up to her and asked her if she was all right. After a few minutes, Juliet stood up, feeling wrung dry and rather dampeningly puffy, numb, as one always does after a long crying session, but a little more cheerful. She had six months' salary. The sun was shining. She didn't have to go to work tomorrow. The children needed her, and she'd be there for them. They'd make cupcakes together. She'd sort Bea out. She'd make sure Isla always had an apple in her bag.

She passed out of the park through Camden Market, up Kentish Town Road, walking steadily, as the afternoon shadows lengthened.

Nearly home. It was funny, she'd never wanted to live in that part of the world – she'd grown up in North London and she wanted a change. But Matt had got the job and he supported Arsenal and wanted to be near the Heath, and she was pregnant and his flat wasn't big enough for three let alone the doll's house – so they'd ended up in the terrace on Dulcie Street. Life was like that. You didn't choose it in the way you thought you'd be able to, when you were younger. You just sort of ended up in places, with people, in lives you didn't recognise as your own . . . She disliked the last bit of the Kentish Town Road, where the traffic was permanently jammed, but at last she was turning into her road, weary feet slapping on the gum-grey cracked paving stones.

Dulcie Street was in shadow – the sun had passed over it already. There was no one around and the only sound above the gentle hum of traffic was faint birdsong. Then Juliet saw a car facing her, outside her house, engine on. The driver had her head down, but Juliet could see the light from her phone screen. She clicked her tongue. Idling was one of her bugbears, especially on a narrow street like theirs, where the stench of diesel seemed to linger in the air no matter the time of year. Zeina, opposite her, had no such compunction, regularly knocking on the windscreen of an offending car outside her house and saying, 'You know idling's illegal?' And if they argued, she could quote the bylaw itself – Zeina knew stuff like that. She knew everything –

While the car was still a good ten metres away Juliet was musing whether she'd be brave enough to do this herself, when the front door of her own house opened and Matt walked down their front path, holding something, and the woman in the idling car looked up.

It was Tess. She leaned forward, and opened the passenger door.

Matt went around the front of the car, and got in. He kissed Tess, on the lips, then, almost an afterthought, grabbed her jaw and cheek with his hands and kissed her again. Her hair was swept back from her face, in its usual artless ash-blonde windswept style. It didn't move as they carried on kissing.

Matt pulled away from the embrace first, clicking his seatbelt in. Tess said something, then put her phone down on the dashboard, and passed one hand over her hair. Matt smiled at her, then looked at himself in the rear-view mirror. Tess pulled away, and the car drove off at speed, past Juliet, standing behind a van, peering out at them, like a Peeping Tom. There was another roar as it reached the end of the road and turned, then there was silence.

Juliet unlocked the door, stepping over the post. Of course Matt hadn't picked it up. Then it struck her as funny that this was what she was thinking about – he never picked the post up if he was first home, as if it was for someone else to do. Bills, circulars, council newsletters, a flyer for a concert and, at the top, a letter, addressed to her, in neat looping handwriting. On the top left-hand corner was written: 'By Hand'.

She went into the kitchen, dropping most of the post in the recycling. 'I've done the post,' Isla used to say when she was trying to be a helpful grown-up, and she'd pick up the envelopes and flyers from the mat and throw them straight into the recycling. 'It's all done.'

Juliet made a cup of tea, but let it stand till it was cold. She stared out of the narrow kitchen window on to the thin garden beyond, newly flowered, unkempt and ugly not through lack of trying but the culmulative efforts of squirrels, foxes, cats and children. There was a worn plastic toy truck, bleached from fire-engine red to pale pink and with only one remaining wheel, upended on the slime-green terrace. The summer herbs she planted every year with such hope were moist black stumps, not one having survived the winter and the dark dank north-facing patio.

He'd done it once before, the year before she had Sandy. A co-worker. Juliet knew she was called Leila and that she lived in Brighton. She was twenty-seven, and had a cat. It had lasted two months, and he had been furious with himself. He'd had counselling – they'd both had counselling, Juliet sitting there as Matt pointed out she was sometimes emotionally unavailable and head in the clouds, and wondering when she got to stand up and scream at him then jab biros in his eyes. But, being Juliet, she had sort of shrugged and then got on with it. And then Sandy had come along, a baby to seal the deal they'd reached to believe things were better, only somewhere along the way it became apparent they weren't.

The silence of an empty family home is unsettling. Juliet blinked, recalling herself to the present, then picked up the letter addressed to her, in its duck-egg-blue envelope. She held it in her hand, weighing it. It was oddly heavy.

Idly she wondered if Tess hated her more because she was screwing her husband, or if she'd always hated her and the husband-screwing was incidental to her feelings about Juliet, and whether, on a philosophical level, the two had to be inextricably linked . . . Where did they have sex? Had they just been in the house, having sex? Would she have to confront him today and say she knew? Would he move out tonight? The children – what would they tell them?

Juliet leaned against the counter as her head started to spin and then it really hit her, as if on a ten-minute delay. Matt. Tess. Her marriage. Matt. Tess. Her job.

She looked down at her hands. They kept being blotted out by black shapes in front of her eyes, as though she had been looking up at the sun too long. Juliet fumbled with the envelope, opening it clumsily, blinking hard. She did not notice when a key fell into her lap, and it made her jump. She looked down at it; an unremarkable dirty gold Yale key. She withdrew the thin, translucent paper and unfolded it, not really concentrating. In fact, she was thinking about Tess's hand, opening the door for Matt, the intensity of her expression as he reached for her, and kissed her, as if he was possessing her, claiming her for himself.

Juliet glanced down at the thin paper, the writing on the final fold, and felt her legs turn to water. It was handwriting she had not seen for years and years. On shopping lists scrawled on scraps of cardboard, on bulb catalogues, on birthday cards.

You were very dear to me. I have kept my word.
   Your loving grandmother

Juliet's eyes darted around the empty kitchen, searching, as though waiting for someone to appear. A joke. Or a ghost. *Your loving grandmother.* Sounds – distant planes, more traffic, some tinny music, far away. There was no one there. The thin paper shook in Juliet's hands. She opened it out and read.

Dear Juliet
   I am dead; don't fear that a ghost writes to you.
   If you are reading this letter this means the sketch has been sold. If it has been sold then I can tell you what I have planned for you.
   Nightingale House is now yours. You have the right to claim it at any time.
   I planned that it should be so. Long before I died I gave your father two paintings in lieu of inheritance; he agreed to this. The deeds are with the local solicitors who will contact you under separate cover. If you do

not wish to have the house, tell them so, it will be sold, and the money divided between three charities.

I planned and planned for you and you abandoned me when you allowed yourself to be made pregnant by that young man whom I knew could not make you happy. I will always love you. I write this not knowing how old your child is, whether it has been joined by others.

It has long concerned me that you do not know the truth of it all, and that at the last I must right a wrong. It was a happy house! And I was happy there, for so many, many years. You were too, weren't you? Weren't we both happy, all those summers together? You, my darling, are the only one left.

You were very dear to me. I have kept my word.

Your loving grandmother
Stella Mary Horner

Juliet let the letter float gently to the floor. She stared at it, and then bent to pick it up. Blood rushed to her head – she swung around, certain this time someone was behind her, watching.

But there was no one. Of course not. Grandi had been dead for fourteen years. Juliet had been to the funeral. She had – for God's sake – seen her grandmother, laid out, the day before the funeral, dressed in her best silk peacock dress, the violet-blue shoes she loved so much.

Juliet put the key in her pocket. She stood up and left the house. She wandered on the Heath for an hour, until it was time to pick up the children, which she did in ascending order: Sandy from nursery first, then Isla, then they walked up the road to meet Bea coming out of school. The pavement wasn't wide enough for them to walk together, and the lorries that juddered up Highgate Road were extremely loud. As they turned into their front path, she saw Bea stopping to wipe a piece of dirt from Isla's face, and suddenly Juliet thought of the painting, in the packing room at Dawnay's, locked away, waiting for its new owner. And then teatime, and bath-time, and bed-time absorbed her, until she could almost have forgotten the day she had had before she collected the children – the painting, losing her job, and the letter, even seeing Matt.

When she was finally alone, sitting with an untouched glass of wine in the little front room watching a TV panel comedy show, Juliet realised she'd been waiting for a change for some time now. Like she'd been braced on the deck of a ship, waiting for it to crash into the rocks. Well, it's happened, Juliet said to herself, as she turned off the TV and sat staring at a blank screen. It's crashed.

What came next though? What came next was up to her. That was the thing. It was down to her.

She put the key on a piece of string around her neck and slept with it; so deeply asleep was she that she did not notice what time Matt came back.

Chapter Four

July

How can you not love July, Juliet? July is for Juliet. My father painted The Garden of Lost and Found *in July. The sketch is all I have left, but my mother remembered the original well enough of course. According to her there were less of those white hydrangeas, and a few more of the rhododendrons, which I find awful blowsy flowers. Mum said she met Queen Mary once, at a viewing of the painting. Her Majesty said to her, well he got the rhododendrons quite right, they drop awfully quickly. And of course in the original there is no shooting star.*

Yes July was my favourite month for ever so long! Most of my life in fact. Until He came – I knew not a moment's happiness after that. That was in July— To business. I trust you will keep up with the sweet peas. When you do please pick them every day, there is a small slim brown jug packed away upstairs in the Birdsnest which I trust is perfect for them. If you don't pick them they won't flower again. Same with the roses. The roses were lovely the day He came and I remember that. There it is again creeping in.

I find a use for the large bank of lavender by the terrace. You should do this. Dry the lavender in the linen cupboard, hang it upside down in bunches. Remove the buds and place them in a Pyrex bowl which you fill with oil – sunflower, or grape. Not olive oil. Heat it gently over a pan of simmering water on the Aga for two or three hours. Strain the oil when cool, then pour it into airtight glass bottles. The lavender oil can be used on sunburn, scalds, cuts – lavender is an antiseptic.

You can also make lavender bags. Take material from the Birdsnest. You may as well know everything old is stored up there. The old children slept there. Old cushions, curtains, children's clothing, furnishings: the old items from the glory days when Dalbeattie designed everything for the splendid new house. The furnishings were threadbare by the time I was born and there were some things Mum couldn't bear to see any more. So she packed them away. I used to go up to the Birdsnest, lie on the floor staring up at the stars painted on the ceiling and listen to the nightingales. I used to open the trunks, see the lives of others who lived in the house before me.

I made you so many little lavender bags, Juliet. To scent the baby's room. I sent you them after you left, do you remember? You never replied. Anyway, Juliet is for July, darling. It is your month.

London, two months later

There was a festive air amongst the gaggle of parents and carers gathered outside the classroom. The dull July heat was puckered by a fresh breeze washing pleasantly over the pockets of adults waiting in front of the stern Victorian edifice of the school. As Juliet, pushing Sandy, hurried towards the Cheddar Class door, she looked up at the pointed Gothic towers on the roof. How many hours had she spent in this playground, rushing to drop Bea off, then Isla, or running into Kids' Club in the evenings? She'd usually been one of the last. Now she'd joined the ranks of pick-up mums. She was there Monday to Friday, she and her little cohort; sometimes they were the only grown-ups she spoke to all day.

Juliet hated being late, and yet she frequently was. She thought this especially today as she caught a glimpse of herself: a sweaty mess in her battered espadrilles and her old worn T-shirts and one of her long floral skirts with pockets; the uniform in which she'd lived for most of the summer. This was the good thing about not working. She was entirely herself when it came to getting dressed now. Her red-gold hair was long, but she didn't care, pulling it into a ponytail every day. She'd let Bea cut her fringe in the bathroom mirror, with mixed results – one side was great, the other uneven as Isla had made Bea laugh at a crucial moment. Juliet found she didn't care about that, either. Like a lot of things, it just didn't seem important. Panting heavily, she merged into the gaggle waiting outside the classroom door.

'What are you doing for the holidays then?'

'I've booked a place in Umbria for two weeks—'

'Oh, how wonderful.'

'Yes, it should be. I did it absolutely ages ago and since then it's been in the *Guardian* in that kid-friendly feature they had –'

'No, the place with the yurts by the swimming pool? Oh, it sounds marvellous, Jude.'

'Yes, yes. How about you, Gemma?'

'We're going to Whitstable for a few days and then the Île de Ré. We've hired bikes – Ash says he won't even try, but I reckon the kids and I can—'

'Oh, brilliant.'

'How about you, Tess?'

'I've no idea. Probably Martha's Vineyard. Robert has friends there.' Tess tapped at her phone.

'Oh, looks so beautiful, I've always wanted to go to that part of the world,' said Katty, smiling. 'How stylish, Tess.'

Tess smiled thinly. 'I'm not looking forward to it actually. If we go at all.' She pinched the bridge of her nose and waggled her jaw, and for a moment Juliet stared at her, drinking the sight of her in; her great, yet fragile beauty, her face, unhinged in that split second. Providentially, Juliet noticed Sandy had dropped his water bottle on the floor. She crouched down next to him and picked it up then pretended to busy herself, taking a bottle of squash out of her bag and putting it in the base of the buggy, shifting things around.

Without warning, Katty turned to her left. 'Juliet? How about you guys? Anything exciting planned? Another one of Matt's crazy extreme-sports holidays?'

'Nope,' said Juliet, standing up, and rocking Sandy's buggy backwards and forwards as if to soothe him. Sandy, jolted out of contemplating a robin on the school caretaker's roof, suddenly straightened himself in the buggy, writhing against the straps.

'Free me! Free!' he cried. 'No! No! *Free!*'

'Are you off to see your parents in France?'

Juliet kept on rocking. 'Nope. Nothing really planned.'

'Nothing at all?' said Dana, staring at her. 'That's a long six weeks you got there.'

'Er – well, no.' Juliet shrugged, bending down to pat Sandy's hair again. She couldn't look at any of them. 'It's – I'm not working, and—'

Katty gave Juliet's shoulder a quick pat. 'Bit difficult this year I expect—'

'My want *food*! My *hungry*! *Please!*'

Dana nodded, chastened. 'Gosh, I'm sorry, Juliet. I should have remembered. Of course you can't go away.'

'Um. No bother.' Juliet nodded. She caught Zeina's eye. Zeina said nothing, but shook her head slowly. Juliet knew what she was saying. *Don't bring me into it. This whole plan is absolutely crazy.*

Juliet changed the subject. 'Farewell to the cheese classes, anyway.'

'Oh well,' Zeina said. 'No more WhatsApp controversy about who got what cheese name.'

'Well I liked Cheddar,' said Louise, another mum. 'There was too many European cheeses in the class names. I think it's nice to have English cheeses shown some respect.'

There was an awkward silence.

'It's just it's really unfair to people who are lactose-intolerant,' said Dana. 'They didn't reflect that in the naming of the classes.'

'It was cheeses,' said Tess. 'They couldn't very well call a class "Something Disgusting Made from Soy For People With Made-Up Illnesses", could they?'

As Dana opened her mouth to reply, Louise said with some relief: 'Oh look. They're coming out.'

The Reception class door opened and Miss Lacey appeared. 'Thank you for the lovely vouchers, parents and carers!' She peered around at the group. 'Have a terrific summer! . . . Isla's mum? Could I just have a word?'

Zeina nudged Juliet, who was staring into space. 'Oi. Ju. She wants you.'

Juliet put the brake on the buggy and went forward, trying not to bash into any of the children streaming past her, biscuits in their mouths, clutching their pictures and exercise books and octopodes with tissue paper tentacles streaming behind them, accumulated cardigans and hats and socks built up over a school year's careless droppage. She turned to Sandy to wave at him. *Won't be long, darling!* she mouthed.

'Eh?' Sandy said, immediately alert like a meercat. 'Eh Mama? *Mama?*'

'Hi,' Juliet said. 'What's up?'

'Nothing!' said Miss Lacey. 'It's only – well, would you come inside for just a second?'

'My son's out there in his buggy—'

'It won't take long.' As Andrea, the teaching assistant, dispatched the last of the children Miss Lacey steered Juliet past her into the cool of the classroom. 'Just a brief chat, really. Isla's been very upset today. She's with Mandy now actually, just going to the loo. She's extremely constipated.'

'Poor thing. She gets like that if she—'

Miss Lacey carried on as if she hadn't spoken. 'The thing is, Mum, she says she doesn't want to have summer holidays. She says she wants to stay at school.'

'Oh,' said Juliet, ostensibly peering at Sandy, who was screaming in outrage outside while Zeina fruitlessly attempted to distract him.

'I just wondered if there was anything going on at home . . .' Miss Lacey paused, delicately. She looked at Juliet, guileless brown eyes peering over her huge round glasses.

Juliet said: 'No. I mean, Isla does really love learning.'

Miss Lacey looked stern. She said: 'Even a child who loves learning should want to be with her family. She should want the holidays to come around. Children who don't – we think that's rather unusual. It flags—'

'Yes, of course,' said Juliet, hurriedly. 'I promise you, there's nothing bad going on at home.' *But I would say that, wouldn't I?* Cold horror, manifesting as an icy snake of sweat, slid down her spine. 'I lost my job in May. Things have been a bit tricky.' That was true, anyway. 'And I've had to, well, I've been – working some things out.'

'I see.' Miss Lacey nodded, sympathetically. 'A difficult time. I wouldn't have mentioned it only today she told me she didn't want to move away.'

'What?'

'She said she wasn't coming back to Marston next term.'

'Why on earth would she say that?'

'I don't know,' said Miss Lacey. She glanced at the clock on the wall. 'Could she have overheard a conversation between you and your husband?'

'Possibly.' Juliet scratched her head.

'If there's trouble at home, and Mum and Dad are fighting,' Miss Lacey said, 'the child really picks up on it. Perhaps you need to talk to her, reassure her everything's OK. That you're not going anywhere and you and Daddy have just been having a few rows about—' she waved her hands in the air. 'Things all parents row about. Holidays, money, jobs, chores.'

'Yep,' said Juliet, deadpan. 'All those. I'm sorry. Look, I'll talk to her. The truth is—'

'Here's Isla!' Miss Lacey said in a bright voice. 'Hello, Isla! All OK?'

'I couldn't do a poo,' said Isla, in a small voice. 'I tried and tried and it hurt and I can feel it, Mum, poking out, but it's really hard and it hurts, I think I ate something like a brick or something without realising it.' Her little face was white, shadows under her eyes.

Juliet pulled Isla towards her. 'Let's go home, honeypot. It doesn't matter.'

'But the poo is there, I know it's there. I've felt it with one finger and it's –'

'OK!' said Juliet a little too loudly. 'Darling, Miss Lacey says you've been a bit sad today. Don't be sad. I've got you a sticker book.'

Isla's face lit up.

59

'Egyptians?'

'Yes.'

'Just Egyptians, not anyone else, not Babylonians or Israelites or anyone? Just Egyptians?'

'It says "Ancient Egyptians" on the front. So if any Babylonians have wangled their way in I'll have something to say about it.'

Isla gurgled with laughter. 'Oh great, Mummy. Oh great.'

Miss Lacey was moving around the classroom, gathering stray pens, geometric offcuts of coloured paper. 'Mum's going to explain to you it's all rubbish about you moving,' she said, and coming over to Isla, she capped her smooth head with the palm of her hand and the tenderness of the gesture stopped Juliet's heart. 'Have a lovely summer, little one.'

Isla nodded, and allowed Juliet to take her hand. At the doorway she stopped and turned.

'But it's not rubbish,' she said. 'I heard Mum talking to Yasmin's mum about it. She said—' She took a deep, juddering breath like the narrator at the school play with the big speech and said in a monotone: "I'll bring the deeds over so you can have a look at them, make sure it's not a hocks." She stopped, and mumbled under her breath, as though recalling the exact wordage. 'I don't know what that word is. Anyway. "One day I'll wake up and pile them into the car without saying a word and we'll drive down there and I'll never come back again."'

Miss Lacey, rolling paper doilies into a craft box, stopped, and looked up in alarm.

'That!' said Juliet. 'That's about us going on holiday with Yasmin and Nawal and Zeina when Daddy's working!'

'It is?'

'Yes! Sort of – well, it's a beautiful house in the countryside, Zeina knows all about it. You'll love it.' She held out her hand again; it was shaking. Surely something would happen, she would be struck by lightning, for lying like this. But, incredibly, Isla seemed convinced. 'Shall we go to the swings and slides? I've got you a special end-of-term treat.'

'As *well* as the Egyptian sticker book?'

'As well.'

'Oh Mummy!' Isla sighed, in her best child-in-a-movie way. 'That's wonderful!' She clasped her hands together. 'Goodbye, Miss Lacey!'

'Goodbye, Isla love,' said Miss Lacey. 'It's been—' She turned to Juliet as if to say something, and Juliet paused, waiting for the inevitable, because people always wanted to talk about Isla, her ability to read anything, even when she was tiny, her aptitude for numbers, the knowledge she had acquired somewhere – where? – about Brunel or Thutmose or Frieda Kahlo. 'It's been really lovely getting to know you this year, my dear. Take care of her,' she added softly, as Isla ran out ahead of her, towards Zeina and Yasmin and Sandy.

Startled, Juliet blinked, her eyes aching, and she turned away from Miss Lacey's gentle gaze. This young woman seemed to know the truth, that Juliet was a bad, black-hearted person.

I'm doing this for them.

On the first full day of the holidays, Juliet woke up at 2 a.m., because Matt had turned off the hall light and Isla had woken up and been afraid of the dark, then at 3 a.m., because Sandy's baby sleeping bag was too small for him (she'd asked Matt to make sure he put him in the larger one, and she knew he hadn't been listening, and she should have double-checked). The second time she lay awake until morning slid around the thick curtains, unable to get back to sleep. Beside her, Matt snored lightly. If she pushed him gently on the arm he got furious with her. Years ago, when they first met, she'd kick him and that would stop the snoring. Sometimes it would jolt him awake, and he would turn to her, and their bodies would join together, both half asleep, waking each other with pleasure then, slowly, drifting back into unconsciousness. That was many years ago now. Since Sandy had been born Matt was so tired, he said, that her waking him up to complain about his snoring meant his productivity was affected all day.

I'm going to get this right, she told herself, blinking hazily. Bea had also broken up, and now all three children were hers for the summer. She didn't expect Bea to hang out with them all the time, but she had extracted a promise from her that they'd spend one day together and this was that day. *I'll put the easel in the garden and we'll all get messy doing finger painting. I'll take them to the cinema. We'll go to Wagamama for lunch as a special treat. We'll make some biscuits in the afternoon. It'll be a lovely London day. They'll always remember it . . .*

Her toes curled up tightly, she pulled the duvet under her chin and tried to go back to sleep, with no luck. At five-thirty Sandy was awake again, so Juliet, eyes already itching with tiredness, took him downstairs and began to prepare for the perfect first day of the holidays.

'Can I watch something on your iPad?'

'No, darling. Eat your pancakes.'

'I hate pancakes. I want Cheerios. Can I watch something on your iPad?'

'No. And no. Now, listen up, everybody. We've got a fun morning – Bea, put your phone down.'

'No.'

'Bea—' Juliet actually wrested the phone from her daughter's hand and Bea looked up, with a hissing noise.

'Jesus, Mum. Don't *ever* take my stuff off me, OK?' She stood up and reached over for the phone.

Bea fucks herself with a ruler in class Ive seen it under the desk

dirty bitch

I saw it yesterday too loool

Yr a fkng pig bea

That ruler must smell disgusting fishy wank

DGAF but I have to sit next to her

What does Fin say? Fin? You ignoring the fishy wank bae now? Plez

Juliet looked up at her daughter. 'Jesus, Bea—'

'Give me the phone.' Bea snatched it back out of her hands.

'Bea. Who's writing that to you?' Juliet twisted herself towards her daughter, craning her neck to try and see her face, bent over the phone again.

Bea's knees were drawn up under her chin. Like a creature, retreating into casing. Like the baby she had once been inside her, waiting to unfurl. Isla was watching, with a blank, uncertain look on her face. Juliet put her hand on her daughter's curved back, feeling the knobbles of her spine. She traced each one, two, three. 'Darling, please tell me.'

'Just people.'

'Is it Molly?'

Bea raised her head. 'People from school.'

Juliet felt slightly sick, as though someone had punched her in the stomach. 'OK. I'm going to talk to your teacher next year now. I'm going to email—'

Bea stood up. 'If you do that, I'll leave.' Isla picked up a piece of paper and started drawing furiously, humming to herself. 'I promise. I'll fucking run away and you won't ever find me, you, anyone else.'

'Bea, darling.' Juliet pushed back the chair, swallowing hard. 'Listen to me, sweetheart! They can't do that to you. OK? It's very simple. It's good I've seen this.' She managed to corral her daughter into a corner of the kitchen and put her hands on her shoulders, all the time feeling as though she was trapping her, not helping her. 'I'll talk to their parents, I'll talk to the school – I'll sort it out, I promise.'

'You're. Not. Listening. To. Me.' Bea pushed her mother out of the way, dark eyes burning. Sandy started crying, and dropped his cereal bowl on the floor. Bea shoved past Juliet. 'Look, there's stuff you don't know. There's stuff *I* have to sort out. Not you. You don't know *anything.*'

'But they can't treat you like that!'

'Mum! Sort yourself out, then worry about me!' Bea's mouth was open, and she was smiling, a ghastly grin, her eyes red. 'You – look at you!' Juliet glanced down, at her grandmother's old dirndl skirt and her battered Birkenstocks, then realised she didn't mean like that. 'You don't have the faintest bloody idea about what's going on in your own life—' She swallowed a huge sob. 'L-let alone mine! Leave me alone!' She backed away. 'I'm going out.'

Isla looked up at her big sister. 'But Beeeeee! I thought we were going to play together today. I wrote out a list, look—'

Juliet saw the agonised twist of her eldest child's mouth, as she tried to work out what to do. The hell of family life, of people who loved you! And then Bea bit her lip, and pushed Isla out of the way. 'Get off me, Isla. I don't have time today.'

Isla's round, jolly face froze into a mask of almost comic confusion; her eyes swam with tears. 'I hate you!' Isla shouted. 'You hairy beast! You troglodyte!'

Juliet shushed Isla. 'Bea, darling, you did say you'd hang out with us—'

'God, Mum, you're pathetic. Dad's right.' She backed away, down the hall. 'Just . . . *Leave me alone!*' The door slammed behind her.

How could she help her? What on earth could she do? Like a rat in a trap, Juliet's thoughts circled around and around the same familiar routes. She sat down with her phone to email the teacher, then realised she didn't have her new teacher's email address, and, besides, she'd be betraying Bea if she did. She rubbed her eyes.

Where was her darling girl now? Walking to Highgate to sit silently in some café with some laughing, drawling girls and languid, cocksure boys? Pacing the Heath? Sitting somewhere in tears? Juliet's heart contracted. She had tried at first to follow her, to be with her everywhere, but that just made the shy, reclusive Bea sly instead. She tried to give her a loving free rein but it didn't seem to be working, and the report she'd had this term had echoed that. Over and over again: 'Beatrice is a bright girl but her studies are not uppermost in her mind and we must all work to overcome the learning deficit she has accumulated during this next most important academic year.'

Oh Bea . . . with your thick dark hair that used to curl and little hands that loved to clap and your dark-brown eyes like Grandi's that used to smile . . . I hate this, I HATE it, I can't reach you . . .

Black despair washed over her again and she pulled herself up straight, leaning on the edge of the chair. Isla scribbled furiously on the paper, looking straight down. Juliet moved around the little kitchen, shoving cereal bowls into the dishwasher, and then clapped her hands. She'd adjust the plan slightly and go out now so she could be in when Bea came back later, which hopefully she would . . .

'Right, chaps. Let's get dressed. We'll do finger painting later. The film starts in an hour and a half.'

Isla looked up suspiciously.

'What film?'

'Minions.' Isla screamed with delight. '"*Bottom*".'

Sandy laughed.

'"Bottom",' Isla said again, then she flung her arms round her mother's waist. 'Thank you, Mother, I LOVE the Minions.'

'Great,' said Juliet. 'Right, let's get dressed, we've got loads of time but we don't want to be late.'

'No!' said Isla, with a cheerily anxious smile. 'We don't! Well done, Mum!'

But they *were* late, of course. Then the cinema wouldn't let her cash in the voucher she'd been given when she'd taken Isla to see *Cinderella* and the film wouldn't start. 'The barcode's indicating the voucher is no longer valid,' the manager kept saying, and Juliet tried not to lose her temper and was snippy and rude instead. On Isla's third loo trip Juliet dropped her phone into the Vue lavatory. During the baffling-yet-dull animated film the phone gradually became burning hot, then switched itself permanently off. Now, at midday, it was searingly hot, a clammy, still kind of heat that seemed to seep into the poorly air-conditioned cinema.

Wagamama was an endurance test where Sandy's buggy, weighed down with shopping, fell over twice, once hitting another child whose father looked at Juliet as though she were a murderer and where neither Sandy nor Isla would eat anything, and Juliet's tired fumbling fingers failed and she dropped a bowl of soy sauce on to her sweaty jeans. As she pocketed the change, smiling manically at the waiter and picking up the large covering of food on the floor with wet napkins, she reflected that that was £38 wasted when she could have given them crisps at home as a treat and they'd have eaten them and been happier.

She had put her Family and Friends railcard in her pocket, not her Oyster card so couldn't pay for the bus and they wouldn't let her on because the contactless machine didn't work. Then it started raining on the way back and Isla got soaked and took her hoodie off, throwing it in a muddy puddle. The buggy fell over again with Sandy in it as she tried to clean Isla's hoodie with her sleeve then realised it was stupid to do so when it was pouring with rain. Obviously Isla stepped in dog shit again, and then Juliet couldn't find her keys and a man said under his breath, 'Fucking hell' as he had to step off the pavement she was blocking with her children while she rummaged in her bag, and she wanted to shout after him. *We held you up for three seconds, you fucking dickhead.* To run after him and punch him in the face, kick him in the stomach, and then she caught herself thinking these thoughts. London. The heat, the dirt, the other people, the relentlessness of it all.

They made cupcakes with cream cheese butterscotch frosting, but there was something wrong with the cream cheese and it went all runny and gloopy, like yellowing cottage-cheese-cum-lemon-curd. It wouldn't stay on the cakes, which had been too long in the oven and were hard as pumice stones. Sandy wouldn't eat them afterwards, and Isla said over and over again, 'Can I watch something on your iPad?'

By this time it was still only 3 p.m. but Juliet made them tea early. Neither of them would eat the chicken goujons because she'd forgotten they'd had chicken for lunch at Wagamama's even though they'd refused to eat that chicken too. The fox that was dying of mange or some long lingering illness kept slinking up to lie on their tiny patio. The smell came in through the open kitchen window. Sandy burned his hand on the pan with the chips in. His scream was high and thin, hammering into Juliet's head.

She let them watch *Peppa Pig* while she cleared up, sweating in the muggy heat of the afternoon, and when she came into the sitting room Sandy had been sick everywhere. He had eaten the corner of *Mog and Me*, chewing away at it while he stared absent-mindedly at the screen. The sick was made up of peas and sweetcorn and bits of carrot though she had no memory of him eating any of these foodstuffs in the last twenty-four hours. Isla accidentally kicked Juliet in the face whilst she tried to change her hoodie and T-shirt and then, eventually, when they were back in front of the TV again, Juliet realised if she didn't go to the lavatory right then and there, she would wet herself.

As she sat on the loo, feeling guilty about not doing the finger painting, about shouting, 'Oh for fuck's sake, Isla' after Isla's boot had made contact with Juliet's cheekbone, worrying about Bea since she couldn't check up on her via her phone, enjoying the release of peeing, Juliet tried to smile. She told herself that one day, she'd laugh about how awful this day was. As another scream came from the sitting room, Isla sitting on Sandy by the sounds of it, and as she smelled something burning and as she couldn't stop peeing, the longest pee in the world, Juliet unclenched her jaw and tried to say it, softly. 'We'll all laugh about this, one day.'

When Matt came back, at seven o'clock, Isla and Sandy were in the little paddling pool in the garden, naked. Juliet was sitting in the deckchair with her feet in the cool water, staring into the middle distance.

'Relaxing I see,' Matt said dryly, and went into the kitchen.

Juliet got up and followed him inside. 'It's been a long day.'

He took off his bike helmet, methodically unloaded his laptop, iPad and phone, winding the cables back around them, then untied his special cycling shoes. 'Really? What did you do?'

'We went to the cinema – and Wagamama, and then we came home and made some cakes—' She trailed off, and smiled. 'Gosh, it sounds rather nice when one puts it like that.'

A vein was throbbing in Matt's glistening temple. 'Yes . . .' He filled a jug with cold water, began putting cups away, in his neat, precise way. 'I'm sure it was hell.'

'My phone's on the blink, by the way. I dropped it down the loo.'

'But you just got it,' Matt said, turning on the coffee machine. He was deliberately keeping his voice even, she could hear the tone, and it made her even more nervous. And angry.

'I didn't chuck it in the loo because it was new. It was an accident. Looking after three children is hard work.'

'Well, two children. Where's Bea?'

'I – I don't know.'

Matt looked up briefly in the middle of pouring water into the coffee machine. 'What do you mean?'

'She left this morning. Listen, I found some texts on her phone.' Juliet rubbed her face. 'Matt, she's being bullied. Some of the things they said . . . they're awful.'

'Like what?'

Juliet glanced back at the paddling pool. 'I'll tell you later. She stormed out because I wanted to email the school about it. She hasn't come back and I can't get hold of her – no phone. Can you call her?'

His eyes were bright. 'She's been out all day and you didn't think to email me to ask?'

'How am I supposed to email you?'

'Your laptop?' he said, with aggravated sarcasm. 'You remember your laptop, don't you?'

'They took it away, Matt. They sent a courier to collect it. Two weeks ago.' She put her hands on her hips, glancing at the children again. 'If you listened to me you'd know. I did tell you.'

The same worn old grooves – that she was flaky, that he never

68

listened, but now there was something tired, automatic about the lines, as though they each of them were glad to find the other one at fault.

Matt ground the coffee beans, leaning into the grinder and pulsing hard with each press of the button. The sound was like drilling. 'So now you have no way of communicating with the outside world.'

'Nope.'

'How are you supposed to apply for jobs?'

Juliet wanted to laugh. It was as if he were questioning her like an employer himself, not her partner. 'Well – I can't. Besides, now we've made the decision to take Sandy out of nursery I'm with him most of the time. Have you tried looking after a two-year-old all day every day recently? It's kind of hard work.'

'Of course I have, he's my child too.' He carefully, neatly spooned the coffee into the filter handle, packing it down, then eased it firmly into the machine, turning it on and taking the tiny espresso mug from the shelf, and placing it carefully underneath the filter. 'They're all my children. Unless, of course, you followed your grandmother's advice and let that black guy what's-his-name get you pregnant. He gave her a cold smile. 'She'd have loved that, wouldn't she?'

She stared at him. 'What the hell are you talking about? What on earth has Ev got to do with this?'

'Oh, you, your family, thinking I'm not good enough for you. The mythical Ev. You know! Charming old bag, your grandmother. *"I do hope she'll come to her senses."* Such a shame she couldn't make it to the wedding! I do miss her.'

She ignored him. *He's trying to blame me.* The therapist had said this the last time around. Juliet tried to ignore the rising tide of anger growing within her. 'Listen, Matt. I'm not getting into this whatever it is with you. I'm merely saying looking after our children doesn't leave much spare time. I have to keep my eye on them—'

'Mama! Sandy's floating in the pool!'

'Sandy,' Juliet cried, running into the garden, as Sandy emerged, shaking his hair into a blond fin and sitting up in the water. 'Don't DO that. Don't put your head underwater.'

'BIG YELLOW FISH,' shouted Sandy.

'Now, Sandy,' said Isla firmly. 'Don't be stupid. You're a stupid boy, aren't you, Sandy. A little stupid poo-poo bum-head . . .'

'I've had a really long day,' said Matt suddenly, as the coffee machine started roaring and expelling hot steam into the already sweltering kitchen. 'I'm going to chill out in the sitting room for a bit.'

'Can you call Bea first?' she asked. 'The landline handset is out of juice.'

'Jesus, Juliet.'

'What?'

'Can't you? I just said I'd had a long day.' He gestured round to the battle-scarred kitchen. 'Can't you even clean up a bit? Unpack the dishwasher?'

'Are you joking?' Juliet laughed, taking a step back. She wasn't sure if he was joking. He must be joking! 'Listen, Matt. Do you understand I know what's really going on?' And suddenly she felt everything teetering.

Matt's expression did not change, but a little pulsing vein began to pump just below his left eye. 'What does that mean?'

Now. I'll tell him I know now.

But then you won't be able to leave.

Juliet shook her head, and looked at the floor, like a naughty child. Hot tears burned in her eyes.

'It's like you're happy things are going wrong. You're taking stuff out on me now. You're letting everything go. They're your children, this is your life. Stop waiting for me, Juliet.' He pinched the handle of the coffee cup deftly, delicately, between his fingers, and swallowed the contents. 'You call her. See you in a bit.'

Standing alone in her own kitchen, Juliet felt something pop inside her, as though she'd been on a flight and her ears were unblocked again. *You call her.* Another screech from the paddling pool made her dash outside again. She stubbed her toe on the door and for a second couldn't breathe with the pain of bone and thin skin on hard metal, but when she started walking again she found of course she could. Just keep on going.

Chapter Five

When Bea returned, a little before nine, she actually came into the kitchen and sat down at the table instead of pushing past the junk in the hall up to her room.

'Hi,' she said. 'I'm back.'

'Oh thank God,' said Juliet, pulling herself up from the table. 'Darling. Where have you been?' She didn't say that she had only just returned from scouring the Heath, Swain's Lane and the cafés of Hampstead for her daughter for the last two hours. 'Did you go up to Highgate?' She didn't say she'd already been up there to check. Bea liked the abandoned mansion next to Highgate church, and the story of the old woman who lived with no furniture in it for years and years, who still haunted the house, so much so that no one ever stayed there. Millionaires would buy it, and then move out again after a few months, vowing never to return.

'No. There's builders in, they're knocking the place down, didn't you hear? I was out and about.'

'OK. Who—'

'With people.' Bea directed her to sit down again, then unhooked her backpack from her shoulders, stiffly. As Juliet watched, not sure what to say next, she carefully untangled her earbuds from the strap of her bag and began winding them round her phone.

'With Fin?'

'Some of the time.' She carried on winding, then put them away, never once looking at Juliet.

'He sounds really nice, do you want to invite him—'

'Oh God, Mum. Just – don't –' Bea's face crumpled and she folded her arms, sinking her head on to her chest. 'I can't be free of it,' she said, so softly Juliet almost couldn't hear it. 'Wherever I go.'

Juliet went over to her, putting her arms around her. 'You can. Just tell me, darling, I'll make it—'

'You!' Bea interrupted. Her voice was still soft. She didn't shout. She sort of smiled, which was worse. 'You always, always say everything's going to be all right. You never really listen to what's going on, Mum. You don't have a clue.' She looked pale, hopelessly tired.

'Darling girl—' Juliet squeezed her tightly, and Bea winced. 'What's wrong with your arm?'

'Nothing.' Bea backed away.

'Did they hurt you?'

'No. No they didn't.' Her small face was panicked, suffused with rage.

A great anger rose up in Juliet, the agony of the last few hours and the fatigue of the long day receding, like a body of water being parted. In the distance, she heard the phone ringing. 'Listen. I'll make this better, I promise.'

Bea said: 'You won't. You always say that, like when I was small and the Virgin Mary costume tore. Or when all the cakes dropped on the floor. Or I did the wrong book report. You can't make this better. I can't tell you what it is.' She stepped back from her mother and glanced around, looking for her rucksack. Scooping it up hurriedly, she said, 'I'm going upstairs.'

'But Bea—'

'Juliet?' Matt appeared from the sitting room. 'Someone wants to speak to you. Landline must be working again.'

Bea had started to go. 'Hi, Dad,' she said, quietly.

'Hi, *bella.*' Matt pinched her cheek. 'I missed my beautiful girl today.'

'Do you want a peanut butter sandwich?' Juliet called, taking the phone from Matt, their hands touching. Her voice was shaky; she felt a bit sick.

'No, thanks,' said Bea, hugging her rucksack to her body.

'He says he's from the removals firm. He's ringing you back with a quote,' said Matt, when Bea had turned the bend in the staircase.

'The removals firm?'

'That's what he said. What on earth is he ringing about?'

'Hello?' Juliet spoke into the phone. 'Yes? Oh, no, not me. No, you've got the wrong Juliet. No, I don't know her. Yes, I'm sure. Oh, I don't know about that! I'll check and call you back, tomorrow, is that OK? How strange. Bye, bye then.'

She put the phone down, and smiled at him, almost sweetly.

'What's that about?' said Matt, looking at her curiously.

'No idea,' Juliet said. 'We use them sometimes at work, they must have called the wrong Juliet. I said I'd phone Dawnay's to double-check and let them know.'

'Why's it your business? Why should you care if Dawnay's have booked some removals?'

She found herself staring at him, at his close-cropped temples, his sharp grey eyes, the smile playing around his mouth. 'You're right. I won't care. Listen, shouldn't you call your mother?'

Matt usually spoke to his mother on Friday evenings. After his English father had died his mother had moved back to Italy, where ten o'clock her time was the best hour to catch her. Dear Luisa, with her extravagant presents, her love for the children, her exaggerated reaction to everything: disdain, horror, intrigue . . . the thought of saying goodbye to her, to Matt's laugh as he spoke to her . . . one of the little props holding up their existence here . . .

'Oh – yeah. You're – I'll call her now.'

Juliet walked upstairs, and her weary legs slightly gave way beneath her. She rested for a moment outside Isla's bedroom door, pinching the cool metal key around her neck, as though it were a talisman, a magic thing that could transport you somewhere else entirely, like the children in those reading books of Isla's. Still, now, she could walk away, she could abandon the whole plan. She could stay here, stay in this life – it wasn't so bad. Bea was going through a horrid time, but that was part of growing up, wasn't it? Isla and Sandy would flourish anywhere, she was sure . . .

Then she saw, with a strange clarity, that it was immaterial whether Matt was sleeping with Tess or not. The point was, they did not have a marriage any more. Their lives together – as she thought this she began to shake at the enormity of it – were over. He couldn't hurt her any more.

That's why I feel so guilty, she thought. I don't care about him. I don't respect him. I loved him once, so much – oh goodness, I thought for years that fate brought us together, the way it did.

But it didn't. And maybe Grandi was right. Whatever, I don't love him now.

And then unbidden, a sentence floated into her head:

The future is yet unwritten; the past is burnt and gone.

The inscription on the frame of *The Garden of Lost and Found*.

The past is burnt and gone.

Juliet reached up and knocked on Bea's bedroom door then opened it, softly.

Bea was sitting on the floor, playing with the doll's house. She had taken her hoodie off, and when Juliet opened the door she folded her arms, defensively. Juliet kneeled down next to her and then she saw her daughter's rucksack, lying between them. It was filthy. Someone had trodden on it repeatedly, the clarity of the imprints like potato printing. She stared at Bea, and then took in her muddy hands and folded arms. They were, she saw now, covered in bruises. She tugged gently at Bea's arms, so they fell open.

'Bea – darling. What happened?' She put her hands gently on either side of her arms. 'I'm serious. This stops now. Tell me.'

'They stamped on my bag and then they pushed me over and stamped on my shoulder. OK? Is that enough detail?'

Moving one hand, Juliet touched Bea's shoulder.

'OK,' she said softly. 'OK, darling. Does it – does it hurt?'

'This? Not much, actually. Mum, you don't understand. Stop trying. They'll always win.' She picked up one of the figures, and put him up on the roof.

'No they won't,' Juliet said. 'They're sad, horrible people, and the thing is, they won't win. I promise you. Honestly. Oh my love. My

74

baby girl.' She smoothed Bea's hair. 'How long's it been going on?'

Bea said in a tiny voice, 'A t-term. A bit longer with making me feel bad.'

'Can you tell me what they've been doing? Darling, I *promise*, absolutely promise that unless it's something illegal I won't do anything.'

In a colourless voice Bea said, 'Putting condoms in my bag, loads of them. Putting shit on the front door step, you think it's a dog, it's not, it's one of them. Writing stuff about me, all the time. Setting up chat groups about me, Airdropping photos of me they've taken and sending them to everyone while we're sitting there. Of me on the loo, or me picking my nose once . . . Molly and Amy, they pretended to be interested in the doll's house then they took all these photos of it and . . . and . . .' She started gulping great sobs again . . . 'They post them too, Here's Bea's Doll's Kitchen with the miniature plates and the very small mirror, Wow, what a fucking loser', that kind of stuff, hundreds of times a day on Snapchat, Mum, it's *all the time* and everyone laughs . . . Leaving stuff on my chair, they take it in turns to pick their noses and then walk past and wipe a bogey on to my shoulder and I sit there and can't do anything. My phone beeps *all the time* and I know it'll be something else from them . . . and I let them do it to me because I have to otherwise they'll tell . . .' She started crying again, broken, small cries of pain.

'Tell what?'

'Nothing. *Nothing.* I can't tell you. It's *nothing.*' She shook her head, and rubbed one eye then said in a small, tired voice, 'Mum, can I just get on with playing?'

Playing. Juliet stared at the small wooden figures, standing outside the front of the painted house. She ran one finger over the spine of the roof.

'I said I'd make it better,' she heard herself say. She swallowed, and took a deep breath. 'What if I told you we were leaving? Leaving here, and not coming back?'

'Ha,' said Bea, mirthlessly. 'If only.'

'I'm serious. Starting again, somewhere else, but a place you know already.'

Bea looked up at her. There were tear trails like silvery streaks on her cheeks. 'What are you talking about?'

Juliet, still squatting on her haunches, kneeled, and took her daughter's cold, dirty hand.

'I've got so many things wrong. I'm afraid you do when you're a parent. You try so hard to make it perfect then you look round and you've stuffed it up and you don't know where it started to go wrong and you make things worse because you're angry with yourself for stuffing it up. And this plan – oh goodness, this might be wrong too. But I don't think it is. I think we need a change, Bea. I'm being completely honest. Things aren't great, not with any of us.'

'What about Dad?' said Bea.

'Well, this is for him too,' said Juliet, swallowing, bowing her head so she didn't sway, blinking back the tears that now brimmed and dropped on to the house, the carpet, because all of a sudden all she could think was that she had loved him once.

'Because he's in love with Tess?'

'What?'

'I know, Mum.' And Juliet could see the shape of her face change, the indent of her cheek as her jaw clenched. 'I-I . . .' She swallowed. 'I picked up his phone to get an Uber about a month ago. I read their messages.'

Very slowly Juliet said: 'You what?'

Bea lifted her eyes to her mother. Her face was white. 'Don't be cross with me—'

'Darling! I'm not cross with you. Jesus. Oh Bea. You knew.'

'He said he loved her. Other stuff.' Bea fixed her gaze down in her lap again. Juliet stroked her arm, very gently.

'Sweetheart, I'm so sorry. I'm so sorry you had to find out like this. Why didn't you say something?'

'I couldn't be the one to . . . How could I tell you that?' she said, shaking her head. 'I thought you didn't know and I was so angry with you for not working it out.' She rested her head on Juliet's shoulder. 'And she's such a skank, Mum, I can't stand her. Even when you used to be friends she gave me the creeps.'

'I don't like her much either any more,' said Juliet. 'But it's – you know what? It's OK.' She rubbed Bea's back.

'Does Dad love her?'

'I don't know. I can't ask him that, not – not yet. I hope so. I've been making my own plans instead because I don't think we can live together any more.'

'Well duh.' Bea sat up.

'I wanted to talk to you about it. Look.' And Juliet patted the doll's house. 'This house. I own this house.'

'Course you do.'

'No, I mean . . . this house. In real life. I own it.'

'What are you talking about?'

Juliet pushed her hair out of her daughter's eyes. 'It's an actual house. And it's mine now. I thought we could go tomorrow.' She tapped the top of the doll's house smartly, as unshed tears stung her eyes. The huge chimney, which sat at the back and acted as a hinge, suddenly swung open and Juliet gazed in at the well-loved figures, the baby in the cradle, the dog, the chairs. The swirling, curved staircase, the huge bay window on the first floor, the Birdsnest at the top which opened with a catch and where you could store sweets, conkers, books . . .

Bea looked bewildered. 'What do you mean, we could go tomorrow? Really?'

'Yes. We are. We're leaving first thing,' she said, kissing her daughter fiercely, and then gripping her shoulders. 'You can start over, leave those girls behind.'

'You've gone mad.' Bea was half smiling, half scared. 'You want us to run away?'

'Not running away. We don't run away,' Juliet said quietly. 'Something's happened – not one thing, four or five different things. And I think we should go. Leave London, start again, and you might blame me for the rest of your life for doing it or it might be the

77

best decision I make. You see, I've realised we've got to a point where something has to change. Something's rotten with us . . .' The effort of controlling the tears was choking her. She coughed. 'It sounds crazy, but the way to do it is to go there. Trust me, darling.'

And slowly, Bea nodded.

Chapter Six

The street was empty; most people were away. Already the dusty, sunbeaten lassitude of summer holidays had descended. Juliet's scratched and dented red Škoda sat in the road with the doors open.

'You're mad,' said Zeina. She blew her hair out of her face, defiantly. 'Just remember, you can change your mind. You can get there and drive straight back to London again, you know. Be home again in time for tea and Matt'll never know you were gone.'

'I won't though,' said Juliet, loading the last of the bags into the car. It was early; her side of the road was still in blissful shade. Matt had disappeared first thing. He'd left her a note.

> Bike ride up on Heath today. Back 7. Pls can u tidy
> up & get some food if it's not too much to ask.

Zeina said crossly: 'You can't simply wake up one morning and decide to transplant your family to some abandoned house in the middle of the countryside because you fancy a change of scenery. You said you were going to sell it. You haven't even *been* there since whoever on earth it is left it to you. You don't even know how it's suddenly become yours!'

'Look, you've seen the lease and the papers. It's all above board. It *is* mine.'

'That still doesn't make this a normal thing to do!' Zeina hissed, over the top of the car.

'Nothing's normal any more,' said Juliet. 'It has to be now, or it'll be never. Look. I don't have a job and I now have a much better redundancy package because of you, you legal genius, so thanks again.'

'My pleasure, sister.'

'My daughter is being badly bullied and beaten up and is going through a lot of shit, some of which I understand, some of which I don't. And finally, for my big finish, my husband is having an affair with a mum at school.'

'*What*?'

'Yes.'

Zeina came round and stood next to her, on the kerb. 'Who? Oh man. *Who*?'

'Tess,' Juliet whispered.

'Bloody hell. Of course. Oh! Oh my goodness, that skank.'

'That's what Bea called her too.' They both laughed, as though it was hilarious. Then Zeina shook her head.

'Oh, Ju. I'm sorry.'

Juliet handed Sandy his bunny. 'There you go, sweetheart.' She shut his door and turned to face Zeina. 'I never told you this but he had an affair with someone in the office, three years ago, around the time he left to set up on his own. Some twenty-something. She got fired. I mean that's what pissed me off the most about it all, the thing that really stuck in my throat, that he got this girl fired. I should have realised then I wasn't as upset about the affair bit as I should have been. That maybe it was a sign things weren't great.'

'You should have told her to come to me, I'd have got her a good deal,' Zeina said, and Juliet laughed again, they both did, and then both gave an identical sigh. 'Oh blimey,' said Zeina after a pause. 'Mate, I'm really sorry about all this.'

'It's not your fault. But you see, don't you?'

'Well . . . OK. What about schools? Isn't Bea starting her GCSEs this year?'

'She can start at the local school in September. I've spoken to them. It's a girls' school, and it's really good. There's space for her. And, listen, plenty of children move schools.' She said, quietly, 'If we stay, I'll ruin things for them. Not overnight. Just . . . gradually.'

'Oh, love, you won't.'

But Juliet nodded fervently. 'We will. I feel trapped. Like the walls are getting smaller and smaller every day. I want space to run around. We need fresh air. They need to spread their wings, to hear owls, to make potions out of grass and mud, they need to get out of this toxic house and this super-toxic family situation. We all do. I can't stay here, Zee. I really can't.'

Zeina said, slightly huffily,'You've literally never mentioned this house before, and all of a sudden your children need to move there so they can hear owls?'

Juliet gave a gurgle of laughter. But she knew it was impossible to describe the hold the place had over her.

'You'll understand when you see it.' Juliet pushed her hair out of her eyes. 'If we don't go now, we'll never go. Bea?' she called down the little path. 'Are you ready?' She opened her car door and turned to face her friend. Zeina pulled her cardigan around her, awkwardly. 'I'm so sorry, Zee.'

Zeina nodded, her eyes swimming with tears.

'I thought we'd live here all our lives and be popping in and out of each other's houses when we were eighty.'

Juliet swallowed. 'I did too.'

'I won't give you the recipe for lamb shaslik now.'

'OK, fair enough.' Juliet smiled and brushed the tears from her cheeks. 'May-maybe you can come down when we're settled and cook it for me?'

'Mum,' piped a voice from inside. 'Can I watch something on your iPad?'

Zeina came round, pulled Juliet up on to the kerb. 'I will. Oh, Juliet. I love you, mate.'

'You understand why, don't you? Please say you do, just a bit.'

Zeina's voice was muffled against Juliet's hair. 'I do, that's the weird thing.'

She gave her a big, steadying hug, and Juliet clung to her for a second, wishing she could stay like that for hours. Zeina always made everything OK.

'I'll text you,' she whispered. 'Bea! Come on, Beatrice! We are *going*!'

And suddenly Bea materialised, as if by magic on the doorstep, her cleaned rucksack on her back, wearing her Grape Purple Converse, holding her phone, which she waved. She was actually grinning. 'OK, Mum,' she said, and hopped into the car. 'Bye,' she said chirpily through the window to Zeina, and Zeina blew her a kiss.

As they drove away, light from the sunny side of the street flooded the car. Juliet could not see Zeina because of the sun, but as they turned out of the road she caught sight of her, waving furiously.

The old ways along the no-man's-land of the North Circular, the vast IKEA in which she'd spent countless unhappy hours, the exotic hinterlands behind the Wembley arch, the Chinese supermarket she always meant to visit, the Hindu temple at Neasden . . . She had not been this way since she'd gone to a conference in Birmingham at Christmas and before that not for years, but it was still all so familiar.

Bea sat next to her, slumped silently, arms crossed, not looking at her phone, her earlier good mood vanished, Juliet could tell. The faint smell of arnica rose in waves from her; Juliet had insisted on rubbing it on her shoulder, much to Bea's disgust. In the back, Isla and Sandy gently bickered, as Isla tried to read Sandy a story he wasn't interested in.

'Guys! Shall I put some ABBA on? There's never a bad time for "Super Trouper",' she said, falsely jolly.

There was a silence.

'Mum, can I watch something on your iPad?'

'No. And don't keep reading Sandy that book if he doesn't like it.'

'I'm only trying to be a caring big sister. Being caring is very important. Miss Lacey says—'

'I know, darling, but I don't think he wants a story at the moment.'

'Where are we going?'

'To a special house.'

'Why?'

'To stay there.'

'Why?'

'Because . . . I want you to see it. It's lovely.'

'Are there Egyptians?'

'No.'

'Are there Babylonians, Mum? Don't tell me there are Babylonians—'

'I promise there are no Babylonians.'

'Well, I still don't want to go there.'

'There's loads of other things.' Juliet scowled into her rear-view mirror at the silver BMW inches away from her bumper. 'There's apple trees, and a cool top floor filled with fancy-dress clothes, if they're still there, and there's – Jesus, this idiot.'

'Who's he?'

But Juliet was silent, edging away from the silver car, trying to change lanes, and into this silence Bea said:

'Mum's taken us away from Dad and we're going to live in some stupid ruin in the middle of nowhere where we don't know anyone,' she announced, fingers pressing into her bruised shoulder. 'The house has got bats, and ghosts, and some children died there, and we're never going back to London, because she's left Dad and got some moronic idea in her head about finding herself.'

There was a pause. 'Thanks, Bea!' Juliet said wildly.

'Mum, what does she mean?' Isla's voice was barely a whisper. 'Don't you and Daddy live together any more?'

Juliet, still trying to change lanes, said, 'It's not quite like that—'

'Oh really?' Bea gave a loud bark of laughter, sounding just like Matt.

'M-mummm,' said Isla, beginning to cry. 'What does she m-mean? I don't want to leave Yasmin. Or Slavka. Or Bonnieeeeeeee . . .' She dissolved into tears.

'Bea,' said Juliet, finally pulling over into the next lane and letting the car overtake her – which he did leaning over the steering wheel, presenting her with a finger gesture and sneering laugh – 'stop it. Don't tell lies. I thought you were with me.'

'With you? This isn't a bloody political movement,' said Bea, acidly. 'You're not a suffragette. You're a bitter old woman who's pissed off cos Dad . . .' She trailed off.

'Last night you said—'

'Last night I was upset. Today I've changed my mind.' She folded her arms again.

Juliet cursed herself. All the parents in Bea's year been summoned to the school six months earlier for a talk by a child psychologist on the rapid and terrifying development taking place in the brain between the ages of twelve and sixteen, the take-home of which was that the brain of your average four-teen-year-old is undergoing such immense hormonal and logistical change relating to risk-taking, opinion-giving, infor-mation retention and identity they should barely be asked to choose their own ice cream flavour, let alone have to shoulder the stress of social media accounts, relationships and exams, so that anyone thinking of imposing any other major life changes on a teenager was no better than a criminal. And she had pitched moving house and leaving her own father to Bea as an exciting *Thelma and Louise* road trip. And got her to agree. She ought to be locked up.

'I'm sorry, my love.'

'Sorreeee,' said Sandy.

Isla said quietly, 'Mum, so you and Dad . . .' There was a long silence.

'Yes, my darling.'

'Well, is it like that stupid reading book *Separate Ways* where the dad and mum don't want to live t-together any more?'

'Oh. Oh, darling. Yes, it is a bit like that.' She looked wildly for a hard shoulder, somewhere to pull over.

'Oh r-r-r-r-ight.'

Juliet glanced in the rear-view mirror, at her daughter, and slowed down, causing the van behind her to beep loudly. Tears were sliding freely down Isla's red cheeks.

'Isla, darling. I'm so sorry.' Juliet wiped a trickle of sweat from her temple. How could she have allowed this to happen? 'Listen to me. We still love you. Daddy is staying in the house. You'll see him very soon. Mummy has a new house. We're going there today. We'll live there for a bit. It'll be different, but I think it'll be – I think you'll like it. Eventually.'

'I want to stay in our house. With Daddy.'

'My want Dadda,' said Sandy, not understanding but sensing the mood. He began to cry too. Bea looked back at them both with satisfaction.

'You've, like, completely ripped the family apart just because you're taking it out on Dad. You're jealous.'

'I'm not. Look,' said Juliet, gripping the steering wheel more tightly, as though it was a life raft. 'We can go back any time.'

'What about Dad?' said Bea, suddenly. 'What did you tell him?'

'Don't worry. I've explained it all to him. He – Bea, he loves you. He understands.'

Another lie. They were past Uxbridge, and the A40 had become a motorway, and the houses were more spaced apart, and there was more light, and space and the land had – just, just a little – begun to open up. Keep going. Not much further.

Dear Matt,

I'm sorry to do this by letter but I don't want to do it by email or phone and I couldn't face telling you in person. As you're always saying, I'm a coward.

I am leaving you and taking the children with me. I have explained it to Bea and she has agreed to come with me for the summer to try the plan out. She will go back to London in September to live with you if she doesn't like it.

Nightingale House is mine, it's come back to me again and I will explain it all when we speak, though I don't really understand it myself. I want to live there, and I want the children to grow up there. Bea needs a fresh start. We all do. I have spoken to the council and Isla and Bea can be enrolled in schools in September. You see I had to make plans.

I know you are having an affair with Tess. I have known for two months. Do you love her, or do you treat her as badly as you treat me? Last time was such a cliché, I see that now. Finding your phone – that girl, those photos, you swearing it was over. I believed you. But the funny thing is this time I do actually hope you love her. It doesn't really matter any more though, does it? I could have stuck it out with you and asked for a divorce, let the children spend another year in that unhappy house where the sun never seems to reach any of the rooms and I could have carried on sending Bea out into the world to be stamped on and bullied every day while we battled over access and settlements and where we'd live. But I can't do that.

You don't love me any more and you haven't for ages. So I don't worry about you missing me. I know you will miss the children. They will be in touch this evening and every night to speak to you. I know you love them.

It's really important you understand something: This isn't me being silly again, me being an idiot. You have made me really unhappy. I thought it was having the children that made me this low and unsure and sad but it's not, it's us. Even if Tess wasn't around it'd be true. When I come into the house sometimes I can feel something in the air, something rotten, dead. I don't want the children growing up in that atmosphere.

I don't think we were the people we thought we were when we met and so perhaps it started from that night. I did love you though, Matt. You made everything fun. You made me feel wonderful. You said I was like a heroine in a Victorian novel and then you told me you wanted to be with me for the rest of your life. Do you remember that? Down by Camden Lock, and we had curry afterwards and walked home and it was Bonfire Night. I lived on that for weeks. But we've grown into the people we are now and we aren't any good any more. And it's OK not to lie any more. Good luck, Matt. Thank you for the children.

Juliet

Chapter Seven

By the time they reached the long, straight lane leading out of Godstow village Juliet's hands ached from gripping the steering wheel so tightly. She had forgotten how uneven the road surface was; the car bounced, then skidded slightly on a verdant, shady bank.

Past the alms cottages that Dalbeattie built the year after they came to the house. Past the little postbox mounted in the wall which was where Grandi told her Father Christmas collected letters himself. Past the ancient church and churchyard, the gravestones silver-white in the midday sun. Her great-grandfather Ned and great-grandmother Liddy were buried there, in the same grave. Next to them the children, angels with folded wings watching over them, like fairies. There had been a time, when she was a child, when the churchyard had a sign nailed up next to the lych-gate directing the many pilgrims to the Horner tombs to avoid the trampling of hundreds of pairs of feet over centuries-old paths and delicate lichen. But that had not been the case for years now – Ned Horner had been forgotten, unless to collectors, until the sale of the sketch in May. She and Ev used to take huge delight in pointing people the wrong way. The first pound coin she'd ever seen was from an American tourist who'd tipped them for showing them towards the grave.

The turning into the house past the church was a sharp right and she had never done it in an estate car. She got rather stuck, having to manoeuvre backwards and forwards. A mud-splattered black Mercedes van hooted at her, and Juliet, furious, glared at it. As the car went past the driver, a man in his mid-forties with close-cropped greying hair, wound down the window.

'What!' Juliet shouted at him. 'Please, just give me a minute!'

'I was only going to ask if you needed a hand,' he said rather sharply, a trace of a Scottish accent in his voice.

'Oh—' Juliet began, but he had driven away with a screech, spraying dust from the road on to their window. 'Muddy puddles!' Juliet said manically, as they lumbered slowly down the drive. 'Look, Sandy! Un-muddy puddles!'

But Sandy was asleep, dried tearstains on his flushed cheeks and Isla was silent for once, sucking her thumb, twiddling her hair and staring blankly out of the window. Bea was tapping furiously at her phone. 'There's no reception here, Jesus. *Jesus.*'

Juliet drove over a pothole, jerking the car sharply so that Sandy woke up and started yelling. Isla began to sob quietly, and Bea sank down in the front seat, pulling her hood over her head. They turned the final corner, and the house appeared before them.

It was two hundred years old but might always have been there, rising from the land in golden Cotswold stone. The roof gleamed. The man who built it for the local rector after the old vicarage the other side of the church burned down had made it a sturdy, bluff house, ready to withstand the harsh winds and frosts that swept over the wold each winter. And Dalbeattie, who had reimagined it for Juliet's great-grandparents, had recast it, dividing up rooms, installing panelling and shelving and hearths and staircases, pargeting and parqueting, making it a splendid pleasure palace, an exotic jewel in an English landscape. Juliet had always loved that first sight of the house, the jumble of different features, the seat, the Dovecote, the windows . . .

The children clambered slowly out, peering around with wary bewilderment, as a clattering sound came from inside the house.

'That's the ghosts,' Bea said to Isla and Sandy. Sandy stared, dazed. Isla nodded mechanically, and walked off towards the garden, which sloped away from the house below a terrace and some steps.

'I want to explore for a little bit,' she said, sticking her hands into the pockets of her pinafore dress.

Juliet watched her go, knowing she had to let her be alone for a little while. She peered towards the house, her heart in her mouth. She saw a figure, pushing a mop along the floor of the dining room, and the spell was broken: the house was inhabited, it was real, it was hers.

She took a deep breath, as though she hadn't breathed properly for a long, long time. She could smell roses, honeysuckle, lavender – it was lavender that reminded her most of Grandi. *I am really here*, she said to herself, staring out at the horizon, at her children, stumbling sadly down the overgrown, tangled pathways.

'Well, I just thought I'd get started, and you'd turn up some point,' said Mrs Beadle, plonking the mop and bucket down on the wooden floor. Above them, Juliet could hear the thud and patter of the children exploring the upper floors. Mrs Beadle exhaled heavily, nudging at her chest with a sideways tuck of her right arm. 'I didn't know, you see. No one told me when you'd be here. If I'd known it was today—'

'Our plans changed,' said Juliet. 'I'm sorry. We came earlier than I'd expected.'

'Oh,' said Mrs Beadle. 'Well. I won't lie to you, dear, the house is in trouble. The roof's about to come in, there's tiles sliding off every hour on the hour, you can hear 'um falling on the ground, it's like rain sometimes. The chimneys have nesting birds. And that kitchen hasn't been looked at for years.'

Juliet stuck her head into the small, dark kitchen, a long galley affair with a little passage under the stairs that led through to the dining room. It was unchanged since Grandi's day, down to the carved wooden knobs on the cupboards.

'Remind me, who were the people who bought it after Grandi died? Mr and Mrs Wilson?'

Mrs Beadle looked at her curiously. 'The Walkers. Retired here from Bucks. Ever so nice, they were. Veronica Walker did the flowers at church. I think the house got a bit much for them towards the end. They didn't have any kids, you see, and kids make a house like this. They loved the garden though. Kept it exactly as your grandmother used to. You'll know all about that.'

'Oh – yes,' said Juliet.

'How long's it been now, since you was last here?'

'Since Grandi died? Fifteen years.'

'Not come back at all? And you here all the time when you were little, I remember it like it was yesterday.'

'I drove past it once,' she said, remembering the one time, late after a valuation of a smart old house west of here, Henry's meaty hand on her leg, late at night, hurrying back to be home for the children but still lying to Henry about the directions so she could drive down the lane. But it had been too dark to see anything, not even the nightingale finials sticking up above the roof. 'No, not once other than that. I'm here now though!'

'It'll be hard come winter,' Mrs Beadle said darkly.

'Oh, I'm sure it'll be fine. It's a tough old house, always was,' said Juliet, trying to sound jaunty, as the sound of the children's voices grew a little louder. It was them, really, she wanted to get to, to comfort. 'Reverend Myrtle built it to last. What does it say above the lintel? *"Thine heart is warm, when home th'art drawn"*.'

Ev used to say it so 'th'art' sounded like 'fart'. They hadn't been able to walk through the front door without dissolving into hysterics. Oh that summer – when he'd eaten so many blackberries he'd been sick, when Grandi drove them to the beach – what beach was it? And they found a mermaid's purse and a sea urchin. That was the summer of playing rummy, and Grandi getting crosser and crosser with the two of them, and with Juliet especially. 'Stop taking it all for granted,' she'd screamed at her, once. 'You never ask me about any of it. You don't care, you little beasts. You don't *know*.'

Juliet stepped out into the large entrance hall and stared up the wide staircase at the light well above, her hand resting lightly on the carved little squirrel newel post.

The week after the painting was destroyed, Ned died of the flu. Thousands were dying of it, all over the country, the world. They laid him out in the Dovecote and there he remained until the day of his funeral, when his coffin was carried out of his studio, into this very circular hallway, flooded with light from the round light well at the top of the house.

His widow, Lydia, had stood apart from the others, head to toe in black, black veil over her face, turning slightly away from the procession, as though she could not bear to look, and as the coffin reached the front door she had swivelled around, snatching her veil away from her face.

'*Ned!*' she had called, falling back against the curved wall of the hallway. '*It was all I had left of them. All that remained of them. Why did you burn them? Damn you, Ned. Damn you!*'

Grandi said the pallbearers were so appalled one or two had turned, the others remaining in place, and the coffin fell from their grip and with a thud, the thud of the man inside, it crashed on to the black-and-white-tiled floor, cracking two tiles, one of each colour. One of the pallbearers had refused to carry on with the burial of a man who'd been damned by his own wife, and so there were only three of them, unlucky, uneven.

The tiles where the coffin fell were still cracked, the lines soft, brown-edged, worn with years. Juliet looked down at them. Hairs prickled on the back of her neck. Figures from the past, family members, lost spirits, jostling to tell their stories.

Mrs Beadle leaned on her mop. 'D'you know anyone here, these days?'

'Well. Frederic? But I haven't seen him for years.'

'Him who's got the antiques shop on the high street? You met George?'

'Who's George?'

'You haven't met George then,' said Mrs Beadle grimly. 'What about the Farmers' Union? You know any of that lot? Naughty lads and lasses, they can get up to all sorts.'

'I'm not a farmer.'

'I don't think they care, dear. Mind you, they're banned from the Crown after what happened Guy Fawkes night. There was no call for it, no call at all, and that German fella ought to have sued.'

'What happened on Guy Fawkes night?' asked Juliet, horrified. 'What German?'

'It's not for me to say, if you haven't heard. Who else, then?'

'There's a few old faces I know, I'm sure. Look – oh, Brenda, at the newsagent's—'

'Dead.'

'Gosh. I'm sorry. And Gordon the butcher?'

'In prison.' Mrs Beadle tapped her nose, significantly. 'No butcher there anyway. It's a charity shop now.'

'Oh – oh dear.'

'They do lovely cards and wrapping paper, very good value . . . You knew the vicar's gone? . . . Had a nervous breakdown.'

'Lovely Leonard? Oh, he was so kind. What a shame, I hope he's OK.'

'Lionel, you mean? Not him. We've had two since then. Now we share the vicar with six other parishes.'

'*Six?*' said Juliet. 'How on earth does that work?'

'Listen, my lovey,' said Mrs Beadle with relish. 'Times are different. You can't come back and expect it to be the same. It's not what it was when your grandmother was alive. That's all a long time ago now.'

'Yes,' said Juliet. She stared at the cracked floor. 'A long time ago.'

Mrs Beadle's voice softened. 'There's still people who'll remember you. Lovely little thing you was, running about the garden all hours of the day with Honor's boy . . .' She nodded at her. 'That's someone you know! Mrs Adair.'

'Honor? Ev's mum? I haven't seen her for years.'

'Well, she'll be ever so glad you're back. She must miss him something chronic.'

'Ev, you mean? Where is he, these days?'

Mrs Beadle shrugged. 'I'd have thought you'd know that better than me.'

Juliet blushed. 'We're not really in touch. I'll ring her though. Be lovely to see her again.'

'Well, there you go. Oh, your gran ud be pleased to know you was back here. The way she used to talk about you! Your poor old dad, never got a look-in, he did.' There was an awkward silence as Mrs Beadle, wondering if she had been tactless, swerved away on to a different topic. 'And what are you going to do down here all day?'

'I-I'm not sure. I lost my job in May. I need to find something in a couple of months. In the meantime I'll make sure the children are settled . . . do the house up, all of that.'

'You make it sound like it'll only take a week or two,' said Mrs Beadle, darkly. 'Forgive a nosy old woman but it's a lot you've taken on. And what about your dad? Ain't he coming over to help you?'

'Some time soon,' said Juliet. She couldn't help glancing round as she talked, staring at everything. It was all so very unchanged. She was back. 'Mum's having an operation on her knee next week so they'll visit when she's recuperated.'

A sudden shriek came from upstairs. 'Oh my god!' Running feet, appearing at the top of the stairs. 'Urgh! A mouse! This is disgusting!'

'I like mice!' came Isla's little voice behind her big sister's. 'Don't hurt it, Bea! Leave him alone! Or her! She might have a nest of baby mice . . . Stop it!'

'Mumma!' Sandy's trundling step, thundering on the ceiling above. 'My want Mumma!'

'Mum.' Bea was standing at the top of the stairs, arms folded, glowering. 'We saw a mouse.'

'Well . . .' Juliet twisted her fingers together anxiously, as though the existence of the mouse was entirely down to her.

'I'm not sleeping somewhere there's mice. OK?'

Next to her, Mrs Beadle began to chuckle, and then laugh, her large body shaking. 'Oh, you are funny. Bea, is it?'

'What?' said Bea, turning to her furiously. A spot of red burned on each cheek.

'Bea,' Juliet said sharply, 'don't be so rude. Apologise.'

'Sorry,' said Bea, flushing a deeper scarlet.

'I'll get on,' said Mrs Beadle. She looked up at the children. 'Listen to an old woman, all right? Country mice ain't the same as town mice. Country mice won't give you any trouble. They've come in from the cornfields over there. There'll be a heap more of them come September. They're nice things.' She turned to Juliet, who was heaving a bag across the hall, as the children melted sullenly into the sitting room. 'When's your husband coming down?'

'We're separated.' Juliet found she couldn't meet Mrs Beadle's eye. 'That's partly why, when the Walkers sold up, I found I could move back here.'

'Oh. I'm sorry, my dear.' Mrs Beadle put one large hand on Juliet's arm, and the dry warmth of it, the kindness of her voice, was almost too much. She took her hand away and then said, as an afterthought, 'They didn't sell up, though.'

'Yes, they sold the house a couple of months ago.'

'No. Renting, they was.'

Juliet shrugged – as if it mattered – then she frowned, realising the significance of what had been said. 'What?'

'They didn't own it. I know they didn't cos they told me. They were given notice to leave.'

'What?'

'Oh, yes. She told me in the High Street, Mrs Walker did. She said it were like someone was watching them. Stepping in just in time to tell them to move. Cos they couldn't cope with this place any more. The garden, and the damp . . . She said it was a relief to hand the old place back again. Oh, they're in a nice bungalow somewhere. They've left their address, I'll look it out for you, post and that.'

Juliet said again: 'What? But – it was sold after Grandi died. Not rented. Who'd have rented it to them?'

'You own the house now, don't you?'

'Yes. It was left to me.' A prickling sensation was running slowly down Juliet's back. 'I have the deeds. I just – I wonder who owned the house, then. Who's given it to . . . to me.'

'None of my business, I suppose, my dear.'

There was a cry from the sitting room. 'Mum! What are these things on the mantelpiece?'

'What?'

Bea appeared in the doorway. 'Dolls! They're dolls like in the doll's house.'

'I saw them,' said Mrs Beadle. 'Wondered who'd left them behind.'

Juliet went into the sitting room. There, on top of the great hearth, were two dolls. They were tied together with a piece of string. Ordinary kitchen string. There was a small piece of paper wrapped around them, like a shield.

'The doll's house . . .' she whispered, and she was afraid now, and didn't know why. 'That's Liddy. That's Ned.'

'Who?'

'He made them for her. I've got the children, but I haven't seen these two for years . . .'

Doll-Liddy's elaborate hair, coiled up on her head, was worn to the colour of sycamore wood once more. The clothes that Juliet had lovingly stroked as a child were almost perfect: exquisite tiny lawn cotton blouse and green velvet skirt, the tiny cameo brooch, the mobile arms and legs that swung so freely, the head with tiny chips of blue glass for eyes. Doll-Ned, with a small painted pointed beard, a paintbrush in one hand (the wooden-pointed brushhead of which had long ago snapped off), had fared less well – his clothes were worn, the black suit motheaten, threadbare.

A noise behind her made Juliet jump half out of her skin; she dropped the figures on the floor.

'What's that?' said Bea, behind her. She picked up the wooden figures, and stared at them.

'They're from the doll's house,' said Juliet. She turned the note over.

Dearest Juliet

I give you this glorious house. Look around you.

Know that in living here you continue a line of women going back to my own grandmother Helena whose father built the house. The Reverend David Myrtle was his name.

He caused the new vicarage to be built on the site of the old manor house. His daughter Helena grew up here. She had three children, Rupert, Lydia (my mother), and Mary. I have told you of Liddy's terrible childhood after Helena died of smallpox. Ned Horner bought the house back for his Liddy and they raised their family there. I was born six months after my father died. Liddy and I grew up here alone — only we were not alone! There are fairies at the bottom of the garden, Juliet. They play at night, when they think I am sleeping.

Enclosed is a little booklet that I have written these last months to stave off winter boredom. You may think of as a how-to guide. It takes you over, this house. She still has secrets to give up, of that I am sure.

You are a very wonderful girl and I loved you. Know that. Find your own way in life, darling. It is there if you look hard enough.

Your loving grandmother
Stella Horner

And underneath, written in rapid, cramped handwriting:

I am not mad, Juliet dearest, though I was made on a mad night and they want to drive me mad. I will tell you what I think: I think they lied to me. I do not think the painting is gone. I think the boy stole it. I think it is somewhere in the house.

'What does she mean?' Bea was reading over her shoulder. 'What painting? What boy?'

Juliet moved away, as though wanting to keep a school secret. 'Don't know.'

Propped up behind the figures was an old lined school exercise book, filled with her grandmother's densely written hand. With a growing feeling of unease, Juliet flicked through it:

March . . . Are all the spring bulbs planted, Juliet? . . . July . . . Lavender oil can be used on sunburn . . . lift the dahlias. Pick the apples. Plant hardy annuals. Clear out the Birdsnest.

She put it down, overwhelmed. Suddenly, she could hear her. See her, standing in the doorway, fists on hips, legs akimbo, tall, slim, the hooked nose and wide dark eyes, the smooth bobbed hair that never seemed out of place. 'Welcome home, darling,' she was saying. 'Welcome—'

The spirits, the ghosts, fairies, whatever they were, seemed louder than ever now, their presence pushing against some boundary between the past and present. Juliet folded up the note, and the exercise book, which felt heavy with the ink of her grandmother's instructions, and slid them both into her jeans pocket. In the doorway, Isla watched, arms folded.

'Isla,' Juliet said, going over and putting her arm round her. 'Come here, darling.'

'I want Dad,' she said, very softly.

Juliet closed her eyes for a moment, and then she dropped a kiss on her soft silver-blonde head. 'I know, darling. Dad's in London. This is our house now.'

She crouched down on the ground. *I am in charge now. No hiding from anything.* She put her arms round Isla, and pulled Sandy on to her lap. She gestured to Bea, who sat down on the floor, stroking her brother's head. 'This is Liddy,' she said, taking the dolls from her. 'That's Ned.'

'Was he the painter?' said Isla, taking her thumb from her mouth.

'Yes. Grandi used to tell me about him and Liddy, when I couldn't sleep.' Juliet stared at the carving of Ned's face, his stiff paintbrush, the seam of wood grain that ran almost along the ridge of his nose. 'I haven't thought about them for years, not like that.' Now, she only thought of Ned as a painter, she realised. Not his story as her great-grandfather. 'I knew about them once. Liddy, her sister, Mary, how they came to live in the house.'

The front door slammed shut, in the sudden breeze, and Sandy and Bea jumped. Isla was still, though.

'He lived here, then?'

'Yes. They both did. For years and years and it was wonderful. Until – well, I'm not sure.' Juliet stood up, holding the younger children's hands. 'Let's go and unpack the car, and make some tea.'

'What happened to them in the end?'

Juliet glanced at the figures again, and out at the garden. 'I don't really know, you see. That, she never told me.'

Chapter Eight

Highgate, May 1891

'Would you care for some tea, miss?'

'Oh hush – hush, please, for a moment, dear Hannah! Just a moment—'

Miss Mary Helena Dysart, fourteen years old and, when seen from the back, possessed of an elegant figure and a neatly turned ankle, was peering on tiptoe around the heavy blue-and-gold-brocade curtains hanging at the french windows of the drawing room of St Michael's House, Highgate. Her burnished-brown ringlets, which unlike her sister's never needed to be twisted into agonising rags, fell over each shoulder, catching the light; as she bent forward, her tiny frame twining towards the open door and the garden beyond, her whole body seemed to thrum with tension. Hannah, their beloved maid, waited patiently in the doorway.

Beyond the french windows was a small path leading in a straight line to a neat garden edged with scented box. The first roses, delicate lemon and blush pink, ran riot along the back wall, threatening to overwhelm the formal lines of the garden, to the consternation of Crabtree the gardener. Mr Dysart took on dreadfully if he found a sprig of box growing out of the low bushes, which must be trimmed twice a week in the summer months. Mr Dysart liked everything just so. 'A garden is to be tamed,' he used to say, waggling his silver scissors at Crabtree. 'We are masters of the earth and sky, Crabtree. Remember that.'

And yet behind the rose-covered wall death ruled supreme, for less than ten yards from the garden was the Highgate Cemetery, built some fifty years previously and still the most fashionable location in London in which to be buried. From the bedrooms at the back of the house and Mary's brother Pertwee's room in particular one could see the whole expanse of the cemetery spread out below – the catacombs sunk into the hill, the Egyptian Avenue with its great stone-carved gates and columns, the meandering rows of tombs, and the headstones poking up like grey teeth out of the dark earth. At all times of day they could hear the shuffling processions and the muffled sobs as the coffins, all too often too small, were lowered into the ground.

The Dysart girls often hid from their nanny, Nurse Bryant, in Pertwee's bedroom, The Rookery – for though to start with Rupert was often caned by her and shut up in the dark for his troubles, lately she did not seem to concern herself to the same degree with him. Rupert, always known to the girls as Pertwee, was eighteen now, and a student at the Royal Academy. He was beyond her power; he was free to come and go. From his bedroom his sisters, however, could and did still watch the funerals and mark out of ten the opulence of each once.

Their mother, Helena, had been buried in the cemetery, in a lead-lined coffin because of the smallpox that killed her. At first, they had been required to go every Sunday to visit her grave. Lately, they hardly went at all, and Mary was not even sure now she could recall where precisely her mother lay. Father used to tell them, they were lucky Mother was buried there, in a proper place, rather than one of the hideous graveyards in Soho or St Pancras, where the stink was unbearable and bodysnatchers still lurked, waiting to carry corpses away and carve them into pieces. Her grave was a small slab of marble, just her name and her dates. Next to the carved hourglasses or the broken columns it made her seem so . . . unimportant. And she had not been, not to them.

Pertwee wouldn't talk about their mother. But Liddy remembered her quite well. She remembered playing with the doll's house, sitting on her lap, her lavender-scented skirts spread out about her, and her telling them about her childhood with her sister, Charlotte. Of the churchyard behind the house. Of the nightingales that sang all night long in May and June. Of the hoop they would chase around the perimeter of the new house with a stick, and the ice on the windows. For Christmas one year when she was quite little her father, the vicar of the church behind the trees, had given her a snowglobe – a large one of figures on an ice rink, for which he had sent to London. She remembered seeing a fox tearing out a chicken's throat, and the dormouse in its nest curled tightly up in a hedgerow, and the throngs of butterflies flickering around the buddleia that fringed the kitchen garden. 'Yes, we ate our own apples, and potatoes, and chickens, and sheep' – for Liddy, when small, wanted a pet lamb. 'One day, my darling. I'll take you there one day.'

It had never happened, for Mother and Lydia had stopped on the Heath one day to help a young woman crying out for help for her child's nursemaid, who had collapsed to the ground in a fit. Mother had escorted the girl – she was no more than thirteen or fourteen – back to Hampstead Road, walking with her arm around her, the mother and her child hanging back, weeping. Afterwards Mary used to wonder: who was this lady? Why couldn't she have helped her own servant? Why was it only their mother who had wanted to help?

Within two days Mother and Mary grew very sick, and only Mary survived. They were nursed together, at the start, until Mary was removed from her mother's room. Her mother had screamed for them not to be parted. Mary remembered that. Mary had nearly died, but now was left only with the scars of her illness.

Because as a young girl she wearied of being stared at, and so went out and about less than the other two, and because she was known to be delicate, having so very nearly died, Mary was generally agreed to be the most docile of the three Dysart children. Which was strange, since her mother had always said she would cause trouble. 'Mary is a world-shaker,' Liddy recalled Mother telling her. 'Mary will change things.'

And Mary didn't feel docile. Certainly she was kind to starving dogs, whom Pertwee tormented with scraps of meat, and wrote letters to her aunt, and listened patiently to Father's interminable stories of his time training at the Bar, his dismissal and rough treatment at the hands of those in his Chambers, his foresight in buying shares in Carbolic Soap Balls at 4 per cent, his foresight in proposing to Miss Helena Myrtle so soon after her aunt had died and left her and her sister the lion's share of her fortune. 'I got to her before the others, you see,' he'd told her daughter, stroking his whiskers carefully. Mary liked to pretend he forgot she was Mother's daughter when he said such things.

The doll's house had been in the nursery. Mother used to open it up every teatime, and they would all play with it, the fire lit, bread and butter and jam served by Hannah. When Mother died, Father decided to hire a nursemaid for the children. He said it would be good for them to have some discipline. After Liddy was rude to Nurse Bryant over not being allowed more jam on her toast, quite soon after Nurse Bryant's arrival, the doll's house was moved to the drawing room, where the children were only allowed to play with it on Sunday afternoons. They spent the rest of the week staring longingly at it. They were lucky children, Nurse Bryant told them, to have such a doll's house.

When, several weeks later, she burned their other toys – Pertwee's wooden Jack-in-a-box, and Liddy's rag doll Anna, and Mary's spinning top – she said they were lucky to have had anything at all and must learn not to complain.

They were also lucky, she told them, to have their dead mother so close by, where they could pray for her soul.

('Such a pity,' Mary had heard Aunt Charlotte say to Hannah on one of her last visits to her poor sister's children. 'Surrounded by all that *death*, most vexing!')

So very much rested on the outcome of this little walk in the garden that May afternoon. Ignoring the rustling in the trees from the cemetery, which scared her even during the day, Mary leaned forward the better to hear what the couple before her might be saying.

The gentleman had long since left behind the travails of youth.

He was a solemn, poker-straight figure in black frock coat and silk top hat, greying hair waxed into magnificent sideburns. He was Highworth Rawnsley, since Oxford days the dearest friend of Mary's father. As he walked, he inclined his head, very slightly, because of his precariously balanced pince-nez, towards the younger figure at his side. This was Liddy, of course, who twisted her figure eagerly to his unbending one, straining to catch his speech, her lovely face turned to him like a flower towards the sun.

Mary watched, her heart in her throat. She adored her sister more than anyone or anything in the world and she had long ago now realised that she had to leave the house to survive. Of that at least she could be certain.

'No, my child,' Highworth Rawnsley could be heard to say to some remark of Liddy's and at that he took her hand in his, holding the little gloved fingers. 'Ah! My innocent little one!'

'But—' Mary heard her sister reply, smiling up at him. The ribbon pulling her carefully ragged curls away from her face had slipped somewhat, and the curls themselves were drooping. Mary froze – this angered Bryant, she knew, but Liddy didn't seem to have noticed. She never seemed to care, she took punishment better than either of the others. Always had done, since she was torn from her mother, one shoulder broken, almost lifeless, a rag doll, Hannah was fond of telling them with relish. 'Greenish blue, twig-like limbs and most ugly, you was. And you just lays there quiet as anything, little bubba, that shoulder must-a been agony, but you never cried, you never did!'

There was a grass stain on Liddy's newly pressed dress, a smudge on her cheek. *Oh Liddy, how will she punish you this time.* Mary turned away, unable to watch any more. She must say yes to him, if he proposed. And he would, today, surely –

They had discussed Mother that morning, sitting on Mary's bed, as she tightened the rags in Liddy's hair.

'She liked Highworth?' Liddy had asked, biting at her nails as

Mary pulled the strips of material tighter again. 'I should like him too if it were true.'

'She did, dearest but . . .' Mary had hesistated. 'Though it is true he was Father's best man and their dearest friend, I suppose it does not necessarily follow that he would make his daughter a good husband. Still . . .' She trailed off.

'But it does not follow that he would *not*,' said Liddy, brightening, for she had been nervy all morning, twitching at the slightest sound – the previous night Nurse Bryant had discovered her looking out of the window when she should have been in bed, and this morning she was so sore down one side of her thin ribcage and leg that she said she had not been able to sleep. Mary, examining the bruises that morning, had felt the rush of anger and shame that followed every such disclosure by her sister and as so often, though she was the younger by almost two years, a protective desire to shield her impetuous older sister, who seemed not to foresee in the way she herself did what behaviour could provoke each beating, each humiliation.

The previous winter she had worked up the courage required to tackle Father about it, venturing into his study one cold January evening. But he had dismissed her. 'It will all come right again, my dear,' he'd said, as though she had been telling him of a carriage's broken wheel or a smashed plate. But he had obviously spoken to Nurse Bryant about it the following day, for a deep bowl of water was left outside on the terrace to freeze over on the surface, exactly where Liddy could see it during her lessons, and that night her head was held down in the bowl for so long she had blacked out afterwards.

So, though Highworth Rawnsley was fifty and Liddy only sixteen, though he licked his lips too much and had a curious sibilant rasp, though Mary thought he grasped Liddy's slim arm too roughly, and though after their marriage he would take Liddy, her beloved sister and dearest friend in all the world, away to Perthshire, where she would be required to keep house for him and his bedridden mother, Mary was certain that this was a safer course for her than remaining at St Michael's House with Nurse Bryant. Mary hoped that perhaps her passionate, impetuous sister was not indifferent to Mr Rawnsley, that she enjoyed his company, the way he made a pet of her, his kindnesses . . . *Oh dear Lord, let him be a kind man. Please.* Often, when someone started at the sight of her in the street, or when a child pointed at the smallpox scars and let out a wail, or when people smiled far, *far* too kindly at her, Mary wanted to stop them, and say:

I am glad of these scars. I am afraid when my sister says that they have started to fade, for with them I am untouchable. I am safe from the attentions of any man. Do not you see? I am the lucky one.

A muddled riot of shouting from the hallway brought Mary abruptly out of her reverie. She blinked, turning away from the couple in the garden, who were locked in close conversation. From the hall the shouts grew louder, so, tidying her lace collar and smoothing her skirts, Mary moved towards the noise, stopping to shut up the doll's house on the way.

'Oh goodness, Pertwee,' she said, as she emerged into the hall. 'What nonsense. Here you are and you'll disturb Father.'

'Father won't mind!' said her brother, his face flushed. He glanced swiftly at her: one of their secret looks, shame and terror mixed with alcohol, and pain sluiced her heart, like lemon on a wound. But, just as swiftly, he was his exuberant, charming self again, throwing his bowler hat on to the coat rack and thrusting two coats at his friend. 'Here, Ned! Here's sport. Hang that up, will you, and Dalbeattie's too!'

'Dash it, Dysart! I'm not your servant,' said the aforementioned Ned, and he threw the coats back at Rupert, who gave a too-loud bark of laughter.

'Ned's a rough and rude chap, Mary. The roughest of them all! But, look, I've promised you for an age that I'd bring him home and see, I have now, haven't I? Ned, compose yourself. Let's make introductions. Dalbeattie, you don't know my sister, Mary, do you?'

A tall figure, disentangling himself from his scarf, glanced at Mary then, obviously flustered, patted his waistcoat with long fingers, blinked several times and held out his hand to her, gazing into her steady brown eyes. 'How do you do, Miss Dysart. Ch-charmed to meet you. Charmed.'

'How do you do,' she said, trying not to blush as he pumped her arm up and down. She had seen him once before, calling for her brother before a walk upon the Heath. This was Lucius Dalbeattie, who was studying at the Royal Academy School of Painting with her brother, though he had recently become apprenticed to an architect.

She liked Dalbeattie, and the way that his eyes met hers directly and didn't range over her shoulders and hair, anywhere but her pockmarked face. Her small hand rested in his large one for a moment longer; each glanced again at the other, as though taken by surprise, before Mary removed her hand gently, glancing up at him once more as she did so.

'I've heard an awful lot about you, Miss Mary,' he said.

I know all about you. He was from a wealthy Scottish family, and he and Ned had talked often of building their own Utopia, where they all might live and work in freedom.

'Only he's engaged to a girl he's known from birth,' Pertwee had told them both. 'So it won't happen just yet, for he has to marry her, though I don't think he's awful keen on it, save for the fact it was his Pa's dying wish he do so. Unite the estates, and all that. So I will carry on painting, and Ned too, until Dalbeattie's ready to build. You can live there if you wish, my dear sisters: we will allow women in Utopia.'

'To pick up after you and get you out of scrapes and mend your clothes? Oh, how very fortunate for us,' Liddy had said, for she had less patience than Mary for Pertwee's schemes.

As he smiled at her and backed away, Dalbeattie collided with Pertwee, who slapped his other companion on the shoulder.

'This is Ned Horner, Mary. I'm sure you must be pleased to make his acquaintance, for I've talked of little else but him since we met. The girls are quite wild to know you now, Ned.' He winked at them both. 'Isn't it true, Mary?'

'It is,' she said, wishing Pertwee were not so vulgar, and terrified

107

he would be discovered in this state. 'It is a pleasure to meet you, Mr Horner.'

'And you, Miss Dysart. How do you do,' he said, and he shook her hand, smiling.

He was fairer and slighter than her strawberry blonde, barrel-chested brother and younger, by a couple of years, Mary could tell. His face was thin, and though he wore a three-piece suit like his friends, it was much mended, far shabbier than theirs. The hand that grasped hers was cold, even on this fine May day, and his eyes were an intense grey-blue. As they shook hands he said, seriously, 'It is a very great honour to make your acquaintance, Miss Dysart. Your brother is a dear comrade of mine . . .' Then he paused and, turning away, emitted a small, slight belch.

'That's torn it!' Dalbeattie whispered, and Rupert said:

'I say, Ned, what? Don't show us all up.' He turned to Mary, frowning. 'Horner here sold a picture this morning. To Charles Booth. Charles Booth, Mary!' His face cleared into a smile, the muscles adjusting slowly. 'A terrific painting, a truly splendid piece, no – don't blush, Ned, it's true.' Pertwee smiled at Mary. '*A Meeting.* We saw it at the S-Summer Exhibition. Liddy was mad for it, do you recall?' Mary nodded, for she remembered the painting, of a group of young people – two women and four men – on the Heath, standing informally and talking. But more than that she struggled to remember, though her brother and sister had been in raptures over it, over the Exhibition itself, so much so that they had visited it again, by themselves. Mary had disliked it: the rooms so close and awfully crowded, the throngs around one or two pictures in each room; everything mostly so brown and sombre and formal. Old men, moustaches, hands twisted behind their backs, watching: watching her, Liddy, the paintings, the crowd. Liddy, however, had adored the whole experience.

Mary said now, 'I remember your picture most clearly, Mr Horner; I congratulate you.'

'That's why I brought old Ned here, so he could see Liddy, and she could tell 'im herself.' Mary opened her mouth, aghast, as

Pertwee scratched his head. 'You see, Mary, we went to celebrate, at Lockhart's Dining Rooms, to toast our future Utopia. Had some chicken, cooked with chestnuts. Chestnuts and chicken. Delisus – delishusus.' He stopped. 'Chicken and chestnuts. Might have had some champagne. Whatnot.'

'That's torn it!' Dalbeattie hissed again, desperately.

'Pertwee!' Mary hissed, but the unrepentant Pertwee was pushing his friend Ned down the wide hallway, past Father's study, towards the dining room.

'Oh, hush, Dalbeattie. You're not a respectable married man just yet – stop being such an old goat. Let us go this way, Ned, and I'll fetch us more refreshment!' He giggled.

'Pertwee,' Mary called again, as quietly as she could towards her brother's retreating back. 'If Father hears you, you'll be thrown out on the street, especially after the last time. Please, dearest. Do exercise some caution.'

But her brother merely threw her a smirk and gave her a small wave. Ned turned to her. 'I'll make it all right, Miss Dysart,' he said, with his sweet, lopsided smile.

'Nearly starved to death last winter, dear old Ned,' her brother had told her recently up in the Rookery, while Liddy wrote and Mary sewed and Pertwee painted them, and where the three siblings were at their most content. 'He won't accept Dalbeattie's charity, and it's fearful hard to help him. There's no money, his circumstances have been most difficult. His mother died when he was a babe, and his father is a carpenter, an honest fellow, too honest, for he takes too long to do the work and charges too little, though I've seen some of his pieces, and they are beautiful. You may see where Ned gets his talent from.'

Liddy, dozing by the fireside, had raised her silver-blonde head. 'Is he good?'

'He's a marvel,' Pertwee had said frankly. 'By far the best student at the Academy and the youngest. He can render in minutes a scene I could not complete in a month, and you're *in* it, when you look at it. Remarkable, really. And he whittles, too – makes little figures in wood. His hands have to be busy, he says. He barely sleeps, eats nothing, wears his clothes to threads – he's not like me, not at all, he lives for his art. I do love him as a brother, he's a most endearing chap.'

Now, from the depths of the house, Mary could hear her father rousing himself from his post-prandial nap. '*Hannah?*'

'Oh dear,' she whispered.

'*Hannah! Dear dear Lord, where's me blasted stick? I can't find it! Hannahhh!*' And there came the jangling of the bell, and, from the kitchen below, the sound of scurrying, of chairs being scraped back, which meant Miss Bryant might soon be on the move, too.

But the gang of three troublemakers had danced happily past her and out into the garden, limbs flailing about like gadflies on a pond, and as Mary peered in terror she could see them, dashing in and out of the rows of box: tall, helpless Dalbeattie, her own darling brother, fat, saturnine as Bacchus, and Ned Horner, leading the way, the sunlight catching his face and throwing its angular beauty into sharp relief.

Footsteps, brisk, quiet, pattered behind her, and liquid seemed to sweep through Mary's person, though her mouth was dry.

'Good afternoon, Miss Dysart,' came a low voice behind her. 'Do you know where I might find Miss Lydia?'

'Yes, Bryant. She's in the garden.'

'I'll fetch her. The tea-gown has come back from the dressmaker's and it's time we measured her.' Miss Bryant, small, sleek, like a blackbird, moved past Mary, who suddenly put her hand on her arm.

'No, don't.'

Miss Bryant turned, and Mary saw the iron anger flash in her eyes, to be instantly replaced with cool politeness. She tasted metal in her mouth. 'I'm wanting to have things ready before teatime, Miss Mary.'

'She's in the garden with Mr Rawnsley, Miss Bryant. Father would rather she wasn't disturbed. I'll tell her – I'll tell her to come to you. She knows not to be late.'

They never knew, because they never asked their father, where Nurse Bryant came from. When she was very old, Liddy sometimes wondered if she had been Welsh, for in her nightmares she heard her voice still and it had a Celtic lilt to it. But Mary maintained she was a Cockney, even if she didn't speak like one.

What horror had happened in her own childhood to turn her into the person she was they never knew either. When she arrived Liddy was not quite seven. On her second day in the house she beat Liddy with a hairbrush, and thence twenty times every occasion Liddy didn't come to her room for tea when called. Ten times on the bottom, ten on the head, so frequently that afterwards Liddy had headaches which blinded her, though Miss Bryant knew never to bruise her face. Because Mary had been ill she didn't hit her, not at first. And then, later, Mary somehow wasn't in trouble the way Liddy was. Her skirts were never torn, her smock dirty, her hair unkempt. Liddy's were.

Now, as Miss Bryant turned and quietly, smoothly left, Mary stepped into the garden, clutching the skirts of her dress so tightly her knuckles were white, and trying to calm herself. Liddy would have accepted Highworth Rawnsley, she'd be married by All Hallow's Eve and gone away from here by Christmas, and Bryant would have to leave. *And I'll still see you, Pertwee, and I shall visit you and Highworth and Mrs Rawnsley every few months*, she'd told Liddy. *We shall write to each other every day, and I will look after Pertwee and Father, and all will be well!*

As she turned the corner she came upon a most unlikely scene – Dalbeattie and her brother, walking upon the rim of the fountain, arms outstretched to maintain balance, and her sister, in between Highworth Rawnsley and Ned Horner, engaged in most serious discussion. Liddy caught sight of her sister's grey skirt, and looked up, a great smile on her face. Behind her, Mr Rawnsley was pulling at the tip of his beard at something Mr Horner was saying. Mary thought with a sinking heart that he did not look like a newly engaged lover.

'Oh Mary, dearest!' Liddy exclaimed, catching hold of Mary's hands. Her fingers were ice-cold, her hands shaking. 'Such wonderful news, I can hardly wait to tell you!'

'What is it, my love?' she answered, trying to draw her sister away, to calm her down. Ned Horner, besider her, patted Rawnsley's shoulder, drawing him into conversation.

Liddy's soft hair fell about her shoulders, the curls so painfully acquired now entirely absent. She chewed at one nail. 'Mr Rawnsley – he and I have had *such* a good conversation about women and art. I told him about the picture I had seen at the Summer Exhibition by Elizabeth Thompson – do you remember it, Mary my dear? It was of the Crimean War. In fact I feel if our talk had not been cut short we –'

Mary sank down on to a bench, overcome. Liddy crouched beside her.

'Dearest Mary, are you ill? May I fetch some water?'

'So he did not offer for you?'

Liddy shook her head.

Mary swallowed. 'Miss Bryant, my love – when you are free she wants you to go to your room, to try on the tea-gown, the dress-makers have sent it back.'

Liddy's face clouded. Then: 'Oh, hang her,' she said, gritting her teeth. 'I shan't.'

'You must,' Mary whispered. 'Darling, of course you must.'

'No.' And Liddy stood up.

'Miss Dysart,' said Ned Horner, suddenly, and when the sisters turned they saw he was watching them both. His eyes fixed on Liddy, intently. 'Will you settle an argument for us?'

'Of course.'

Highworth Rawnsley cleared his throat. 'Mr Horner is under a misapprehension,' he said, and he pursed his lips, briefly. 'Now I, who have known you from a babe in arms, know this to be true, but you may disabuse him yourself, my dear. You too, Miss Mary. Is it not true, as you yourself have owned, that the disabilities of your sex preclude you from a full appreciation of art?'

'Oh!' said Liddy, and she bobbed up on her feet and down again, and then was very still.

'For myself,' said Mary, after a pause, 'I should not place credence in such an idea and it grieves me that you should, Mr Rawnsley.'

'My dear,' said Highworth Rawnsley, smiling thinly, his hooded gaze watchful, and he pushed his glasses up his fine Roman nose. 'I trade in facts, not in figures like your wily old father. It is accepted fact that a constitutional weakness in the female form prevents full dexterity with finer brushes. Besides which, the idea of woman as Great Artist is so abhorrent when one thinks of what her role *should* be. One thinks fondly of Patmore's *The Angel in the House.*' He rocked on his feet, pleased with himself. '"Man must be pleased, but him to please is woman's pleasure." Hm? On my previous visit your sister and I discussed this very subject and she and I agreed—'

'Indeed, sir, no, for you misunderstood me then, and you do now!' Liddy said, hotly. 'Elizabeth Thompson's paintings are as fine as any others in the exhibition. Finer, to my mind, for she brings a subtler understanding of the human condition.' Her eyes flashed. 'Tell me, sir, this constitutional weakness from which we suffer, is it a physical one, or a mental one?'

Her little hands clenched and unclenched themselves into fists: beside her stood Ned Horner, watching her in astonishment.

'She's right, Rawnsley. How do you answer?'

'I'm with Highworth,' said Pertwee, carelessly. 'Don't care how you say it, women don't have the stamina to paint. Charming watercolours all very well, but 'snot possible for them to attempt the great subjects. War. Love. Heroism.'

He sat down suddenly on the side of the fountain, and wiped his nose on his sleeve, before, catastrophically, expelling a quantity of air from his mouth, loudly. Highworth Rawnsley looked at him with cold disgust.

Dalbeattie muttered: 'Oh Pertwee, you absolute—'

'Miss Dysart, perhaps you and your brother forget yourself,' said Rawnsley, as Mary placed a cooling hand on Lydia's arm, and suddenly her sister's anger subsided.

'Perhaps you are right,' she said, after a short while, and she gave a small, resigned shrug. As though she could see the inevitable.

Then, from nowhere, a tiny piped voice began singing.

'Oh Rawnsley, Oh Highworth, Oh Highworth it is so,
Oh Rawnsworth, Oh Highley, Oh Fol-di-rol-lo!'

Highworth Rawnsley spun around.

'Who's that! Who sings that nonsense! Rupert! Is that you, sir?'

'This is the surname and this be the first!
But to say both together, I'd laugh fit to burst!
Oh Rawnsley, Oh Highworth, Oh Highworth 'tis so . . .'

'Hi!' Highworth Rawnsley called, his voice thick with fury, the tip of his nose entirely white. 'Stay there,' he said to Liddy, pointing at her, abruptly. 'I will return, momentarily, to clarify with you a subject about which I came to call.' Mary saw the cold fury of the look he gave her, the dismissive way he turned from her. *He doesn't mean to marry. He never did. He is an old woman, not a husband. Father must have known this.* He marched off towards the back of the garden, where to her horror Mary saw two figures, Pertwee and Dalbeattie, climbing over the back wall, on to the lane which led into the cemetery.

'Bad, awful, awful boys,' Liddy muttered. 'Oh . . . oh dear . . .'

But she was smiling, just very slightly.

Mary turned to her. 'Please go and see what Nurse Bryant wants, darling.'

'Yes, I should, shouldn't I? Come with me.' Liddy set off towards the house, pulling her sister's arm through her own. As they approached the french windows they heard feet thundering behind them and Ned Horner was beside them.

'I say, Miss Dysart,' he said, breathing heavily. 'May I call upon you again?'

Liddy turned to him.

'You're a boy,' she said, almost scornfully. 'Pertwee is a boy too, and an idiot, and Mary and I suffer because of his dissipation. Do not seek to please me, sir, by embroiling yourself with him.'

'But he is a good boy. He is my friend. He suffers—'

She turned away from him, wearily. 'Good day, Mr Horner.'

'Miss Dysart. Please allow me—'

'No,' she said, sharply, and there was a note of hysteria in her voice Mary had never heard before. 'If he was your true friend, yours and Dalbeattie's, with all your fine talk of utopias and friendships, you'd stop his drinking, find him a way out, a way he can leave this place and help his sisters. But you don't care for that. You *or* Dalbeattie. Mary and I must look after ourselves.'

Ned nodded, teeth gritted, hair falling in his eyes. In a low voice he said, 'I swear to you we will help him. From this moment I swear it.'

Liddy did not react. She said blankly, 'I wish that you meant it.'

'I do. You have my word. I – I will act for Rupert. I know he suffers. But he is a dear fellow to me. Lydia – you must allow me to tell you – to help you – I have wanted to say, since our meeting –' His eyes were hollow, his voice hoarse. 'Here—'

And from his shabby coat pocket he took a piece of carved wood, and handed it to her.

'I saw you the day you visited the Academy again with your brother,' he whispered, and he folded a kiss into the palm that held the small figure, as Liddy gasped. Mary took a few steps back from them, watching. 'You were in brown watered silk with a cream gathered skirt. We discussed painting. Your eyes were dull, you had a bruise on your arm, I saw it. Pertwee told me in his cups what she does to you. I've thought of you every day. I made this for you.' His hand tightened. 'I want – you.'

He was staring at Liddy with a bright, feverish gaze; Mary turned away, uncomfortably stirred by this display of private passion. Liddy stood straight-backed and silent.

'I know you understand me. I – I want to take you away. To make you beautiful things. A house. People to go in it. Please. Please let me show you I can.' His eyes searched hers for a reaction. 'Please!'

She nodded, mutely, and put one hand over his.

For the rest of her life, Mary would always think of them in that moment. Framed by the formal lines of box and the red brick of the wall behind them, clutching hands, as if a pact had been made. An undertaking.

And then he was gone, running down the path towards the back wall, and he had climbed it in a trice, and disappeared out of view, as the sisters stood on the step, astonished, and the voice of Miss Bryant could clearly be heard calling with fury to her charge. Liddy opened her hand again and resting on her palm was a girl, half turning as if to catch a sound, in a swirling dress whose skirt rippled as though it were water, not wood, and a smile upon her face, and she was the living image of Liddy, a tiny replica.

Chapter Nine

Pardon me, dear sir! Pardon me –
For I am but a foolish maid
And foolish maids, unlike thy sex
Their hearts oft feel betrayed –
Dear sir! Allow me one small gift
A crumb dare I present to you
Were I to love – ah – to give mine heart – 'twould be you
But alas, 'tis not, and I must say – adieu.

Liddy watched as her sister put the verse gently down on the writing-desk. 'And?' she said, without much enthusiasm.

Mary hesitated. 'Well, dearest, it's very – *feeling*. I feel the writer is sincere.'

'I'm the writer, Mary. You know I am.' Liddy checked a lock of hair that had escaped from her bun.

'Yes.'

'So what did you *think* of it? As a poem? As a – a *work*.'

Liddy followed her gaze as Mary looked politely away, out over the gathering autumn afternoon, at the ruffled citrus-coloured tree-tops of South Grove. A carriage drew up outside the Flask Inn, opposite the house; the nearest horse was old, dead tired, saddle sores blooming on his side, his mane matted with mud. Liddy's nose twitched; she blinked, and turned away from the sight, drumming her fingers on the wall.

'Oh, Mary. I used to want to paint, before Pertwee took it on, and I am sure he is better than I would have been. And I had such plans of opening the hat shop, too, do you remember?'

'And of writing music. Those songs. Very good they were.'

'Oh, they were not. I want to *do* something. To *be* something.' They were both silent, contemplating the futility of this dream. Then Liddy sighed sadly. 'I do not think I shall ever be a poet. At least,' she corrected herself, with a glimmer of humour. 'Not a good one.'

'You must be honest.' Mary stood up, pushing her chair away from the table, and gathered up her embroidery work-bag. 'That is all. With yourself and with the reader.'

Liddy would not return her gaze. After a moment she muttered, 'Highworth is gone today, off to Scotland, did you know?'

'Yes. Yes I did. And your plans must be delayed again.'

'I asked to go with him and for you to accompany me.' Liddy rolled her pen between her fingertips. 'But his mother felt it would be unseemly, before he had even asked for my hand in marriage.' Her voice was high, almost shrill with tension. 'Oh, I wish he'd declare himself, instead of this delay!'

'If he did offer for you, would you still want to marry him?'

Liddy said: 'Yes, to have it done with. I – There is no other way. I see that.'

After that spring afternoon several months ago, Highworth had written to Liddy.

> *. . . behaviour unbecoming in one so young and in my future wife . . . standard of decorum expected . . . grace and poise absent. It is clear that I shall have to reconsider my position, and shall also be required to prepare you most diligently for married life if our union is to be sanctioned by me, and gain the approval of your father, and God Almighty, Maker of All Things . . .*

Pertwee had been severely punished by his father, his allowance docked, his final year at the Royal Academy School cancelled, and he had been banned from seeing Ned Horner and Lucius Dalbeattie, simply for being intoxicated and causing high jinks. The sisters felt for him most acutely. Pertwee was now left without the one activity that gave him release and distraction from his other vices, and since painting was the only occupation for which he had ever shown any aptitude, his sisters felt this to be extremely foolish of their father, but there was no hope of changing his mind. Their father was like a clam when he did not like something: he simply closed up.

Dalbeattie had gone to the Continent, having completed his apprenticeship as an architect; his family's hopes rested on him, and it had been understood for many years now that he was expected to earn a living as soon as may be before his marriage. Ned Horner had not been mentioned since that day, nor had he been back to the house.

At the doorway Mary paused. 'Did you have it in mind to attend the lecture at the Highgate Literary and Scientific Institution this afternoon, dearest?'

'No. Mary . . .' And Liddy hesitated for a moment too long. 'I don't care for the subject today. I shall work a little longer then perhaps persuade Pertwee to get out of bed and take a turn upon the Heath with me. Do you go?'

'Miss Madison is attending, as she has a keen interest in the supernatural. I have said I will meet her there.' Mary put her head on one side, her eyes bright, and swallowed, as if she were controlling herself tightly. 'Take – take care, dearest.'

Liddy nodded at her sister, her lips pressed together, and picked up her pen, but as the door closed she laid it gently down again, and ran to the window. *You must be honest.* The carriage was gone, the horses watered. 'Though what relief that will give them and for how long,' she said aloud, her voice shaking with scorn.

Fingers trembling, Liddy put on her small-brimmed teal velvet hat trimmed with the single egret feather, a much prized birthday present from Aunt Charlotte, and quickly donned her dull-grey woollen cloak – for October was cold this year, with a wet chill that sank into the bones. She glanced in the mirror, pinching her cheeks, then moved swiftly about the room, gathering up her little reticule, taking out her own embroidery sampler, hiding the sheets of poetry, setting out a letter she had previously half written in the expansive, untidy scrawl which had so often earned her the oppro-brium of both her father and Miss Bryant. When she had finished, she looked around. It was, to all intents and purposes, the room of a young lady who had stepped out of the room for a couple of minutes in search of – what, exactly? Another silken thread, a lost glove, a book.

Footsteps sounded on the stairs – Liddy started and, creeping into Mary's room through the connecting door, she made her way down via the back stairs. Her father was in his study. Hannah was out: it was her afternoon off. Mrs Lydgate was at the butcher's, Mary gone to the lecture, Pertwee asleep in his room, snoring loudly. And Miss Bryant was nowhere to be seen in that moment and that was all that mattered.

In less than a minute she was crossing the road, the sweet, thick scent of woodsmoke mingling with coal, and manure, and the mulch of the autumn leaves. She made her way towards the hackney carriage that she had earlier seen pull up outside the public house. It was waiting for her.

Liddy stroked the horses' shivering flanks, then climbed up into the cab, averting her gaze, biting her lip, for the treachery of it, the betrayal of all her fervently held beliefs! Miserably, she settled on to the back seat of the cab.

'Cold day, ain't it? Where to, miss?' said the lantern-jawed driver, arranging a rug over her knees, but she flung his hand from her lap, frantic to be off, not to be seen, to be away.

'Blackfriars – oh, hurry, please, Blackfriars Bridge. As before, sir.'

'Aye, if you please, miss,' he said, and he sucked his breath in grimly, as though he'd like to say more on the subject. One of the horses whinnied in a pathetic fashion, he set about them with a whip, and they were off, Liddy in the back, a pear-shaped tear rolling down her cheek, for she hated it, every time, though she could no more have stayed away than stopped breathing.

The road south of Smithfield market was clogged with livestock of all kinds – when she had first started doing this journey, she'd seen lambs just like the ones she'd wanted when she was a little girl, whites of their eyes rolling in their silly heads, bleating pitifully as they were shoved roughly into pens. Now, several months later, they were young sheep, fluffy grey-cream clouds being being herded inside the great iron halls, along with the mass of cattle and goats. Liddy had learned to cover her ears now as they approached, to block the screams of animals being slaughtered, and she stayed like that for a minute or two, eyes tightly shut, as the cab driver bellowed at various animals and humans to clear out of his way. Down towards Ludgate Circus, where, as they waited for a way to clear through the cabs, carts, omnibuses and wagons, several lads outside the Dog and Bowl peered inside the carriage and made several off-colour remarks, which she ignored. A street-sweeper, a curly-haired boy younger than her, leaped hastily out into the traffic, frantically sweeping up the stray straw and detritus on the road before retreating swiftly to avoid being knocked down by an omnibus. Then further on to Blackfriars Bridge. The first couple of times the ragged, filthy women scrabbling desperately at the small mounded shores of the foul Thames had aroused her curiosity, until she had had it explained to her by the driver that they went through every last piece of rubbish to collect items that might be valuable, and could be recycled – leather, glass, wood.

Sometimes there were children with the women, ragged and painfully thin, sitting blankly on the cold, slimy riverbanks, faces black with dirt, expressions blank. Once, hurrying across in the safety of her luxurious cab, she had seen a fight over some small scrap, two women tearing each other to pieces, blood dripping from the ear of one, an older woman, while the others around them simply carried on with their search.

As they crossed Blackfriars Bridge Liddy held her nose, and tried not to think about them, about the baby she had seen as the carriage thundered past on her previous visit, a tiny thing, in the arms of its mother, who was leaning against a low wall before the bridge, insensate, maybe asleep, maybe dead, the baby coughing, making a piteous mewling sound and she had not really taken in the meaning of the scene until they were past and the driver would not stop. She had left them behind too. She was so innocent. She knew nothing of life, nothing at all.

She stared at St Paul's Cathedral, and thought of what Father had told her, that the tip of the spire was exactly the same level as the front door of their own church, St Michael's in Highgate. How lucky she had been to grow up high above the stinking city, with a father who had money to care for them all. She had known nothing of real life before. How lucky she was to have soft feather pillows and warm soup to eat, and people to help her get undressed! She was, as Miss Bryant would say, extremely fortunate, unlike so many of her fellow humans. These last few months had utterly opened her eyes to the truth of the world in which she lived. She couldn't ever see things the way they had been, could not go back and put it all in the box, close it, again. 'We shall all be changed in an instant, in the twinkling of an eye, at the last trumpet,' St Paul said. He had changed it all.

Over the bridge the carriage veered sharply to the right, clattering down a narrow, dark lane that led down to the river. The driver halted. 'Here we are, miss.'

'Oh, thank you,' said Liddy, clambering down by herself before he had the chance to offer to help her, for she did not think he would. 'And you will return at four o'clock? No later than four, for I must not be missed.'

'I'm not sure this time, miss,' he said, his jowls working as he chewed on some licorice root. 'I – I ain't comfortable with it, this sneaking around. Might be as though your father'd want to know something like this.'

He stared at her, and she saw his black, beady eyes, the jawline grinding, the pockmarked, heavy face.

'You were comfortable enough bringing me here,' she said, frankly.

'Aye, but it's different, when you're wanting to come back too, and I don't know as this gentlemen is right and proper—'

Liddy stamped her foot, chewing the inside of her mouth in

irritation. 'Sir, here is your money. If you wait for me I will pay you the same again for the return.'

He pulled his cap down over his forehead and said flatly, 'Three guineas.'

'You know full well that is not something I can give you.' She gave him one of her most charming smiles, for she knew old cross men like this could be easily appeased by sweet, charming young ladies. 'Please, sir, your kindness to me overdoes everything. I have no more money, but you have my undying gratitude.' She looked up at him through her lashes. 'Is that enough?'

He folded his arms. 'Mebbe.'

Liddy hurried down the uneven cobbled lane and, despite it all, she began to smile, her heart quickening as she drew close. For she was almost with him.

She climbed the wooden steps of the old tenement cottage grafted on to the side of one of the great wharves that overhung the Thames, clinging to it like a limpet to a rock. At the top of the stairs she clung to the slippery railing, and looked out over the churning, muddy river to the city spread out in front of her. Her heart thumped painfully in her chest. The door was suddenly flung open.

Ned Horner stood before her, rubbing a paintbrush with a cloth, his hair wild, his shirtsleeves filthy. His eyes drank her in, all of her, and yet all he said was:

'You came.'

And because of the boys outside the pub or the scrabbling women, or her sister's face as she read the poems, or the sad broken horses who had been whipped to bring her here, Liddy pressed her palms to her eyelids and began to softly cry, and he put his arms around her, for the very first time.

His scent was of dirty coal and sweat and the clean metallic oily smell of paint. She buried her hands and eyes into his chest, not quite able yet to look up at him yet but merely content to be in his arms. They were both of medium height but he was a little taller than her and her head was comfortable against his chest. And oh, he was so steady, so strong! How, when he was such a slight thing, painfully thin, for any money went on ale or porter and paints, not on good food. As he held her he whispered into her ear:

'I love you, Lydia. You will, won't you? You will . . .'

He left the words unsaid and she broke away, looking up at him now.

'Yes.'

Their grey eyes met, her mouth slightly parted and he kissed her.

Since the afternoon she had seen him again in the garden she had thought of little else. Often she thought she must be going slowly mad with love for him. Nothing so far in life, other than the huddled, private affection she and her two siblings had for each other had led her to understand what love could be like. His lips on hers were soft, and firm. He pressed against her, his buttons digging into her dress momentarily before the sensation ceased, as if they were fusing, top to bottom, melting into one another. She clutched his head in her hands, feeling his shiny hair, the scroll of his ears. She pulled away, looking into his liquid grey eyes, gently pushing his hair out of his face, and then she leaned towards him and kissed him again. Her heart pounded, somewhere in the back of her throat; her breathing came quickly, rising and falling. He put his left hand gently on her chest; she felt the pressure of his fingers on the curve of her breast, the thudding beneath it.

'Your heart,' he said, simply, staring into her eyes. His other hand was on his own chest and there was nothing except the two of them.

'It is like this, isn't it?' she said, moving towards him again, so his hand pressed against her breast again. He moved away from her after a moment, turning his head.

'I cannot – no more. Liddy, we must not forget ourselves.'

She met his gaze. 'But I don't care about anything else. Don't you understand?'

What might have happened next no one knows: but a seagull

cawed outside, too close, and Liddy jumped, just as the casement window of the dark room sprang open, flooding the place with stinking river air, and the spell was broken.

Liddy said, 'I hate this place. I wish you were not here.'

'Where else can I go?' Ned said. 'There is nowhere else.'

She tried to sound light-hearted. 'Dearest . . .' But she was so young, and had no experience of handling grown-up matters, much less men. 'But this place – your boots leak – the chimney smokes – don't you tire of aping Mr Rossetti, and living like this?'

He did not smile back, but slid his hands from her grasp. 'I do not ape Rossetti. I am not Dalbeattie, or your brother, given a generous living by their families.'

'Can't you sell a painting for a great deal of money, so we might set ourselves up together?' She moved towards him but he had folded his arms, his untidy hair falling forward into his face. 'You sold *A Meeting* for fifty guineas.'

'Yes, and I owed my landlord rent and Dalbeattie even more, and there are others I had to help, and paint, and canvases . . . I thought you understood.'

She stared at him, bewildered. She had believed that a river had been forded, that they were on the other side and all would be simple now. 'Yes. I understand that you choose to live like this when Mr Galveston and Mr Booth both say they will buy anything you paint if you paint more like *A Meeting*. Galveston said you could take on commissions—'

'I won't!' he said, loudly. 'You don't understand me, Liddy, if you think I'll hand over my work, which comes from my very deepest soul, the vision I have of – of everything, how the world should be, how you and I – you and I . . .' He trailed off. 'Booth's retiring soon, and I won't sell anything to that showman Galveston. He convinced poor Evelyn Peck to sell the copyright of *Larks at Play* to that train company, and Peck did it for he was near destitute and has three younger brothers and sisters to clothe and feed. And now the man's a laughing stock. It's on every other page in the newspaper. Evelyn's greatest painting and they're wrapping fish with it.'

'But what's *wrong* with that?' she cried, wringing her hands. 'He had very little, now he has much! His little sister has money for the doctor for her hands, and the children have shoes—'

'You said I was a boy once,' he said, his eyes glittering with unshed tears of anger. 'You said I behaved like a child. Well, I've been trying to show that I am not. That I'm a serious artist. Liddy, you must understand – I'm good, awfully good.' Now he caught hold of her hands. 'But I have to be the best there is. And that means there's no money yet, not for marrying, not for – other things like that.'

'Like what?'

'Family. Children.' A faint blush bloomed on his cheeks. 'Not until I establish myself, and not until you have distentangled yourself from that awful old man who wants to pluck you and take you to his Scottish prison.' He was never able to say Highworth Rawnsley's name. 'Dash it, Liddy – you must tell your father you will not marry him!'

'He has retreated, and I do not believe he still wants me. I do not understand why Father encouraged him.'

'Well there, you see! All will be right if you are honest, and your father lets me court you properly – don't you *see*? There is only one other alternative, and I will take it now.' His hands tightened on hers; she felt lightheaded, the hurried journey across town, no food all day; everything swam before her eyes, and she held on to him tightly. 'It is that you marry me now, Liddy, out of hand. Run away with me today. Yes, Liddy, honest artisans, we can live like that – we can!'

If she had said yes then!

'Oh, Ned. My love . . .' Liddy shook her head. 'My dearest friend from school, Imogen Cozens, she married a curate for love. I visited her last year, in Wales. She has lice and fleas, Ned. Rats chew all the food, she has the same grey stuff dress to wear come summer or winter. I won't.' She shook her head. 'We ate turnips. Three times. And her husband had the effrontery to tell me it was a pleasure for me to live like an honest peasant. I told him I expected peasants honest or otherwise would give anything for some ham to go with the turnips and he said something about Babylon and Mammon I thought it was best to ignore. Mary and I left after two days. Even Mary said it was really most unfortunate.'

He turned away from her and she bit her lip, watching him, then realised his curved back was shaking.

'Darling—' she began, then heard a sound coming from him and realised he was laughing. 'I don't understand quite what's so amusing,' she said, uncertainly.

'No, don't you?' he said, upright again, and he wiped his eyes. 'It's that your pragmatism is extremely refreshing, my darling – in fact, it's one of the things I love about you.'

She watched him cautiously; she simply wasn't used to being laughed at, and suddenly he said 'turnips' again and she found herself smiling. He put his arm around her, as though they were friends, as well as lovers, laughing together. He was like sunshine, golden warmth after the years at home. Liddy smiled at him and, curling her finger, beckoned him towards her.

'I must go,' she said. 'I cannot stay, I cannot be here—'

'One more kiss,' he said, and pulled her towards him, and they kissed, she thrilling to the touch of his hands, his lips, the promise of greater pleasure to come. He whispered in her ear:

'At night I close my eyes and I see us in our own world. You are in charge of this world. I paint. We have children – three children. We are very happy, Liddy.'

'*Yes.*' And she wondered if she wasn't making a terrible mistake. If she ought to stay with him now, as she so desperately wanted to do. *Yes.* She saw it now, the shining house on a hill, hidden away. Safe, warm, certain. And she at the centre of it all, in control.

She shivered as his lips lightly brushed her ear. He stroked the side of her head and moved away. 'Even your ear is beautiful. I want to paint it. My nightingale, in a cage.' He looked serious. 'I worry for you, my love. Trust me, and I will come good. Soon. And in the meantime, you must be brave, and break with Rawnsley.'

She said, dully, 'It is easy to say it. But if I break with him Father

127

will be angry, and that gives Bryant greater licence than ever. She is monstrous now, but must contain herself for fear I marry and my husband speaks out against her.'

Ned shook his head. 'How can someone be made this way?'

'I do not comprehend it.'

'Pertwee says he hears her muttering to herself at night, her room is next to his.'

'She told Crabtree she'd grown up in a debtors' prison. The Fleet. She said she used to have to beg for food, any sort of food, for the family, from passers-by through a grille in the wall on to the street. Crabtree said she was four. And she told him when it was demolished she walked through the night to stand outside while they pulled it down.' She shivered. 'I can believe it. I almost feel sometimes she is trying to do the best for me. But at other times I do think she is mad, Ned, that something's rotten in her soul. She holds up Mother's dresses against herself in front of the mirror. This look in her eyes – like a mechanical doll. A machine. You know what I mean?' And she shivered.

'I know exactly what you mean.' He nodded. 'As if there were something good in her once . . .' He went over to his notebook, perched on the windowsill and scribbled something down. A small brown bird, nestling against the leaded window, was startled, and flew away.

'What's that?' she said.

'Don't anger her, please. I want you. I want us. Remember the dream I had, and keep it safe.' His grey eyes were stormy in his kind, boyish face. 'Kiss me, Liddy.'

So she kissed him, allowing that extraordinary warmth and desire to flood her once again and as she stepped back, pulling on her gloves, she looked up. 'Ned, the door was open all this time.'

He glanced at it. 'I'm sure it wasn't. How vexing. The catch must have gone. It's not a good door, the grain is wrong, the quality poor.' She had collected up her gloves and reticule and stood watching him as he turned the handle, confused. 'Oh well. You'll come back next week? You will, won't you, my dearest?'

She drank in the sight of him: for he was here, in front of her, his lovely, liquid eyes, the scent of him, the fine bridge of his upper lip, the wild hair, so romantic. How could she not come again, despite the risk? How could she live without him? She patted his anxious face and realised something had changed, that she had grown up, somehow, at some point.

'Of course I will.'

And she walked downstairs alone, having dismissed his requests to see her into the carriage. The door banged on the hinge as she emerged downstairs on to the streets, and one of the horses neighed; Liddy looked up, half in a daze. Surely there had been only one horse before? But there were four now. She rubbed her eyes, knowing she was tired, and then a voice said:

'Get in.'

A hand with a grip like steel closed around her upper arm; the coach driver with the lantern jaw was escorting her to the carriage. She cried out –

'Ned! Help! Ned!'

But she was bustled into the carriage, and as she tumbled forward, gathering her skirts around her, she found herself gazing at the pale, glistening face of her father. As Ned Horner appeared in the dirty yard, calling out her name, her father leaned out of the carriage window, and said:

'You may proceed, driver.' He tapped the roof with his silver-topped cane and they were off, Ned shouting after her.

'Liddy! Liddy, where are they taking you?'

Mr Dysart said, in a sad, strange, faraway voice:

'Oh Lydia. They warned me about you, when you were born they said that hair of yours was a sign of sin, hair that silvery-yellow.' He plucked out a strand from her bun, pulling it lazily with two thin, long fingers. 'But I didn't believe them. And now I'm afraid I must punish you.'

'Father – Ned is a fine man, he is a friend of Pertwee's—'

Her father tapped his cane on the floor and pulled at his gloves. He was in a fuss, she could tell; he hated to be crossed. *'Don't interrupt me.*' She turned to him and saw his strange amber eyes, glowing in the gloom of the carriage. He was like a cat, prowling, lazy, dangerous. 'You wicked, wicked child,' he said, in a hissing drawl. 'The shame you have brought upon us. Imagine me, climbing the stairs to that vile shack. I should have listened to Miss Bryant from the start, when your sister came to me carrying these ridiculous tales of mistreatment, and what do I find? That it was all to cover up your own behaviour. I will deal with you at home, my dear.'

She could just hear Ned's voice, carried on the wind from the river:

Liddy! Liddy, send word to me!

'Deal – *deal* with me?' Liddy clutched her head, as the carriage juddered and rolled up towards the bridge, back over the river, back towards home, where it would all be over. 'You can't deal with me, not any more than Miss Bryant has already seen fit to over the past few years. I won't submit. You might as well kill me.' She laughed at her father. 'Yes, kill me, for it would be preferable to my treatment at her hands.'

'I won't kill you, nor will I allow such melodramatic nonsense to be spoken,' said Mr Dysart, coldly. 'But I can take your liberty away, which is the correct course of action for wayward daughters.'

'I will accept Highworth, the second he asks me!' she said, laughing at her father, for in that second she knew she would, to effect some form of escape, to allow her to leave the house. 'I will take Mary with me, and find her a husband, up in Scotland! How Mother must suffer, looking down on us—' She stopped, for her father was laughing, rocking backwards and forwards in the stuffy carriage. 'Yes, I shall marry him as soon as I may.'

'Rawnsley! Lydia, dearest, you are very much mistaken on that front. Dear, dithering Rawnsley has been sent back to his mother with a flea in his ear. I have told him you were unstable, a most unsuitable wife for a man of his position. Oh yes' – he was still laughing –'he was most relieved; do you not understand, my love? I encouraged his courtship knowing he'd never have the gumption to come up to scratch. My dear child.' He gazed out of the window, smiling as they crossed the river again, peering at St Paul's, as if it were all most diverting. 'None of you will marry. Not while it affects my portion; I shall be honest with you now! You see, no one will want Mary, thankfully, and Pertwee is on his way to ruin with no assistance from me. You were my only concern; I encouraged Highworth to that end knowing he'd keep the others at bay; but now you will understand the course I am regretfully forced to take.'

'Mother left us our own money!' Liddy spat, her face burning. 'She and Aunt Charlotte had the inheritance from their own aunt! There is the house in the countryside! The one w-with the night-ingales! It is to come to us, in due course!'

'Your mother was a fool, and was advised by fools, but for the question of my share. The beloved house about which she used to prattle incessantly is worth no more than the doll's house. Yes, my dear. It's a ruin, her father lost his money on poor investments, and ran the place into the ground. The man was a fool – ah, look at that fellow, the sailor, with the parrot! The inheritance she left you was dependent on your marriage. If you're not wed by the age of twenty-five, it passes to me.'

'You hope Nurse Bryant is finished with me before then?' Liddy's voice shook. 'You will see me dead before then? I understand.'

Her father's eyes opened wide, and she saw a thick, snaking red vein in his right eye, inching towards his tear ducts. 'My dear, such vulgar language. So hysterical! Of course not.' He dabbed at his forehead with his handkerchief. 'Now, we shall return home, and you will be confined to your room, until such time as you can be trusted. Nurse Bryant shall have the care of you. She is waiting for you.' He leaned forward, so she was inches away from him, and she could smell his sour breath and the oil on his yellowing whiskers. 'You thought she was your enemy. My dear, you are your own enemy. How you shall soon see it.'

Chapter Ten

Mary dreaded Tuesdays now more than any other day of the week. Before she knocked on Liddy's door a creeping fear consumed her like a fog, as she wondered what her state would be now, what fresh torture Miss Bryant would have found to visit upon her. At first, every Tuesday she was made to sit on the chair, her hands tied behind it around her writing slate for several hours and when Mary saw her she was too weak to talk, merely lying on the narrow cot bed, face buried in the bolster sometimes emitting a broken sob, her arms too sore to be of use, much less to embrace her sister.

Miss Bryant had made up a song with Liddy, had pretended it was a game, and now Liddy had to sing it every time Miss Bryant or Mary entered the room – if this was not done, a beating with the slipper followed, and there was no food that day. In winter, she said, there would be no coal for the fire. So when Mary entered, her sister would greet her thus:

> '*I am bad, I am bad, I am truly very bad,*
> *I'm the worst little girl that you'll see,*
> *I think vile thoughts and I do evil things,*
> *I bring shame on my fam'ly*'

She sang it in a sing-song monotone, head bowed, some of the notes catching in her throat, as Mary watched her, Nurse Bryant nodding in approval. 'There, we see you can be good, if you apply yourself!'

One week after bringing Liddy back from Ned Horner's, Father had left for Paris, where he had investments, he said, and this time he was away for six months or more. The night before his departure Mary had begged her father not to leave them in Miss Bryant's hands, but for this defence of her sister she received only a spell in her own room, three days with no food.

'I must feel that you are willing to submit to Miss Bryant, otherwise who knows what ills might befall you again?' he'd told her. 'Can you not understand that Lydia's behaviour imperils you? Can you not, my dear, see how she nearly ruined us all? Rawnsley will not touch her now . . . no one will.'

'Ned loves her, Father—' This was the one time Mary had mentioned his name, and her father had been roused almost to fury. She had thought of him until this last summer as a stern but distant father. She knew him now. He was such a small man.

'She will not marry him. She will not marry anyone.'

On the third day locked into her own room Mary was half asleep, half delirious with hunger and fear, and once she had the image, of Liddy and Ned, laughing together in the garden, his fingers pressing the wooden finger into the plump ball of her palm, his lips on her hand, her sister's flushed cheeks, the desire even Mary could see. And the thought came to her, as she woke, sweating in the freezing chamber. *It's not fair. She caused all this.*

But she dismissed it, for she already understood subconsciously that she must stick firm to her sister. They would try to break them both.

They had already broken Pertwee, ordered from the house the day before Father's departure for some trumped-up business over the girl who worked at the hat-shop on Cranbourn Street who had retrimmed Liddy's summer bonnet. (Miss Bryant had taken possession of the velvet hat with the egret feather, as a warning to Liddy, she said, not to covet worldly things.) Pertwee had been made to watch as his name had been scratched from the family Bible in Father's study: Miss Bryant had performed the deed while Father wept crocodile tears. Mary felt keenly it was intrinsically wrong she should do it, though it infuriated her that this of all the horrendous details was the one she latched on to. The Bible had been Mother's; before that, it was her father's. The names of his children were carefully written in it. 'Helena Alexandra Myrtle 1850' and 'Charlotte Gwendoline Myrtle 1852'. Mother had done the same with her children. It was not for Miss Bryant to erase them.

But she had, and what were they to do? What could be done?

On Tuesday afternoons Mary was permitted an hour with her sister, and to bring her her tea. Since Miss Bryant kept her on the strictest rations, tapioca or rice and stale bread, Liddy had lost the bloom of her youth. She was waxy and grey. She was allowed out once a week, to walk in the garden, wearing the red cloak she had been made to sew herself with fabric she had been forced to ask Hannah to buy. Across the back of the cloak were sewn strips of white calico, with the words 'Sneak' 'Liar' 'Fool' tacked in thick black thread. The only time Mary had seen Liddy cry was when she'd had to show herself to Hannah in this cloak and Hannah had shaken her head and quietly said: 'Not to me you're not. Never will be, Miss Liddy. You're my darling. Your mother's watching over you, so's my darling Ma.'

They knew that was a lie. Hannah's mother had gone to the bad and had died in the workhouse and their own mother had taken Hannah with her as a maid when she came from Godstow to London for her marriage. They knew Hannah loved them but that was because she had loved their mother. Gumball the butler, their greatest friend as children, had shaken his head and moved away, as if he could not bear to see Miss Lydia in this state of shame, for shame is what Miss Bryant traded in, shame and secrecy and silence.

'Dearest? May I come in?'

She opened the door quietly, clutching the little bundle she had smuggled upstairs. Liddy was sitting on the bed, bare feet on the floor, her hair down. She was in her nightgown. The room seemed emptier every time she visited; the previous week Mary had rolled up the carpet from her own room, Persian, with patterns of knotted roses across each end. It was her mother's rug from her childhood home. She had carried it to Liddy to brighten the room up, but it had been returned that night, laid out perfectly smoothly, while she slept.

The air was stuffy, heavy with the smell of tallow candles. The shutters were kept closed most of the day. At first Miss Bryant allowed her to open them for an hour but after a while Liddy stopped opening them altogether.

'Dearest, aren't you getting dressed?'

'Not today, for I did not eat my supper. There were worms in the rice. I hid it under the bed and lied to Miss Bryant about it. So I am to wear my nightgown now.' Her voice was dull.

'What about your trip around the garden?'

'That is to be no more.' She did not even raise her eyes to look at Mary.

'Liddy . . .' Mary sat down next to her on the bed. 'See, here, I brought you fresh forget-me-nots and here is an almond biscuit Mrs Lydgate thought you might like.' Hurriedly, she palmed the soft diamond-shaped cake into Liddy's hand. But her sister dropped it to the floor.

'I'm not hungry.'

Her eyes were ringed with purple; her mouth was cracked at the sides. Panic thudded in Mary's throat, her head, through her body. 'Dearest, it's a treat for you.'

'A treat.' The word fell heavily into the stifling air of the room.

'You must. You must see what that is.' Mary gripped her sister's bony hands. 'Darling – please . . .'

But Liddy turned away from her. 'Oh Mary. I think you'd better go for today, I am not myself, more than usual.' She gave a small smile, and that was the worst of all. 'I deserve it all, as I have come to see, and Miss Bryant says Father will be pleased with the change in me when he returns, which is soon – and I shall not bring shame on any of us. But sometimes it is rather hard to bear and I'd rather live alone than have the misery of watching you go and missing you . . .' She swallowed, and might have cried – a small sob caught in her throat. She unfurled one little hand and

Mary saw the figure Ned Horner had given her, the tiny wooden Liddy, as she had once been, carefree, her shoulders turning back in a laugh –

A sound came from outside; Liddy curled her fingers over again in a trice and then slid the wooden girl under her mattress.

At first Mary had kept her up to date with news – the Highgate Literary and Scientific Institution had had an interesting talk on spring flowers, and she had heard that the tramway was to close again for more repairs, to the amusement and fury of local residents, the Reverend Mander had preached a most fascinating sermon on loving thy neighbour. (Yet Mary noted the Reverend Mander himself showed no curiosity at the absence of Mr Dysart's elder daughter, his own neighbour, from church services.)

Liddy had pretended to be interested, but after a couple of months of Tuesday visits she would look away and begin chewing at her nails while Mary talked, and Mary knew it was another kind of torture for her, to hear about it all.

So the two of them sat in silence, in the dank room. Mary's hand moved towards Liddy's; the younger let her older sister hold it, gently, but then she lay down, facing the wall – 'Sorry, Mary. I am rather tired today', and Mary felt that this was the darkest of all moments. Liddy, from whom life poured forth like birdsong, reduced, at eighteen, to this carapace of a girl. The wooden figure under the mattress had more life than her.

Mary turned for the door, and then, looking down, handed her the rest of the bundle.

'Dearest, I brought you paper and pens. You should write. Write some new poems.'

There was a silence, then Liddy said:

'She'll find them. She goes through the room. I have to hide the figure in my bodice, and now there's nowhere for her. She'll find her next and I'll have to burn her. She makes me choose something to burn, every week. To make me understand I should not covet earthly possessions. Last week it was some of Mother's letters to me when Father took her to Paris.'

Mary steadied herself on the back of the cane chair. 'Burn these afterwards then. Memorise them first.' She came forward again, and pulled her sister so she rolled on to her back and lay blinking up at Mary, her sallow face expressionless. 'She doesn't have your mind, Liddy. She can't have that. Remember it. It is your greatest gift!'

But Liddy only shrugged, and rolled back towards the wall. She screwed the scraps of paper into balls, and tucked them into the small gap between the thin mattress and the wall. She wouldn't speak after that and so Mary left, stopping to pick up the dropped biscuit first, then quietly closing the door.

Outside, she breathed in the fresh air of the house, the beeswax polish on the staircase, the faint scent of lilies, the breeze coming through her own bedroom window, next door. She felt guilty at the relief of leaving that room. It never occurred to any of them that the door was not locked, that Liddy could have wandered out when she wanted; so complete was Miss Bryant's campaign of terror.

Mary went downstairs, meaning to gather more flowers outside, and ask Miss Bryant if it might be possible to leave them outside Liddy's door. The garden at the front of the house was slowly unfurling into spring; early bees droned in the budding lilac. A high wall ran around the front garden but, through the wrought-iron gate, Mary could see two gentlewomen on horseback. They were elegantly sidesaddle, glowing with the first sun of spring; the younger one smiled politely at Mary as she peered at them. She saw, as always, the shock and then concealment as the stranger caught sight of Mary's scarred and pitted face, and for once Mary did not smile to put her at ease: she returned her curiosity with a hard, cold stare, full of fury at this careless, cruel stranger and her friend, at the fresh spring day and feeling of hope, furious at it because it was all a lie. She turned towards the house.

'Miss . . .' A voice called to her from down the road, and she started, then peered out of the gate at a figure, moving slowly towards her.

'What is it?' she said, briskly. There was no room for charity in her heart, not today.

'Miss – Miss Dysart, please: could you spare me a moment of your time?'

It was a young man, by the voice, shuffling as though walking were difficult. He wore a drooping, oversized cap concealing his face. Mary started: could it be – was it? – dear Pertwee, gone for months now and so very much missed by his sisters? She moved towards the gate, looking fearfully behind her; Miss Bryant had eyes – and spies – throughout the house.

'Go away,' she said, clearly. 'We've nothing for you.'

The stranger raised his cap. 'Mary . . .'

Mary saw with a jolt that it was Ned Horner; though so pale and haggard she should hardly have known him. 'Ned?'

'Tell me' – he caught at her hand through the railings – 'is she still alive? Has that woman killed her?'

His face was, if anything, thinner than Liddy's. He was a living skeleton. His jacket had once been respectable enough she could see, though it was now filthy, but his trousers were held up by a frayed piece of rope, his shoes splitting so she could see one or two toes, purple and rotten, one of the nails missing. Loose skin lay below his eyes, on his cheekbones. Mary tried not to flinch, as the women had flinched at the sight of her.

'No, not yet. She lives. Dear Ned,' she whispered, as low as she could. 'I am sorry to see you here in this state.'

'I walked all day and night from Blackfriars, but I wasn't well – I had to stop – I can't seem to get far these days.' He coughed. 'I have had trouble with my chest as you can tell. But it is quite better now.' His eyes were too bright.

Mary peered through the iron railings of the gate at him. 'Dear Ned. Can I fetch you some food?' To invite him in was her Christian duty; it was also madness. 'If you wait here, I will hurry inside for some soup—'

But he shook his head frantically. 'I – I do not want anything, I do not want to imperil her. I want you to give her a message. We argued, the last time – she felt I wouldn't give up my ideals so that she and I could—' He was racked by a coughing fit that caused him to cling to the railings: Mary grasped the bones of his hands as he coughed. When he stood up again there was blood on his dirty handkerchief.

'You *are* ill,' she said. 'Oh, dear Ned—'

'All will be well.' He gave her the ghost of a smile. 'Honestly, Mary. I want you to tell her I'm painting again. A picture that will sell for thousands of guineas, and we'll be rich. Do you believe me?'

She smiled, as if soothing a child. 'Yes, Ned.'

'I tell the truth, Mary! It's called *The Nightingale* – it's of Liddy. I don't need studies, it's from memory – she's holding a mechanical bird that sings all day, they're both trapped in a room, she and he, in a cage, but she is free, really, her mind is blissfully free . . . We talked of mechanical objects, the last time I saw her, it gave me the idea – "The Emperor and the Nightingale", do you know the story?' He started coughing again and this time it seemed to almost consume him, as though he would not be able to stop, as though he were mechanical himself now, able only to repeat the racking motion.

Wretched, Mary made for the gate, not caring now if she were caught. She opened it, but he backed away. 'No!' he gasped, edging into the lane.

Mary held up her hand. 'Dear Ned,' she said, helplessly, again. 'I wish to assist you – but I cannot, I fear! You need a doctor, and warm bedding and soup and – and . . .' She wrung her hands together. 'Are there not friends to aid you? Where is Dalbeattie?'

He was quiet, and squeezed his eyes shut. Like a small boy, utterly alone in the world. 'Dalbeattie is still in Germany. I cannot disturb the poor fellow, he has too many demands on his time.'

'Dalbeattie is a kind man,' said Mary, warmly. 'He would help you. Do you not have a pact to assist one another?'

There was something of the old, kind, eager Ned who smiled and answered, 'Perhaps – yes, perhaps I'll write to him. "Chestnuts and chicken", that's our signal for help, you know. He'd be glad to know I've seen you, Mary, he – he asks after you every time he writes to me.'

Flushing slightly, Mary said, 'And where is your father?'

'Alas, my poor father is most dreadfully ill and not long for this world.' He drew himself up, painfully. 'You must understand this – I will come for her. Will you tell her? Will you ensure she lives? Tell her about *The Nightingale* . . . and one day I will come. When – when I am recovered.'

She reached towards him again, but Ned shook his head. 'Goodbye, dear sister,' he muttered and he scuttled behind the Flask Inn and then out of her sight.

Knowing she must not linger, Mary turned and went inside. But on the doorstep she paused, looking back at the flowers. *I did not collect any for Liddy. Instead I shall tell her of his visit.*

Then she thought of the yellow eyeballs, Ned's sunken face, the blood on the handkerchief, his feverish state, and slowly bit the tip of her finger. With an aching heart she knew she could not mention a word of it. But she would pray for Ned, for his soul shortly no doubt to be received in heaven. And so she did, every night, and another six months passed and no word came from him.

Chapter Eleven

September 1892

Father was back – but Liddy did not see him, not for ten days. The event which caused her most distress was Mary's departure to stay with a cousin in Lyme. Liddy had begged her not to leave her, but Mary was strangely obdurate. *I need a change of air, Liddy. Dearest, please try to understand, it is a most difficult situation for me, as well as for you.*

Liddy saw that the moment had come when everyone else peeled away from her, grew distant, went towards the sun and away from the shade of the unhappy house. And there had been not a word, not one, from Ned. Mary had told her Pertwee had gone to Paris to paint, encouraged by Dalbeattie. Now, for the first time, Mary was to leave her, to breathe in the sea air, to be with dear Aunt Charlotte, to go to dances. She had even been allowed to purchase a new bonnet and gloves; Miss Bryant had accompanied her to Marshall and Snelgrove to procure them.

Miss Bryant was in favour of the trip, which meant Liddy would partly be left alone in the house with her. Gumball and Lydgate had both been dismissed while her father had been away, by Miss Bryant, for reasons of household economy, she said. Hannah was visiting her sister.

When Mary came to say goodbye to her sister on the morning of her departure, she said:

'I will not be gone long, dearest. Now Father is expected back . . .'

Liddy lay on her cot-bed, wrapping and rewrapping the worn blanket tightly around her narrow frame. Both girls were too thin these days. Miss Bryant kept saying so, as she held open Liddy's mouth, force-feeding her the gruel and rancid tapioca she insisted she eat.

Liddy said furiously, trying to keep herself from weeping, 'Go then. You should have liberty, and enjoy yourself, even if I cannot. I know Aunt Charlotte will want to see you—'

'I wish I were not going,' said Mary, blinking back tears in her eyes. For they dared not cry, for fear of Miss Bryant catching them and scouring their cheeks for she said children as fortunate as they should have no cause to weep. Quietly she added, 'I have to go, Liddy. I wish I could make—' She stopped.

'What do you mean?'

'Nothing.' Mary shook her head, almost frantic. 'Nothing, only be patient, my dearest—'

'Will you try to speak to Aunt Charlotte about our situation, Mary?'

'I will try, but I scarce know how to go about it, and I fear for you, so very much, and that if I do, something worse will happen, when we are so close . . .' She cleared her throat.

Liddy's dull grey eyes glanced at her again. 'So close to what?'

'I wish I were not to be parted from you.' Mary kissed her sister, her warm lips on Liddy's cold cheeks. 'Dearest sister, keep well, keep your mind engaged, and clear of doubt . . .' She unwrapped her mother's Paisley shawl, which had been hers since she was wrapped in it the day she fell ill, and handed it to her sister. 'Take this. It is warm.'

Liddy fingered the soft, fine wool. 'No, thank you. I am warm enough. No, I tell you' – for Mary was pushing it towards her. 'Leave me be!'

Mary stood back, bundling the shawl up in her arms. 'Then . . . Pretend you are in the Rookery, with a warm fire, and Pertwee toasting crumpets for us, and everything cosy. Think of the three of us, and the love we have. F-for I will see you again, I will—' and she pressed a palm to her mouth, gave a small sob, and dashed from the room. Liddy turned on her side, gazing at the blank wall again.

*

Two days after Mary's departure, their father came up to visit her. When he went up to see his one remaining child in the house he found her rocking in a tightly furled ball, singing her special song.

I am bad, I am bad, I am truly very bad,
I'm the worst little girl that you'll see,
I think vile thoughts and I do evil things,
I bring shame on my fam'ly –

Mr Dysart stood in the doorway, watching. He did not refer to this, nor her emaciated frame, her lank hair, the smell in the room, the nightgown that was almost indecent by now. He stayed for two minutes, then excused himself hurriedly. 'I will return tomorrow, dear child. I am tired now.' It seemed Liddy was not even aware of his departure for the singing continued as he retreated down the stairs in search of Miss Bryant.

The following evening, he came back up again. He had Mary's dressing gown with him, which he handed to Liddy, and a plate of cheese and biscuits, from his own supply, he said, as though the rest of the food in the house were nothing to do with him. 'Now, Lydia,' he said, seating himself carefully on the fragile cane chair at the centre of the empty room. 'Miss Bryant tells me that you have begun to mend your ways and I must own that I am glad. For you—'

THUD!

Mr Dysart jumped half out of his skin as something landed heavily against the window. Liddy froze, a piece of cheese halfway to her mouth; father and daughter looked at each other in alarm.

'What was that?'

'I do not know, Father.'

'Open the window then,' he said, peevishly, drawing the little chair back from the window himself. 'See what may be there.'

Liddy hesitated. She never opened the window any more. She could not tell him the outside terrified her now, so complete was Miss Bryant's control of her.

'Lydia. Did you hear me?' Her father's voice rose. 'Open the casement, for heaven's sake.'

Clutching her little hands tightly into fists Liddy ran to the dormer window, flinging it open and letting the sweet evening air flood the stuffy room, then stood back. It was September, and still light. She glanced up and around her, and then down, blinking in confusion at what she saw, then she opened her mouth to speak, and shut it again. Eventually she said:

'I see a dead bird, Father, on the roof below – dead or dying, I'm not sure.' Her fingers tightened on the windowsill, the sensation of the sounds and smells of outside almost overwhelming her. 'Do you think that is the cause?'

'Undoubtedly. Stupid creatures, flying at the window. Come, Lydia, sit down. The bird will die, there's an end of it,' said her father, gruffly. He looked down at his foot. 'The boot has let me down here; see that mark? Hm? Now, I require you to listen. Do you understand, my dear, that your punishment has been necessary?'

'Oh,' said Liddy, trying to concentrate. 'I understand Nurse Bryant finds me to be a sore trial, and for that I am sorry. I have promised to mend my ways.' She lowered her eyes. 'I have suffered greatly at her hands and she will tell you I have accepted it all.'

'That you have, and it's as well, for you should mind what she says, and your father too, for every girl should. After all, the burden of your food and watering and clothing and the marriage-portion –'

'Yes, Father,' she said, meekly, pulling Mary's dressing gown around her and staring at his gouty foot, the thick mulberry silk lining of his tail-coat, his florid cheeks. But, inside, her heart was beating even faster, as though it were starting up again, pumping blood to all parts of her after months of inactivity.

And suddenly she heard Mary's voice, remembered what she had told her with that curious expression which had then made Liddy so angry. *Keep well. Keep your mind engaged, clear of doubt* . . .

'I will leave you now, but I am glad to have brought you these little rewards, and to have seen you in a state of such repentance.' Her father stood up very slowly. 'Hand me my stick, my dear.'

144

She gave him his silver-topped malacca cane and he twirled it in his hand, in the same way the family legend had it that he had done when he caught sight of their mother in Hyde Park all those years ago. Watching him preening, and twirling his cane, Liddy thought of her beloved mother and, for the first time, wondered that she should have fallen for his shallow tricks, like the magician in Covent Garden who only knew one illusion, how to hide a tiny bird behind your ear. She felt a bolt of rage judder through her, that her clever, wise mother should have chosen him.

As she was thinking, her father took her chin in his cold smooth hand and, pushing aside Mary's dressing gown, he fingered the worn and dirty nightgown. Liddy shivered, and he said quietly:

'I'll have Bryant bring up one of your dresses for you to wear, no more rags now. Something simple, though. I admit it's a shame – you'd be a fine catch for any man, my dear, a plump little bird ripe for plucking. They'd plough you happily, any one of them, but they shan't have you. No one shall. Not that any of 'em would want you now.'

He gave a little shiver, and she saw saliva pooling in the corners of his mouth.

'Father . . .' She slid free from his grip, ostensibly to be able to grasp his hands. 'Dear Father, thank you.'

He gave a grunt. 'Ah. Well.'

'Dare I hope to have the pleasure of your company again soon? Mary – Mary says you are awful lonely lately, since Rupert's disgrace.' She cocked her head and looked at him, smiling.

He frowned. 'You know then that Rupert has returned? Is that why you mention him? Is that why?'

She shook her head, instantly afraid. 'No, Father, upon my life I did not know.'

'The scoundrel is back from Paris and says he wants to see me. I shall meet him, for I am a forgiving father, but why, when his name is garn from the Bible and I have said he'll never darken our door again – ' He looked up at her, scanning her, mistrustfully. 'You really don't know about it, do ye?'

Liddy shook her head. 'I do not, Father, I'm sorry.'

Mary had said nothing to her about Pertwee's return – did she know nothing, too? Then Liddy remembered the thud at the window, and her eyes darted to the window in terror.

'Now,' said Mr Dysart, 'Miss Bryant and I have discussed your being allowed out of the room in the next few months. This is not a prison, after all, Lydia dearest! It is your home!' He spread his arms wide, in the small hallway, and Liddy felt her heart fill with hate for him, actual hatred; it was a strong, black, poisonous thing, like oil.

And then suddenly she felt her heart, beating in her chest. A soft, fluttering thing, still weak. She smiled.

'Thank you, Father,' she said. 'I should like that very much.'

'I shall tell her so. And that I am pleased with you. After all, it's I who – she cannot – I am your father.' With that he left, tapping his cane and grunting as he made his way down the stairs. Knowing how much he hated others to see how the gout slowed him down, Liddy went back into her room, closing the door gently behind her.

She heard her father calling for something on the stairs – it was muffled, just the light upper tones, querulous, pleased, and then she froze, as the voice of Miss Bryant answered him. Her clear, clear voice, which slid like a shard of glass through any crack.

'No, sir. I agree. She seems better. To me, at least, sir, she seems less hysterical.'

Liddy knew Miss Bryant knew Liddy would be listening, and that Liddy would know she knew this, too. She waited until the thud of the cane and the low voices grew faint. Then she turned towards the window and opened it again, carefully. Slowly, she stared down at the small brown paper parcel resting on the window-sill below her.

She knew then this was luck playing on her side for once: luck that she had not given herself away and told her father, luck that she had found it so easy to lie, luck that whoever had thrown the parcel up there had done so with such skill, though she knew no one but Pertwee who could throw that well and with such precision . . .

Pertwee!

Liddy snatched it up and, utterly silent and still, strained to hear the voices of her father and Miss Bryant, now at the bottom of the stairs. She tore at the brown paper, making a spiral that unravelled, and a small wooden figure fell into her hand: a man holding a paintbrush, cap askew, hand on hip, smiling. The wood felt warm to her touch.

She began to tear the rest of the wrapping away – but then stared at it. Someone had written on the inside of the brown paper. She unfolded the rest of the bundle, smoothing it out on the floor.

My dearest bird

Here is your second figure, a willow husband for you. He comes from me with all the love I can carve into him. He is a token, he says I will never leave you again.

Dearest bird, we have one chance and thus I write in great haste. It is most likely that this plan will fail, but we have tried. 'Say not to the struggle naught availeth.' If they chain you up for life afterwards, you know you are loved by me, your brother and sister. <u>Know you are greatly loved, Liddy.</u>

I was very ill for several months – a ridiculous nonsense but I cannot live without you – my father died, Liddy, he left me 80 pounds, and grieving for him though I did so greatly, his dying delivered me for they came to my rooms and found me and took me to hospital . . . Dalbeattie's had the care of me since: he's come back from Europe and has been the best friend a fellow could want.

I have made the picture of you that I always said I would, Liddy my darling, it was in the Summer Exhibition, and it was a great success. Now Mr Galveston says he wants to buy it for his gallery, he means to pay me 70 guineas for it. It is called The Nightingale. It is you, my Liddy.

Please forgive my mentioning these financial matters in a letter swearing my love for you but our situation is unusual as we have always known: this is by way of saying I have now in total 150 pounds and a heart full of love for you as the first time I saw you.

I have a plan for your escape and it involves our marriage, my dearest, there is but one chance and it is tomorrow. Tomorrow, Liddy — everything is tomorrow.

For tomorrow morning (Thursday, 10th September 1892) Miss Bryant will be called from the house — you will see — all our plans are well laid and they are good plans. Please wait at the window until you are sure she is gone. Your father is meeting your brother tomorrow also; Pertwee has come back to England at my request, first to deliver this message to your room, then to bait the trap. Wait until his carriage has departed.

With your father and Miss Bryant both absent you will be free to leave the house at 10.30 a.m. dearest. I will be at St Marylebone Church at 12 p.m. Dalbeattie, Pertwee, and Mary too, if she can be back in time, for her trip away has been engineered so that no blame attaches to her in the event of failure. I will wait inside the church. I have a special licence. Our names are writ upon it in black ink; I see them now as I write to you, hands shaking. Please say that you will come, that we will be married then!

I feel your fear as you hold the figure, I know you must be most terribly scared. <u>Be brave, dearest Liddy, please be brave and come</u>. I cannot fetch you myself, the risk is too great we have all agreed. Come to St Marylebone and we will be married.

Come tomorrow — will you come? For now I doubt it all — Dash this pen for it makes my writing so weak, I am strong, Liddy, I promise you. I will be strong as A TREE and I will shelter you, that is the promise I make to you now, our own promise now and in the years to come. The future is yet unwritten; the past is burnt and gone. It must be so.

Yours always more than my own —

Liddy threw the letter aside. She shook, at first with what she thought was excitement, then recognised as pure, seething rage.

Rage that they should pluck her from her room, where she finally felt comfortable, where Father was arranging for her to have a dress again, where she was confined but cared for.

She tore the letter into tiny pieces, scattering them like snow on to the flames, then crawled around on the floor in the flickering light of the fire to ensure none of it was left behind. *She* would not upset Miss Bryant, unlike foolish Pertwee, or deceitful Mary sighing over her, her lies about missing her.

The remains of the letter sparkled and spat in the grate, as if coated in dynamite. Liddy crawled on to the bed, where the mattress still showed the indentation of her father's heavy frame. She curled into a ball, thinking, listening to her heart pounding. Of course she would not go. The betrayal to Miss Bryant, who truly understood how bad she was, who was the only one, as she frequently reminded Liddy, who could make sure she was cured.

The sound of the fire now seemed like knives jabbing inside her skull, so she buried her head further under the bolster and began to sing the only song she could remember, its very familiarity giving her comfort.

I am bad, I am bad, I am truly very bad,
I'm the worst little girl that you'll see,
I think vile thoughts and I do evil things,
I bring shame on my fam'ly.

Chapter Twelve

'My good fellow . . .' Lucius Dalbeattie plucked at his friend's sleeve. 'I say – what about if we were to wait inside, as you said?' Ned ignored him. 'You told her you'd wait inside the church. She knows that.' He gazed anxiously about the Marylebone Road, as though expecting the Four Horsemen of the Apocalypse to appear.

Ned twitched his arm away, and carried on staring in front of him, out from under the vast portico of the church, towards York Gate and the entrance to Regent's Park. The Marylebone Road in front of them was thronged with hackney carriages, buses, horses and riders, even a Daimler motor car. There were men in bowler hats striding towards the City and children tugging on the arms of their nursemaids. Below them, a boy was roasting cob nuts, the acrid burning smell catching in their nostrils. Ned said quietly, 'I want her to see me as soon as possible, if she comes.'

'If she comes . . . Horner . . .' Dalbeattie trailed off, and his kindly face creased into a concerned smile. 'She's an hour late. Let's wait inside, eh? It's chilly here. I don't want you taking ill again. You know I'm no good as nursemaid.'

He led Ned back inside the church and they stared about them at the great white-and-green stucco decoration and the tall, glittering stained-glass windows below the huge curve of the ceiling, the two of them as specks in its vast empty finery. Dalbeattie clapped his friend on the shoulder.

'Do look at the stucco work on the ceiling, Ned. Most fine—' Dalbeattie broke off, at a sound, and they both looked over towards the door.

But it was only a sparrow, fluttering about in the upper reaches of the portico. Ned took a deep, heavy breath, and closed his eyes, holding on to the edge of a pew. Dalbeattie looked at him in alarm and said, gently, 'She's taking her time, isn't she? But she'll be here . . .'

'Dear Dalbeattie.' Ned clutched his friend's hand. 'What a friend you are.'

Dalbeattie looked bashful. 'My dear man. I'm so very glad to be able to help you.'

'Why did you go away for so long? Don't do it again, will you?'

Dalbeattie's long, kind face twisted. 'I won't. I wish that I had not, you know.'

Ned said quietly, 'How is she?'

'Please,' Dalbeattie replied. 'Don't ask me that.'

'You concern yourself most intensely with my affairs, my dear fellow. You must let me help you with yours!'

'Not this,' said Dalbeattie. 'I agreed to the engagement, and I alone must see it through.'

The vicar hurried towards them. 'Mr Horner? Ah, good morning.' He put the tips of his fingers together and smiled mirthlessly. 'I am needed most urgently by a parishioner who is gravely ill. Might I ask when you expect the bride?'

Ned shrugged helplessly; Dalbeattie could feel the desperation rolling off him like steam from a bath. 'I don't know, sir – we hope at any moment! She has a letter, with the address—'

Footsteps thundered outside; a voice called his name, a familiar voice – both Ned and Dalbeattie started, with joy. 'I'm here!'

The door creaked open, and they sank back in bitter disappointment.

'Ah, Dysart,' said Ned, quietly, smiling at him. 'Hello, my dear friend.'

'I've not missed it?' cried Pertwee, shedding his gloves, looking about him eagerly, and clasping Ned by the hand. 'Where is my sister, Mrs Horner, my dear fellow? Well, Father has been well and truly baited, I confessed all my sins, including an ever so lively one about a lovely bit who worked in the cheese shop in Pigalle – he went quite pink, the dirty feller— But she's not here yet? Really?' His expression changed. 'Oh, I say. I met Father at his club at eleven, she'd have had ample time to leave and get here . . . Ned – old boy. Has she changed her mind? Could you not persuade her?' He noticed the vicar, for the first time. 'Good morning, Padre. Ready to join two people, and all that?'

The vicar cleared his throat.

'Forgive me, gentlemen, for voicing my concerns. But I was told by you that the grounds for the licence were owing to the lady's most delicate family situation and a recent bereavement therein.' Ned glowered at Pertwee. 'I must be entirely happy on that point if we are to proceed with this marriage. If there is any suggestion of coercion—'

'No!' Ned said, hurriedly. 'None, sir, of that you may be certain!'

'My sister is very much in love with Mr Horner, sir,' said Pertwee, at his most sincere and charming. 'I regret having given you any other impression. She walks slowly, however, always did dawdle. Most likely something in the park caught her eye—'

'That's it, isn't it?' said Ned, weakly, though for the first time it felt as though he was buoying himself up with false hope, and false hope, he had come to learn, was the worst of all. 'She's found some ducks or some gentleman selling birds in a cage – yes, that's it.' For a second he almost might believe it was true, for Liddy *could* spend hours wandering in the park or in a garden, finding something new to exclaim over; as a child, rescuing an upturned ladybird from a path in the cemetery, she had fallen and grazed her hand most painfully. Pertwee had told Ned this, before he'd met his sister, Lydia: Ned had loved her perhaps a little from that moment.

Please come. Please come. Please come. Please come.

His stomach was hollow, leaden, empty. Liquid acid rose in his throat.

'Ned,' came a quiet, female voice. 'Dear Ned . . .'

They all turned at the sound, and Dalbeattie muttered under his breath, 'She's here – dear God, thank heaven for that. Oh – oh no.'

A small figure peered anxiously around the door, her face lighting up as she caught sight of her brother; Ned's heart sank again, and he wondered if he would actually be sick.

'Mary, dearest,' Rupert exclaimed, folding his hands around his sister's. She kissed his cheek, tears trembling in her eyes, clinging to him. 'My dear sister, you have come! This is more than I dared hope.'

'I told Aunt Charlotte that Father was unwell and I came back on the train this morning. May God forgive me. But I could not tell her the truth and I was driving myself quite mad for wondering,' she said. She clutched at Ned's hand, her brown eyes fixed on him. 'Dear Ned. Where is she? Oh Pertwee—' Her voice broke into a sob. 'I do miss you, you terrible boy.'

'And I you, dearest sister.' He gripped her again. 'My, but you're in fine looks, now those scars have faded. When did they go?'

She stared at him, and clutched his hands as they rested on her shoulders. 'Do not jest with me, Pertwee!'

'I do not jest. You are a great beauty, my dear. Dalbeattie, ain't it so?'

Dalbeattie was watching Mary. 'Anyone can see that you are, and always have been,' he said, quietly.

'But her smallpox scars,' Pertwee said, a little too loudly. 'They were chronic when she was little, weren't they, Mary? What a miracle. You may marry now! I tell you, anyone would have you!'

Mary frowned, closing her eyes at her brother's words. Dalbeattie stepped forward. 'I say – Pertwee.'

'Understood,' said Pertwee. The vicar stared at him, at his glazed expression, his scruffy appearance, and took out his pocket watch.

'Where is Liddy?' said Mary, looking around. 'Has she not arrived by now?'

Ned shook his head, and her face fell.

'Are you sure you threw the note to the right room?' Dalbeattie demanded sharply.

Pertwee laughed. 'On this alone you may be sure of me. I've had enough practice over the years. We used to throw notes to each other when we were in purdah for something. I hid behind the railings of the Flask, till I saw her reach down and take the letter. I saw her hold it with her own hands.' He turned to Ned. 'Pon my honour, old chap.'

'Something must have happened,' Mary said, in a small voice, and Ned saw that she was very pale, and trembling.

'Is there a chair for Miss Dysart?' he said, to the vicar.

'She can sit on one of the pews while you wait.' The vicar flung his fobwatch up into his palm with a small neat flick. 'Twelve eighteen I have the time, gentlemen. You have until twelve-thirty, and then I must ask you to let me take my leave of you. And this wedding, it seems to me, has some appearance of irregularity to it, about which I surmise I should be better off not knowing.'

He bustled away, casting a look back at their small group, and once again Ned felt the vastness of the empty church.

'Should we post people out in the park, go and look for her?'

'No!' hissed Mary, turning pale. 'For if she should turn up and one of us is missing, you'll have no witnesses and have to go into the street and she's so late there's no time for that now, not if Miss Bryant or Father discovers where we are and comes here, which they may do, oh they may do!'

'They can't,' said Ned, queasily. 'You said nothing, and Dysart, you did not reveal it to your father, did you?'

There was a short silence.

'Rupert?' said Mary, quietly. 'Dearest, you did not say anything to Father about our plan, did you?'

'Well, so what if I did?' exclaimed her brother, angrily. 'He was damned unpleasant. He as good as told me he'd overturned Mother's will and he'd arranged it all so we'd never marry. Imagine that, Mary! He sat there and laughed at me when I asked for a raise on my allowance, which is the one expenditure he makes on our behalf and a tiny portion of what is owed us! Said there wasn't a penny for any of us, not any more. Said he had all his plans in place. I couldn't stand it. There at his club twirling his glass of Madeira in his new silk waistcoats, surrounded by grinning servants standing guard as though I were a dangerous footpad instead of his son, and it's Mother's money, not his! I saw red, Mary. I told him his plan hadn't worked and even if there was no money left one of us would marry anyway. I'm sorry.'

Dalbeattie swore, and turned aside; Mary clutched his arm.

'Oh how wicked. . . oh, Pertwee,' she whispered, sinking into a chair. Dalbeattie turned back and dropped to her side, gently lifting her so she was standing again.

'He's a monster, Mary.' Tears were in Pertwee's eyes. 'I couldn't let him think he'd won! I told him he'd failed. I said – oh, darling Mary, don't cry, you'll come and live in Paris with me, you can't go back to them, that's for certain. I didn't say where they were marrying, don't worry. Then he said – oh.'

He stopped.

'What?' Ned demanded, furiously.

'Well, he said she'd never come. He said, "You haven't seen your sister for a great many months, have you? You'll find her very changed. Very changed indeed."' Pertwee took a handkerchief from his waistcoat and pressed it to his mouth, then his face.

From the choir at the other end of the church the vicar cleared his throat again. The sound was like gunfire in the echoing cavern. Ned pressed his hands to his ears, and then let them drop to his sides. He said weakly, 'I – I thought she might not come, you know. I had a premonition, just before you arrived, Mary. She can't. It's been too long, now.'

Mary was crying against Dalbeattie's sleeve. She said, 'Perhaps. I think you're right. I shouldn't have left her. I don't think it's possible for her. Not now.'

Ned leaned forward, to Mary. 'You must go back to Paris with your brother, Mary. They will not blame Liddy. Indeed, perhaps they will be kind to her, and shut these two out. It may be for the best for you to cut ties with her altogether now, though I will never give her up . . .' He choked. 'I regret most heartily causing you any pain, any of you – I only desired to free her, to make her happy, to—' He broke off. 'Dalbeattie, you must comfort Mary. Speak to her.'

Dalbeattie said brokenly, 'Oh my dear fellow . . .' He turned to

Mary. 'Miss Dysart – dear Mary.' His usually gentle eyes burned fiercely. 'The very great pleasure of seeing you is tempered by the prospect of failure.' He had one arm around her shoulder, still supporting her. Her head was turned towards him, her eyes looking up at his

'Miss Mary,' he said softly, as Pertwee went to Ned, to comfort him. 'Dearest –'

'No,' she said. 'Not now, please, dear Mr Dalbeattie.'

'I wish you would call me Lucius,' he said, smiling gently at her.

'Oh, I couldn't do that. To me you are and always will be Dalbeattie,' she said, trying to smile, but her face crumpled again, like a child's.

'Oh,' he said, softly. 'I can't stand to see you in pain, that's all. I am a great fool.'

'You are anything but that!' She gave a watery smile. 'It's only that she is all I think of.'

'It cannot always be this way,' he said, and she looked up at him, two small lines between her brows. 'You must have your own life, and concerns, your own home.'

'I have never considered it, you see,' she said.

'Mary, when they are married, they will not need you.' His deep voice was still quiet, and she leaned against him without meaning to, then pulled away.

'I know, I know. I will find another cause, you may be sure.' She glanced at the door again, in an agony of suspense. 'Dear God. What freedom do we have? On one point I am sure,' she said, almost viciously. 'I will never marry. Never.'

Beside her, Dalbeattie did not move, but he shifted his hand so it was under her elbow, supporting her should she sway, or fall.

'Gentlemen,' said the vicar, his voice sounding loud in the empty church. 'I am very much afraid that I cannot stay longer. I have waited past the hour at which I said I would depart—'

'Oh no,' said Mary, with a sob. She pressed her hand to her mouth, and they were all silent, the enormity of the failure washing over them.

'It is over,' said Pertwee, quietly.

'*Hello?*'

Ned froze, as a small voice came from the other end of the church, near the vicar. 'Hello? Are you there? Yes, it *is* you. I dared not enter at the front; I came through the garden at the side.'

And there she was, a small posy of jewel-like berries and daisies in her hand – he never remembered afterwards where she found them. She was walking towards him, her feet sounding loudly on the echoing tiled floor and at one point she stopped, looking down at them for the sound they made, blinking, as though unused to it all. Which she was, of course.

Ned found he was unable to move.

'Liddy!' Pertwee cried, with a shout. 'You're here! All will be well! Capital! Capital!'

Mary was weeping and smiling, clutching Dalbeattie's arm – Dalbeattie himself, quite undone, was murmuring, 'Dear God. A near thing. Dear God!'

'I presume this young woman is Miss Dysart?' said the vicar and Liddy clasped his hand, smiling into his eyes with such charm that he was instantly mollified.

'I am here,' she said, and Ned ran towards her now, down the long nave of the church, the longest journey of his life until he could reach her, hold her hand, claim her for himself, for fear she might be whisked away from him again.

'Forgive me, my love,' she said, smiling at him, tears falling from her eyes. 'It took me a while to be able to come. I was very afraid . . . everything is rather overwhelming.'

'I asked so much of you—' He was shaking his head. 'I am sorry.'

'It had to be this way,' Liddy said.

He held her face in his hands. She was pale, dull through lack of sunshine, her hair scraped back against her head, but her eyes shone as she smoothed down the skirts of her pale-blue dress. 'My father persuaded Bryant to bring one of my old dresses up to my room last night,' she said, her smile fixed. 'Her last act.'

157

They were married then, that day, no bells, no organ music, no orange blossom, but the five of them, dear family and friends and, at the centre of it, Ned and Liddy. At one point, he stared at her thin, waxy face, the bright dancing blue eyes fixed happily on him, her hand clutching his arm, and he felt the most powerful sensation of transformation. As they walked out of the church, Liddy leaned heavily on his arm, the exertion of the day catching up with her and at one point, she stumbled. He was afraid that it had all been too much for her, but then she looked up at him, and whispered in his ear:

'Now, my love. It all begins now.'

Mary had brought rose petals from Aunt Charlotte's garden, and she threw them over the newly-weds, the faint scent rising up to Ned's nostrils. The boy roasting cob nuts and a passing gentleman on horseback smiled, raising their hats to them. Even the vicar unbent as he hurried past them on the way to his next appointment, waving his tasselled hat at them. 'God bless you, my dears. A lifetime of happiness to you both.'

'I should think so,' Liddy said, seriously, to Ned. 'It's the very least we deserve, wouldn't you say?'

Part Two

Chapter Thirteen

September

There's a fig tree growing next to the Dovecote. Your great-grandfather Ned planted it after they came here. He loved figs and the tree symbol-ised new beginnings. They are usually ripe in September. They are delicious with honey and sharp cheese.

Mum loved the fig tree. She loved the shelter it gave my father in his studio as he painted – keeping the outside cool, even as the glass roof let the light in. Now the tree has overgrown and when you look up at the glass roof it is dark, covered by a canopy of fig leaves. You might climb up there as the fruit falls, Juliet, clear it from the glass. And again in October. Take care not to fall.

When he burned the painting, the heat of the fire shattered the glass roof. Part of the tree was burned, too. When I was little Mum had the glass ceiling replaced, a clean, unblinking round eye on the sky above. The doll's house was put in there for me to play with. And it was as though the fire never happened.

As you grow old, one's childhood draws near again. Events of seventy, eighty years ago, which seemed obscure and long abandoned in the past, are now to me crystal clear. I cannot stop thinking about them.

Cut the dead sunflower heads off. Store them in the shed and you will be glad of them come Christmas. I will later explain why. In the meantime, relax into autumn. 'My favourite time of year' some nitwits will claim. They are idiots. Everything starts to fall apart in autumn. Be on your guard, Ju. Be ready.

September 2014

'Mummy . . .'

'Yes, darling?'

'I had an accident again.'

'OK, OK.' Juliet had thought she was awake already, but as she swung out of the sagging divan bed, her bare feet hitting the smooth floorboards, her head began to spin, her heavy eyes peering at the little figure in the doorway, and she realised she'd been fast asleep.

'I'm sorry.'

'That's OK, darling,' said Juliet softly, opening the bedroom door. 'Let's get you changed – oh.'

'I changed myself.' Isla was in a shabby sundress, green with tiny white flowers. It was far too small for her and, in places, stained a dark rust colour. 'I found this in a chest.'

'That's OK.' Juliet smoothed her hand across her daughter's face, blinking in the dim light from the hall lamp. Out of the empty bedroom window next door to hers, the full moon shone like sunshine. She looked back at her alarm clock. It was 2 a.m. 'We'll find you something to wear.'

'All my pee-jays are in the wash.'

'Well, something else. You can't wear that. It's too tight – Isla? Come back, darling.'

Juliet followed her daughter upstairs to the Birdsnest, where the girls had chosen to sleep. Only Sandy was on her floor, next door to her in the room in which she had slept as a child, with the window seat carved with squirrels and foxes and the carved hinge which lifted up and where Sandy kept his toys now, just as she had done.

The Birdsnest had been the nursery, but Grandi had put a plasterboard partition up, dividing it into two still-large rooms. Isla's half overlooked the Wilderness, the Dovecote and the lane. Juliet thought Isla was too little to sleep up there. She wanted her next to her, in case she woke in the night. But Isla wouldn't sleep in that room. She said it gave her a bad feeling. She said she wanted to be with Bea.

Juliet went into the bathroom, as quietly as she could, and fetched a towel and a bucket of warm water, praying as ever that the banging pipes didn't wake Sandy. She hunted through the linen cupboard, and went back up to Isla's room. Isla had taken the duvet cover and the sheet off by herself, and was sitting by the window, her feet tucked underneath her. 'I washed the pee off me,' she said. 'But I couldn't find a sheet.'

'There aren't any,' said Juliet. 'They're in the wash. Sorry darling, I should have done it a bit more quickly. Getting ready for school tomorrow and everything . . . Come here, and give me a hug. It doesn't matter.'

'I don't want to go back to sleep.'

'You're bound to be nervous, first day of school, and all that, sweetheart. But you need to get some sleep.' Isla shrugged. Juliet went over to her, and just as she reached the window, Isla darted out of her way.

'I'm fine thanks, Mum. I'll sleep on the mattress.'

'You can't, darling. Come and sleep with me.' Juliet stripped the sodden sheet, balling it up, and began scrubbing at the mattress with the wet towel.

'No *thanks*,' said Isla, swiftly.

'Booooo,' said Juliet, with a theatrical downturned mouth, doing the blubbery baby voice that used to make Isla and Sandy shout with laughter. 'Waaahh!'

'I don't want to have a bed with you.' Isla stared at her mother, her huge grey eyes shining in the dark. ''Cause I hate you. I hate you more than anything in the whole world.'

'Oh Isla. Look I know – oh darling. Come here—'

'Bea's right. You don't ever listen to me, Mum.' Slowly, deliberately, Isla picked up the beloved Moomin mug she had been given for her last birthday. She held it out, her mouth downturned almost comically, only it wasn't funny. 'You pretend everything's OK, and it's –' And Isla opened her fingers and the cup fell to the ground, smashing into three. 'NOT.'

'I can mend this, it's fine,' said Juliet, bending down to pick up the pieces, fingers clumsy with fatigue. 'Listen. I know you're upset about leaving your old school, but you can't throw things, Isla—'

'*Shut up, Mum*,' Isla shouted, so loudly Juliet jumped. Juliet looked at her. Her chest was rising and falling under the too-tight dress, her moon-face a picture of misery. She picked up a photo Juliet had put in her room, of the five of them at London Zoo the previous summer and threw it across the room, her bottom lip wobbling as it hit the corner shelves with a sickening crack. 'I'll keep throwing things if you d-don't go away,' she said. 'I will, Mum. I will. You should have got some more sheets when you went to see Daddy without me. If you don't have a new sheet then can you just go, please, and leave me alone. I hate you, I k-keep telling you.'

She was crying now, fat tears rolling freely down her small face. Juliet put her hands up. She moved towards Isla again, spreading her arms wide as though trying to catch a stray chicken. She grabbed her daughter who squirmed, hitting Juliet, scratching her, her mouth open in outrage, a high-pitched, wailing whine coming from her. Juliet pulled her close and whispered in her ear. 'I'm so sorry,' she said softly. 'I know you're cross I didn't take you last week. But Daddy's coming to see you soon.' Isla's sobs increased, and she shuddered in Juliet's arms. 'There wasn't room in the van, and I had to bring back lots of our stuff. He's coming in two weeks. Didn't I say so?'

'Y-yes,' sobbed Isla, her body rigid. She was not hugging Juliet back. 'But you said I could g-g-g-go home! I miss him! I want to s-s-see D-d-daddy. And Yasmin and Slavkaaaaa. I d-d-don't like it here. Why can't I just go for one night, Mum?' She kneeled up. 'Just one night. Mum? Please? Pleeease.'

Juliet stared out of the small dormer window to the fields outside, the newly harvested stubble glowing silver in the moonlight. She closed her eyes.

'Daddy needs to sort the house out.'

Isla's shoulders heaved and she said suddenly sharply, 'Why is he sorting the house out? Is he selling it too?'

'I – no, darling.'

'I'll be very good. I'll just sleep in a small corner of my room if he needs it for other things. I'll be very quiet.'

She was looser in Juliet's arms now, sucking her thumb and twirling her hair around. She looked exhausted. 'It's your first day tomorrow,' Juliet said, trying to draw her a little closer. 'Why don't we call Daddy afterwards and tell him how it's gone. And we can work out what biscuits you're going to make to give him when you see him. He loved those chocolate chip and raisin ones you baked for his birthday, didn't he?'

Isla nodded. She gave a deep, shuddering breath. 'Y-yes. OK.'

'What's a treat you want tomorrow after your first day of school? Ice cream? A magazine?'

Isla said, 'It's all right, Mum.' She turned from her, pushed Juliet gently away. A movement in the doorway made Juliet jump and she looked up, to see Bea, in her Kate Bush T-shirt, her hair ruffled.

'You all right, Iley?'

'My Bea,' said Isla, pleased, and she padded over to her.

Bea patted her head, affectionately, and rubbed her eyes. 'I like your dress. Do you want to come and sleep with me?'

Isla said, in a small voice, 'Yes, please, Bea.'

'That's a great idea,' said Juliet. 'If you don't mind, Bea . . .'

But as though their mother had not spoken, the two girls had already left and gone into Bea's room. Juliet watched them go, then gathered the wet towel, dirty sheet, and broken mug all in her arms. She glanced into Bea's cluttered room, piled high with old dressing-up clothes pulled from abandoned trunks, along with the dusty green and orange Penguins Bea had discovered and was devouring, and the curious odds and ends she'd found around the house: a blue and white miniature china cat, a silver egg cup, a teal velvet hat with an egret's feather sewn on to it. Bea was a collector, Juliet had realised, an old soul who liked old things. Who had used them? When?

Bea was bending over her little sister, tucking her up before climbing into bed herself. In her weary resignation there was something grown-up that Juliet found almost unbearable. She cleared her throat. Both daughters looked up warily at her.

'Goodnight, my darlings.' As she went downstairs she heard Isla saying:

'I can't sleep, Bea.'

Bea's soft voice seemed to float after Juliet, following her back downstairs. 'Yes you can. Do what I do . . . Imagine you're back on the Heath. Walking up to Parliament Hill. When we flew that kite with Dad after Sandy's birthday, remember? Imagine you're on that path. Going higher and higher. Trace the steps. Every bit of it. Close your eyes. You can see the bushes, and the playground on the right, and the path . . . keep walking, that's right . . .'

She could hear her soft voice, reverberating through the empty house, as Juliet retreated.

Back in bed a few minutes later she crawled under the sheets, praying she would drop off soon: since her return from London the previous week Juliet hadn't really slept. After a while there was silence from upstairs, and quiet through the house; but Juliet lay there, stiff, heart thudding, janglingly alert. Her jaw ached from clenching it too tight. Every night since she'd gone back to London the previous week. At five she climbed out of the creaking bed, and went silently downstairs.

Sunlight was spreading across the treetops behind the house, pearl and coral. Juliet pulled on her wellington boots, and opened the kitchen door. The dawn chorus encircled her, lifting her up. She went to the abandoned potting shed and, after several attempts, with a huge groan managed to yank open the stuck door. Reaching past what seemed to be hundreds of spiders, Juliet took out the rusting shears. Without knowing why she knew this, she rattled an almost empty tin of linseed and put some on the stiff blades. She took a wobbling spade too and went out into the garden, stopping first at the overgrown borders and pathways of the Wilderness. She hacked away at the brambles, the ivy, the knots of rambling roses, bindweed and honeysuckle. By six-thirty she was exhausted, but underneath the cover she could see plants beneath. Strangled

166

lavender and red-and-white flowers she thought might be a kind of salvia. Salvia? Was that even a word for plants? She wondered if Grandi had written to her about it. If not, she'd look it up.

This I can control, she thought, dubiously, leaning on her spade, flushed, sweaty, already bone-tired but feeling slightly less miserable, she thought, than if she had stayed in bed chewing her nails. She thought of Ev, and wondered where he was right now. If he was looking out over a garden like this, too. If he missed this place. If he ever thought of her. How she could do with his help now.

Chapter Fourteen

When Juliet had suddenly decided to take the children that July day, cancelling the removal van the following week, she had had to leave most of their possessions in London. She'd packed a fair bit, everything she could fit in the car, but throughout the wet summer and the beginnings of that golden autumn she realised having the rest of the children's books and toys would help make the place seem more homely. Especially since come Wednesday, 10th September, they were all starting somewhere: Bea at Walbrook Girls' School, Isla at Godstow Primary School, Sandy at nursery.

So she had returned to London for the day, leaving the children with Mrs Beadle. In order to bring back as many of the children's possessions as possible, Juliet had even hired a large van from Godstow's sole industrial area (a three metre by four metre concreted strip behind the bakery, next to some bins).

It was eleven o'clock when she arrived back at Dulcie Street. The moment her key clicked the lock and she opened the front door she could tell something had changed. The house smelled different. It had a different air to it.

Moving slowly down the hall Juliet frowned as she saw a pair of children's shoes. She didn't recognise them. Up the stairs, photographs had been taken down, leaving marks on the wall. On the door of Bea's room, a childish hand had scrawled directly on to the paint in felt tip:

THIS IS MY ROOM NOW SO KEEP OUT

Juliet rubbed her eyes – she really thought she might be dreaming. A thought occurred to her: Matt had redecorated, for the kids' next visit. He'd bought them new shoes! Then she went into Isla's room.

Her own children's things were piled into open bin bags in the corner. Drawers of their clothes had been, she saw as she peered in, simply upended into the bags, unfolded. Their toys were jumbled together into huge zip-up canvas bags, Lego and Duplo and Playmobil mixed into one along with piles of Ladybird books, pens and pencils, paper, paints and fancy-dress costumes, as though burglars had simply tipped everything off the shelves into them. One arm of Bea's spare pair of glasses had been snapped off and thrown in with toiletries from the bathroom. The small pile of the children's old babygros and first clothes she had kept, not sure what to do with (things like a ridiculously small pair of shoes and a pretty pintucked top from Matt's mother in Italy) was balled tightly into a plastic bag. She could feel the rage of the person doing it.

In Sandy's room was a brand-new IKEA bed, draped with Sleeping Beauty-style curtains hanging from the ceiling, and a chest of drawers from the landing filled with another boy's clothes. Sandy's toys were herded into the corner, his old baby blanket which Juliet's parents had sent from France thrown over them, as if to hide them from the new occupant's sight.

This, then, was how Juliet discovered Tess and her children had moved out of her husband's house and in with Matt.

'You said you were coming Thursday.' Matt stood clutching the door frame. He had come back from work after Juliet called him, anger and disbelief rendering her almost speechless.

Juliet thrust her phone towards him, still shaking. 'Wednesday. I've got the texts in front of me. Look. *Look*. So – if I'd come tomorrow all this stuff *wouldn't* have been here?'

'I was going to call you tonight. Explain. Yeah, I would have made some of it look a bit . . . better.' He was flustered for once, following her from room to room, watching her as she rifled through the bin liners. 'She needed to get them settled ASAP.'

'She? I assume you're talking about Tess, your mistress? The one you've been shagging for eight months. Or is it longer than that? I'm not quite sure of the actual timeframe of it all,' Juliet said, tying up a bin bag. 'I can see she had time to order a new IKEA bed to replace my child's bed. Or perhaps you did, but it seems unlikely, since you haven't had time to come and actually see your own children.'

Matt had gone to visit his mother in Italy and when he'd come back in late August kept saying it 'wasn't the right time for them to come to London'.

'You know it's Tess. Don't be childish.'

'Well, please thank her for doing all this packing. She's saved me hours. Although it's strange it doesn't bother you she's treated your own children's possessions like rubbish.' They were in their old bedroom. 'I don't care about my stuff. But it's—' She searched for the word, bin bag in hand. 'It is *so* bizarre. It's nasty.'

'Her kids needed to feel at home,' Matt said. 'Robert threw her out on the street when he found out.'

'My kids though, Matt. Your kids.'

'You fucked off. You don't get to tell me what to do.'

Juliet realised that, since she'd moved away, she had acquired a muscle memory, some hunching of the shoulders when she thought of Matt, of what she had done by moving away, which told her she was at fault. And it wasn't like that at all. She shook herself a little. She moved back into Isla's room, holding a tiny woollen hat Bea had worn home from the hospital. Outside on the landing the cheap carpet was worn thin and the string underneath showed through, from years of all of them standing outside Isla's room and the bathroom, chattering, yelling, cajoling . . .

She said, wearily, 'You were having an affair.'

'Listen!' He leaned forward, laughing. 'Whether I was or wasn't is immaterial. You took my kids away without telling me. You are screwed.'

'God,' said Juliet, and she pushed away the tip of her ponytail which she had been chewing, and actually laughed. She faced him, her eyes glittering. 'Matt. Do you know what?'

'What?'

'You're a total, fucking idiot.' She saw his face, incredulity spreading across it, like water on blotting paper. 'I'm so sick of you. You're a second-rate person. You always were. And wow! It is so nice not having to put up with you making me feel crap about myself. All the damn time.' She picked up one of the bin bags. 'Come down for the last weekend in September and stay at the house, otherwise I'm telling them what you've done.' She smiled, not caring if this turned him into an enemy and she turned, picking up two bin bags, and went downstairs.

'Look. I'll come that weekend,' he said, when she'd finished loading up the van. 'I – I can't come before then. But how about, weekend after next, I meet you halfway somewhere, and I take them out for the day. How about that, for the meantime? We can go to Whipsnade, or something.' He rubbed his face.

'Fine. Another time we'll have to work out how you have them to stay, now there are other children living in their bedrooms.' She gave a despairing laugh. 'Isla likes most people but she can't stand Elise. She thinks she's rude and farts on purpose.'

'How are they?' he said, suddenly. 'How's Bea?'

'Bea is doing OK. She actually told me a couple of weeks ago that she liked it there.'

Matt nodded and said, solemnly, 'You haven't really talked, though, then.'

She stared at him with irritation. 'I talk to her all the time.'

He raised his eyebrows. 'I see.'

'Would you tell me, if you know something about her you think I should know?'

Matt hesitated. His eyes darted from her face to the near-distance, then back. 'I don't think that's for me to tell you, Juliet, actually.' He patted the side of the van, and stepped back on to the pavement.

As she drove down the narrow street she saw Zeina peering through her front window at her, eyes round as saucers, and it was all Juliet could do not to stop in the middle of the road, pull over and bash down the door, just for a hug, to feel someone who loved her hold her. To smile with someone. 'Can you believe what he's done?'

She'd thought bringing back their possessions would help make the place look homelier, but even when their things were scattered throughout the house they looked all wrong, the plastic dolls looked out of place, the Lego and Duplo got lost, the dressing up was too plastic-y. The house needed proper, substantial items, like a wicker laundry basket, not the collapsible IKEA one made of tea bag material. Back home – back in London, everyone had these items, jumbled in their cramped homes. Back in London everyone was the same as her.

'Isla, eat up please. We're leaving in five minutes.'

'But I don't like my Cheerios. I hate Cheerios. I want some Weetabix.'

'You used to hate Weetabix. I got the Cheerios as a first day of school treat.'

'They're too sweet. They make me want to *vomit*. I mean literally, yes, Mummy I do know what that means. That's how too sweet they are.'

'Ugh. Too sweet. Sit down here.'

'OK, Sandy. Isla, you need to eat something. It's a big day. Imagine if you can't play with any of your new friends because your tummy's rumbling so loudly!'

'My . . . t-t-tummy's not going-going-going t-t-to rumble, Mummy . . .' Here Isla dissolved loudly into tears. 'D-d-don't say that!'

'Oh sweetheart –' Juliet hastened down the long table to her daughter. 'Isla, darling, sorry, I was just being silly – Sandy, don't put your arm out, you'll knock over your mu— DON'T, Sandy – oh, darling, Mummy didn't mean to shout – oh Jesus. Matt!'

There was an awkward silence. 'Silly Mummy,' said Isla. 'You left Daddy behind. He's not here.'

She wiped her nose on her too-large red school sweatshirt, emblazoned with an oak tree in white. Juliet looked away. Isla was small for her age. She didn't look old enough to be going into Year two. She should still be in nursery, with Sandy.

'You'll see him next week. He's taking you out for the day.'

'Why can't I see him now? Mummy, please, can't we go back home this weekend?'

Juliet hesitated. 'I'm sorry, darling.'

'Is it because you've taken all our things back here? I can sleep on my floor, promise,' said Isla, her eyes huge.

'Darling, we can't stay at the house.' Juliet chewed a loose piece of cuticle, tearing it away from the nail. A pinhead-sized bead of blood popped out, glinting in the sun. She wiped it on her already muddy jeans. 'It's – Daddy has some lodgers staying there. So he's going to meet us halfway between here and London, and you'll do some fun things for the day.'

'What?'

'My play with doll's house?'

'No, Sandy. Eat your toast.'

'My no like toast. My like Cheerios.'

'Oh good grief. *Bea! Darling! Are you ready? We need to leave in five minutes!* Isla – more toast, sweetheart?'

'I DON'T WANT ANY TOAST MUM!' Isla screamed, so loudly her voice sounded hoarse. There was silence as the words rang around the dining room and Isla got up and stomped out, trying to make her feet stamp on the solid wood floor. Juliet glanced out over the garden. She could actually see the difference her efforts that morning had made. Later, she would buy some cheap bulbs. Sort out the shed. See if there were any potatoes in the old potato bed. Go to the library and get them all cards. Buy: gaffer tape, a new rake, batteries. Bulbs – this time for the lights. Look at the fusebox, as four different switches didn't seem to work; she remembered her grandmother, bent over the wooden casement in the scullery for hours. Call Honor. Call Matt's mother. Buy more socks.

Sandy was still at the table, swirling pieces of muesli around on the table-top.

'All right, little one?' she said, gently stroking his flaxen hair, which curled and bobbed around his head. He nodded, not really understanding. 'My get down,' he said, and slid off his chair, pottering out of the room, calling after her. 'Isla! Isla?'

Of all of them only Sandy had adapted with any equanimity. He didn't seem to have noticed Matt wasn't there. Juliet had bought him some new red wellies and he'd liked helping her on the few previous times she'd tried to tackle the garden, watching her cut things down, sow new seeds, tie branches to walls. He loved getting lost in the Wilderness. He didn't mind the mice in the sitting room, or the constant rain, or the loneliness of the echoing house which Juliet felt was peopled with ghosts, watching them, every day.

We should all be more like Sandy, Juliet thought. She glanced at her watch.

'It's eight-twenty!' she yelled. 'Everyone! In the car! Now!'

Somewhat to her surprise there was a thundering noise on the stairs and Isla appeared, flushed and cross, followed by Bea, glowering, barefoot, dressed in her new school uniform. Her slender neck and small dark face with its bobbed black hair rose from a navy sweatshirt that swamped her thin frame, her new navy nylon trousers far too long. She stood at the bottom of the steps next to Isla, who clutched her bookbag.

Juliet felt her heart clench. She said, 'Darlings, you both look very smart. I'm – I'm so proud of you both.'

Bea twitched her nose and then rubbed her face, a sign she was trying not to cry. She pulled on her black trainers. 'Shut up, Mum. I look like a bloody Passport Control guard.'

Isla peered forward to stare at her sister then clapped her hands. 'You do, you look like that man from the Arr Ess Pee Pee who rescues sweet guinea pigs on Pet Rescue, oh the darlings with their fluffy fluff, remember chinchillas have two hundred thousand hairs per square inch, do you remember?'

'Shut up.'

'Annie says none of the girls wear trousers at Bea's school.' Annie was Mrs Beadle's granddaughter and Isla set great store by her opinion. 'They *all* wear skirts. I told Bea this. She didn't listen.'

'Literally no one wears skirts, it's gendered bollocks. So shut *up*, Isla, OK?'

'Isla, darling, get in the car. You're the one who'll be late, Bea doesn't start till this afternoon.'

'I don't understand why I can't bloody stay at home anyway.'

'Because I want you to come into Godstow with me. There's someone special I want to say hello to.'

'Who?'

'An old friend of mine.'

'Well I don't see—'

'Get in the car! All of you! Or else I will get really cross! Really soon!' Juliet bellowed. They stared at her, her two girls in their new uniforms, Sandy in his red wellies, and then Isla smiled.

'It's funny when Mum shouts, isn't it?' she said to Bea, as if Juliet wasn't there. 'She's so terrible at it.'

Bea nodded. 'Mum has no clue. At all.' She looked at her phone.

Chapter Fifteen

'I'll stay in the car.' Bea slumped down over her phone as Juliet eased into a parking space on Godstow High Street.

'No,' said Juliet, pushing her sunglasses up on her head and grabbing Grandi's old green string shopping bag which she'd found at the back of a cupboard. 'You're coming with me.' She rubbed her eyes. Sandy had screamed inconsolably for ten minutes at his new nursery before she had brutally cut him loose and left him in the arms of an apparently nice woman named Janet whom Juliet had never met but had to trust wasn't a child murderer. And Isla, perhaps more heartbreakingly, had gone into class without a murmur. She had hugged Bea tightly, clinging to her as a drowning man to a liferaft. But Juliet she had dodged a kiss from, brushing her lips against her arm instead.

'Bye darling – I hope you—'

Isla had turned away. 'My dad gave me these hairclips,' she said to Miss Fraser at the classroom door. 'He lives in London. I'm seeing him next weekend. He's picking me up from school. My sister says some other children live with him now.'

One of the other parents had stared in horror at Juliet, as if she had three heads.

'Come on,' said Juliet now, opening Bea's car door for her and waiting while she got out of the car. She put her arm around her daughter, so grown-up in her new uniform. 'It's time you met someone important.'

'Hello, Juliet.' Frederic Pascale looked up at her over his half-moon spectacles and laid his fountain pen gently down on the table. 'Ah! And this must be Beatrice. Good morning, my dear child. *Enchanté.*' He stood up slowly, kissing first Juliet, then Bea's hand.

'Hi,' she said, awkwardly.

'I'm sorry we haven't been in to see you yet,' said Juliet, hugging him. 'I wasn't sure when you were back.'

'We came home four days ago. And I have been feeling most guilty about not paying you a visit. It has been rather hectic since our return: six weeks in France and I have forgotten everything about running a business. George says next year we can only manage three weeks. George is more practical than I, as you can tell.'

'George? Oh – of course.'

'My partner. He believes you know each other.'

'I don't think so,' said Juliet. He was watching her closely; something in his direct gaze unnerved her. She smiled at him. 'How lovely it is to be here again. It hasn't changed at all.'

Frederic nodded. 'Dear child. You haven't, either. No, don't protest. You are still a Pre-Raphaelite innocent in a big bad world.' His gaze took in her unbrushed hair, her dirty mud-and-blood streaked jeans which she hadn't had time to change, her worn plaid shirt, but Juliet felt flattered, for the first time in ever so long. 'It is true, my dear, you are a greater beauty now than you were at twenty.' He reached under his desk, a long-forgotten gesture that clutched at Juliet's heart, and took out a wooden box. 'Beatrice,' he said, and she looked up.

'Yes?'

'Would you be able to look at these pieces for me?'

Bea said, in a rush, 'Well, I really don't know anything about old things—'

'You do,' said Juliet, stoutly. 'You're brilliant at it.'

'These are items for a doll's house, Bea. As your mother knows, over the years, I collected them. Some are not the right shape, or size. But Juliet told me over the phone that you love the doll's house, too, and have a fine eye. I am so very pleased it is back at the house. Could you see what in this box might be suitable for it?'

There was a light determination to his tone, as he handed the crate to Bea. 'Sure,' she said, nominally unenthusiastic, but Juliet saw, with a kind of wonder, the soft glow in her eyes as she peered inside.

'Thank you so much, my dear. It is much appreciated.'

'Let me know what we will owe you, Frederic.'

He waved his hand. 'This is my treat. I am in your grandmother's debt for many reasons. You must indulge me on this. I will explain why, one day.'

The shop – named Pascale & Co, on Godstow High Street, was narrow and long. The sound of traffic grew faint the further you retreated into the shop. In the first room was jewellery, velvet-covered trays studded with pieces worn in the ears, on the fingers, around the necks of those long dead. Juliet used to wonder about them, who they'd been. The second room was shelves lined with gold-tooled books. There were etchings and prints in upstanding cases for one to sift through and a stand of old umbrellas and walking-sticks. In the back room were large, dark items of (good) Victorian and Georgian furniture: 'Antiques, not Junk' read the sign in the shop window.

In fine weather Frederic would place cane chairs, upturned wicker baskets and a dogbowl in front of the shop. He himself sat in the first room behind his desk, ledger book and cash till by his side, and thirty years since he'd first opened, the set-up had not changed. Frederic had taste, was honest, and did not suffer fools, and thus had built a reputation for himself beyond the village and the towns nearby. London dealers dropped in en route for weekends away to see what he might have, or to ask his advice.

Frederic had been in Godstow since the eighties. Originally from a small town in Brittany, he had decamped to this forgotten corner of the countryside almost on a whim because, as he said, he loved the English. He had become one of Grandi's closest friends – by the end, one of the very few with whom she hadn't argued at some point.

Juliet, having spent many happy summer hours skulking round the shop and in the tiny cobbled garden at the back, knew the place like the back of her hand; every time she came in she found there would be something new to covet. A Tiffany-blue travel set, with tiny crystal bottles to be filled with rose-water, cold-cream and talcum powder. A set of photographic plates of a Victorian fancy-dress ball. The tiny edition of Jane Austen's *The History of England,* no bigger than a matchbox, and, of course, the doll's house furniture.

So it was in that shop, not at Nightingale House, with Frederic telling her about Rococo art, or Whitby jet, or Clarice Cliff, that Juliet first acquired her love of old things. And it was in that shop, as a long-haired, moody teenager in flowing skirts, that she learned from Frederic that to follow the crowd is all very well, but forging your own path serves you best in the end. He, as much as Grandi, had taught her to trust her eye, her instincts. Without him she suspected she would never have found the Millais sketch in the Oxfordshire junk shop, nor bluffed her way into a job at Dawnay's when she had no auction house experience.

Now Frederic turned, and the light from a passing car mirror bouncing off the late-morning sun caught his face for a second, and Juliet could see for the first time the lines around his eyes, the sag of his skin, how slowly he moved.

'We had a very pleasant summer. We were in Paris for a fortnight, then to Brittany, to Dinard. We saw your parents.'

'Yes; they said.' Juliet jangled her keys in her pocket. 'Dad told me you were worried I'd made a terrible mistake moving back here.'

A faint glimmer of amusement played around his mouth. 'That is not how I would put it; either your father exaggerates, or you do.'

'But you don't deny it, Monsieur Pascale,' she said, smiling.

'I do.' Frederic put his hand on hers. 'Ah my dear. It's so lovely to see you, after all these years. I've been wondering so very much how you're getting on.'

'Oh. Well, it's been – a bit strange.' She hesitated. 'I don't want to moan—'

'Please. You may moan to me. I think you have every right to.'

'Well . . .' Juliet looked at her hands. 'We moved back at the start of the summer holidays, not knowing anyone. We've hung out a lot. That's been terrific. Played a lot of board games . . .' She cleared

179

her throat. 'And the children have got things out of their system, as it were. They've obviously been – ah – affected by the move, and our marriage break-up.' She thought of Isla one lunchtime two weeks ago, refusing to come in for pasta, head bobbing out from the Wilderness in the pouring rain as she bellowed: 'I wish you would understand *I hate you* and I don't want your horrible pasta!'

'Anyway, our stuff is here now, and we all know the house inside and out, and the garden. So it was OK. But – well, I had all these dreams of them running wild. And it rained. You know, it never really rained when I was a child.'

'You remember it like that. I remember it rained an awful lot. It is England. It is the West Country. I remember you and Ev bouncing off the walls, your grandmother quite distracted about what to do with you indoors all day.'

'Oh.'

'Memory plays tricks, my dear.'

She nodded, unsettled. 'Oh, you're right. I thought I'd sink into some rural idyll and of course it's not like that. Well it is, but not in the way I thought.' She gave a self-pitying chuckle. 'Besides, we don't have enough furniture and the garden is a jungle. We're just getting used to it all. And it has been tough on them. Sandy is fine, he's two. Isla is very, very sad. And Bea – well.' She lowered her voice. 'I think it's the right thing for her. But I know she's still not telling me everything. It's a lot for them to take in.'

'A huge amount. I am very impressed at your bravery in going through with it. I had no idea when I – Well done.'

'Oh, it was liberating to be honest.' She smiled into his kind eyes, and put her elbows on the desk. 'You know, some mornings I'd wake up and hear the rain and realise there's another day stretching ahead to be filled and wonder what on earth I'd done.'

'Don't they play, these children?'

'A little. They really want WiFi.' Juliet shrugged, ashamed of her London children, creeping around inside instead of rushing out to find beetles and wild snapdragons and blue speckled eggs. 'Like I say, if they were used to it, to being here . . .' Juliet looked around, at the sound of voices: Bea was chatting to a stranger towards the back of the shop. She heard her laughing.

'They will get used to it. It takes time.'

'Yes. But I wish there were some way of making them understand. That I did it for them, as well as for me.'

'Did you?'

She thought for a moment. 'I hope so. I thought I was doing it for them. When you're a mother you gradually lose any sense of what is best for them and what is best for you. They become the same thing.'

'Not all mothers, Juliet.'

'Well, I felt by coming back here I would . . . make everything better. You understand.' She looked at him frankly. 'It's the house. You know? I stand out in the morning with my coffee and look out over the garden and I hear the birds in the trees in the evening and I see eight peacock butterflies on the white buddleia and there's room to breathe, and I feel this little certainty inside. That it was the right thing to do. And the children have found all my old dress-up clothes and books, and when it's sunny they do actually disappear for hours in the garden. They've taken over the Dovecote.' She was nodding to herself; Frederic watched her. 'I assumed this was purely a selfish, self-indulgent move. I was so scared, Frederic.' She paused. 'Everything's unravelled since I took the decision to come. But you know what? I feel at home.'

'It *is* your home,' he said, very quietly. 'For whatever reason, it is.'

Juliet hesitated, trying to read his expression. 'Yes . . .'

'And you? You have told me about them, but not you.'

'I'm OK. I'm sad. They're all sad. But it comes in waves. You know, listening to a love song. Or staring round at the wiring. I feel overwhelmed, somehow. It's all linked up.' She laced her fingers together. 'I don't miss Matt, I don't think. I am just sad. Sad it didn't work out. I hear about how greatly other people love or are loved, on the radio, on TV, even on Facebook or something and I want to weep for myself, is that self-indulgent? And then I am angry with myself, for not standing up to him. For all of it, all those years.' She looked up at him, pulling a piece of hair between her fingers. 'I don't have any identity, at the moment. That's what makes me sad.'

Frederic put his hand on hers. Bea was telling the stranger at the back of the shop something, her voice rising in excitement. 'No!' Juliet could hear her saying. 'He never said that.'

'Forgive my rudeness,' Frederic said. 'Can you afford to stay there? Your parents were concerned – '

'I think so. I have six months' pay, thank goodness, but I'll need to start looking for a job as soon as possible.'

'That house needs attention.'

'Attention! When Grandi left Nightingale House to me it was obviously in better condition than it is now. It absolutely eats money.'

The quarterly gas bill had come in, and the invoice for fixing the kitchen lights and the oddly wired electrics. She had bought new garden furniture, because the old set had rotted away. She was sure Liddy and Ned would have had some fine, carved oak table and chairs for the terrace but she'd got a plastic table and four chairs from Argos in a murky sage mysteriously called Barbados Green.

'I mended some guttering the other day with gaffer tape. Special dark green gaffer tape.'

'This is very impressive.'

'It is. But I want to do things properly,' Juliet said. 'I don't want everything to be plastic furniture and gaffer tape. And then I tell myself it's my house and I shouldn't worry about that stuff, that I'll be there for years and years.'

'Well, exactly. So, to other matters: I have a chest of drawers, very fine, and a bedframe, if you have need of a new bed. Some chairs: two armchairs and dining chairs, also a sofa, which I wondered if you would do me the very great favour of taking off my hands and removing to Nightingale House.' He tore the page from the book and handed it to her. 'Here it all is. Can George drop it round tomorrow?'

'George?'

'My boyfriend. As I said.'

Juliet rubbed her eyes. 'Sorry – yes.'

He glanced up. 'My hearing is terrible. Look, he's been here all along. George! Ah, I see he's found Bea. George,' he called. 'Come and meet Juliet. Stella's granddaughter, as you know.'

Out of the shadows stepped an angular man, only a few years older than Juliet. His salt and pepper hair was close-cropped, his eyes were a flinty grey, fringed with thick black lashes. He and Juliet stared at each other.

'Hi,' said Juliet. 'Don't I know you from somewhere?'

George said tersely, with the faint Scottish accent she'd heard before, 'Yes. I met you the day you moved into the house. I was driving past and offered to help you turn into the driveway.'

'I –'

'You shouted at me. I think you might even have given me the finger.'

'Oh, yes,' said Juliet, her eyes still searching his face. 'You're quite right. I'm so sorry about that.'

George gave a shout of laughter. 'It's lovely to meet you properly,' he said, and he shook her hand. 'Very nice to have some new blood in the village, too. And this one.' He put his arm round Bea. 'This one is a very lovely girl. Even if she does have some crazy ideas about Bowie.'

'Mum loves ABBA,' said Bea, in disgust. 'I discovered Bowie on my own.'

'Nothing wrong with ABBA,' said George. '"The Day Before You Came" is one of the best songs of the last thirty years.'

'That's what I say!' said Juliet, staring at him. 'God. Well done, George. At last.'

Bea glowed, smiling at them both. 'Thanks for letting me look at these,' she said, handing the box back to Frederic.

'It's my pleasure. I hope that you will pick some yourself, to put in the doll's house.'

'I'd love to.'

Juliet said, 'We need to get you to school, Bea. I have to do a bit of shopping beforehand.'

'So soon? Will you come back?'

'You won't be able to get rid of us,' said Juliet.

'I am sure there's still a lot you have to catch up on,' said George, slowly, looking at Frederic. 'Isn't there, F?'

'It can wait for another time.' Frederic raised himself up slowly, and stepped out from behind the desk. He put his arm through George's, and did a small heel-toe shoe shuffle, then slid his hands outwards. George applauded, enthusiastically.

'He'll win *Strictly* yet, you wait and see. Listen, come again soon.'

'Thank you.' Juliet hesitated, and turned to Frederic. 'It is so wonderful to see you again. Thank you for listening to me go on.'

'It is my pleasure,' Frederic said, walking her through the shop. 'Ev's mum is looking for you, by the way. She's back from Jamaica. She wants to come for tea.'

'I must call her. She can be the second person I know here. Third,' she said, to George.

'You're determined not to remember me, aren't you? Who's Ev?'

Juliet laughed. 'My best friend. Well, he *was* my best friend. He's – gosh, I haven't seen him for twenty years now.'

'Honor's son,' Frederic interjected. 'You know Honor Adair, George, we went to their house for dinner. Barn, rather. Bryan is her husband. Lawyer. He's Jamaican, she grew up here –'

'Those Moroccan tiles,' said George, clicking his fingers. 'The amazing garden.'

'That's her. Ev is her son. He and Juliet used to play together as children. You met him last Christmas, I think, when he was back.'

'Oh . . . yes,' said George, in a hard-to-read tone. 'I remember him.' Juliet could feel George's eyes on her, and thought he could see her blushing.

They were standing on the pavement. One of the parents from Isla's class, a nice-looking woman in a potentially Boden skirt, whom Juliet had noticed earlier that morning at the school, nodded at her.

'Hi.'

'Hi,' Juliet said, smiling at her.

'I had to drop Emily's inhaler back at the class just now,' she said, in a rush. 'Your daughter was playing very happily with her. Just thought you'd like to know.'

Juliet could have clasped this stranger to her bosom and kissed her. 'That's so kind of you. Thank you! Thank you so much.'

'No problem.'

'Well thanks again. See you – see you later.' The others watched as Juliet waved frantically after her as she disappeared into the Co-op.

'The fourth person I know,' Juliet said, turning back to Frederic and George. 'She was nice. Wasn't she nice?'

George looked at her, with a raised eyebrow. 'That was a bit desperate,' he said.

'Yes,' said Bea. 'Calm down, Mum.' As George and Frederic turned back into the shop, Juliet heard George say:

'You should have told her.'

Frederic was turning to go inside but she saw him shrug his shoulders, his face hidden from view. Juliet stood for a moment and then, becoming aware of her surroundings, she checked her watch.

'We'll be in loads of time to get to your school.' Bea nodded; Juliet was pleased to see the colour in her face. 'Well, well,' she said, fumbling in her bag, to hide the emotion she felt. 'Old Frederic. I never knew he was gay. Silly me.'

'Seriously?' said Bea.

'Well – I just thought he was asexual.' Juliet fiddled in her pocket for her keys. 'Some people are, you know.'

'That's rubbish, they're not. Everyone wants someone.' Bea was biting her nails.

'That can't be true.'

'It is true. You're born with desire. It's, like, a biological thing.'

'Is it?' said Juliet, uncertainly. 'Really?' She literally couldn't remember the last time she felt desire. She desired many things, not another person. A watertight house, a garden free of brambles, and a good night's sleep, both for her and for her children.

Chapter Sixteen

October

When you used to come to me for half-term in October, do you remember what we'd do? We'd rank all the apples in order of usability and attractiveness. But Ev used to just eat them no matter what. A child out of time, your Everett, wild and elemental. He never slept, as a baby. Honor would bring him over at seven in the mornings during the holidays. Whereas you – you were like an enchanted princess in a bower. You slept all the time.

Pick the apples. Store them in the wooden trays in the cool and the dark of the Dovecote. Make sure each fruit is not touching another or they will bruise. Pick the quinces from the tree by the stream. Quince, when boiled up with sugar, makes delicious jam which you can eat with cheese. Your child – WHAT IS HER NAME – can live on apples for months – ours are Russets, and Blenheim Orange – my favourites.

I don't know her name, I'm old and sometimes can't remember myself. Sorry.

What else? Lift the dahlias after the first frost, cut them and plunge them in sand or ash in the greenhouse for winter.

Sow the sweet peas in little pots in the greenhouse.

You must tackle the garden with pruning shears, ready for winter. Cut back, always cut back. You will be rewarded come summer.

The weather changed when October arrived. Having rained for most of August suddenly it became achingly warm, an Indian summer where the light was that peculiar rich gold of autumn. The days were noticeably shorter. On 2 October the thermometer on the wall by the kitchen door said twenty-five degrees, and they sat outside amongst the last of the listing sunflowers and had home-made pizza which Juliet did on the old barbecue. Isla and Sandy rushed around the Wilderness playing hide and seek and Juliet watched them, and the darting birds, and the heart-shaped Small Copper butterflies basking on the lawn below her. Lacy, pink-fringed daisies crept along the borders and the steps along with the final wild strawberries, prinking the luminous lichen-green and the soft grey flagstones with coral and red. The apples were gloriously ripe now, reddening to blush on one side.

Bea set herself up in the Dovecote, where she'd put the doll's house, much to Sandy's disgust, for he wanted it in his bedroom. She did her homework in there. The north-facing windows still gave light; Ned had lined the opposite wall with wooden shelves himself – in fact everything in the Dovecote had been made by his hand, not Dalbeattie's. An old easel, rarely used by Ned, stood in the shadows; mostly he had painted his larger canvases on an old wooden child's cradle, still propped up against the wall and spattered with paint. The whole room was covered in paint – smears and blobs of colours hardened over time into a nobbled texture.

Juliet had not yet paid attention to her grandmother's advice about the sunflowers, because the weather had been so terrible they hadn't flowered until very late on. But she had remembered about the figs. Bea loved figs and could eat five in a row. All three children grew adept at picking the ripe ones, and Bea kept a bowl of them in the studio, resting on the table Ned had made for his paints and brushes, a semi-circle whose side was lathed precisely to run flush with the gentle curve of the wall.

One such warm afternoon, when you could hear the bees still buzzing lazily in the purple salvia, Honor came for tea, and was press-ganged into droping off one of Frederic's latest offerings into the Dovecote.

'I don't understand why George couldn't have helped you with this,' said Honor, pulling at the eighties office swivel chair, which was caught on a small rock. 'This path is in a terrible state. Ah, I see the dahlias and asters are still out in force. Look at that yellow. And that bright red. She'd be delighted the Walkers kept it up.'

'Yes,' said Juliet, herself wheeling a small cabinet on a trundle George had left behind. 'I have no idea what to do about dahlias, do you?'

And as she said it she knew it wasn't true, that somewhere in Grandi's little book of instructions there was something about dahlias.

'Here we are, the scene of the crime – oh, you have got it looking nice in here.' Honor swung the chair around, and pushed it into the Dovecote, then fluffed out her blonde cropped hair. 'Lift them out, cut them, store them. Darling, I must go. Bryan is off tonight and I want to catch him before – Hi, Bea!'

'Hi, Honor. Nice to see you again. Thanks for bringing it over.'

'When did you meet Honor?' said Juliet, as Bea leaped happily into the office chair and started to swing around.

'Oh, with George.'

'George?'

Honor was hugging Bea. 'Listen, Ju. It's wonderful to see you. I'm giving your number to Ev, you can ask him all your garden questions if I'm not around. He wants to be in touch again.'

'Really? How is he?'

Honor rolled her eyes. 'Same old Ev. It's rather wonderful in a way to be that childish still. But his old mum thinks he should be more futureproof – is that the term? Right then.' She jangled her keys in her coat. 'When he's back in the summer you two can catch up properly – but he's the one to ask about it all, the professional gardener and all—'

'Frederic says you're the one who taught Ev everything he knows.'

'I am, but it's the lot of the mother to teach them only to lose them.' But she was smiling. 'Toodle-loo, Ju, darling. I'll come back, if I may. Love to everyone.'

Juliet watched Honor's car drive away. Funny, it was, how someone like Frederic seemed so much older and Honor seemed exactly the same, if anything slightly younger. Younger than Juliet felt. She had always been like that, bursting with energy, direct, funny. She'd grown up here, like Juliet's father.

Bea was still spinning round in the chair as Juliet turned back, her feet skimming on the stone counter that ran one side of the studio. She pulled her hoody up over her head.

'Oh this is great. Thanks, Mum.'

'George brought it over.'

'He's the best.' She spun around again. 'I like George. Did you know he saw Bowie live in Glasgow? Have a fig.'

'Thanks, in a minute.' Juliet climbed up on the high mezzanine ledge and began hunting for a booklet she'd co-written on Leighton at her first job with the Tate Gallery's publications team. She thought it'd be useful to look it over again. Darryl, her old friend from Dawnay's, had emailed her to let her know the Fentiman Museum in Oxford, with its peerless collection of Horner sketches, might be looking for someone. 'Wouldn't working there be totally ideal except isn't the new man there the guy you hate?' he'd written. Juliet winced as she read it. Hate was too strong a word, she told herself nobly. But, yep, she couldn't stand Sam Hamilton.

Since the sale of *The Garden of Lost and Found* sketch he kept cropping up, on the radio, in those ridiculous 'What I'm Reading on Holiday' pieces in the papers which never gave any decent recommendations like a Virago Modern Classic you'd missed or a Georgette Heyer you'd forgotten about. And, as expected, Sam Hamilton had said the book he was taking probably somewhere pretentious like Micronesia or Yerevan was a translation of an Italian poet's new epic in thirty stanzas about the death of Europe as seen through the eyes of a dying bull. He'd even done a short Q&A in *The Times*. 'Sam Hamilton, new director of the Fentiman

Museum and at 40 one of the youngest gallery directors in the UK. Divorced, lives in Oxford alone.' In answer to the question 'What has most disappointed you?', Sam Hamilton answered: 'Social media as a means of democratisation but in fact a purveyor of narcissism and entrenchment.'

Pretentious idiot. Twitter had a field day with it, as Juliet could have predicted it would.

Along with many art historians, Juliet was tired of new directors coming into galleries and feeling they had to put their stamp on a decent, well-run museum by doing something ideological like ordering a rehang that displayed everything in alphabetical order or by themes. She couldn't work out what Sam Ham, as she thought of him, would be like now, but at Oxford he was very much the kind of person who went up to you and explained how clever he was. At *Oxford*. Still, it was literally the one museum in commuting distance, and she had to email him . . . She wondered if Sam Ham still only wore T-shirts from nineties Britpop bands. There was no photo of him in the *Times* piece, which was small.

'Any luck finding that leaflet?' said Bea, rearranging her books and computer on the stone surface.

'Nope.' Juliet climbed down, gingerly. 'There's loads of apples up here. You must make sure the others don't climb up and knock them off. You understand?'

Bea squirmed in her chair, her good mood evaporated. 'Of course I will. I'm not stupid. Can the Dovecote be my place, Mum? My special place? Please?'

'Um – we'll see. The winters here are really cold,' Juliet said, her mind still on Sam Hamilton and feeling rather sick at the thought of heating bills and those old windows.

'I know, I know. I found an old cashmere jumper of your granny's up in the Birdsnest. Wrapped in plastic so no moths get to it, clever, huh? And we could. . . maybe. . . couldn't we run a socket out here? So I could have a light, and a radiator?'

'We'll see. When I've got some spare cash. It'll be pretty chilly, you might not want to leave your computer in here overnight.'

Bea folded her arms. 'Isn't it supposed to be safe around here? Isn't that why we moved?'

'It's safe, I'm sure, but the computer might freeze in the night. It happens.'

'Oh. Well, I'll burn a fire. That's what they used to do in the olden days, didn't they?'

Juliet peered doubtfully up at the ancient mellow-gold stone of the chimney. The Dovecote was actually an old banqueting house where guests would repair after supper to eat sweetmeats and listen to music, the last relic of a formerly great Elizabeth manor which had been demolished to build Nightingale House. 'God knows when it was last swept, I don't remember Grandi ever burning anything in it.'

'Wasn't there, like, supposedly a huge fire that destroyed that painting?'

'Yes, you're quite right. But it wasn't in the fireplace.' She indicated with one scuffed Converse exactly where she was standing, a purple-red circle staining the stone floor around her. 'That's the mark the fire made. Right there.' They stared at it in silence. 'Fires in here make me a bit uneasy, that's why. Besides, we've no money for logs.'

'"We've no money for logs, Father, and Tiny Tim coughs something terrible." Oh come off it, Mum.'

Juliet gave a hollow laugh. 'Logs are expensive. Unless you chop down trees and dry the wood out, and we haven't had time to do that yet with the rain . . .' Bea snorted with derision. Juliet said mildly, 'I don't enjoy saying all this, you know.'

Bea moved her feet around in the chair so that she was facing her mother. 'It's the one bit of this stupid house I like, so of course you want to take it away from me.'

'Yes. Yes, I do. I exist to make your life hard and difficult.'

Bea had swung away from her. In a quiet voice she said, 'You joke about everything. You pretend everything's fine. I want to talk to you and you make things into a joke. It's not a joke, sometimes.'

'I have to make a joke of it otherwise . . .'

'What?'

191

'I have to.' Juliet looked at the darkened floor again. 'Oh, Bea. Tell me what you want to talk about. Anything. Anything at all.'

'No, it's OK. I'm busy. Please, Mum, can you just leave me alone?' She half turned her head again, and gave her a bright smile. 'Thanks. Here, take your book.'

Chapter Seventeen

Hi ju. I heard u moved back to the birdsnest hows that going?! In Jamaica atm but coming back in summer. Be great to catch up. Ev

Hi ev. So great to hear from you! Your mum said you were a gardener now, that is so great. please say you'll help me when you come back, as you may remember this place is pretty wild . . . x

Hit me up what you want to know

What should I be doing atm? I read an article which said I should be kuching. I don't know what that is. Also Grandi said to cut the dahlias but she didn't say how much. Basically not sure what to do for winter

Mulching not kuching stupid auto-correct

Don't worry about mulching or kuching it can wait another year – dahlias need trimming of foliage to about 3–4 inches then storaging somewhere cold and dry in sand. What else?

Wilderness is a mess the leaves are rotten and stink now it's nearly november and there's slime all over the ground bc rain.

OK. Rake up the leaves as much as you can. And on the grass, leaving leaves on grass stops light getting to them. Cut back the foliage. Get some cheap bulbs, grape hyacinth / narcissus / anemones / crocus plant them where you can. Get that earth open to the air not covered with decay. Honestly if u spend 10 mins planting bulbs now you'll be glad in jan / feb. see u soon

I've done some of this already, that's honestly so helpful, thank you! How are you getting on? x

Matt and Juliet met in what was then referred to as a Bar Stroke Club just after midnight on New Year's Day, 1999. Prince was playing loudly in the background, and they were serving Cosmo-politans for 99p, and if either realised this was a pretty cheesy beginning they never said it. They never said the bar was loud and sweaty, and they were both drunk and slept with each other that night without remembering it the next day. They never said one of them was sick on the way home, or that the next morning they couldn't remember the other one's name. They reimagined it, as one does, refashioning the myth so it fitted what came afterwards.

When they got engaged, a pregnant Juliet went back to the bar, a lurid pink building in Fulham Broadway, and took a photo which she had framed along with the front page of *The Times*, 1 January 1999, an exclusive detailing how in three years' time Britain would adopt the euro. It hung in the kitchen in Dulcie Street, and so they were able to tell the children later: we met then, and there.

Why they felt the need to mythologise it Juliet was afterwards never quite sure, but Matt was obsessed with symbols and outward signifiers: personalised Christmas cards, family portraits in silver frames. Juliet, having grown up surrounded by symbols and mean-ings, couldn't really care less. Early on, he laughed at her low-key approach to life, but it was true; she didn't need anything else girlfriends were supposed to demand: bunches of flowers, anniver-sary presents, weekends away. She liked Matt; she fancied him; she loved how he stared at her, as if he'd never met anyone like her. He would wind her hair around his hands and pull her towards him, smiling; the sex was amazing, drawn-out, surprising, the two of them engulfed in awe at how they could make the other one feel. He was furious, passionate, mocking, hilariously traditional; he

194

was like no one she'd known before, a curious mix of Italy, where his mother was from, and Kent, where he'd grown up. He aped the style of the age, of urbane Britpop art students, nineties Mod props – moped, manbag, a tweed cap and a gramophone. Amongst his records was an old 78 of Audrey Hepburn singing 'Moon River'. She played it that first night with him and every night she stayed over for months; she could never again hear the opening chords and that tight, sad voice, without recalling the strange, happy thrill of those first cold winter weeks with Matt.

But one evening, not long after she had moved into Matt's flat in Camden, Juliet found herself staring at the photo of the Bar Stroke Club hanging in his tiny kitchen. Without thinking she said aloud, 'It is strange, isn't it? That we're not like Gav and Lisa, or Tom and Gem.'

Matt was clearing up after dinner, carefully sealing the packet of orecchiette. She watched him, smoothing it down, then putting it in the correct Kilner jar before stacking it neatly in the cupboard next to the other pastas. She had laughed the first time she saw him do it, little realising as one never does, that what now was a charming oddity would later reveal itself to be the minute opening of what would become a grand fissure. Juliet believed one could simply open a cupboard and fling a bag of pasta inside and if some fell out, well, so be it – it was dried wheat, after all, not soft cheese.

He looked up. 'Well spotted. I'm Matt, you're Ju.'

Juliet scraped the leftovers into the bin. 'Ha ha. I mean, we have no background in common.'

'What do you mean?' Matt was putting the herbs away now, each one in order. Juliet watched, mesmerised, then turned back to the sink.

'Well, like these other couples we know. The ones who met at university or through mutual friends.' She propped her elbows on the table, looking up at him. 'It's like there's a sort of destiny about it for them, like it would have happened at some point. But it's coincidence we met. Marie and I weren't supposed to be at that bar, we only went in to use the Ladies.'

Matt turned back and, leaning against the kitchen counter, he folded his arms, and said, 'We're together now. It doesn't matter how we met or if we would have met otherwise.'

Juliet laughed. 'It's just funny our life together is because I needed a pee.'

Matt said sharply, 'Shut up about it, will you?'

'Fine.' Juliet had said nothing else, merely flopped down on the sofa and rolling her eyes a little, to disguise that she felt rather upset. She stroked her small baby bump, as 'Moon River' mournfully floated into the little sitting room. 'My huckleberry friend' – 'my huckleberry friend' – it always made her remember Ev, that, the boy picking wild berries in the hedgerow.

She didn't think of it again, but a few months later, the day before their wedding in fact, she was on the bus home from work, tired and fat and gazing vacantly out of the window, when a chance remark by their friend Gav from months back came floating out of her subconscious into her conscious thought. 'Best mistake he ever made.' She realised Matt had gone to the wrong place that night too. And not at that moment, but afterwards, she slowly came to understand what his touchiness meant: Matt really believed that the fluke of their first encounter should never have happened. They should never have met.

'Here – here's the sitting room – we don't need to bother with that now, we can come here after supper. Mum! Tell Sandy to get *off*! Here's the dining room, it sounds posh, Dad, but it's not, not really, it's where we eat but we play card games in here, and Monopoly, there's a super old version, we've got pretty good at it, Isla beat us once, can you believe? Dad?'

'I did, Dad. I did. But I'm not into games any more, I'm into dancing, Dad, I want to be a dancing queen—'

'Shut up, Isla, you can tell Dad about that later. Look, Dad, look out over the garden, that's the Wilderness, it's always been called that, did you know that?'

'I did, darling. I remember it from when your great-grandmother was alive. I see not much has changed,' Matt said, turning to Juliet with a smile. 'Is that room up on the top floor still there?'

'Yep.' Juliet bent down to pick up a reading book and some socks from the sitting room floor.

'Dad—' Bea was pulling on his arm. 'Look out of the window, you can see beyond the valley almost towards Wales, that's what they say. Come and see Ned's studio, Dad – will you? That's where he burned the painting, you know, no one knows why. That's where I hang out, Mum's getting me WiFi in there after half-term so I can do my homework there—'

'The whole point is it *doesn't* have WiFi, I thought, Bea.'

'Shut up, Mum. Dad, come and see, you'll love it—'

Matt shrugged, and held his other hand out to Isla. 'Come with us, bella? Have you kids had tea?'

'No, not yet,' said Juliet.

Matt stretched out his arms and rolled his head around his neck. Sandy watched him in awe. 'The Friday afternoon traffic was pretty terrible. Can I take us all out to dinner? Is there a pub nearby?'

'The Owl and Ivy, just down the road. That's a great idea. Tell you what, why don't you have a bath, relax with the kids and I can drive us there in an hour or so.'

'Yes!' the two older children cried, clapping their hands and dancing around the room. 'Hurrah! A meal out!'

Sandy joined in, waddling from side to side. 'Huwwahhh!'

Matt raised his eyebrows. 'This from the children who were bored of Wagamama and Pizza Express.'

'Country living,' Juliet said. 'Or rather, middle-of-nowhere-with-no-money-living.'

'Tess's children eat out about four times a week,' he said. 'Us, cinema night, their father, once with friends. It's crazy.'

'Lucky them,' she said, glad he had mentioned Tess first. Perhaps this was going to be fine.

'I know, Dad! Dad, come and see my room—'

'In a minute, pumpkin. Just want to talk to your mum. You go and get it ready, OK?'

'Sure!' Isla said, and the two younger children ran out of the room, whooping with excitement. Bea melted away, looking at her phone. Matt turned to Juliet.

'You OK?'

'Absolutely.' She smiled at him.

'I'm going to be nice this weekend,' he said, quietly. 'I don't want to be a dick. I've been a dick to you, Ju, I'm sorry.'

'You—' she began, then she shook her head. 'It's fine.'

'It's not. We have to talk – about the future. Yes?' She nodded, but didn't look at him.

'That'd be good. It's great to see you.'

'Me too.' He cleared his throat. Oh, the familiarity of him, his square jaw and funny dimpled chin, his smell of rosemary and soap and sweat. He put his hand on one of the spikes of the coat rack.

'I remember this,' he said, stroking it. 'I didn't have children then. What a good idea, all these different hooks at different levels. Clever.'

'It was Ned's idea, most of the little things like that are his,' she said, proudly. 'And Dalbeattie, but Ned had most of the ideas, thinking through what a family wants.'

'That window seat in the child's bedroom upstairs.'

'That's your room. Well, it's Sandy's, but you're sharing.'

'I loved it . . . that's great. I'd forgotten the nightingales on the roof.'

'Yes,' she said, pleased. 'Wow, you remember it really well.'

'Ha.' He rocked on his feet. 'Well, it's sort of imprinted even more strongly on my brain cos of when we went to tell her we were engaged and you were pregnant, do you—' She was nodding. 'We left so suddenly. You can see the nightingales up on the roof now the leaves in the trees have almost gone. It's limestone isn't it?'

She had forgotten how much he loved design. They used to go out for day trips in the car, taking turns to pick a place to go – Ernö Goldfinger's house in Broadstairs, or Ham House, and Dalbeattie's one and only country mansion in Sussex. 'It is. All of Dalbeattie's papers have just come up for sale at auction, actually. There must be some stuff relating to Nightingale House. I'd love to see it.'

'Who's selling it?' He was smiling politely.

'Oh some museum in Canada has gone bust and they're having to sell everything off. So sad . . .' They were walking into the hallway. 'Look. There's a row of shelves in the sitting room, look – floor to waist high, then there's cupboards and hooks for adults and look, this is my favourite bit, they've got birds—' She broke off. Matt was looking at his phone.

'No reception here,' he said, and shrugged, and grinned. She realised for the first time they had no secrets to keep. He didn't need to sneak off to call Tess. She didn't need to hide the clothes she was bagging up and taking to the charity shop, the others she was secretly packing, the bills she was reallocating. If he wanted to call his girl-friend, Matt could use the bloody landline. Juliet grinned back at him. She handed him his overnight bag. 'I'll run you a bath. Take your time. They're so pleased you're here.'

Sandy did very well at supper, but by the time pudding came around he was so tired that, even though it was ice cream, he fell asleep. His parents left him where he was in the chair, curls bouncing gently as his head nodded, while Isla wrote a story in her exercise book about demonic dancing spiders released from a tomb in Egypt who take over the world by putting on an amazing show. Bea sat next to her father, arms linked with his, head resting on his shoulder, listening as Juliet and Matt chatted. About Gav's new business, and Frederic, vague, pleasant talk of people they had in common.

They walked home from the pub in the end. Juliet had had three glasses of wine, partly at Matt's urging, and it was a beautifully warm autumnal evening, so Matt carried Sandy back. They put him straight to bed, just taking off his shoes and trousers. Matt read to Isla, and Bea disappeared to the Dovecote, and Juliet tied her hair back in a scarf, and pottered around the kitchen. She opened another bottle of wine. A faint trace of golden fire on the horizon in the inky blackness showed the sun had just set. Owls called quietly, urgently, from the trees beyond the garden. From far away on the other side of the house she could hear Isla's roars of laughter as Matt did his best set of voices.

Perhaps he's like this with Tess's kids, she thought. Perhaps it's just the five of us together where the chemistry's all wrong. Coming back, they had walked in their old family pack order: Matt carrying Sandy, Juliet with Isla, Bea in between. Were they still that family, even though they were apart? In the lovely fading light, the mournful stillness of the evening, surrounded by the quiet and beauty for which she had longed for years, Juliet was not sure.

'Hello there.' She jumped, and turned around. Matt was in the doorway.

'Isla OK?'

'I said she could read by herself for a while.' He paused; she nodded, awkwardly, both afraid of what the boundaries were, wanting to be polite. 'Her reading's really come on, hasn't it?'

'It has. The school is great for that. They let her go into Year two and pick her own books. She talks about some people – there's a girl called Emily who seems nice and likes the Egyptians, which is crucial, obviously—'

'That's great. Listen, Ju—'

'Yes?'

'Thanks for having me here. I know everything's still up in the air . . .' He came towards her and put his wine glass down on the table.

She gave a nervous laugh. 'No trouble. Really, Matt – you must come as often as you want. You can have your own room, your own set-up – the kids would have you here all the time—'

'You're a great mother. I'd forgotten that.'

'Hardly.'

'You are.' His eyes shone in the gloom. The last of the light outside was almost gone. 'You talk to them. You let them be themselves, not how you want them to be.'

'That's nice to hear.' Juliet could feel the wine warming her. She felt relaxed. 'Really?'

'Yes. God, yes. You're so – lovely. I – I miss you, Ju.'

He put one hand on her hip, the other around her neck, and leaned in towards her. As if in a trance, Juliet mirrored him and then she inhaled, smelling him again, the hair gel, the aftershave, the rosemary. Matt.

The spell was broken: she pulled away.

'Sorry,' she said, trying to stay calm, not to show how this upset her, but merely to laugh it off – she knew Matt's fragile ego of old. 'We can't—' She held out her hand. 'You know that.'

'Sorry. Yep. I know,' he said, neutrally, and walked back to the other end of the table and picked up his wine glass, as if none of it had happened. He gave a little frown, and stared down towards the garden. 'Bea's in that little studio again, is she?'

'No, I've corralled her back into bed. But she loves it in there.'

'Must be a bit lonely. How's she getting on?'

Juliet realised her heart was thumping, hard, as she tried to answer normally, calmly. 'Good. I'm making sure she does her cello practice. She's very keen on Frederic, and George has been so great. There's some play she's in at school, too. I'm keeping her busy.'

'I didn't mean that.' He put the glass down on the table and stared out at the sunset. 'Has she mentioned Fin to you again? Do you know if they still see each other?'

'Fin?' Juliet passed a hand across her head, then realised she had foam on her hairline from the washing up. 'Oh, him. I've seen some weird texts. But to be honest, he seems to have passed out of the picture since we moved away.'

'Who?' he said, as though he hadn't understood her.

'Fin. That boy I thought she was seeing. She has some friends at school here – there's a girl called Jack, and Betty, and some twins . . .' Juliet had been keeping track of everyone Bea mentioned down here, determined to stay on it, to make sure she knew as much as she could about her Sphinx-like teenager's existence. 'It's a different set-up at this school, much smaller, and everyone knows everyone else – the parents seem nice, Matt, you should come down for her birthday, you can meet some of them. But, to be honest, Fin always seemed OK – it's Amy and those other girls who were so vile—' He was staring at her, with a half-smirk she couldn't decipher. 'Why are you looking at me like that?'

And then Matt started laughing. A loud, ringing laugh that rang, strange and wild, round the old house. He smiled nastily.

'This is what I'm talking about. You ask me down here, you prattle on about some stupid window seats and how I can have a bath, like you're lady of the bloody manor and I'm some bit of scum you accidentally had three children with. And you – you don't even know what's going on under your own fucking nose.' The expletive took Juliet by surprise; she flinched, and he laughed again. 'You drag them down here, to this *pit* – I mean, Juliet, have you looked at this house through anything except your ridiculous grandmother's rose-tinted spectacles?'

'It's not a pit.' She shook her head slowly, allowing her disdain for him to show itself on her face as she twisted her gaze to meet his. She knew she was breaking her pact with herself, not to antagonise him, but she didn't care. 'It's our home.'

'Oh, my God!' He wiped his eyes. His voice was loud, almost as if he wanted the children to wake, to hear them. 'You really have lost the plot. It's starting to make sense now. You know I never understood why your grandmother riled you more than anyone else.' He leaned towards her, eyes shining. 'It's because you're *identical.* You seem all sweetness and light and you're exactly the same as her. Single-minded, selfish, head in the sand . . .'

'You keep forgetting this small detail, Matt. *You were having an affair!*'

'You *left,* my dear girl.' He laughed. 'This is why I get to tell you what to do. You took the children and you *left.*'

Juliet said in biting tones, 'You know, Matt, you're going to have to get past that bit, otherwise you're in for a nasty shock. You were squashing me. We were crushing each other down, the children, too. Bea especially.' She took a deep breath. 'You don't understand. She wanted to come. She asked to leave.'

Matt turned and shut the door on to the hallway. 'You don't know the first thing about your own daughter,' he said, softly, walking back towards her, only now he seemed menacing, and she remembered with cold horror the chameleon-like way he could utterly change himself.

Juliet's jaw was clenched so tight she realised it was actually hurting. 'Bea was like a hunted animal back in London. Don't tell me I don't know her.'

Matt looked down at her, picked up one lock of her red hair. It caught in the light. 'Fin is a girl,' he said, and dropped the hair again.

'What?'

'Fin. Is. A. Girl. She was Bea's girlfriend. She came out to me a few months ago.' He laughed again, shortly, and stepped back from her, arms outspread, like a magician, concluding his final trick of the show.

Juliet put her hand on the back of the chair. 'A girl. She—' She exhaled. 'Of course.' The pit of her stomach felt hollow. 'Little one—' She put the other hand over her mouth. '*Of course*. How could I have been so stupid!'

He was watching her. 'This is what I mean.'

'Why didn't you tell me? How could you—' She let her hands drop to her sides, and said blankly, 'I don't understand you.'

'She asked me not to tell anyone. So I didn't and, besides, you live in a fantasy world. You *never* talk to your parents. What's that about? Your grandmother was completely mad when she died. You don't even know your own children. You shouldn't be in charge of them. So don't threaten me. Robert's got me a solicitor.'

'Robert who?'

'Tess's husband.'

'Tess's husband has found you a solicitor?'

'Yeah, OK? And – and by the time I've finished with you, you'll have sold this house, and the children will be back in London, nearby, where I can see them. It's happening, Juliet.' He started to say something else, then stopped. 'I don't know what you're up to down here, what little plans you've got, but this is happening. And I'll make you so sorry you made a fool of me, taking them away like that.'

'I want to talk about Bea—' she began, but he had turned. 'I'm tired. I drove for three hours to get here. I'm going to bed.'

She watched as he climbed the curving staircase at the centre of the house, a slim figure in navy-black, looking ahead of him. And I can't ask him to leave. There's nothing I can do. He has to stay here.

She dreamed vividly, of Bea in the Dovecote, playing with the doll's house, and woke upright in bed, arms gesticulating as she talked to her. Of Frederic's face, staring at her and smiling. Juliet lay awake blinking in the dark, almost until the first, grey light, the last day before the clocks went back. Then she got up, as she had done so many times lately, and went out to the garden again. To rake up the leaves that had fallen in the night. To pick more apples and quinces, plant the bulbs she'd bought.

Chapter Eighteen

'What do you guys want to do today, then? You should show Daddy some of the local sights.'

'Here?' said Isla, in surprise, pushing away her Sugar Puffs. 'Dad, there's nothing to do here.'

Matt smiled into his black coffee.

'Oh,' said Juliet, 'I know it's nothing compared to London. You could take him round the garden, show him the Dovecote—'

'Bea doesn't like people going in there.'

'Well, I'm sure she wouldn't mind Daddy seeing it. Where is she, do you know?'

Isla turned to her father. 'She is literally so unpredictable lately, Dad. If you go in there, you might get it in the head.' She looked momentarily confused, and whispered, 'Is that right?'

'Sure, honey,' said Matt, not looking up from his phone.

'Sort of,' said Juliet. 'Get it in the neck.'

'Oh. Well, that makes no sense. I think you should write to the people who make the dictionary.'

'Yes, OK—' Juliet said. A creaking floorboard behind her made her spin her head around, hoping for the flash of a smooth black head, but there was no one there, just the house, settling, sighing. 'You can take him for a walk down the lane, to pick some damsons, they're still everywhere—'

Isla looked at her with pity. 'A walk down the lane.'

'Mum's very good at all that country stuff, isn't she?' said Matt to the children. He put his phone down on the table. 'Listen, kids, do you both have swimming costumes?'

'My like swimming,' said Sandy intently to his father.

Isla nodded, cautiously. 'We do, Dad. But why?'

'How about we go . . .' Matt slid the phone across to them. 'How about we go here! The Walbrook Wild Waterpark and Pirate Ship! It's got a 4.8 rating on TripAdvisor!' They looked blank. 'You can jump off a pirate ship into the water and they've got a wave machine!'

'Yay!' screamed Isla, knocking over her bowl and rushing round to her father. 'Yay, Daddy, the waterpark! Everyone at school has been and I am the only one who hasn't!' Tears shone in her large blue eyes. 'Sandy, we're going to the Pirate Waterpark!'

'Yay!' shouted Sandy. 'My love Pirates!'

'He can't swim,' said Juliet, pointedly, her arms folded. 'You'll have to watch out for him all the time—'

'I know he can't swim.' Matt had picked Sandy up and was jiggling him about. 'We'll go in the little rascals pool, won't we, mate? We can watch Isla on the ship. And we can have an ice cream afterwards!'

'Yay!' said Isla.

'Apples?' Sandy looked at his mother, questioningly, but Juliet beamed at him.

'Yes, you can take an apple. Guys, you'll have such a brilliant time. Let me find your swimmers.'

'Hurrah!' Isla started dancing around the kitchen, as Matt said, 'What about Bea? I'll go and ask her.'

Isla stopped dancing in the doorway to the kitchen. She turned around. 'She said she told you she was going out.'

'No,' said Juliet, looking at Matt who shook his head. 'She didn't tell us. Do you know where she was going, Isla?'

Isla shrugged. 'On her bike to see a friend. Her bike with the blue handles.' She frowned. 'I didn't *actually* pull off the rubber coating, I just wanted to play with the handlebars to see how it works and she was really mean. She said I was a baby and she pushed me away . . .' She gave a big, dramatic sniff, looking around to gauge sympathy, but her parents looked on unmoved. 'I bet she's gone to see George.'

'George?' said Matt.

'That skarkastick man who lives with Frederic. She *loves* him.'

'When did she go?'

Isla shrugged. 'I can't tell the time. This year some time.'

Juliet stood up. 'I have to go into Godstow anyway to thank Frederic for the furniture.' She felt if she didn't see another adult other than Matt soon she'd scream. 'I'll bring her home if she needs a lift. You guys go without her. Right, I'll get the swimming costumes and pack an apple, and Sandy, you *have* to promise you'll wear the armbands all the time. And afterwards you can have as much ice cream as you want, Daddy wants to treat you both to the biggest one there is,' she said, maliciously and, carrying her breakfast things, she glided out of the door.

He caught up with her, as the children resumed eating, their spoons clattering on the china. He put his hand on her arm.

'We didn't properly finish our conversation last night,' he said, under his breath, the pressure of his fingers increasing. 'I just wanted to make sure you understand I'm on to you, Juliet.'

Juliet shook her arm free. 'Oh good grief.' She pushed her hair away from her eyes, and went into the kitchen, dropping the bowls into the sink with a clatter. 'Look, I know I'm the worst person imaginable to be in charge of your children and it's a wonder they're not all crack addicts or in jail, but stop muttering threats like some third-rate villain, and *stop* speaking in riddles. You are a total dick not to have told me about Bea and you know it.'

'Don't call me names—'

'Matt! You deliberately withheld information from me. She's our daughter, and she's been being horribly bullied because she was in a relationship with a girl, and she was trying to come out to us and couldn't face telling me and you found out and instead of sharing it with me so we could be there for her you. . . *you didn't tell me so you could have the power*. I mean, have a word with yourself.'

'It wasn't like that.' But he was staring at the floor.

'Mate!' She shook her head. 'You know how shitty that was. You know it.' She paused, looking at his blank face, and breathed in. 'It's great you're taking them to the Waterpark. They've been nagging me about it since we moved here.' She dried her hands on a teatowel. 'OK? Do we understand each other?'

Matt wiped his face with his arm, collecting himself. He fiddled with his phone. 'Sorry – just doing this,' he said, then put the phone in his pocket and cleared his throat. 'OK, I'll stop speaking in riddles. But I've been thinking. I don't understand how you got this house. Something doesn't make sense. How did you afford it?'

'The house? It was left to me. I've told you.'

He leaned towards her. 'What have you found, though? Have you found the painting?'

'The *what?*'

'The original *The Garden of Lost and Found,*' he said, impatiently. 'Or the sketch. Is that why you had to leave Dawnay's? Because it was your property? That's how you've paid for all this?' He tapped the side of his nose.

Juliet was twisting her hair up more tightly into a clip. She stared at him in astonishment. 'What on earth are you talking about? Why are you suddenly asking all these questions?'

'Robert's investigating you. He's sure you must know more than you're letting on. Cos something about this doesn't add up.'

'Tess's Robert? Oh, good grief.' Juliet stepped back, and opened the back door, letting a fresh, sharp burst of warm October air in, along with bright sunlight and a few drifting yellow-gold leaves. 'Not him again. The three of you want to know what you can get out of me, do you?' She smiled – it was so cartoonish.

Matt drained his coffee. 'I know you're lying.'

Juliet breathed in again, drinking in the air. It was cool, with a spiced edge of woodsmoke. 'Oh, my goodness. So he doesn't want to have to pay maintenance, you don't want to have to pay maintenance, and the three of you have started to wonder how you can get your hands on some money, have you?' She laughed. 'You're like a sort of modern-day Lavender Hill Mob, only led by a man in a Savile Row suit with a blacked-out black Range Rover.' Sandy appeared in the doorway, and stared at his father curiously. 'Look,

I'm sorry to disappoint you but Grandi left me the house. You're welcome to see the roof and the guttering, but if not let me assure you it is in a terrible state and will probably bankrupt me. The sketch was bought by a soulless billionaire who hates publicity and it won't ever be seen again in public.'

'He's an old friend of Robert's actually.'

'Who? Julius Irons?' Juliet realised, were it not for worrying about Bea, she would almost be enjoying herself. 'Of *course* he is!'

'Robert's a fascinating guy when you get to know him, Juliet. You're such an inverted snob, I'd forgotten.'

'Matt, are you in love with Tess, or with her husband?' She shut the back door and walked through the dining room to the hall, Sandy following them at a distance. Morning sunshine flooded the light well above them.

'You're so juvenile. You expect me to believe she just left you a house fifteen years after her death and there's nothing more to it than that? Come on, Juliet.'

Juliet lowered her voice so Sandy couldn't hear.

'No,' she said, with a big, cat-like grin. 'I expect you to believe I left you because I don't want to be with you any more. Because you're an idiot. Other than that, you and friend to billionaires Robert can think what you want.'

She picked an apple out of the crate, and went upstairs, taking a bite out of it as she went.

'Juliet? Hi!'

'Hi – hi there.' Juliet paused outside Pascale & Co, and smiled, trying to remember the name of the woman in front of her. 'I'm Juliet,' she said, pointlessly, after a few seconds.

The other woman laughed. 'Yes. Yes, I know. I'm Jo. Emily's mum.'

'Oh. Hi,' said Juliet. She held out her hand, knowing this wasn't the correct next step, but lately her ability to read social cues seemed to have totally vanished. She pumped Jo's hand up and down, enthusiastically. 'Isla goes on about Emily all the time. She saw her the other day, near the almshouses.'

'Yes, we're just opposite the church in one of the newbuilds on Mill Lane actually.' Jo shifted her cloth bag over her arm. She had a heart-shaped face and a big smile. 'How are you settling in, then? You're at the old Walker house, aren't you? Sounds like an amazing place.'

'Yes,' said Juliet, and she hesitated. 'It's my family's house, actually. My grandmother died about fifteen years ago and her . . . it was . . . well, I'm just trying to sort it all out.' How did you explain it all? You didn't. This woman was simply being polite. She didn't want to know about burned paintings and divorces. *Just be normal.* 'Anyway, can we get Emily over some time?'

Jo ruffled her short hair. 'Emily would love that,' she said, briskly. 'Maybe we could come to yours.'

'That'd be fantastic. Isla doesn't know anyone yet really and it's been a bit hard on her. Her dad and I . . .' She trailed off again.

I've split up from her father and he's moved his girlfriend's children into Isla's old bedroom.

It was my grandmother's house, she used to have people over all the time. There's a stain on my bedroom windowsill where Grandi used to break an egg into a glass every Midsummer's Day, and by the end of the day if the white formed into rigging it meant you were going to marry a sailor.

I'm really quite lonely and have no friends, please like me.

'Anyway,' she finished. 'I'd love to organise some playdates for her.'

'If you don't mind me saying so,' said Jo with a small smile, 'I think she's OK. I was in there yesterday doing reading volunteer support and Isla had four kids sitting around her at lunchtime. She was telling them a story. She made one of them cry.'

'Oh. Oh dear.'

'Yep.' Jo grinned at her. 'But he came back for more. He kept saying, "I'm not crying because I'm scared, go on."'

Juliet found herself laughing. 'That sounds like her.'

You seem really nice, can't we just skip the bit where we dance around each other for a while and go straight on to being friends? Do you like rosé? And Monster Munch? And do you believe 'Mamma Mia' to be a genuinely well-made film, and that it is a testament to the patriarchal subjugation of women that it's still so derided, when people actually write theses on bloody 'Transformers'? Are you worried about 'Mamma Mia 2'?

Thankfully there came a faint cry behind them. 'Muuuuum! Can I have some money?'

'I'd better go, that's my son.' Jo grinned, shrugging her shoulders. 'He's in the Co-op. I'll message you.'

'I don't have WhatsApp, or is it Snapchat? I can't remember which one's which,' Juliet admitted. 'It's beyond me. And Facebook Messenger. I'm never sure how to get in touch with people – How do you do Snapchat?'

'It's like any of these things, Juliet. You just do Snapchat,' said Jo. 'Hey Bea.'

Juliet spun round to see her daughter standing behind them, fringe covering her eyes, bike lock slung across her chest, hands sunk into her jeans pockets. She could feel her heart beating wildly in her chest and opened her mouth, unsure of what to say but to her surprise Bea spoke first.

'Hi, Jo.' She raised her hand then let it drop, heavily. 'Ben needs money.'

'Hi, baby!' said Juliet, too loudly. 'I missed you this morning! I didn't know where you'd gone. How are you?'

Bea fed her fringe through two thin fingers, flattening the hair against her forehead. She looked at her mother suspiciously. 'Good, yeah, thanks. Oh, hi, George.'

'Good morning all.' George appeared behind them, a magazine advert come to life: navy polo shirt, sandy chinos, a turquoise blazer and immaculate trainers that had never seen sweat, much less country mud. He smiled at them. 'Well, hello, Juliet sweetie, how are you? I see you've met the lovely Jo, queen of the village.'

'Morning, Jo,' said an elderly man, walking past with a greyhound that was straining at its lead.

'Hi, Jeremy!' said Jo, waving cheerily. 'Hi, Tugie!'

Juliet stared at her. 'Do you know literally everyone?'

'Pretty much,' said Jo. 'Hi Ciara! Hi Georgina!' she called to a mother and daughter walking along the other side of the road. She turned back. 'She's nice. I didn't know a soul when we moved here. So I just decided I'd have to make an effort, and it was terrifying. Listen, forget about Messenger or WhatsApp. Just text me when you've got a bit of spare time. You've got a phone, haven't you?'

'I have and I will,' said Juliet, nodding at her. 'Bye, Jo.'

Juliet followed Bea and George inside the shop. The door banged loudly behind her, the bell jangling with fury.

'Hi, Frederic,' said Bea, wriggling out of the bike lock and hanging it up on the hooks with one fluid motion. She came towards him and kissed him on the cheek. Frederic looked up from his large lined ledger.

'My dear, hello. George told me you were rather upset – I've saved you some Jaffa ca— Oh! Ju!' he said, catching sight of Juliet, behind George. 'What an unexpected pleasure. George, will you put the kettle on?'

'I'm just going to get Bea some toast. She hasn't actually had breakfast, silly girl. She wanted to show me something in the window of Harcourts. For a Halloween costume,' said George, airily. He disappeared into the tiny galley kitchen at the back of the house, calling out, 'Marmite, Bea?'

'Great, thanks,' said Bea, following him. 'I sorted out those old *Girls Annuals* for you, by the way,' she called back to Frederic. 'And the shoes, too.'

'Wonderful. Do you want to pick something for the doll's house?'

'Yeah. Thanks, Frederic. Bye, Mum,' she called, as the door banged behind her.

'Bea,' Juliet called after her. 'Darling – come back for a second, would you?'

Bea's head appeared in the stairway. 'Yes? What?'

'Can we talk? I want to have a word with you about something.'

'Oh . . .' Bea looked back up the stairs. 'Maybe later.'

'No . . .' Juliet went over to the stairwell. She put her hand tentatively on her daughter's arm. 'Now.'

They walked along the path by the rushing stream that skirted the edge of the village, fringed by a tangled cloud of old man's beard studded with orange and jewel-red rosehips. Behind them, the smoke rose gently from the low long rows of cottages that made up the village, silver and warm in the grey autumn sun. Juliet shoved her hands into her pockets: there was, for the first time, a chill in the air. She stared at the cottages, at the birds flying over the woods high up on the other side of the valley. 'I wanted to ask you about Fin. Dad told me last night she was your girlfriend.'

Bea froze. Only her eyes, darting from side to side like a cornered animal.

'He told you that.'

'Yes, darling.'

'What did you say?'

Juliet took a long breath, exhaling as gently, as slowly, as she could. She put her arm round Bea's narrow shoulders, to pull her towards her, but didn't look at her. They kept walking. 'Well I wanted to talk to you about it.' She could feel her daughter's panic, almost like radiowaves, coming towards her. She squeezed her shoulder with her fingers, gently, knowing she could not crowd her. 'I wanted to know if you want to ask her to come down for the weekend.'

'Oh.'

'Or if you need to go and see her in London. Whatever works. But you must let me know.'

Bea's head was bowed. 'Dad said you'd be upset. He said I mustn't tell you.'

Juliet sucked her lips in, buying time, trying to stop herself saying something she shouldn't. 'Oh. Did he?'

'He – he thought it might just be a thing. He said I was only fourteen and I should wait and see how I feel. But I've always felt like this. I don't even hate boys. I like them. I just don't ever want to kiss one.'

Juliet tried breathing slowly again. She found she couldn't. But as carefully as she could she said, 'That's good you know you like girls. Daddy's wrong. I'm not upset. I'm upset I didn't realise.' She stopped. 'I'm very proud of you, Bea. Do you want me to make a speech? Say something official?'

'Mum – oh my God, Mum, please *don't*.'

'I thought so.' Juliet stopped and turned to face her daughter. 'Listen to me. I should have realised. I felt I was losing you before the summer. I would have done anything to change that. To make you feel better.'

'You did,' Bea said simply.

'But I should have asked myself what else was going on. Is that what the bullying was about? That you'd come out?'

Bea stared up at a skein of birds, flying south, away from the hills towards their house, black pintucks in a puffy grey sky. 'But I didn't, really. It was just Fin and I started having feelings for each other and we kissed one time. But then everyone found out and started sending these messages. We never made some big declaration. But they'd been after me before that. It's like that was another stick they could use to beat me. And Fin and I were arguing, I was sure but she wasn't, she likes this boy, Frank, but I knew I didn't like boys and it all . . . you know . . . I didn't really care what happened to me to be honest.' Bea's voice was dull. ''Cos I just couldn't stand it any more, with you and Dad hating each other and the kicking and taking my bag, and making me feel crap—'

'Oh, Bea.'

'Then I found out about Tess and then there was this idea of coming here and I thought it'd be for the best, you know. But then we got here and I panicked. I was sure it was a mistake. You always make out everything's for the best, and it means I don't trust you, sometimes, Mum. Because sometimes it's not for the best.'

The sky was clearing over to the north. Juliet stared up, at the golden break in the cloud.

'I'm still not sure yet whether we did the right thing, moving. I hope we did, that we can all be really happy here.' She pulled the collar of her jacket up around her, and tugged at her daughter's denim jacket, doing the same. 'I get things wrong. But I'm trying to do what's best for you. To protect you.' She kissed Bea, very gently, on the forehead. 'Tell me about Fin, then.'

Bea tugged at the fastened button. 'Well, she's got cool short thick brown hair and she dyed it pink this summer. I've seen photos. She really likes Kate Bush, Mum, do you know her?'

'Er, yes.'

'OK, well she gave me a T-shirt of her before the holidays. Fin says she's the greatest singer-songwriter this country's produced.'

'I like this girl.'

'You would like her, Mum, she's really funny. And clever, and interesting. And she's *into* stuff, you know? Like, she loves dragons. Loves them. And she likes me telling her about the doll's house, and the history. All the other girls at school, they were into their hair and their phones. Or what their boyfriend thinks or what their other friends think. Like, who cares?'

'Who cares?'

'So you're not cross?'

Juliet resolved that she would never throw what he'd told Bea back at Matt. That she would do her best by her children and help them love their dad. But that some time, some day, she would make him pay for what he'd done, to this lovely, anxious, passionate, kooky girl in front of her. *I burn with rage for you*, she thought, looking at Bea.

'I'm not cross.' She tested her own feelings gingerly like probing a sore tooth. 'I don't think it's that big a deal.' She squeezed her daughter's thin shoulders. 'Don't get me wrong, realising you are, and then actually saying out loud, "I am gay", must have felt like a huge deal. But when I hear you say it, knowing you . . .' She stopped, for suddenly her heart was flooded with love, so powerful she could not speak. She thought of Bea's baby feet, so slender, not chubby at all, and her first scraped knee, the spongy bloodied patch of skin, of her story about the chimney sweep girl that had won her a special Gold Star at school . . . of how she held hands with people at playtime until she was eight or nine, how she rarely cried, even with that knee, but turned white and pinched, how she loved fruit, and hated cooked vegetables, loved sitting very still with her feet tucked underneath her . . . All the things that made her . . . Juliet struggled to find something to say to convey this love. She wanted to squeeze her tightly, so tight it hurt. Her heart ached. 'All I want to say is it feels to me like just one part of who you are. A very important part, but it doesn't change you for me. I am so proud of you and happy you know this about yourself. Does that make sense?' She was shaking her head, smiling through the tears brimming in her eyes. 'I'm hopeless.'

'You're not. It's OK, Mum.'

'Anyway. Yeah. I love you, my love. Fin sounds great. Let's invite her down.'

'Yes, Mum, oh yes please.' Bea's eyes shone, and she slipped her arm through Juliet's, as they turned back towards the village, and the bridge that led on to the single-track street behind Frederic's shop. 'I'm so relieved. Dad said you wouldn't be happy.'

'Dad's wrong sometimes, darling. I'm very happy. You've always made me happy.'

'How often does Bea come here?' Juliet asked, after Bea had disappeared back upstairs to see George.

Frederic was in the back of the shop in the office, sorting through old box files, his glasses perched on the end of his nose. He indicated an old mahogany dining chair, and Juliet sank gratefully onto it. Her legs were feeling rather cotton-wool-ish. She stared around her, at the decades-old paperwork, the postcards stuck into the cork tiles lining the small section of wall.

'Most days after school. She does her homework here. George feeds her.'

Juliet took off her coat. 'I know nothing about my daughter, it turns out. She said she was having a snack at school and cycling straight home.'

Frederic said in his quiet, even voice, 'Dear Juliet. We adore having Bea here. You know, she is very like your grandmother. So fresh, and alive, so passionate. With those dark eyes just like Stella's. It is an absolute tonic – why are you crying?'

Juliet pressed her hands into her eyes. 'Frederic, I'm screwing everything up.' She found she couldn't stop herself. Tears rolled down her cheeks. 'I didn't know she was gay. You did, didn't you?'

Frederic took a sip of tea. 'You didn't?'

Juliet's voice was muffled. 'She tells you and George, she told her father . . . I hadn't twigged, and I'm the one who spends hours awake at night trying to work out what to do to make her happy.'

'I apologise for not telling you myself.'

'Matt told me.' Juliet gritted her teeth. 'Grandi, oh, you were right about him, you were right . . . *He* told her it might be a phase. Can you imagine that?'

Frederic nodded. 'I can, for it happened to me, with my first lover. My mother said my father would die of shame were he to find out.'

'I'm sorry.'

'It is of no matter. Except that – but that, my dear, is *une histoire* for another day.'

The shop door swung open, the bell clanging. A customer came in, a middle-aged woman with a basket on her arm. Frederic nodded politely to her.

Juliet pulled at the string of her green bag, and said under her breath: 'I don't know *anything* any more. Literally nothing.'

'There is liberation in that.'

'Goodness,' said Juliet. 'Perhaps there is.'

The sound of laughter came floating down to them. 'George is wonderful,' said Juliet. 'He fixed her bike last week, did you know? Of course you did. And Frederic, the office chair is perfect in the Dovecote. And my new old bed – thank you so much, again. It's bliss. What did I do to deserve you two in our lives?'

Frederic said, very seriously, 'I am not so sure you can say that.'

'I can.'

The customer was poking around in the tray of Victorian glazed tiles. Juliet was still. She could hear the sound of magpies, chattering on the branches of a rowan tree outside the shop. There was the gentle creaking of the floorboards upstairs, the low hum of voices.

For the first time in a very long while, longer than she could remember – before she had come back, before having children, before meeting Matt; for the first time since she was a teenager perhaps, sitting at the bottom of the garden at Nightingale House, wiggling her toes and watching dragonflies circle the stream, the heat of summer sun, the smell of ripening apples and honeysuckles, Ev's humming faint as he climbed a nearby tree – Juliet felt calm. At peace.

She said:

'If I ask you something, Frederic, will you promise you'll tell me the truth?'

The clear blue eyes looked steadily at her.

'My dear, of course. Do you trust me so little?'

'I knew I'd seen George somewhere before, you see.'

'Ah.' Frederic slowly shut the box file.

'He was there on the day of the auction, wasn't he? Did you send him? Did . . . did you know about the painting?'

Frederic leaned heavily against the shelves. 'Well, well. Yes, my dear. I thought you might recognise me, so I sent him. We felt one of us had to be there, since I was the one selling it . . .'

Juliet blinked. 'You sold it? It – she left it to you? Or – the house?' But he was shaking his head. 'They were renting it, the Walkers. I *know* they were. So *someone still owned* it before it was given to me. She left you the house *and* the sketch?'

'No.' He gave a small sigh. 'Not really. We had an agreement. She left the sketch and the house to me, and I rented the latter out to the Walkers after she died. I arranged it all. The rent was my income for many years. So very generous of her. When the tenants decided to leave, or I decided the time was right for them to leave, the rental income would have stopped. Your grandmother planned that I was then to put the sketch up for sale, and give you the keys to the house the very same day it sold with that letter. She sat at that desk day after day writing it all out, the letter, the notes . . . Oh, she thought it all out, you see.' His eyes twinkled. 'The sale would make me some money for my old age, this shop not really providing much in the way of pension, and the house would then pass to you. I am not sure I didn't get the better end of that bargain, but it is what she wanted. I gave the Walkers notice when I saw the house was getting too much for them. Besides, I am getting old, too. And I wondered about you – your parents sometimes seemed to hint all was not well, so –' He said, solemnly, 'Ah, Juliet. It must be a shock – I am sorry.'

'It's not a shock, precisely . . .' Juliet laced her fingers together, trying to find the right next question to ask. 'Why not just leave it to me when she died?'

'You know why, Juliet. She felt you weren't ready, not then. She wanted you to be able to come back here even though when she died you two had fallen out, because she knew – How do I say it? She thought you might need the house at some point. I daresay she underestimated the challenges of coming back here to live, but her intentions were good. Does that make sense?'

He looked around him. Juliet stood up, and gestured towards the chair. He sat down heavily, clasping her hand, and she nodded.

'Yes, it does.' She took a moment to absorb it all, rubbing her fingers across her forehead. 'Boy. And she was completely right. I wish I could tell her she was right about so many things. Tell me something else, then.' She touched his arm, gently. 'Frederic – oh, why did she change so much, towards the end? Why did she hate the doll's house so much?'

'How do I explain it? Picture your grandmother. She grows up in the house alone with her mother. All that remains from the glory days is the sketch of a burned masterpiece. There on the Dovecote floor is the very scarring from the tiles where the fire destroyed her father's dream. There in the trunk upstairs in the house are the fancy-dress clothes in which the beloved children who came before her dressed up. There are the letters of praise from great men, the books and paintings autographed by others. Yet . . . There is no money for new clothes: they refashion everything. They have to sell a painting to repair the roof, and another to pay her school fees, and then her mother sells Ned's sketches to the Fentiman Museum in Oxford when she is eighteen to send her to university. And there in the middle of it is this doll's house, which was her mother's and her grandmother's, and which Dalbeattie refashioned for those children before the great breach occurred with him, which she must have heard about. And she is expected to love it, to play with it. I did not know Liddy.' He hesitated. 'I knew several people who knew her. And they loved her dearly. She was, I believe, a quite extraordinary person to have survived that childhood.'

'Grandi told me about it.'

'Exactly. *Mais, Juliette* – what Stella didn't tell you, because she was part of it, was that Lydia never really recovered from her childhood. How could she? And then with what came afterwards . . . my God, how did she bear it?' Frederic began coughing.

She waited for the hacking to subside and then said, 'Are you all right?' She pulled a bottle of water from her bag, but he was sipping his tea, calm and collected again.

'Yes. I am sorry I could not tell you sooner about my role in your inheritance. She was very generous and I have profited enormously from her generosity. It seems wrong that I have the proceeds of the sketch, and you don't. That's why I keep trying to give you things. To help you. I stand as your family. That is how I see it, that is what sh-she would have wanted.' He patted his chest.

'Oh, Frederic, you dear man. I am so grateful for your help. It's your money and it's your reward for looking after her, all those years.'

'It seems unfair though.'

'No, no!' Juliet said, firmly. 'You mustn't ever think that, or say it again. Money isn't important. I know that now and I haven't got any. I might have to sell the place, if Matt gets really nasty. But it doesn't matter.' She smiled at him. 'All that matters is Bea, and Isla, and Sandy.'

He shrugged. 'I am sure that is right. But still—'

'Can I ask you something that sounds absolutely crazy?' He nodded, and Juliet swallowed. 'Well. OK. Do you believe in ghosts? Not ghosts, exactly. People – spirits – something unfinished, needing to be completed . . .' She shook her head. 'I don't know what I'm trying to say.'

'I do.' His expression was suddenly sober. 'In Stella's case, yes, perhaps I do.' The shop door banged shut suddenly as the customer left, the bell jangling then abruptly stopping. 'For me it is unfinished, the business of that house, and your family.'

Juliet took a deep breath. Into the stillness of the shop she said, 'Frederic – do you think Ned Horner destroyed the painting? Do you think he burned *The Garden of Lost and Found* on the fire?'

'Why do you ask me?'

'I don't know why. But there's this feeling I get in the house. I've studied him for most of my adult life but I never lived in the house, properly. The way he did. With his family.' They looked at each other. 'Do you know, I can't explain it. But I don't think he could have gone through with it. I just don't. Neither does Grandi. *Did* Grandi, I should say.'

'I agree with you, and with your grandmother. Somehow, I do not believe he would have been able to destroy it. It was, after all, his truest record of the children. And he lost them. He lost everything, remember.' Frederic pushed away his tea. 'Where is it, then?'

'I don't know,' said Juliet. 'That's the trouble.'

The words fell into the thick silence of the room, crammed with things from the past.

Chapter Nineteen

March 1893

The loquacious cab driver had said he would set her down outside the cottage, but as they approached Ham Common he grew suspicious.

'Too narrah, rahnd by the pond,' he declared, shaking his head. 'Nothing but mud, 'cause of the river. Funny, out of the way place, in't it? I won't get them hosses back if I goes down there. Best I drop ye here, and ye can walk along the path. That way, you'll have a constitutional, some fresh air.' He handed Mary out of the carriage, staring at her and she lowered her eyes, pulling her mother's old Paisley shawl around her. She had no money for a tip, and he muttered something under his breath as he drove away, but Mary did not care: for once in a long while her heart was light.

Liddy was over there – a bare few hundred yards from her, she was there! And, though this part of the world was utterly unknown to her it was Liddy's home, and so she must love it. The clear blue March sky arched overhead and the last of the snowdrops and the early daffodils made a brave showing at the foot of the hulking trees fringing the common. The track alongside it had indeed been churned into sludge, and Mary was obliged to walk on the damp grass itself, which she did, slipping and sliding, the wind slicing her face. It had been a cold, wet winter.

Ahead of her, Mary could see a fetid-looking duck pond, a row of cottages and, set back from the common, two small red-brick lodges, the old gate houses to Ham House. The one on the left was dark, discoloured, the windows broken. But the other showed signs of life, smoke rising in a black twirl from the tall chimney. Mary clutched her bag tightly in her small gloved hand. Her stomach churned. She was about to see her dear sister, the person she loved most in the world, for the first time since her wedding day.

'Come in, come in, and let me take your coat – look, Mary – see, how housewifely I am. For we have hooks. Dalbeattie made them – oh, anyway. You may hang your dear old shawl just here. I love this little hat, Mary, is it French? The black straw is so chic. Your scars, dearest – they are remarkably faded, I can hardly see them— do not blush, for it's the truth! We shall have some tea, shall we? – Alas, the candles do smoke so, does it inconvenience you, Mary? You are coughing, I shall open the window. It is tallow, for we cannot afford beeswax and the smell is rather heavy. Dalbeattie sent beeswax, but we used it all up. The passageway is rather tight so indeed – mind your head on the door, dear – oh! Oh Mary. I am sorry . . .'

'It is of no moment, my dear.' Mary rubbed her crown then caught Liddy's hands. 'Stop fussing, dearest, and let me look at you now!'

'You cannot in this poor light, it is a mean, dark house I'm afraid!' Liddy answered, gently disentangling her hands. She had barely stood still since Mary arrived, instead darting here and there and chattering, nonstop. Mary's head ached – she had looked forward to this reunion ceaselessly. She had supposed, foolishly, that relations would be unchanged between them. But how could they be? Here was Liddy, formerly confined to the house in a shift and shawl, now a young wife, in a pretty white cambric blouse with wide sleeves and a square yoke and a velvet coverall of peacock feathers over her shoulders, concealing a suspicious thickening around her middle. Her skirt was a deep garnet-coloured velvet; her little boots polished and clean. She was completely herself, the wife of a promising young artist at home in her cottage, and at the same time utterly alien to Mary. Suddenly, Mary realised she was nervous.

'Come and sit in the parlour, we call it, Ned ribs me about it, for I have made it ever so cosy yet I won't let him take his boots off. He leaves them all about the place and the corridor is so narrow one may trip. We will sit together on this little bench – see, are we not snug together? And the fire is still burning – excellent. We will have tea, Mrs L. has laid it out here, bread and butter, Mary, look!'

In the tiny, dark room, Mary peered towards the fireplace. A small tray of bread and butter and what must be rock cakes sat upon a small iron trivet, keeping warm. A kettle of hot water swung from a stand in front of the puttering, weedy flame. The log smoked slightly. Liddy lifted the kettle up carefully, brushing the strands of pale golden hair from her flushed face, and poured the water into the large, brown teapot. Mary found these simple little rituals of teatime brought a tear to her eye. She had missed them so very much.

Drawings and paintings lined the walls – with a start, Mary saw a sketch of Dalbeattie, his long, lanky frame sprawling over the very bench upon which she sat. Liddy caught her looking at the picture and her eyes fell.

'Is that Ned's work?'

'Oh – yes, yes it is. Dear Dalbeattie, he has been so good to us. All our friends have been so good to us.'

Mary recognised nothing in this house – not the teapot, or the books, not Liddy's dress. She had taken nothing with her when she ran away – there was no trace left of their former lives together. Mary glanced at her sister and felt her heart beating faster, filling up with love again. 'How wonderful it is to be here, and see your home, dearest.'

'Oh yes and to have you here – but I wish Pertwee would come too. You must tell me all about him, and whether he has too many portrait commissions to spend time with you, and how it is keeping house for him, and Paris, and everything else. Why is he not here? Did you tell him I long to see him?'

There was a silence. Mary stared around her again, wishing the room wasn't so small, the air so close. 'He hopes to visit you tomorrow. If he is well.'

He had returned home as the sun rose. She had left him at the lodgings this morning, surly and barely able to speak, one eye swollen shut, turning black.

'Capital.' Liddy clapped her hands. 'I think of your home so often and wonder about it! I am not sure this tea has brewed for long enough, but hey ho. Tell me – tell me all!' She poured the weak-looking tea with unsteady hand.

Mary shook her head. 'I am very boring, Liddy. I want to hear about you and Ned, and married life.' She swallowed the word 'married'. 'Are you – are you happy, dearest?'

'Wildly so. Yes.' She handed Mary a cup of tea and said seriously, 'Mary, my love, you must know something. You mustn't concern yourself about me again, do you understand?'

Mary's throat had a catch in it as she spoke. 'I cannot breathe and not concern myself with you, dearest.'

'No, Mary, I am serious. For all is well.' Liddy's eyes sparkled with tears. She put one hand on her breastbone, as though taking a vow. 'You alone cared for me. You saved me from her, on so many occasions. I will never forget what you did. And look. You see I'm happy, I always will be, now Ned and I are married.' She turned towards the window, and the dull March light fell upon her creamy skin, illuminating her delicate profile. 'We have always felt we are two halves, and now we are joined . . . Oh, it's wonderful, dearest one. Truly wonderful. All of it. Our ah, *relations* – I knew nothing of it all. It is marvellous, we are quite transfixed by each other and what we find we can do . . .' She touched her rosy cheeks with the tips of her fingers, and Mary felt even more awkward. 'I will not be indelicate, but you must understand me, Mary!'

'Yes,' said Mary, uncomfortably. 'Yes, of course – I am so glad of it. Dearest Liddy. I suppose you knew the first moment you saw him.'

'Not the first moment, no. But when we looked at each other in the garden at home that afternoon . . . then I knew. It was very simple. I think,' said Liddy, carelessly, 'it always is like this. Men, and women . . . I embarrass you, Mary, for you cannot know of what I speak but oh, one day, perhaps you will – no, it's too much for me to talk to you like that.'

Mary bit her lip. *I have seen things between men and women that would curdle your stomach, my darling big sister. I will never talk of Pertwee's depravity, the cries they make, the sights I have seen since we last met. The hopelessness of it all. No, my naïve little bird, I pray you never find out what the real world is like!*

'And you, Mary? Has Pertwee introduced you to any of his dashing French artist friends?'

Mary gave a small laugh. 'He is very busy. Now, tell me, how do you spend your days as a married lady? Is it so very different to what you expected?'

'I had no expectations, that's the great thing! Well, I walk Ophelia on the common and wait for Ned to come back to me of an evening. He brings friends sometimes. I keep house. Very badly, as you see.' She spread her arms around the room and displayed her hands, which were red and raw. At the mention of her name a small, wiry-haired border terrier came trotting into the room, rough little tail wagging, and sat pointedly beside her mistress.

'Ophelia,' said Mary with pleasure, and a little pang, for they had longed for dogs as children. She patted the animal's ruffled neck. 'I am glad you have a companion, Liddy, it makes me happy to think of her with you all day.'

Liddy's restless hands stilled for a moment, and she stroked the dog gently. 'Oh yes, she is my greatest friend now, and I tell her everything, just as formerly I would have told you, only a little more perhaps, for she is not embarrassed by what I have to say.' Her eyes danced wickedly. Mary simply smiled and patted Ophelia's soft head.

'How does Ned's painting go? Does it progress well?'

'Yes. Since *The Nightingale* he has been in high demand, and he is working all the hours he can to submit another painting to the Summer Exhibition.' Liddy held out a plate of bread and butter. 'He works in Dalbeattie's studio, most days, in Barons Court. He takes the Underground train from Richmond. He says he is like a stockbroker, leaving every morning for the City. Sometimes he has to work very late, or dines with friends, and then—' Her voice faltered. 'I have Ophelia for company, you see. But he is always sorry if he stays away too long, and he brings me sweetmeats if he is particularly pleased with a day's progress. I do not worry about him. He is my dear Ned. And then we have tea and are tucked up cosy as may be in our little cottage, safe from the winds . . .' Liddy's eyes shone; she chewed the nails on one of her small raw-red hands.

'It sounds like a veritable paradise,' said Mary, fondly. 'Ah – has he actually sold anything lately?'

'Not much. That is to say, nothing since *The Nightingale*, apart from a sketch of a dog he made on Ham Common which he sold to the owner before Christmas, and we were so pleased! But I wish he were not so high-minded. I wish he would just paint another picture as popular as *A Meeting*, or *The Nightingale*. If it wasn't for Dalbeattie – he has been such a great support, you know. We rowed rather, before Christmas, about it. He always says he has plans, but you know—' She broke off and then said flatly, 'Let us speak of something else. Dalbeattie said he had seen you, I believe?'

Mary's heart seemed to be in her throat. 'Oh. Dear Dalbeattie,' she said, carefully. 'Yes. He – he came to Paris, to visit Pertwee.'

Her brother had been asleep for most of the day, and tradesmen kept banging on the door, and one girl who claimed he'd stolen her brooch. Dalbeattie had called around for tea, quite unexpectedly, but Pertwee, when roused, wouldn't let him in.

Dalbeattie had stood in the drab little courtyard of their apartment, turning his hat over and over in his hands, as Pertwee raved and shouted at him. It was a bad day for him. He had bad days. Mary had watched Dalbeattie trying to reason with her brother, his eyes constantly darting to her, a mixture of shock and despair.

She had forgotten things about this man who had done so much for their family – how pleasing his long, charismatic face was, how dark and gentle his eyes. How his mouth twisted. How his movements were rapid and decisive and yet he was always calm and in control, the very opposite of her poor brother.

'Here is my card,' Dalbeattie had said, his kind face furrowed with concern, after Pertwee had turned and gone back towards their own door. 'Please, dear Mary – Miss Dysart, write to me if the situation becomes urgent. You must know you are not friendless, though I cannot help the poor fellow as much as I'd like – you see . . .' He had trailed off, his eyes searching hers.

Their hands had touched, and he had gripped her tightly, and Mary had swallowed, her head spinning. 'Will you be back?' She had closed her eyes but only heard his voice, dull, flat.

'Mary – Miss Dysart – I am afraid not. Not for a long while. I am needed elsewhere.'

'I wish you would come again,' she had forced herself to say, the boldest words she had ever uttered. But he had simply pulled the bolt of the heavy wooden door and stepped back out on to the street, not looking at her.

'Dirty old dog, Dalbeattie, sniffing around,' Pertwee had called as she'd entered the room. He'd sunk back into the winged-back armchair. 'Got more money than sense since he won that competition. Started building houses for those dreadful aesthetes and the like out in the Home Counties. He's forgotten what art is, what it is to suffer, to struggle . . .' He had got up, shuffled out of the room with the blanket around his shoulders, and hadn't emerged from his bedroom for another day.

'Dalbeattie said something strange about Pertwee when he came to visit. "He is not too wild, is he?" I was not sure what he meant, and he was locked up with Ned for a while afterwards. Am I to worry about you?' Her fair face turned towards Mary and she shifted towards her sister on the bench. The dark, cramped room grew still and it was only her voice, the two of them again. 'Does he treat you kindly?'

'He must do for he is my brother.' Mary gave a small smile. 'But – oh dearest, it is—' She could not speak.

Liddy's face was pale. 'Whatever it is, I will understand it, I am sure.'

The joy, of being with one who knew it all, the one person who did! 'Oh, Liddy. H-his heart is black, my dearest. I never knew until I went to keep house for him quite how black.'

Liddy pushed a lock of hair from her sister's face. She said seriously, 'Does he – hurt you?'

Mary laid down the cup. 'Hurt me? Yes, in a thousand different ways but he does not mean to. We know how we grew up, Liddy, the three of us, and I try every day to forgive him, when he spends the housekeeping money on absinthe – do not be shocked.' She found she was shaking with the liberation of talking freely. 'Even if I could speak French there is no one to whom I can say these things, for I know no one. I am his silent sister who keeps house for him and lets the people with whom he fraternises come and go. Such people, Liddy!' She knew she must hold back, but she could not conceal the whole truth from her, or Ned, for she knew Dalbeattie must say something to them when he next visited, too. She could not keep it all to herself. 'Thieves and cads and downright dirty sots, and g-girls whom I cannot like, some I do.'

'Girls from where?' Liddy said, mystified.

'Oh darling. They are not quite proper, do you understand, and they – they seem to me to be so young. Sometimes – anyway. I am not allowed to be there when he entertains, but often I cannot help but hear, or see. Our rooms are not large.'

Liddy was shaking her head. 'But what of the painting? He writes to Ned and Dalbeattie that he has commissions a-plenty! He painted the daughter of the conductor of the Paris Opera!'

'He did, and he was drunk, and tried to kiss her, and her father has spread it around that he is no one to be trusted.' Mary bit her lip. 'It was so unfortunate, for the portrait was finished but for a few strokes, and it was awfully good – he *is* good, Liddy, not as good as Ned, but he has a real feeling for faces. If he could have held out for five more minutes, only until the painting was removed to their salon.' She looked sadly down at her hands. 'I used to imagine he needed a piece of luck. But now I am not sure. I think he is damaged and it can't be undone. He misses Mother the most of us, I think. He often talks of her. He was the oldest, after all.'

'Yes . . .' said Liddy. She was silent for a moment, pressing her fingers to her lips. 'Oh, my love. This is all awful. How do you live?'

'He translates crude novelettes and magazine stories from French into English for a publisher, who brings them out over here.' Mary stumbled on the words. 'They are horrid, Liddy. It pays very little – I don't know if it would be worse if it paid a vast amount, but I don't believe so. He reads them to me – he forces me to listen. He is without shame—' She buried her face in her hands.

'How cruel, how rude he is.' Liddy was red. 'Tell him he must come to us tomorrow. If not, I shall write to him. He never answers me, but I shall persevere! Dearest, you must not be treated so. We will make him see the error of his ways.'

Mary looked up at her sister, brushing the dead embers from the grate and flinging open the casement to empty the ash on to the daffodils outside the window. Liddy was strong, a core of steel running through her tiny body, and Mary saw for the first time that she herself was not made that way.

'When he is well, oh – Liddy! He is my dearest brother again. It is extraordinary, the change in him, in the atmosphere in our little house.'

'How are the lodgings?'

'In a quite pretty part of Paris, not far from Abbesses. We are in a *cité*, a small courtyard off the street, and it is charming.' Mary gave a small smile. 'You see, I am quite dreadful at housekeeping and I do dislike it so! Oh, that *I* were a man and someone else shifted for me. I am overcharged for bread, the meat is frequently gone bad. I do not get the best candles, the linen is not of the right quality, because I do not know how to ask for better things.' Her eyes filled with tears. 'Oh, Liddy, I do not know. Around the time of Epiphany they were selling sugar biscuits in the *cité*, patterned doves, iced with little coloured strands of sugar. There was a young man with an accordion, and dancing. It was all so lovely. I watched the couples from my window and I wanted to go down and ask for a biscuit, one or two . . . But I can't really speak any French, I try to learn, but I see so few people. It is a silly thing, but it stuck with me. I keep seeing that pretty scene, only a few feet from my window. Just out of reach, but Pertwee was in his cups and I could not leave –' She bowed her head, then looked up. 'Enough of Pertwee! He tires me, even in absentia. He takes all my energy. When I think what plans we used to have for ourselves, what plans Mother had for us – that you would teach, and I would train in medicine, do you remember?'

'I do,' said Liddy quietly.

'But you are my concern now. When are you to be brought to bed?' Liddy flushed, a hot pink. 'I may be a cloistered spinster, Liddy, but I can use my eyes. Your figure is not increasing merely because of the sweetmeats Ned brings you, my love! You are to have a child, are you not, before too long?'

'Oh,' said Liddy, in great confusion, and she stood up. 'I – I do not know, and have not seen the doctor – Ned wants to call someone named Dr Corps, but I cannot deal with a man with such a name. And here's the thing. I wanted to go into town to ask old Dr Forsyte, though it mortifies one, rather, the idea . . .'

'Oh, I quite see. What does he say?'

'He wouldn't answer my letters. And so I went to see him in Marylebone, having written, and I heard him tell his nurse I was not to be let in.' Liddy leaned against the wall and the light from the window threw her swollen shape into greater relief. 'He has had the care of us since we were children and he would not even see me. Father has told all his acquaintance to cut us out, you see. I wonder – don't you? Is he controlled by Nurse Bryant, do you think? Who rules the house?'

'I don't know,' said Mary, quietly. 'I cannot think of them, I find, still. It will be a great many years until I can.'

'We will be revenged one day, do not fear,' said Liddy, evenly. 'Ned does not understand why I wake sometimes screaming, and I cannot stop. The house. When I think of being back in that room I—' She pulled at her collar. 'Sometimes something will happen; a horse neighing, for example. It reminds me of the sounds of the horses outside the Flask. While I was still allowed to have the shutters open I used to watch them for hours on end when I was cold, and hungry, even though leaning on the windowsill hurt my bones. Now I jump, when I hear one, and I feel nauseous. You understand.'

'Yes – Oh, Liddy. Don't torture yourself.'

'Or tapioca. If Mrs L. makes tapioca I must absent myself, for even seeing it makes me faint. I wish it were not so – I cannot tell her why.' She laughed. 'How would she ever understand?'

'She would not. No one would, quite, not even Ned, I am sure.'

The smoking log in the grate seemed to have extinguished itself. Liddy said:

'You know I've come to see Bryant might have gone to another family, and she might have destroyed them. But she couldn't finish us off. I think about that, often, you know. When I was missing you one day, and feeling really quite tragic, dear Dalbeattie told me there is a saying in the Koran. *God never gives you burdens greater than you can bear.* He understands everything, you see.' Beside her, the little dog whimpered. 'It is oppressive in here, when the fire smokes,' she said, suddenly. 'I want fresh air! Let us walk towards Ham House, and see the river.' Liddy stood up and struggled into her cape. 'It moves inside me, Mary, it is most strange!' She ran to the door, and flung it open, Ophelia yapping wildly at their heels.

The feeling of liberation after the dark, dank house was almost intoxicating. The sisters linked arms up the long walk that led towards Ham House, glinting in the silver spring light. 'I often take myself out to remind myself – I am free, we are all alive –' She turned to Mary. 'We will triumph over Nurse Bryant yet, my dear love.'

Mary nodded. 'I hope so.' She squeezed her sister's arm. 'May I come again tomorrow? We still have four days together before Pertwee and I must return.'

Liddy's glowing face fell. 'Not tomorrow. We have – Dalbeattie is coming for tea.'

'I know,' said Mary, shyly. 'Pertwee told me, for he hopes to see him here, if he is welcome.'

Liddy cocked her head on one side. Mary thought she was

watching Ophelia, chasing a duck around the pond in the distance. Then she saw her face. 'My love. Dalbeattie was married last week.'

Mary raised her head up, looking at the treetops above her. 'I – oh, I see. This is wonderful news.' She gave a small smile. 'Please, Liddy, will you give him my best wishes.'

'Oh, dearest.' Liddy turned back to her and her face was a picture of misery. 'No. I am wretched about it and furious with you! Forgive me, Mary. But I've been wanting to tell you since you arrived,' she said, blinking. 'He told Ned he'd have broken off his engagement and offered for you, only you told him most clearly you'd never marry! It's not true, is it?'

'It is, my love.'

'Mary!' Liddy actually stamped her foot, splashing mud on both their skirts. 'Oh goodness, you are silly. You could have had Dalbeattie!'

'Liddy.' Mary hated this feeling of separation from her sister – a greater separation than the hundreds of miles that were usually between them. 'I'm not like you.'

'I know, but—'

Mary said gently, 'Oh, my dear. I couldn't stand in his way! We barely knew each other.'

They had reached the swollen, rushing river. Ophelia barked at it, and Liddy reined her in. 'He – he told Ned that at first sight he knew he wanted to marry you.'

'Well, oh – I will – I will never marry.' Mary blinked, to hide the effect these words had on her, the heavy ache in her eyes. 'Liddy, when I think of domesticity, and dogs, and babies, and laying a fire for tea – I cannot do it.'

'It's only because of Father, and that awful woman, curse them both. You do it already, for Pertwee,' Liddy pointed out, sharply, and the sisters stared at one another, trying to fathom the other's thoughts.

'I have to. Without me he will die. He will die anyway, but I can help him. Please, Liddy. I – I can't ever marry. I wish him all happiness. He is the best of men.'

'Oh, Mary. He is and it's wretched. He's gone ahead with it for his family – he's their only hope, he has to support his mother and siblings up in Perthshire somewhere. But I've met her. Rose. *Rose*. Oh, she was all wrong for him, all wrong, Mary!' Her eyes were swimming with tears. 'I used to think how very lovely it would be, us, Ned and Dalbeattie, working together, married, babies – everything just so. Everything just so.'

'Rarely is everything just so,' said Mary. Her neck ached from staring up above her. She looked down at the mud on her boots, her heart in her throat, not trusting herself to speak. She thought of her mother's last words to her as Mary was carried out of her bedroom, away from the deathbed towards life, her whispered urgency. *Never marry, my bird*. 'My darling, it's of no matter. Let us keep on walking.'

Chapter Twenty

Summer 1894

Very early one morning, at daybreak, Liddy woke to Eliza's thin wail. She lifted her up out of her cot and held her close, waiting and watching in something like abstract revulsion as her daughter's mouth searched for Liddy's scaly, wet, long nipple and found it, settling down to suckle. Liddy gazed out of the window of her tiny bedroom.

It was the first *really* warm day of the year. A deep-blue sky fanned overhead, and the budding trees swayed in the wind. The pulling, sucking motion of Eliza's mouth on her breast lulled Liddy into a state of calm. She rubbed at her eyes with her free right shoulder: for the first time in days, weeks, she felt different, and then she realised what it was. She had slept. She had slept for a little over five hours. No wonder Eliza was hungry. Something crackled on the blanket beside her as she shifted around a little. She looked down; it was the letter from Ned.

I am sorry to have left so suddenly but I must return to work. I love you dearest Liddy and I am sorry I make you angry. Hang it – all I seem to do is apologise! Please understand I work only for you – I think only of you, and Eliza. Now I have sold 'The Artist's Hovel, etc' I am making plans for another series. These plans are very near completion Liddy. In the meantime, I meant to tell you, before the deterioration of our evening, that Galveston wants to produce a limited set of engravings of 'A Nightingale' and has paid me two hundred pounds. You will hang on walls around the country, my Liddy.

I know that being a mother has not been what you expected and that you feel we live a hobbledehoy life in this little cottage. But you must be patient, dearest. Do not doubt me. Did I not say to you that I plan only for you? And now our Eliza, who will grow up surrounded by beauty and happiness, and for whom, along with her mother, I carve and paint and build a paradise. No more now –

Do not be cross – for I love you most of all

Liddy screwed the letter up into a ball, roughly, with her one free hand. Eliza sighed, giving a half-cry as she fed, and Liddy tensed. But she went back to suckling, and Liddy relaxed, hurling the balled paper across the small room. It bounced off the wall and under the bed.

Mention of *The Hovel* pricked at her tired ego. Ned had submitted a painting to the Summer Exhibition, and it had been a great success, but Liddy, while admiring it greatly, disliked it hugely. It showed Liddy, in her moth-eaten velvet walking cape, holding on to her feathered hat – which she had snatched back from Nurse Bryant's room on the day of her wedding – on a breezy Ham Common, Ophelia pulling at her lead, in front of their little Gate House. The feeling of spring winds, of fresh air, of Ophelia's desire to be off the lead, was very strong. It had been received rapturously, even by the stuffy old nabobs in charge. Ned's ability to capture personality and light, to work quickly and skilfully, was extraordinary.

But he had called it *The Artist's Wife, the Artist's Dog, the Artist's Hovel.* As if it were all a joke. As if they lived only through him, existed because of him. Ned had said, smiling nervously, that it was a satire on English manhood. Liddy, tired, bewildered by Eliza's screaming and fury, cross at constantly being told by visitors that the child should have a wet-nurse, stuck out in Ham not knowing anyone and missing Mary dreadfully, said he was being awfully pompous and she did not care to be part of a list that included a dog and a perfectly nice house that might be cramped and rather dark but was in no way a hovel. Ned, his smile more fixed, had repeatedly said that she'd told him hundreds of times that now Eliza was here the Gate House was not the home for them. He knew this. He was working all the hours he could to change this. She was being rather unkind.

Oh, hang it all. She thought about what Ned might be doing, and the familiar ribbon of anger snaked through her. She was very tired, tired of being cross with him, of feeling so sad and the worst of it was he didn't seem to care. Something was afoot, she knew this with a calm certainty. It wasn't simply that he was enjoying a bachelor's life without them, it was that in some way – and she understood this, because she knew him as well as she knew herself – he was hiding something from her, something fundamental. This hurt her dreadfully.

Liddy held her little daughter close to her, and noticed for the first time, as the spring sunshine dappled the child's bare legs, the plumpness to them, the pleasing perfection of her toes, like fat little beans. Her delicate hands, though, had fingers like her father's, thin and quick. Love, pure love, flooded Liddy, like sunshine flowing in through an open door.

It was sunny. She knew then she could not stay in bed. Not on a day like today. Not when she had had five hours' sleep. Who knew when Ned would next be back? She would stop waiting for him now, and go out herself, do something herself. Liddy wiggled her toes. We will go out today, she said to herself, pulling Eliza a little more closely towards her. And I know where we shall go.

She sat up, rather lightheaded at the thought.

'Yes,' she said, looking down at her baby. 'One last time.'

It really wasn't such a big house after all. In the midday sun it seemed shrunken, the closed shutters like eyes sewn shut.

'There,' she whispered, out of breath from carrying Eliza the last several hundred yards up the hill. 'There it is.' Liddy caught hold of the railings, and peered in through them to her old home.

She had taken the first train into town, and from there the omnibus which ran up past Heals on the Tottenham Court Road. As the crowded bus rumbled through North London, horses jostling on the road with other carriages and carts, she held the baby tightly in her arms, terrified for any bump, pothole, loose wheel. She was a stranger in this city now. An entirely different person.

Somewhere towards Highgate Eliza opened her huge blue eyes

and stared up at Liddy, taking in everything she was shown out of the window. 'That is the church your grandmother attended, my sweet. Over there is the zoo, and we shall go there when you are older. This is the boundary mark your Uncle Pertwee used to jump from. You will meet him one day.'

Eliza waved her fists at the window, swaying slightly with the motion of the tram, and Liddy held her tight, staring at her anew, bowing her head constantly to let her lips brush the perfect, slightly knobbly sphere of her silken skull.

Alighting from the omnibus Liddy took her large silk shawl and made it into a sling for the baby, as Mrs Lydgate did when she'd stroll on the common to stop Eliza's mewling. Eliza fell promptly asleep again, and so Liddy walked up the hill, looking around her as the old sights appeared, one by one: the Flask, the church, the same grand houses opposite hers . . . She turned to look through the gate at her old home.

The garden was bare, the box and lavender and roses ripped out. The lion door knocker had gone, there was a bare square of wood where it had once been nailed in.

After a minute or two, the front door opened, very slowly, and a figure appeared. She passed between the bare beds set into the flagstones, and stood on the other side of the railings. She looked up at Liddy. Liddy blinked, and found she couldn't see her. She was just a blur.

'This is your child, I take it, Lydia.' And she gave a shuddering, drawn-out sigh.

'Yes,' Liddy said. She wondered, for the first time, if this was a dream. She snatched her hands from the iron rails as if they were molten hot, the sun blinding her. Eliza's body against her was warm, almost stifling, and she gave a small cry, and Liddy opened her eyes.

Nurse Bryant was in a purple tea-dress, cream lace at her throat and cuffs. The dress was too rich and smart for a Friday lunchtime, too opulent for her short frame.

She was a small person really, nothing to her. Not fat, nor thin. Her face, too – it was not the face of nightmares, but a plain, simple face. Grey eyes, a slightly potato-ish nose. Her mouth was unusually wide, her jaw square. And yet she was everything evil in the world. To be in front of her, now, made Liddy understand something with startling clarity: evil comes in disguise, it seems drab and grey at first, and then it blossoms, transforms, assumes new ribbons and bibbons and lace at its throat.

Nurse Bryant's smile widened. The pale-brown eyes, like buttons in her head, were without expression. 'Come inside, Miss Lydia. Your father will be delighted you are here. Let me call for some tea. Hannah!'

On the way there Liddy had thought of so many things to say. As she felt the weight of the sleeping little body against her, she knew she could not go inside the gate. She could not step into the garden, walk up the path.

'I won't. I don't want to come inside,' she muttered.

'What's that? I don't hear you. What do you say, Lydia?'

'I said: I don't want to come inside.' Liddy raised her chin. 'I just want to look at you again. I'm glad to have seen you. This is my daughter. Her name's Eliza. She is mine. You can't touch me, now.' Her voice trembled, but she smiled on, matching Bryant's manic one with her own. 'I'm very well. I'm very happy.'

Bryant lowered her voice, and frowned, muttering something Liddy couldn't hear. '. . . *a shame* . . .' Then she called out again. '*Hannah!* Well, the servants will be most disappointed not to see you, Miss Lydia, and your father. Allow me to tell you your treatment of him has been most cruel.' She put her head on one side, fingering the lace at her collar. The sun cast her hollowed eyes into relief. Liddy hadn't realised before, how high and soft her voice was. 'And you shall receive the judgement of God when the last trumpet sounds. He is your Saviour and Lord and you will be found wanting when we are all called to answer for our sins.' She was nodding. 'For your sins can never be made clean. You murdered your mother and nearly did the same for your sister. Yes, Lydia dear.'

'No I didn't,' said Liddy, shaking her head, her vision blurring again. 'I – I didn't.'

'Oh, but you insisted she take you out on the Heath that day when she was tired and it's there she stopped to help the little boy whose nurse was ill with the smallpox. But you know that and have prepared for the Day of Judgement.'

Liddy steadied herself against the railings. She could see Hannah, appearing at the door, her face a picture of disbelief.

'Where's your lovely clean-faced artist now?' Nurse Bryant said, closer than ever at the railings, as Hannah bustled towards them. 'When does he come home? He's bad, Lydia, bad to the bone. Rotten, like you, my dear, everything you touch is rotten.' Her tongue passed over her lips, quickly, and she inhaled; she knew she'd hit her target. 'So you deserve each other. I hope he comes back to you, so you can make each other happy.' She laughed, showing a bottom row of rotten, brown teeth.

Liddy turned her daughter towards the house. Much later, she wondered if she should have done, if showing her child to this woman had, in some way, cursed her.

'Good day, my darling Hannah.' She fumbled in her pocket, as Hannah, bringing her apron to her mouth, pressed a sob down into her throat, and Liddy pressed the bolt of paper with her address into Hannah's hand. Bryant was staring into the middle distance, muttering to herself. Liddy cleared her throat and said: 'I say it again, for you. Here is my daughter. Here am I. We are well, and happy, and healthy. You didn't win. You couldn't break me. Please tell my father he has a grandchild. He will never meet her.'

'You are wicked. Wicked through and through. And you will suffer for it. May the Lord bless you,' intoned Nurse Bryant, shaking her head.

'No,' Liddy said. 'May the Lord bless *you*. I am free of you now! We are all free of you.'

'I said, you will suffer for it!' Her voice rose, cracking as she screamed. 'You can never leave me behind.' But Liddy did. She turned away, blowing a kiss to Hannah. 'Don't you understand?'

Liddy simply pretended she had heard nothing. She sang sweetly to Eliza, as she tramped towards the Heath, and, taking a hunk of bread from her pocket, she ate it. She walked and walked, until her legs gave way and she had to sit down on a hillock, staring out over the city. *I am free of you. We WILL be happy. Just you see.*

When she arrived home she was very dusty and tired and Eliza was crying, and Liddy wondered if she ought to have gone. She soothed Eliza, kicking the bootscraper out of the way to pass through the tiny door to the sitting room so she could sit down and feed her, her wails growing louder while Ophelia barked: she hated the baby's crying. Only then did Liddy notice there was a paper package on the mat. Untwining Eliza from her sling, she set her down carefully on to the floor while she undid the string. Eliza protested even louder.

'You'll have to wait a moment, girls, I'm sorry,' said Liddy, fondling Ophelia's ears. 'A curse, indeed. I must write and tell Mary – no, I won't tell her, she takes these things to heart. Now, patient for a moment while I unfasten this and—'

Out of the brown paper, falling on to the floor with a sharp clatter so that Eliza's mouth opened comically into a little O, tumbled three wooden carvings. A smooth, plump baby, in a dark wood, fat with grain and polished to silk-smoothness. A cradle, of lighter wood, into which she fell, and which rocked perfectly within a wooden frame. A switch of hazel, thin and curved, which stood in a stand, upon which was fixed at the top a kite, in light sycamore, and a tiny real ribbon, fluttering down. It bobbed in the spring sunshine as Liddy, legs splayed, baby gurgling, possessions around her, read the note that was tied around it.

In haste my beloved
I will come to collect you later. Be packed – be ready to leave 'The Hovel' – pack Eliza's things. I have made us a home – our home Liddy, I can't wait for you to see it.
I have agreed to sell some paintings (I am very tired). 4 of 'em, scenes of Ham and Richmond. I didn't give them to the Academy, but to the Grafton Galleries – well, I barely unpacked them from the crate and someone – remember his name, Liddy, Sir Augustus Carnforth, who

has made all his money in steel, bought them all for £500! There and then! I wish you had been there to see it. They are my best work and cheers to it that a chap like Carnforth, who has money and wants to buy taste but not old fangled dead and gone men but a taste of something British, something new. He is to hang them in his new house – Dalbeattie is building it – it is in Richmond, very grand, and he likes the views of Ham House you see. Well he is welcome to them, for we will not live with them for much longer. The Hovel is to be our home no more. I am sending this by messenger.

Kiss to Eliza, all other kisses to you – I live for you – I work only for you – everything is for you – please, Liddy, believe me!

She felt rather odd. She gazed around her at the little house, rather astonished at the day she had had, then back at Eliza, at the sling and at the floor. She swayed a little and suddenly her ankle gave way underneath her, with a tearing rip of agony that caused her to scream, Eliza to cry out, Ophelia to commence barking most pathetically.

When he came, the lines of strain were etched on his face as though drawn on by charcoal. It was an hour later, and she had not moved from the floor, though she had managed to pull herself over to a rigid, screaming Eliza and had picked her up and fed her. She had fallen asleep, Ophelia curled up reproachfully beside them. It was quite peaceful, on the wooden floor, the call of birdsong outside, and for once the walls seemed to have stopped moving in on her. When he came, Liddy had fallen asleep, holding the baby, and she woke to find him lifting the child out of her arms, and she grabbed at her, fiercely, and then felt for the second time that day what maternal love was – a primal, odd instinct, one she was not quite used to, but now as much a part of her as the scars and the tears and the fatigue.

He looked dreadful as he bent over them, his thin, handsome face waxy with tiredness, his eyes sunken. He kept pinching the bridge of his nose. But he was smiling his tender, sweet, happy smile.

242

'She is very like you, you know,' Liddy told him, her voice stuffy with tears, for the twisted ankle continued to hurt. 'She must be your child for when she smiles at me I am unable to do anything but grin wildly, like a fool.'

'Shh,' he said, looking down at his daughter, though Eliza still slept. 'You must rest for a while, and I am going to pack our things and then put you in a hackney carriage. It is waiting outside.'

An hour later, she was sitting in the carriage, her possessions in a bag, the doll's house figures in another bag, one trunk of books and painting materials strapped to the roof, waving fond but not entirely regretful goodbyes to 'The Hovel'. They took an early evening train from Richmond, pulling out of the station into the late-spring countryside, a riot of cow parsley and blossom. Liddy slept, her foot bandaged by Ned and resting on a smaller trunk whilst he held Eliza, singing to her. Ophelia stuck her nose out of the carriage window, ears flying in the wind.

For the rest of her life she could not recall much of that first journey. They were met at the tiny station by a horse and cart – who was it? She was afterwards never sure. Late evening was spreading gold light across the hills, shadows were shifting and lengthening, and by now Liddy, jolted about by the carriage and the train and now the cart and already tired to the bone, felt very lightheaded.

The road out of Godstow village ran around a hill before disappearing into a small, secret valley. Then – a narrow, curling lane, a row of cottages, in honey-coloured stone, and next a sloping hill. After a high wall below a church, the cart drew to a halt in a driveway.

Ned lifted Liddy out of the cart. He was shaking. Ophelia had disappeared, shooting out of the carriage and bolting into the green mass below them. Liddy peered down the hill – they might have been at the edge of the world. It was silent but for birdsong and the sound of water somewhere. She peered ahead, blinking tiredly: she could see the side of a building. Yellow and white roses scrambled along the soft golden stone. She looked down: she could see nothing but green, and at the end the hint of landscape beyond, distant blue hills.

But the curving rose-gold roof of the house was visible, nestled further below them.

'Can you put any weight on the foot yet?' he asked, after the cartman had left, and they stood alone in the middle of this strange driveway.

'No – no,' she said. 'I think it is sprained. Where are we, Ned? What is this place?' And then she spotted the birds on the roof. 'Look – Ned. Goodness. Mother's doll's house has the same birds, look—'

'One moment,' Ned said, and he took Eliza from her, and disappeared. When he returned, a minute later, he picked Liddy up, in his arms, and carried her down the bumpy drive towards the open door of the house where their baby daughter lay on the threshold, neither out nor in, staring up at them in utter surprise at this peremptory treatment.

The house was golden too, with a large porch and doorway, with a great oak door. The windows, leaded and pointed, glinted so brightly and exactly in the setting sun that the whole place looked as though it were on fire, or gilded by some strange force. A frill of slim roofing ran around above the ground floor like a ribbon. Beyond, a wilderness of a garden, sloping down towards an orchard, and the sight of rushing water through trees.

Ned gently set Liddy down, holding her arm. Her hands flew to her hair, where the pins were threatening to come loose.

'This is Nightingale House.' Ned pushed his hat back on his head.

'Nightingale –'

'That's what I'm calling it, do you agree?' He bent down to pick up Eliza, who was gurgling on the floor in front of them. 'Liddy – listen! There are nightingales in the trees, I've heard them at night. I've heard the songs they sing.' His thin face was extraordinary, part pain, part ecstasy, and she realised what an ascetic he was, for the first time, how single-minded his vision. 'I hunted for it until I found it. I had so little to go on! But I had to try and find it, for you. It was a wreck. Dalbeattie and I have brought it back to life. We have no past, you and I, not now. We have to make our own family, out of the bones of what we have. Tell me.' He was smiling, mischievously. 'Does it remind you of anything yet?'

'The rectory in the countryside, an hour's drive from Oxford. My sister and I used to get lost in the lanes, they were so narrow, the hedgerows were so high – it had a . . .' She stopped. Her throat was dry. 'It had a banqueting house. Part of the old house. You'd go in there and eat sweetmeats after dinner.' Liddy shook her head. 'You found the doll's house. You found it. This is it, isn't it?'

He nodded, slowly. 'It is. No one's lived here since your mother left it and came to London. Her parents died and it was abandoned. I don't understand why, but I'm glad of it.'

Liddy put both feet on the polished new black and white tiles of the entrance hall, though it hurt her ankle greatly to do so.

'It is our home now,' she repeated, quietly, and she leaned gently against him, and the baby patted her cheek with a squeal of delight. She thought of Nurse Bryant – so fleetingly, her face passing before her like a creature on a carousel in the park – she shook her head, foot more firmly on the ground. The pain was receding.

Birds sang in the distance – oh the noise!

Chapter Twenty-One

Oxfordshire, six years later

Ned Horner's idea for the most famous painting of the age came suddenly to him, without warning. Walking in the dappled shade of the rambling Wilderness to escape his baking studio late one afternoon he came upon his children, crouched on the lichen-spotted steps that led from the house into the garden.

'Now, John,' his daughter was saying. 'Put on your wings.'

'No thank ooo.'

'Put on your wings please.'

'Dolphin.'

'No, John, not dolphin today. Let's be fairies.'

Eliza was wearing a pair of wings Liddy had made from the old box of costumes Ned had kept for sitters in his Blackfriars studio. Gossamer silver gauze they were, purchased by him from Leather Lane market. She had made a pair for John but he refused to wear them, because he said he was afraid he'd turn into something with wings and fly away. He liked to stroke Eliza's though, watching her as she flitted around the garden. Eliza was a do-er, John an observer.

It was their seventh summer at Nightingale House. Ned had tried to draw both children several times but the results were too arch, something Millais could have produced to great acclaim but which he couldn't seem to pull off. *Spirit of the Age*, his vast panorama of the Strand, and *Man and Wife*, the triptych of a modern wedding painted at St Marylebone Church, had won him further acclaim and riches. He had sketched the children for his and Liddy's own record, but not painted them: *The Artist's Wife* . . . was the last painting he had made of his own family. It was also true that increasingly he wanted to pull up the drawbridge, to keep this world private.

Liddy agreed. She was busy with the house, making, mending, cooking, gardening, for she did much of it herself. Most of all she was with the children, teaching them their abacus, how to tie boot-laces, to recognise birds and flowers, all done with an extraordinary kind of patience. Ned could only marvel at her self-taught aptitude: it was the vogue, in those days, to be a 'natural' mother, but in the county drawing rooms of the other families they knew it was clear from the brief, impressive appearances of the inhabitants' offspring that most of them lived in the nursery ruled over by Nanny. Liddy simply enjoyed the company of young children, preferred it to that of adults, in fact. She adapted herself to their rhythm, she walked at their pace, she saw the world through Eliza and John's eyes. Ned was, he knew, mercurial, impatient, wanting them to understand how lucky they were to live in these glorious surroundings; they tired of him more quickly. Their mother asked nothing from them, and in her company they flourished.

Liddy could persuade vegetables to grow in rocky, acid soil. She made clothes for the children, intricately smocked and trimmed. She found money from seemingly nothing, managing the household accounts with an eye for finance which Mr Gladstone would have found impressive. She had transformed the garden, which they had christened the Wilderness all those years ago, into an earthly para-dise, where flowers seemed to burst out in different beads and splashes of colour year round. She even buried Ophelia, who dropped dead of a heart attack two years after they came to the house. Ned had watched her digging the grave, hacking methodically away at the frozen earth, lifting the small, grizzled brown-and-grey body into a sack and gently lowering it into the ground all without shedding a tear, shaking away his offers of help. 'Thank you. I've watched enough gravediggers from Pertwee's window to know what I'm doing. She was my dog; I must bury her.'

He supposed it was no surprise she was so adept at creating all of this wonder: control was what she had longed for all her life. When he said this to her once she had laughed. 'Dearest Ned. I longed to write, and be free. To walk and smell the flowers. I did not long to sew ruffles back on to pinafores which is how I spend most of my days.' She had stood up and come over to him, slipping her hands into his pockets, drawing him close for a kiss. 'But you are right. I wanted to make a home. So did you. They must change the world, these children, not I.'

The following year they came to the house John was born, and in the same year Ned had sold both *Spirit of the Age* and his entry to the Royal Academy Summer Exhibition the following year, *The First Year*, of Eliza surrounded by the chaos of her toybox, grinning widely. So there was money, more money than before, and they hired servants. Liddy had found a housekeeper, Zipporah, a cousin of Hannah's from Godstow village and a good, sensible woman whose own father had been baptised by Liddy's grandfather, the Reverend Myrtle. There was a maid, Dymphna, from County Cork, and a gardener, Darling, who was old as the hills, sprightly as little John himself, and knew everything there was to know about the clay soil and the plants best suited to it. They had no nursemaid.

Their life was very simple, day to day. They did not seek company: in those early, happy years, they only wanted each other. Besides, Ned was always working, and Liddy was content. Every day there was some new joy: when John said 'Dolphin'; when they found the dormouse, sleeping in the corn the day before the fields were harvested. The first roses they grew themselves, and Ned's joy when the glass ceiling went into the Dovecote. Midnight mass, and carol singers gathering outside the door on Christmas Eve . . . more and more lovely things every day, week, year, rolling forward, time speeding up . . . Of course, there were visitors too: lovely, jolly Hannah came, when she was released from Highgate, and the children's adored Aunt Mary, who would read stories from *The Arabian Nights* to the children for hours on end, making the nursery at the top of the house – 'The Birdsnest' – recede and a palace in the desert, a cave of thieves, or a magical genie come alive. There too was Uncle Lucius, Ned's best friend, who came at other times, and shut himself up with Papa in the Dovecote, smoking his cigars and talking till late. No other family. There was no one else. Just them.

And so it came to be after long enough in that beautiful place that Ned found himself wanting to capture this feeling, if not the specifics of his children's faces, but unsure how to do it. Until he came upon them, that June day when the summer heat rose from the old stones and that and the scent of roses and honeysuckle flooding his senses acted like a powerful drug: he stopped, and stared, quite transfixed.

'Oh,' he said, softly to himself. 'Yes . . .'

Then he turned and ran back to the studio for his sketchpad.

Perhaps he knew how astonishing the finished painting would be – glimmers of golden late-summer sunshine flecking the long grasses of the garden, the nodding silver-purple rows of lavender, the pink-and-white daisies that sparkled in lichen-crusted pathways and on the steps up to the house. That it would be his greatest work, perhaps the greatest Victorian painting – that by the time it was destroyed, eighteen years later, millions would have seen it around the world. Men and women for decades after it was gone could say with a smile: 'I saw the fairies.'

For they queued for hours on end, in Johannesburg and Toronto and New York and Adelaide to see *The Garden of Lost and Found*, to marvel at the coral-gold light, the little figures with their backs to the viewer, one with the lopsided silvery wings glowing in the late-afternoon sun. People would stare for hours at these children who represented hope and childhood, an innocence that despite everything else in this terrible world had not yet been snatched away.

Perhaps he knew this, too. They were his children: quiet, determined John, golden forelock falling in his face, one hand outstretched towards the windows, and Eliza, one leg dangling, the haze of hair, the fine sculpture of her cheek and ear, the hunched, curved shoulders in concentration, watching the figure in front of them. It could only be them.

Their mother, having finished her writing, was called upon to entertain her poor children while they complained bitterly about having to stay still for yet another of Father's 'monstrous paintin's', as John put it. For three days she wandered in the garden as he sketched first with pencil then with oil on a tiny primed canvas, right there, singing to them while he worked. She would sing old folk songs, songs of the countryside her mother had taught her. 'Tomorrow shall be my dancing day', 'I had a little nut tree' and songs she adapted herself:

> *'John John, the painter's son*
> *Stole a cake and away he rund.'*

Her voice, rising and falling, hypnotised them into some kind of quiet, sometimes clear and cool, as she walked in front of them, feet crunching on the gravelled path, waving solemnly to them but saying not a word, while behind them their father frantically worked.

She would collect flowers, heavy, nodding sunflowers, fluttering hollyhocks, dahlias like puffballs in coral, cerise, midnight purple. She would wander back up towards the house with her arms full, looking up at the steps where her children posed, that natural moment of childish rapture now frozen, now posed, an artificial scene. 'Just a little longer,' Ned would mutter, steadying the easel on the sloping ground, and Liddy would echo him. 'Dears, just a little longer.'

For three days they posed, until they rebelled and said they could stand it no more. Liddy agreed – once Ned had the bit between his teeth it was impossible to persuade him otherwise, and she had suffered at the hands of his intense concentration, standing for hours on end till her shoulders ached, her head swam, her foot went numb. 'The poor children, they've had enough,' she told him, though in truth she had loved those days, when she could look up at the dear, warm, curved house, french windows flung open, all over the south-facing wall the dark green creeper and the scrambling hydrangea flecked with white, star-like flowers.

The moment the children, released but still complaining mightily, climbed down from the sloped coping of the steps they fluttered away like birds, into the garden for more adventures, with the promise of Welsh rarebit for tea. Later it was discovered that Eliza immediately tore off the wings, threw them into the stream. Ned picked up his easel and the finished sketch and almost ran towards the studio. He had prepared the main canvas the previous night, stretching and clipping it firmly himself over the wooden frame, priming it himself, covering it in a brilliant white.

Now Ned rested the canvas on the easel, staring at the blank space. This was the purest piece of the process – the moment of empty calm. Then he picked up his palette, mixed his paints and, like a man possessed he did not stop painting until a few days later when the work was completed.

This painting was the culmination of his life's work: truth, beauty, naturalism, humanity combined. For the only time in his life he did not care if it sold. He kept the oil sketch and the pencil drawings, for every scrap of preparation relating to *The Garden of Lost and Found* was to be treasured, as representations of his wife, his darling daughter with her cloud of soft honey hair and quizzical smile, his solemn little boy with the light mop and darting, anxious, dark-blue eyes.

When it was finished, Ned brought the painting out into the garden, and left it amongst the flowers and the summer heat to begin the long process of drying. It remained there for two days, and this was part of its mythology: they said that trapped in the layers of paint were flecks of seed, of grass, pollen, the golden dust of summer. It was a living work of art.

While he kept it outside Ned would walk past it, first thing in the morning, last thing at night, chewing on a pipe, looking at it, searching for flaws, but he found none, for it was to him the perfect expression of what he wanted to say about the life they had made.

Perhaps that is why he painted the picture. Perhaps he knew he had to capture it, the four of them together. Perhaps he knew.

Chapter Twenty-Two

June 1901

There were puppies at the farm.

'Aunt Mary won't ever notice! We shall be away, and back again by the time she realises we've gone!'

John shifted awkwardly, his corduroy culottes rubbing against the damask of the dining chair with a strange squeak. He clapped his hand over his mouth. 'Aunt Mary notices ev'rything, though.'

'I think it's because she's not used to children.' Eliza, whittling a piece of wood with an old rusting penknife shook her ringlets, biting her lip in concentration. John nodded, though he liked that about their aunt, her intense alertness over them. She was different to their mother, the calm centre of their world. 'Mama says we aren't ever go to away from the house by ourselves.'

'She won't know! It's up to you, Johnny. Well, I've told Mrs Tooker I'll come to see them this afternoon.' Eliza pushed the chair away and stood up. 'They won't be puppies for ever. They'll grow up. Don't you know about nature?'

John scratched his head. He really wanted to go and lie under the apple tree by the river and read his book. That is what he really wanted to do. It was most awfully good, about a boy called Alfred and his dog, Blaze, the runt of the litter, whom Alfred had rescued from drowning and hand-reared. It was John's great ambition to have his own puppy . . . there were puppies at the farm, real, live puppies . . .

Eliza was watching him, head on one side.

Mrs Tooker's sister was Hannah, and Hannah was up from London and was staying for a week. When the puppies were born Mrs Tooker had said they had to wait a month before they could have visitors – they were too small, their eyes hadn't opened yet, and in a month Hannah would be there. Eliza preferred cats, but puppies were puppies, as she said to John. She had waited patiently, crossing the days off on a piece of paper in Mama's study, and now a month had passed, and it was surely permissible to visit them, and Hannah too! They loved Hannah, who had known Mama and Aunt Mary as children. Sometimes she would tell them about when Mama had been a child. Tiny details, like the fact that Mama had wanted to own a hat shop and had once retrimmed Hannah's best Sunday bonnet all over with lace.

But Mama, who never said no normally, was very strict about such things. No wandering into the village alone, much less out past the village and down the lane to Marsh Farm. The Tookers were good people, and so was Hannah, but still – last year, two children had caught typhus from the well in the village and in April a young maidservant of thirteen had run away from Godstow Hall, leaving a note saying she missed her ma too much and was going back home to her. She had been found dead in the lane, torn to bits, her body scattered wide. John had overheard his mother and Zipporah whispering about it: killed by someone, or something.

They had not been able to trace her parents, so she was buried in a strange village, with no family at the funeral. John could not stop thinking about her; he begged to be allowed to go to her funeral but was not allowed. Instead he left ox-eyed daisies and rosemary on her grave: *Ella Watson*, it said. *At rest. 1886-1899*. But she wasn't at rest, he'd think. It bewildered him, and he used to lie awake at night blinking as he thought about it. Who could have done such a thing? To John life was a paradise. In his small span of existence he had seen only kindness and beauty.

But Mama and Daddy were away, in London. Daddy was being given some food because there was a dinner in his honour. He was also showing his new painting at the Royal Academy summer show, the one of them waiting for Mama. The picture was already sold to Mr Galveston with the twirling moustaches, and this was marvellous news. Everything was better when Daddy sold a painting.

'The puppies are going in a week, in a *week*, John. If we don't go today we won't get to go a second time. We'll only go a first time. D'you *understand*?'

Aunt Mary had refused to read him another story last night, and he was jolly cross with her. And the call of the puppies was so strong! He looked out of the window. He could see fairies dancing in the morning sunshine, dots of white-gold catching the light . . . and the stream would be sparkling and cool, and the path well-hidden . . . puppies! He looked at his sister, and then nodded.

'Yes please. But let's go now.'

'No, no, no, no,' said Mary, depositing them firmly in each chair on the terrace, and standing back, arms folded, glaring at them. 'Bread and dripping for tea, and no cake. And no sardines, no, nor any cocoa! How could you, darlings! I'm heartbroken. What would Mama say if she'd caught you paddling upstream like that. She'd never ask me to look after you again and what would I do if I couldn't come and see you, please tell me?'

'You'd stay in London and sew those banners for the rowdy women who want to vote.'

'Rowdy women, tsk. Well, I'd miss you, Eliza. And what about poor Mrs Tooker, having to entertain the two of you out of the blue, and then Darling, saving your lives like that?' She clutched her hands to her chest, very swiftly, then let them fall, breathing slowly. Poor Aunt Mary – her face was still white. She had been standing on the terrace scanning the valley and had given a great howling cry of relief when Darling had appeared bearing two soaking children, black and wriggling like tadpoles, bellowing in outrage – well, Eliza bellowed, Johnny howled in contrition.

Eliza had found the old boat in one of the outbuildings. They had only got as far as the almshouses beside the church when Darling spotted them – he was tending the graveyard. John was secretly relieved – was that terrible? But rowing hurt his arms hurt so much, and he was scared of falling in, and then Eliza had rocked the boat so they'd fallen anyway, and it was freezing cold, the chill biting your legs, green weed wrapping itself around you like mermaid's hair . . . He sat on his chair, shivering, tears pouring down his small face.

'What am I to do with you?' said Mary, half smiling, but a frown creased her brow and she smoothed her forehead with one hand. 'Oh darlings. Let's go upstairs. You have been naughty.'

'No we haven't!' burst Eliza, furiously, her face puce with shame, and misery. 'We were being brave, and shouldn't be chastised like this!' She caught her lip in her teeth. 'Besides, you mustn't punish Johnny. I made him d-d-do it.'

Mary hugged her niece's wet head against her breast, stroking her hair, her cold cheek, her clammy hands. 'My angel, you are brave, and wondrous, but you must listen to me, d'you hear?' She looked down at Eliza's tangled hair. 'You musn't go off like that.'

Eliza pulled away and stood up. 'I promise.'

Mary smiled, and patted her damp front, the skin of her chest showing pale peach through the wet pintucked linen. 'My love, you have your mother's bravery, in any event. Tomorrow, would you like it were I to take you both in the boat up to the village? I can row – after a fashion.'

'No! Perhaps!' shouted Eliza, bursting into tears again, but a voice behind them said, 'Well, well. What have we here? Has Aunt Mary lost control already?'

John saw the look on his aunt's face as she stared up at the tall figure on the terrace, who was watching them and smiling, hands in the pockets of a tweed suit. He advanced, and said pleasantly, 'Good – good evening, Mary – Miss Dysart, rather.'

She had turned pale, and looked down at her see-through blouse, hands clutching at her skirts and then she paused. She took a deep breath and walked towards him, holding out her hand.

'Dalbeattie,' she said, and her voice was different, light, not an aunt's voice any more. 'What a great pleasure it is to see you.'

He had taken her hand in his, and was staring down at her, eyes fixed, his expression very grave, and for a moment they were both utterly still.

255

'My dear Mary. I am so glad to find you here.'

He gestured to the driveway, where a drayman was lifting a large wooden crate from a cart. 'Into the hall, there's a good fellow,' Dalbeattie said. He turned to the bedraggled children, who were staring at him, eyes wide as saucers. 'I came to deliver a commission of mine, knowing your parents are away – though I thought Zipporah would have the care of you, not your aunt.' He spoke as if to them but he was looking at her. 'Come and see what I've brought you.'

In the round hallway, with the afternoon sun streaming in through the roof, Dalbeattie took the large case and set it gently down upon the tiles. His firm hands pressed the packing-case; his eyes, grey and steady, his back straight as he bent to the ground to catch each board of wood as it fell away, revealing the cargo within, and they gasped.

It was a house – their house. It stood in the centre of the hall. As high as John's shoulder, the roof rendered in dazzling carved fishtail pattern, the pointed Gothic windows fitted with real glass.

'This is—' Mary swallowed, and said quietly, 'This was Mother's. It was ours. How did you get it?'

He nodded. 'Ah, Mary. Pertwee carried it out, on his last trip home. I waited for him, in my carriage outside, while he asked your father for more money – it was the last time, and he was sent away pretty smartish, but he came out with this. I couldn't work out what it was, at first – he'd thrown a rug over it and only his legs visible underneath – the poor chap was staggering along the path not able to see where he was going.' Dalbeattie's eyes crinkled at the edges. 'Oh, that old nursemaid, she tried to stop him – but his blood was up: you should have seen the look on her face as we drove away!'

'Pertwee did this?'

He nodded. 'He said I was to give it to the children. Well, I took it to Ned, and told him, and he agreed I should "do it up" – and here it is. Mary, I hope you don't mind them having it?'

She put her hand on his arm. 'You are very thoughtful. I think it's the kindest thing I've ever known. Poor Pertwee.' Her eyes brimmed with tears. Dalbeattie, on the other side of the house, watched her, hands clutching and unclutching behind his back.

'I'm so sorry, Mary.'

'Uncle Dalbeattie,' Eliza said, 'please, does it open?'

'Yes, of course.' Dalbeattie tucked up his trousers and squatted down. He flipped the catch and the house swung open, like a cracked walnut, revealing its interior – the curving staircase, the hedgehogs on the bannisters, even the little cupboards and window seats that lifted up and where treasure could be stored. There, in their rooms, were the iron bedsteads, the trunks, the casement windows. The house was curious in one respect – the hinge was to the right, not the left. The great chimney of Nightingale House, with the huge fireplace in the sitting room, had been made, in the doll's house version, into the hinged side.

'Here,' said Dalbeattie, lifting off a chimney-pot. 'Here's a magic thing – a hiding place.' Eliza, standing on tiptoe, peered down into it.

'It's wide enough for my stick collection,' said John, coming forward timidly.

'Sticks,' said Dalbeattie, putting his arm around John's small frame. John stared at the house, down into the chimney. 'Or sweets. Did you know about this, Mary?'

'No!' said Mary. 'Not in all the years . . .'

'I found this,' and he handed her a note. She opened it, fingers trembling. It was a thin scroll of paper and written on it in a neat, childish hand:

I am sorry I broke your bear's tea set your loving brother Rupert Dysart

Mary clutched the note tightly, staring unblinking at it. 'So like him. To be sorry and not be able to say sorry so to hide it somewhere.' She couldn't remember anything of this tea set. 'Oh, Pertwee.' And she turned away, clutching the paper.

'You could hide anything down there,' said John, much taken with this idea, his shy eyes raking over the different rooms of the house, his hand reaching up to waggle inside the chimney.

Dalbeattie took something from his pocket, and dropped it down the chimney stack. It landed with a clunk. 'A ha'penny for you, if you can get it out.'

'Treasure,' said John, shivering with pleasure. He turned to Dalbeattie, smiling a toothy, happy grin. 'Thank you, sir.'

'It's my pleasure, young Master Horner. I hope it brings all of you many years of pleasure.' Dalbeattie ruffled John's fine blond hair and John caught his hand, then scuttled away. Dalbeattie replaced the chimney-pot lid, shut the house up again, and turned to Mary, who had folded up the little note and tucked it into her sleeve. He went to take her hand, almost without thinking it seemed, then stopped. She met his eyes, smiling.

'You, who are so busy, found time to do this,' she said.

'It is a pleasure to help my friend. He allowed me to practise all my ideas on this house . . .' He looked around. 'It was my playground, my attempt at a family home – I look around and that is what I see.' He rested one hand on the chimney-pot. 'It is a home.'

'Run and get into the bath, children,' said Mary. 'Zipporah has filled it nice and high and is warming your clothes. You mustn't catch cold.'

'It's summer—!' Eliza began.

'Yes, and you're wet through. Go, please, to your room, and on the way back down you may fetch the wooden figures from your Mama's desk drawer. They belong in the house.'

'Yes,' said Eliza. She stood on one foot and said seriously: 'Uncle Dalbeattie – thank you, it's a most fantastic house.'

They were gone, running upstairs as fast as they could go, and they left Mary and Dalbeattie, staring across at each other in the dying light of the afternoon.

A cold breeze rippled across her skin; Mary shivered as she looked up at him. At his long face, the still grey eyes, the muscle in his cheek that twitched. He said nothing, meeting her gaze, his hands gently clenched by his side. The shadow of that morning's shave was on his jawline – she longed, then, to reach up, feel it against her fingers –

Mary knew then, without anything else being said. All the natural impulses Nurse Bryant had said were inside her and her sister that needed controlling; all the times she had stared in despair at Pertwee, disporting himself so shamefully with some young woman; the way Liddy described her first night with Ned, the ecstasy obvious from her expression, her tone.

She cleared her throat.

'Thank you. Pertwee would be glad, I think.'

He did not speak, but nodded, still staring at her, or past her, she could not tell.

'About Pertwee – I am so sorry I did not see you in Paris—'

She put her hand up, and was annoyed to find it shaking. 'It's of no concern now. Thank you for your help.'

'Mary, I must explain it to you—'

'No, sir. Dear Dalbeattie! Please do not. Now excuse me – I must attend to the children.'

He hesitated. 'Mary – Miss Dysart—'

But she was gone, hastening upstairs.

He came to her room that night.

A soft tapping at the door, deadly soft, so much so that at first she thought it was – what? The spirits she had long suspected ran throughout the house and the garden, leaving mischief and magic in their wake? The full moon shone through her thin curtains, as Mary wrapped herself in her shawl. It cast milk-white shadows over her bare feet as she padded quickly over the dark floorboards. *The Arabian Nights* was still open on her dresser; John and Eliza had joined her in bed to have it read to them, their little bodies, warm and dry again now after their adventure, squashed against hers.

She opened the door, hesitantly, just an inch to find him there. He did not bend, nor whisper. He merely said, calmly:

'May I come in?'

Fear rose in her throat. 'Is it the children? Is one of them ill?'

'No. I have to talk to you. May I?'

Mary, too surprised to say no, simply opened the door. It was

Dalbeattie, after all. He had saved Liddy and Ned from sinking into poverty, he had remodelled this very house. After Pertwee had been found dead in his rooms, a brain haemorrhage they had said, he had arranged everything: had sent Mary the next day to an hotel with Alphonse George's sister acting as escort; he had brought back Pertwee's body from France himself, and had settled his debts, sold his paintings and possessions, and given her the money from which she now eked out her small, quiet existence. She had seen him irregularly: at christening parties, the last time in London several years ago, at a preview of the Summer Exhibition.

His wife, Rose, was usually in Scotland, but she had accompanied him on this occasion. She was as tall as him, slim, hollow-eyed, dressed most exquisitely in a tweed day dress of soft purple and green, and a beautiful hat trimmed with curling peacock feathers. She did not like London, she told Mary. It was loud, and terrifying. This dress was new, Mama had had it made for her and it was uncomfortable. She wanted to be at their home, stabling the horses.

'I should think,' Mary had said kindly, watching over her shoulder to make sure Pertwee was not saying something unfortunate to the wife of the President, 'that Dalbeattie is most glad to have you in London with him for once, and to show you off.'

'Oh,' said this unusual creature. 'I shouldn't think so. I'm most unhappy here.' A tear had formed in one eye, and she brushed it away. 'I want to be back at home.'

She was young – but Mary and Liddy were young. She was beautiful, and tall, and she and Dalbeattie had had the same upbringing. But Mary could see with utter clarity that she was the wrong wife for Dalbeattie. They did not speak once to one another except when Dalbeattie asked if she was ready to leave.

'Lord, yes. The train home tomorrow morning is very early. We must be ready for it.'

'He doesn't hate her,' Liddy had whispered afterwards. 'It would be better if he did. But she is the kind who should never have married. Oh, not like you, Mary, don't put on one of your mysterious faces. You have a capacity to love as deeply as I do.'

Now Dalbeattie stood inside her doorway holding the candle. He was wearing the most magnificent dressing gown, dark-aubergine velvet, embroiderered all over with birds, in gold and silver thread.

'Why are you here?' he said quietly.

She laughed. 'You disdain supper and then come to my room at midnight, dressed like – like a sultan, off to inspect his harem, and ask me this question?'

He glanced at *The Arabian Nights* behind her and smiled. 'I'm so sorry. Forgive me. I meant, why are you at Nightingale House?'

'Again: I might ask the same of you, with better reason.'

'I thought you'd stay in Paris after Pertwee died. That is what you told me.'

'I found I could not.'

'I would have helped you arrange things, had I known.'

'Thank you; I was happy to do it by myself. It was not your concern.'

'I promised your brother I would look after you,' he said.

'And I was happy to arrange matters to my own satisfaction.' She lifted her eyes to his. 'Thank you for your kindness to him.'

'I loved him dearly. You know I did. He and Ned stood as family to me when I came to London from Scotland, knowing no one. We promised to help one another, we three, and we have. We did. Where do you live now?'

'In Hammersmith, by the river, in rooms. It is far enough for me to feel certain I won't bump into Father or – or anyone else, and near enough to the railway that I am able to visit Liddy. I have a quiet life, perfectly pleasant. There is the lending library, and the hospital, and societies – I have various friends whom I meet. Clubs, and so forth. The suffragists, the Fine Arts Society, the Socialists—'

'A socialist *and* a suffragist, Mary. How have you time for Fine Arts?'

Mary met his gaze, steadily. 'The hour is extremely late. Liddy and Ned do not care much for convention but their servants would, were they to see us. You are married. What do you want with me, Lucius?'

'Mary – if I may. I understand that my arriving here today places you in an awkward position. I tried to talk to you but I couldn't do it in front of the children. I'm sorry to ambush you in your room.' He stopped and looked around. 'Is it very late? What hour is it?' She was smiling; he glanced at the carriage clock on the mantelpiece. 'Good heavens, I had no idea – oh, hang it, Mary. I must talk to you.'

Outside, the wind shifted restlessly in the trees. It was just the two of them, in the dark wood-panelled room. Mary put her hand against the old wooden bedframe, steadying herself. 'Yes?'

'I am sorry. I came to explain myself to you. To say that I am very sorry.'

'Sorry for what? How could you ever be sorry?'

'I am sorry I married. I know you said you would never wed, and that is why I was persuaded by my father to offer for Rose.' He was staring at the book, intently. 'We have never spoken of these things before . . . I have wanted to, so many times, and yet, not knowing you well enough, and yet . . . and yet knowing you . . .' He shook his head, a bittersweet smile twisting his kind face. 'My wife and I – I hoped that perhaps we would rub along together well enough . . . We have a love of the Highlands, of the heather and the hills. She is not stupid. But it was, from the very beginning, a disaster. I will be frank. I cannot be a husband to her. She does not want it. She admits she should never have married.'

'What do you mean?'

'I am –' He smiled and said carefully, 'I am not a husband to her. I was, once, but not since then. Our honeymoon, in Germany.' He rubbed his face in the old Dalbeattie way. 'God's teeth, Mary, what a disaster.'

You should not be saying these things to me, she should have said, but she did not.

'How so? I know nothing of honeymoons.'

He was leaning against the bedstead. 'You know enough to understand the act must take place for the marriage to be consummated and the wife must not drive a fork into the husband's leg when the husband tries to – oh goodness.'

'Goodness indeed.'

'Yes. I was not able to – persuade her to be my wife. I didn't try

262

very hard, in all honesty, but before I could pursue the matter further she had taken a fork out of her skirt and driven it into my thigh.' He was rubbing his face so much his hair stood up on end. 'I passed out. She locked herself in the bathroom. The maid thought I'd been murdered. It was all rather like Scheherazade, trying to avoid death—' He looked up. 'Why are you laughing, Mary?'

Mary was closing the book, her face turned from him. 'I am not, I swear it. Where was this?'

'Weimar. It's a beautiful town, cradle of the Enlightenment—' He stopped as she faced him again. 'You *are* laughing.'

'I should not . . . oh Dalbeattie.' She covered her mouth. 'But that poor girl – poor you. Did you hurt her?'

'Her?' Dalbeattie practically shouted in outrage. 'Not her, I put my hand on her shoulder, that was it! Out came the fork . . . I've never seen anything like it.' And watching her, he began to laugh too. 'I told no one. Not even Ned.'

'I can see why. Is your leg fully recovered?'

'It is, thank you. Poor Rose.'

Her mirth subsided as quickly as it had flared up. 'Yes, poor Rose. Was she in love with you, ever?'

He shook his head. 'No. She loves the horses. And her little sister. She's wonderful with children. I hoped perhaps we might have a family, and that would give her something to do, other than sink into misery over her dissatisfaction with her husband. She ought not to have married, she told me so herself. The whole family, hers and mine, I think, would like to stab me with a fork. She let me, once. Said she had to know, that I must try, though I did not want to . . .' He passed a hand over his face. 'It was awful, Mary, I – I – the sounds she made . . . I hurt her . . .' He stopped, and said quietly, 'Her damned father – forgive me, but he's a brute and for that reason alone I'm glad she's out of his house – he's after me all the time, for money, for not staying up in Scotland.'

'A woman's lot,' said Mary, quietly. 'Good Lord, Dalbeattie.' She swallowed, staring into his gentle face. 'I am sorry to hear it.'

'I am sorry that it happened. I should – oh, I don't know what

I should have done.' His dark eyes were dilated in the dim light of the room. 'Please tell me, Mary – would you ever have changed your mind? Would you ever have married?'

She shook her head. 'Never.' What else could she say?

'I suppose I should be glad. Perhaps not.' He watched her; it was so strange, the understanding between them, how normal it felt to be standing there talking, her in a nightgown, he in his dressing gown, the very picture of domestic intimacy. 'I did always want you, you know. I can't dress it up, you see. I wish I could.' His voice was low, quieter now; she moved towards him. 'I wanted you, Mary. Know that I do. I will never speak of this to you again. I should not have come to you so late – I should not be here at all – and yet I am glad, for –' His voice was hoarse; she saw almost with disbelief that he had tears in his eyes. 'I have loved you from that very first day in the garden.'

'I—' she began, tears in her eyes, but then a terrible cry tore through the whispered hush of her room – an unearthly scream, and both of them jumped. 'John—' Mary hissed. She grabbed her own oil lamp and made for the door, then was still, as other cries echoed around and above them.

'It's the owls,' she said, with a shuddering sigh of relief. 'They're in the trees behind the house. It's the Milk Moon, Zipporah says. They're all a-fluster. Sometimes it wakes me and I think it's John – he has the most terrible nightmares, poor thing, and then I realise it can't be him, but the noise might wake him nonetheless – I'm most awfully afraid of it, to be honest!'

'I can well imagine.' Dalbeattie was still staring at her.

Silence fell again and this time it came like a roaring rush into the large, moonlit room. Mary's heart thudded sharply in her breast. She was afraid of going up in flames, one spark on the touchpaper, and she would be lost . . .

Don't give in. No matter how much you would like to.

'My dearest.' He took her hands, folding them in his own as he had done earlier that day and she allowed herself to look at him then, at his dear face, huge, kind and serious.

Raising herself on tiptoe, she said, 'Thank you for coming. I am glad you did.'

They were formal, both nodding. Her hair, which had been twisted behind her back, fell over her shoulder. She pushed it away, and looked up at him. 'If I were to give myself to anyone – Dearest, you know that it would be you. You must know too that I have loved you for many years now.'

'I see,' he said again, and in the silvery moonlight his eyes flashed.

She moved towards him – only an inch or two, shifting her hand so it circled his arm, and moving his hand on to her shoulder, shaking her own hair behind her back. Then, very gently, he wrapped his long, strong fingers around the top of her neck.

The pads of his fingertips were warm, sending liquid shooting through her where they touched her skin. They stood very still, holding each other in this way, and Mary thought she might faint in his arms. She could not breathe; she did not want to. No one had touched her like this – Pertwee had gripped her roughly, when he was in his cups, the children twined their arms around her neck, Liddy hugged her, but this . . .

Dalbeattie bent his head, and their lips met. She felt his mouth against hers, and it was wonderful. His body pressed forward, against her, and desire unfurled inside her, starting in the stomach, where his dressing gown pressed against the thin lawn of her nightgown.

I am here . . . we are here . . . this is real.

Another cry, this time softer, and she drew back, her mouth wet, her hair disordered, holding onto the cord of the dressing gown.

'That was John,' she said.

Dalbeattie's breath was ragged. 'I think it was.' He gripped her shoulders, and kissed her again.

'*Mary*—'

With huge effort, and a low moan, he drew himself away.

'Stay,' she said.

'No, no. I will go now.' His hand gripped hers; they stared at each other, all reserve gone. 'Dearest Mary. I should not – I will leave tomorrow.'

'Do not go on my account. Ned and Liddy do not return for another week. The children crave company – they are too isolated here. Stay and keep them amused, if not me.' Mary heard her voice as she spoke. It was not her normal voice. It was full-throated, passionate. 'I will not marry you, but I will love you. Stay here, if you may. The children will be glad. And I will be glad.'

He twisted his mouth. 'Mary, there is no woman alive like you who would talk in these terms.'

'You forget the circumstances of my life thus far, Dalbeattie, which surprises me. I went from the care of Nurse Bryant to living with Pertwee. I saw things in Paris you would struggle to comprehend.' She shrugged her shoulders. 'I choose to ask you to stay knowing what might happen.' She swallowed, knowing that if she crossed the river now there was no going back.

'Aunt Maryyyy – I am frightened.'

'I take a nap in the afternoons after lunch, when the children play outside and they do not come back until teatime.' Suddenly she could hear Liddy's most earnest instructions to her as the carriage pulled away a week ago. *'Don't let them go roving far on their own, darling. Don't let them meet any strangers – oh, darling, have them take care!'*

She blinked, shutting the high, clear little voice out. 'Hannah, our dear maid from London, is visiting her sister at Tooker's Farm, this week. She is coming to collect them every day. They will go with her to the farm, to play with the puppies.' She could hear her own voice was shaking. 'Do you understand me?'

'A devoted family retainer with a puppy at a nearby farm?' He gave a small laugh. 'One could almost imagine you placed Hannah there merely to be rid of them.'

'Perhaps.' She smiled, and then paused. 'They're delighted to see her—' She stopped. Something about Hannah's pale, withdrawn face, her tiredness, had made her uneasy. Something she could not quite unpick, which she meant to – Bryant blackmailing her about something, she thought, or perhaps she was simply fatigued, unwell . . .

She was at the door. She took a deep breath. 'I must go to John. Will you come? I will not drive a fork into your thigh.'

His face was half-shadow. 'By God. Yes. Mary – yes. Yes. I will come to you tomorrow. In this – in this house.'

He took her hand, and kissed it as she opened the door. She caught his face to hers, and kissed him again, astonished at herself, at the response. 'In this house.'

The next day, when the children had gone to play, and the afternoon haze settled over the house, he came to her once again. Zipporah was shut away in the kitchen, Dymphna was chattering to Darling in the garden, and upstairs their voices floated up to them, as Mary locked the door and stood in the centre of the room, and slowly, shaking, removed her worn and much-mended cotton tea-gown, with his help, his clever fingers deft on the tiny buttons. 'I'm nervous,' he told her, as his lips skimmed the soft skin on her neck, as he pulled away the straps of her underclothes, peeling away layers of her, like an unfurling flower. 'I will be careful—'

'I am nervous too,' she said, though she was not. She had never been more certain of anything. After these obstacles, of worldly clothes and conventions, were removed, they were naked, on the bed. His hard, lean, tall body drawn in to hers, like coiled springs, released. That day, he made her his own, and she possessed him, and the day after, and the day after that. The cleft of his chin; the base of his spine; his hooked toes, his wide, muscular thighs, the dark hair everywhere. The strength of him, when he was so gentle. The fury of her, the feverish longing, when she was so demure.

The sound of the children, returning, chased out of whatever tree or boat or lane they'd got to, was the sound that they must get up, rise, smooth out the smiles from their cheeks, the wrinkles on their clothes, the fingers that soon became yet more deftly adroit at fastening buttons and hooks, the better to restore themselves as they had been. To pretend.

It lasted for five days.

Chapter Twenty-Three

'What dear children, Mrs Horner.'

'I've told my husband, we shall come to the Academy every day of the Summer Exhibition. I must see this painting every day! Their little faces . . . !'

'It's awfully interesting . . . I suppose it's a meditation on the fleeting nature of childhood, of time. I really do think it's quite remarkable, Liddy. Ned has taken an apparently decorative subject and made something truly profound from it. It is art in its purest form: the two-dimensional rendered into a scene, into an ideal, and thence into our deepest psyche: life, death, time – nature – Poussin. It's a modern Poussin.'

'I love the wings. They're so pretty. I do so awfully want the wings, Mama.'

Day after day, standing beside Ned at dinners and receptions, hearing the exclamations and adulation, watching people staring at *The Garden of Lost and Found* and at her children, and missing them so much after a while it was a pain she didn't notice but carried with her. And though she had been the one to suggest to Ned that they go back together to London in triumph, after only a day or two she was sick of it, and longed for Nightingale House again.

'The future is yet unwritten; the past is burnt and gone'

She had written it down on a piece of paper for him when he was struggling to find an inscription for the plaque on the frame of *The Garden of Lost and Found*. She had left it in the Dovecote, on his mixing table, before they left for London – he had rushed into her in the study. 'Yes,' he had said, eyes shining, and pulling her to her feet, laughing, had kissed her, hard. 'Yes, my darling, that is the one.'

Every detail of the hanging was supervised by Ned: where it was placed, so that the varnish did not catch the light. The frame carved by Ned himself, a wide, swirling, sweeping decorative gilt edging, to emphasise the subject matter within. The lettering of the inscription: the past was dead, the future was theirs, they must look forward . . . keep on going, no matter how hard at times.

But that was before she came back to London. Liddy had to admit she found Piccadilly and Regent Street terrifying: motor cars were everywhere in London now, and there were more hackney carriages and horse-powered buses than ever, too, as well as street-sweepers, hawkers and newspaper-sellers taking their lives into their hands every time they stepped into the road. Buildings were still draped in black for the old dead queen: the new king and the new century not quite things one was used to, not after so long. In London, it seemed reality was different, it was all noise and acclaim and chatter, not the reality of mending torn clothes and planting seeds.

Thank God John was too young to fight if the war with the Boers dragged on, as it seemed likely to. John was a timid chap – already Liddy could see he would be unsuited to fighting. He might be an artist, like his father, perhaps an illustrator of stories, like Arthur Rackham, for he loved observing others. Or a teacher. Then Eliza – she should be denied nothing: if her brother must go away to school, though Liddy could scarcely bear the idea, then so must Eliza. She might even go to university. Might drive a car, even vote: Mother had told Liddy and Mary it would happen in their lifetimes.

Standing in the crowded main gallery of the Royal Academy, Liddy looked around, wanting to enter into the festive feeling. This was Varnishing Day, the crucial moment before the opening of the Summer Exhibition when artists were invited to view their work hanging in its allotted place and were allowed, if they so desired, to make final touches to their canvases. The great beasts of the Victorian era – Leighton, Millais – were all dead and gone.

Something had been released with the end of the late Queen's reign; the atmosphere here, as out on the streets, was different. Electric, buzzing with something.

She smiled mechanically at the wife of a society portrait painter and inclined her head politely at an old and decrepit essayist who had criticised Ned's work in the past. There was M. George surrounded by a crowd of admirers, leaning forward to make one finishing touch to his *Leda and the Swan*. He was stroking his moustache like a villain in a Gilbert and Sullivan operetta. Liddy's mouth twitched – Alphonse George was always so certain of his own genius; she rather admired him for it.

At her side, Ned grasped the arm of someone firmly, roughly shaking hands with him. She turned to see Thaddeus Galveston, smiling at him intently.

'A great day, sir.' He raised his top hat to Liddy. 'Madam, your servant. I was glad of your company yesterday.'

Galveston had thrown a dinner party for Ned and Liddy in his rooms in Berkeley Square. A collection of old friends and new investors, rich men. It had been a late night: Ned had stayed behind to talk to Galveston over port and had not returned to their hotel until the small hours. 'We were discussing what we might do after the exhibition, with this painting. I stand firm this time, Liddy! This painting must transform our fortunes.'

Poor Ned, it had transformed his immediate fortunes: he looked the worse for it this morning. His face was pale, his eyes were bloodshot in the stifling heat of the crowded room.

Liddy shook hands with Galveston and allowed her mind to drift, imagining she was back at home, feet dangling in the stream, Ned beside her, children on the rug, eating mulberries from the tree . . . a fresh cooling breeze . . . the smell in her nostrils, not of heavy perfume but of June summer flowers . . .

'Liddy!' Ned was tugging her arm. 'What do you say to Galveston's proposal?'

Liddy blinked. 'Forgive me.' The riverbank, the dancing figures, the garden, the scents of home vanishing, like a scene from a toy theatre being slid back into place out of sight. Galveston tapped his cane smartly on the floor.

'You have driven a hard bargain, Ned! But here we are. It is as follows: that I buy from you *The Garden of Lost and Found* for an agreed sum. This sum to include the copyright of the painting. Do you understand?' She nodded, patiently. 'And that we tour *The Garden of Lost and Found*, in the manner of *The Light of the World,* and so forth. I have associates in Canada and Australia whom I have telegraphed ahead of the exhibition's opening. They have all expressed a great desire to see it. This—' He raised the cane, levelling its silver point slowly around the crowded room, as if it were the barrel of a gun. 'This has already proved my interest correct. They're queuing up to see it already, look: why not charge them to do so? It'll be the making of you. You can paint what you want for the rest of your life.'

'What do you say, Liddy?' said Ned.

'Wise of you, to ask your wife's opinion, for she'll have one, no matter what you say!' said Galveston jovially, and Ned turned back to him, with a dangerous note in his voice.

'I make no decisions without Liddy. She must decide.'

'Don't do it,' said Liddy, flatly. 'Don't sell the copyright. Give Thaddeus the painting if you want, for the right sum. But not the rights. Look at *Bubbles*.'

'Mrs Horner, I'm grieved you'd suggest I'd sell *The Garden of Lost and Found* to a soap manufacturing company and allow it to be used in such a cheap way. Millais was a fool – he should never have—'

'Dear Millais was an artist, not a businessman, as well you know,' said Liddy, smoothly.

'I . . .' Ned hesitated. 'I'd a mind to do it, we'd agreed last night, Liddy, my love. Galveston will pay us . . .' and he leaned towards her, and she caught the aroma of last night's cigar smoke and port wine on his hair and skin, and underneath it all the same old Ned smell, '. . . one thousand pounds.' He stepped back, and watched her reaction, smiling his boyish smile.

'Exactly,' said Galveston, carefully. 'If you agree to this, the final debts on the house will be paid off, and the future of your children entirely secured – you'll have made the final step necessary. A legacy.'

'Ned – what kind of legacy is it if you have no control over your work?' she began, urgently, but then there was a disturbance in the crowd, a parting of the ways. Idly, she turned, and as if in slow motion saw the crowd swell, then vanish, melting away until one man was left, a fellow in a suit with tassels around it – she couldn't understand it for a second. Look, there he was closer now, the tassels bouncing: what a strange thing to wear to Varnishing Day! He was a young fellow: his moustaches were nothing like Georges's, she found herself thinking, sandy, bristling, very poor—

'Mrs Horner,' he was saying, and he handed her a note, and before she opened it the dread caught at her heart, her legs turned to water – the note was wet with his sweat, his forehead was glistening, and his eyes – His eyes did not meet hers. His voice was too high-pitched as he said, 'You must go home at once.' And the words started to swim in and out of her hearing *'Your daughter – the carriage—'* and she could not understand him, wondered if she was mishearing what he said.

And through the waves of terror and nausea, she heard Ned's voice. Eliza. Eliza, Liddy – oh dear God. We must go. We must go.

And they were running, running out into the Great Courtyard, and when she saw the horse and carriage already waiting, the crowds parting, fear written on their faces, she knew she had not misheard. It was bad. Something was very bad.

Chapter Twenty-Four

They had moved her to the studio, out of the house, so she might not infect anyone else. She was in there as the carriage screeched to an almost-halt and Liddy flung herself down to the ground, Ned following. Mary was waiting, an apron working between her fingers, her face pale as a ghost – she grabbed her sister by the arm, pulling her towards the open door of the studio.

Little Eliza sat up propped against an easel on a mattress on the floor, gasping for air – her eyes bulged, her small hands clutching and releasing a wooden object in her hand. When she saw her mother tears came to her eyes, but she could not speak, only rasp, stridently trying to catch more breath. Her face was a ghastly yellowish white, her nightgown rucked up around her knees. Her fingers opened and closed more frantically.

'My God—' Liddy sobbed, pushing the doctor out of the way and falling to the floor beside her daughter. 'What is it? What's – please say it's not—'

'It's diphtheria, I'm afraid, and it's well advanced,' Doctor Carritt said, moving out of the way. He put his hand on Liddy's shoulder. Behind Liddy, Ned gave a strange choking noise. Liddy turned to look at him, terror in her eyes. She saw Mary, her face buried in her apron, her shoulders heaving with silent sobs. 'There's an outbreak at Tooker's Farm. The farmer's wife has already died, and her sister who's visiting from London is mortally ill. Hannah Blount – they said you knew her.' He smoothed back Eliza's hair, shaking his head, a momentary flare of despair flickering across his face as he looked at the young girl propped up against the easel. 'There, my dear.'

The Strangulation Disease – that was what they called it in Highgate, when the funerals of those who died were held at dead of night to avoid the risk of contamination. Liddy shook her head.

'The milk,' Mary said, her voice tight. 'Was the milk not treated properly, is it the cause?'

He turned to Mary. 'I suspect it's Miss Blount. Hannah Blount at the farm. She complained of feeling unwell when she arrived, but she was sent away suddenly by her employer from London to visit her sister. Most irresponsible of them.' He looked at his fob watch, then at Eliza's thin wrist which he was holding. 'I fear she's the cause . . . Her fever is very high. The pulse is extremely fast. She can't breathe, I'm afraid. The membrane builds up on the throat, it grows at this stage with—' He broke off.

Liddy cried out then turned to her husband. But she saw that he, too, did not know what to do.

'There are antitoxins one can administer, but I do not have them, and we are running out of time . . .' And Liddy saw Dr Carritt glance at Mary with a curious expression, which then she did not understand. 'The only option left is most risky. I have to consider administering a tracheotomy,' said Dr Carritt, his thin, elderly face hollow with weariness. Eliza made a grunting, horrifying sound and her mouth fell open, gasping for air. Then Liddy could see, at the back of the throat, the white coating on the tonsils – like putty, or mouldable plaster, as if someone had stuck it there. So incongruous. She pulled her daughter into her arms, pushing her hair out of the way – the cloud of unruly, tangled gold, stroking her forehead. She was very hot.

'No! Liddy, you must not – the infection risk—' cried Mary, as Liddy cradled her daughter in her arms, smelling the sweet honey scent of her soft hair, feeling her cool smooth skin against hers, but Liddy ignored her. Eliza's eyes, cobalt-blue chips of colour in the gloom of the room, bore into Liddy's. She tried to say something. Liddy kissed her, and Mary gasped again and Ned turned away.

Looking around her, Liddy saw canvases knocked to the floor, or listing against the walls, paint powders knocked over, feathered spots of bright, bold rainbow colours in this awful scene. Gently, she released Eliza, stood up, stumbled against the wall, steadied herself and walked out into the bright sunshine. Birds were singing loudly, rudely, in the bushes.

'What – what is a tracheotomy?' she said.

'They cut the throat open to aid breathing, but it is very risky,' said Dr Carritt to her and Ned, without preamble. 'One in four fails. And she is very young. Nevertheless, without it I am certain she will die. I don't have the antitoxins to hand to treat her. She will die without them. I am sorry, Mrs Horner, I must be frank with you. This is a dreadful business – diphtheria has been on the decline but where it occurs it is a most awful disease and it is partiularly virulent in children.'

There was a gold-and-grey dappling of the sun through the new leaves on the branches. Yes. They were leaves that had appeared while she had been away. Liddy turned to look at the house, the dear house, saw the church, the graveyard behind.

'How is Hannah?' she said, after a while.

'Very unwell. I am afraid I do not expect her to survive.' Doctor Carritt stood up straight, and exhaled. He gave Liddy a careful, kind smile. 'You must decide now, I'm afraid. I can perform the tracheotomy here and now – but Mrs Horner, there's no time to waste.'

A voice behind them said, 'God's sake, Liddy, you must do it.'

She jumped; Ned started out of his skin and they turned to see Dalbeattie, standing behind the doctor. 'Dalbeattie? What on earth are you—?'

'I came to – to deliver the doll's house. I have been staying, with Mary.' He clasped Liddy's hand. 'My dearest Liddy—'

'I – I am so glad you were here,' said Ned. Liddy nodded, scratching at her cheek, what to do, what seconds they wasted! She turned to look back into the building again, at the little figure on the mattress.

'I – they've been so happy, these last few days, before she started feeling ill,' he said, without meeting her eye. 'I'm so awfully sorry, m'dear. Ned.' He put his hand on Ned's shoulder, and turned. 'You must let him do the operation, Ned. You must.'

'Mm,' said Ned. He caught Dalbeattie's hand. 'Liddy . . .'

'Mrs Horner – come . . .'

Liddy looked back into the studio, into the darkness. She could see the small figure on the mattress, rigid, her hands around her throat. *How is this to be borne?* she thought. *I always thought I could stand anything. I can't.*

'No,' she said. 'No operation.'

'Liddy—'

'Mrs Horner – I must—'

'No. She hates knives, sharp things, violence. You can't do that to her. If she's to die—'

'She might live with this operation, Liddy,' said Ned.

'She won't let me cut her hair. She hates it. She is dying before our eyes and you want to hold her down and cut her throat open? She's not yet eight, Ned. She won't understand. I won't – I can't let you. I am sorry.'

'Liddy,' said Mary, desperately. 'You must, you must let him do it.'

'Mrs Horner,' said Dr Carritt. 'You must allow me to tell you I disagree.'

'The risk is too great, and she's – she's little. She can't – you can't treat her like that. Like a medical – a body.' Those bodies snatched from graveyards, the stuff of nightmares that Nurse Bryant used to warn them about. *Waiting round corners they were, still warm the bodies were, they'd slice off your face, slice open your eyes . . .*

Her throat seemed to be closing up too. 'Cut a hole in her throat while she's conscious, dig through the muscle, scrape it away – you can't. I'm sorry.'

She turned, and went back into the stone building, and scooped Eliza up into her arms again. 'Mama will take you inside now.' Stepping over a bundle of rags, she caught a small framed picture with her heel, tearing it slightly. She shook it away, kicking it to the corner, then carried Eliza, out of the studio into the light, across the forecourt of the house, through the open door. Her slight frame shuddered under the weight once or twice but she kept on going, past the wooden hooks, the squirrel, the watchful owl, past the singing birds, and up the stairs to her and Ned's bedroom overlooking the garden where the children had played. Not the nursery. She would not have John sleep in that room. She put her in the bed, gently, prising Eliza's fingers off her shoulders. Eliza pulled at her mother's form, tearing the lace on her blouse, frantically scrabbling at her hands, her arms. Her cheeks were flushed, her face otherwise utterly white.

Liddy propped her up with cushions, and waved the rose water Eliza so often begged to wear around the room. She took out her jewellery box, laying the pieces on the bed. 'Here's the one you want, Eliza, here's the star, here's the brooch Daddy gave me when we moved here, it's a nightingale, here's some earrings, here's a bracelet with your hair, darling – your hair—'

Every time she put on any piece of jewellery, she was back there, that last afternoon in that room. How Eliza tried to look, to play a part even, to be distracted, and how very soon she could not. How Ned tried to help but could do nothing except look on. To watch your own child's strangulation, slowly suffocating, as you watch, any semblance of power you had in the home you created, in the walls you built up around them, utterly gone. You have no power now. A greater force is at work.

Hell is not dramatic. It is slow, cruel, repetitive, once again it is slow. Eliza's agony, her gradual suffocation, took hours, she weaker and weaker trying to fight, then, not wanting to any more, until evening began to fall across the wold, stripes of orange and violet in the spring sky, darkening to blue-black, pricked all across with stars. Eliza saw the stars and her eyes finally closed, as though now night was here she could finally give up, and Liddy leaned forward and kissed her forehead.

'Just a little longer now. We are nearly there,' she whispered. Death was to be welcomed when he came creeping into the room. Death was the release, their friend. 'Just a little longer, my darling.'

Eliza's small face was bloated, her limbs useless, her body a leaden, motionless sack on the bed. She died in Liddy's arms a few minutes afterwards, eyes still closed and when it happened, Liddy could feel nothing except relief. She smoothed the fluffy gold hair out, watched the plump still-childish face slowly relax again, the little still-warm fingers with the nails, their tiny crescents moon-white.

Liddy touched a small twig in Eliza's hair, then a pale green leaf. Twigs, leaves, insects – the outside was always becoming caught in her hair. Outside, the moon was waning. The Milk Moon, she remembered suddenly. A strange, strange time. Who had said that? Hannah. Hannah was a country girl. But by now, of course, Hannah was most likely dead too.

Tragedy causes tightly knotted secrets to unravel at remarkable speed. It was the following day that Liddy, wandering aimlessly through the house, not yet able to cry, not even yet able to understand, but finding all she could do was tidy, order things when there was no order, found the cord of a most elborate man's dressing gown, aubergine velvet, embroidered with gold and silver, under Mary's bed.

Liddy ran the velvet through her fingers, knuckles catching on the embroidery. She stood gazing at the wooden frieze on the wall. She said nothing, then.

In fact the silence of that time was what Liddy remembered most. There was simply no noise in the house. Eliza's thundering feet, her cries of outrage, her laughter, had been silenced. John was confined to the nursery, forbidden to see his parents, given soup and comforted by Zipporah, whose steadfast support and kindness during those days Liddy was never to forget.

Eliza's funeral was held two days later, as soon as the lead lining for the coffin could be arranged, which it speedily was: the risk of infection was still great. Ned had insisted he make the small coffin of ash himself, staying up all night, ceaselessly working the lathe, planing the rails of the wood himself, inserting the heavy lead lining, lifting his daughter's cold, still-stiff body in, his face riven with grief. And as she watched the pallbearers stagger under the weight of the lead, though the coffin itself was little, and slim, as she saw Mary sobbing over the coffin, black lace draped over her head, her thin hands red raw and scabbed with chewing them – the old habit – she felt the metal spike enter her heart, pierce it, twist it. Afterwards, as the sound of the men throwing the earth back over the coffin, the clink of their spades, floated down towards the house, Liddy summoned her sister to the study and told her to leave. Dalbeattie had been spoken to by Ned, that morning. He had gone back to Scotland, the letter he left for Liddy burned, unopened, on the fire.

'I know you let them go wandering, to the farm.'

'I let Hannah meet them halfway. They weren't wandering. She had charge of them. I didn't know she was –'

'You blame someone else.' Liddy was looking out over the garden, wondering what to do with it now. Perhaps someone should simply set it alight, raze it to the ground, start over.

'It's not blame. I'm telling you what happened. It's my fault, of course—' Her voice was flat. 'Oh God, Liddy. What did I do? What have I done?'

Galveston had written to Ned, his letter arriving before the news of Eliza's death. Queues stretching around the courtyard the following day. Thousands the day after that. All there to see his painting. Liddy wondered if she could go up to town, slash the painting into pieces, so she'd never have to look at it again.

And suddenly, she thought of Bryant. *You will greatly suffer for it.*

'I only asked you not to let them wander too far from the house,' she said, and she clutched on to the bureau, fearing she might lose her composure utterly. 'I wanted to keep them safe. Make sure no one . . . No bad fairies could get them . . .' She trailed off.

'Safe from what, Liddy?' Mary's dark eyes were huge in her white face. 'They were always safe, my dear – ' She shook her head, tears flying. 'This is bad, bad luck, it is not – revenge. It's not some . . .'

Gritting her teeth, Liddy said, 'Bryant knew Hannah was ill. She put her on the train. She paid for her train fare. Did you know that? Mr Tooker told me. She sent her here to kill my children.'

'Liddy, you can't believe that—'

'It's not a question of believing or not believing, Mary. It is the truth.'

Liddy knew now, when she had taken her sweet, plump, happy little girl to see Bryant, to see the house, that she had angered her, and laid a trap for herself and her little birds.

'Do not seek to explain it to me. You betrayed me. I don't ask what you were doing. I don't ask why Dalbeattie was here.' Her bottom lip curled over her teeth, she leaned forward, curling over, head between her legs, keening like an animal. She did not care how Mary saw her.

Mary kneeled down by the chair. Her lip was bleeding, where she'd bitten it. 'Liddy – my darling. Don't make me go. Let me stay. Let me help you.'

Liddy drew the chair back and stood up, turning away from the garden. She could hear John, crying out for her upstairs, and she could not go to comfort him.

'You are not my sister. I have no sister any more.'

As months turned into years, Liddy tried not to think about either of them. The house became her world and the world shrank to only that, to John, her darling boy, and the grave of her little girl, buried still with the twigs and the leaves in her hair.

Part Three

Chapter Twenty-Five

December

You should of course have saved the sunflower seed heads in September.
Fasten them to bamboo canes and stick them in the beds just below the
terrace, watch the greenfinches and wrens and robins methodically extract
seed after seed. Now, though you are in the depths of winter, you may
start to understand how the garden is working year-round.

I find comfort in that you see.

There is mistletoe in the hawthorn trees by the churchyard, next to
the yew. I always cut some there. Do not bring yew into the house, it is
bad luck. It means death.

Here I am at the end of my little exercise book and the end of the
year. I have enjoyed scribbling these hints and tips down over the past
few days. Will you ever read it, Juliet? Will it come off? Will you ever
live here? I trust Frederic, and yet . . . The idea of the house gone to
someone else but you is painful to me I must say. I have a stack of
acorns saved up. I always place a new acorn on my windowsill every
New Year's Eve. It means the house will not be struck by lightning.
My room was my parents' room. Mum told me once there were no acorns
left on the windowsill the year her daughter died. 'My daughter died.' It
is hurtful when she talks like that. I am her daughter, no matter what
he said. I am here after all, and they are all gone. All of them.

Years later Juliet liked to recall that first Christmas back at
Nightingale House and shudder before telling herself no matter
how bad things were, it wasn't as bad as that Christmas. It was

freezing cold, not deep and crisp and even but with a misty fog that felt as though it was swirling into your bones. Juliet could only see as far as the terrace on Christmas morning.

Like orphans in some sad Victorian painting, the children huddled together on the wooden settle in the dining room, pleading for breakfast, as Juliet ran in and out of the house fetching wood, cutting the holly and ivy it had been too wet to collect on Christmas Eve, all the while letting in cold air and treading fox poo throughout the house.

She'd meant to get them all matching pyjamas, as though they, too, were Boden people, but realised she couldn't afford to splurge on some pyjamas Bea might refuse to wear after Boxing Day due to them having robins on them. The stockings – economy version – were a disaster.

'I've read this book. The puppy dies in the end.' Isla slid it grimly across the table towards her mother. 'Perhaps give it to a charity shop.'

'My no LIKE Chase!' Sandy had screamed, throwing his miniature Paw Patrol toy across the room.

'Mum? Sandy hates Chase. I hate Chase too. We like Marshall. Marshall's cute . . . he has these little puppy paws and a funny smile. . . We *hate* Chase.'

'Oh dear.' Juliet rubbed her face, red with exertion, and took a sip of coffee. She had burned the cinnamon Christmas buns she'd prepared the day before, and the kitchen and dining room reeked of acrid sugar and scorched bread, the scent of the former catching in the nostrils and the back of the throat.

'You've marked the floor, Mum,' said Bea, hugging Sandy, who was softly crying, his mouth almost comically downturned. Juliet looked back at the long scratch on the wooden floor, a line leading from the front door to where the log basket rested at her feet. She stuck out her jaw, and pursed her lips. 'It's OK, Sandy. My stocking is way shitter than yours. Look at my bracelet. It's broken, all the beads have come off.'

'Don't use language—' Juliet began, and then stopped. 'Darlings, come and help me. Put on your boots and warm up.' She clapped her hands. 'It's Christmas! Let's bring some more logs in, then we'll light the fire and be all cosy. Frederic and George are—'

'Dad!' Isla screamed, and Juliet jumped, swivelling round in horror, but it was Matt, FaceTiming from London on Bea's phone. Bea carefully propped the phone up on the dining room table and answered the call.

'Dadda! Dadda!' shouted Sandy, hurrying towards his sisters. 'There my dadda!'

'Hi guys!' said Matt. He was in the old sitting room, surrounded by large glossy-looking presents and torn wrapping paper, other children running back and forth behind him, the mayhem of a busy family Christmas fully apparent. 'I miss you guys. Happy Christmas! Elise! Jack! Come here, say – oh, they've gone off. Hey! Have you opened your presents?'

'Mum said we couldn't yet,' said Bea. They turned around to look at Juliet, who was frantically trying to dress the set of the FaceTime view by sticking a sprig of holly into the dresser and sliding the meagre quantity of Christmas cards she had received into view. 'She said we'd do it after we were dressed and after church. But she never goes to church so why's she going today of all days, plus we've got hardly any presents to open.' Bea leaned forward and said in a penetrating voice: 'Dad, Mum said yours weren't posted in time. Is that true?'

'I'm sorry. It's not Mum's fault she wasn't in and hasn't been able to arrange redelivery . . . Don't blame her, OK?' said Matt sadly. 'She did let me know.'

Juliet hid her own face behind a card she was putting on the mantelpiece. It had arrived only the previous night, sent on by Honor, with her own Christmas card. She reread it once again.

Hi Ju – Mum says you listened to me about the dahlias & all cool. Happy Xmas. See you 2015 I hope. Luv Ev PS Remember the Royal Wedding? Do you? Been thinking about it. It's crazy. Can't wait to see the old house again – great stuff!

'My presents?' said Sandy, as the noise at Matt's end grew louder, and Tess could be heard calling something from the kitchen. Matt leaned in closer.

'Hey, little guy! I miss you, mate. Listen to me, OK? You'll get them when we go skiing day after tomorrow. And we'll see Nonna! And Nonna has loads more for you, too. So it'll be worth it . . . Promise. Hey! Hey!' he said, catching hold of Elise, and giving her a kiss. Isla's old classmate stared into the camera, unsmiling. Juliet saw Isla taking a step back, as though she had been slapped.

'OK,' said Bea, watching Matt, her eyes narrowed. 'We have to go now.'

'Yes, Daddy, bye,' said Isla. Bea leaned swiftly forward, and ended the call.

Then it was very quiet in the too-large, echoing house. Juliet gathered up some just-picked holly and ivy, and came towards the children, keeping her voice level. 'Hey,' she said. She pinched Sandy's cheek, kissed Bea and Isla's heads. 'I've got crumpets in the freezer. And Nutella. How about that for a Christmas breakfast?'

'Nutella!' shouted Sandy, joyfully, slapping his hands against his face.

'Oh, Mum! You're not usually so kind,' said Isla, sitting back down at the table with a sigh.

'I'm not hungry,' said Bea, picking up her slim stocking. 'I'm going back to bed.'

'Nutella!' Juliet shouted, desperately. 'Special treat!'

'It's got palm oil in it. Palm oil is the worst.' Bea turned round in the doorway. 'Thanks, Mum, but I'm going to just chill in my room and message Fin till Frederic and George arrive. Happy Christmas and all that.'

'I hate palm oil too,' said Isla, watching her sister leave. 'I hate it. I hate oil. I won't eat it.'

'It's chocolate spread,' Juliet said. *I've got nothing. If I've gone to Nutella at 8.30 a.m. on Christmas morning, I've got nowhere else to go.* 'It's lovely.'

'I still hate it. But I will have some.' Isla swallowed, with a great gulp. 'Mum, I want to go home. I want to see Dad.'

'Oh, love.'

Juliet pulled her middle child into her arms. She looked out over the white and grey fog, the bowed and black branches of the bare creeper like spider legs, clicking against the window. 'It won't always be like this, my darling. Promise.'

'I hate winter.'

'Oh, winter's OK. It has to be like this so summer can come.'

As she stroked Isla's hair, and rubbed her tummy, which she had always loved, Juliet realised they needed, all of them, to be anchored to the place more. They had to understand their mum worked here, and that they lived here. That this wasn't an extended break, an experiment in living. She had to start looking for a job. To put down more roots.

Bea reappeared in the doorway. 'Fin's busy. I'll speak to her later. Can I have some crumpet and Nutella, please?'

'Yes!' Juliet cried, practically throwing Isla off her lap and herself towards the freezer, fingers fumbling to get the crumpets out and in the toaster before Bea could disappear again. And as she heard the children chatting quietly in the dining room she let her shoulders rise, and fall, as George kept telling her she needed to do.

'Scrunch them up around your ears, high as you can. Let everything that's bothering you be scrunched up in there. OK? Then you let them fall, see?'

Dear Juliet Horner

Thank you for your email, which my office forwarded to me. We are looking for an assistant curator. Do you have a CV? Email it over and I'll take a look.

Yours
Sam Hamilton
Director, Fentiman Museum

PS Are you the Juliet Horner with whom I studied at Oxford? Hope you're well.

Dear Sam:

Yes that's me. I'm well thank you. You didn't have to reply so soon; I know it's still Christmas. I have recently moved west of Oxford and wondered if the position you mentioned is still vacant. I'd love to come in and discuss it with you if so. I attach a copy of my CV and look forward to hearing from you.

Juliet Horner

Dear Juliet

Thank you for your job application.
Unfortunately the position you mention is no longer vacant. I will be in touch with you on my return to the office, 4th January 2015. I'd be happy to meet you to discuss what you feel you might be able to offer the Museum.

Yours sincerely
Sam Hamilton

P.S. Happy New Year.

Matt took the children for a week's skiing two days later, and Juliet began her week alone with terrific intentions. She wrestled with damp patches and mice and collapsing curtain rails, with dusty trunks full of Grandi's junk, waterlogged plants, slimy pathways. Every day brought some new challenge and she ended it always exhausted, sleeping like a log in only the way fresh air and physical exertion can make one.

She had parted from them in high drama, Sandy having to be torn away from her at the gate screaming *NO AIRPLANE STATION*, Bea whistling casually as she strolled towards her father, then shooting a heartbreakingly scared look back at Juliet from under her fringe to see if she'd seen her, and Isla howling angrily at everyone in Departures and calling a poker-faced Tess *that horrible lady.* Juliet made the drive back to Nightingale House in an equally cliched howling gale, sobbing loudly as she listened to ABBA's *Arrival* on repeat. It was all awful, and clichéd, and hysterical.

Yet when she had been alone for a few days, Juliet began to realise something. As the year drew to a close, she was out every morning in the garden with the sunrise, raking leaves, cutting back branches and staking things to sticks. Slowly, she came to understand that she felt different, that she was changing. No longer was she the sad, low-level unhappy being whom the slightest thing could make cry, as she had been when she was still with Matt. She had been sleepwalking through life.

At midnight on New Year's Eve, sitting alone at the bottom of the curving staircase, a headscarf tying her hair back, her limbs aching from dragging furniture and unpacking her own cookbooks and novels and the children's books and games, shaking out rugs and quilts, Juliet opened a bottle of champagne given to her by Zeina and slowly, luxuriantly drank two small glasses from a coloured plastic beaker.

As she sat there, head spinning slightly, she promised she would make these last twelve months count towards something.

On 1 January, she woke up early and relatively un-hungover for the first time in years. She went for a brisk walk through the wind-swept, empty lanes, collecting broken twigs, husks of silver birch bark that had peeled away, discarded pine cones. She made a hearty leek and potato soup and built a 'roaringly' successful fire, then huddled inside in the study, and reread every published word she had ever written, and all the articles she could find online about the Fentiman, Sam Hamilton, current critical thinking on Victorian painting, and so on.

Unfortunately the position you mention is no longer vacant . . . Even the tone of Sam Hamilton's emails, the careless repetition, set her teeth on edge; she could practically taste his self-satisfaction, oozing through the pixels on the screen. On 31 December, two days before the children were due back, Juliet gritted her teeth and emailed the directors of three other museums with significant collections of Victorian or Edwardian art: the Tate, the V&A and the Walker Art Gallery in Liverpool.

That was the other thing she'd realised during this period of solitude: she was not adept at pushing herself forward. When she'd started working, job vacancies were in newspapers, and it seemed more democratic: you applied, you had an interview, you got the job, or not. But Matt, she kept recalling, had been given a promotion and a pay rise at his old company *because he'd told them he ought to have one.* Juliet would no more have done that at Dawnay's or at the Tate than she would have bought a pair of jeggings or eaten beetroot.

Somewhere down the line the women she knew started getting pregnant, and boys who were five years younger were suddenly running some department or other, and friends of hers didn't come back to work, but appeared sometimes in the park, smiling with anxiety, their story down pat. 'It's been really great taking this time while he's so small.' Then they started getting jobs: a boy at her college was, at thirty-nine, the youngest ever managing director of the CBI. One guy she'd been with at university was an MP already; another was a TV journalist; what happened to the women? Juliet knew the answer. *She wasn't quite right for the job. Didn't have quite the commitment necessary for the hours. Wasn't quite on top of the brief. Quite.*

Alone with her thoughts these memories kept bobbing to the surface. It made her think of the apples she and Ev used to drop in the stream that would eventually reappear, floating along until carried out of sight by the eddying water. For how long had she been simply carried along by the tide? How long had she let it happen?

The replies were swift. The V&A had nothing, they said, with regret, but the director invited Juliet in for coffee, 'to discuss future options'. The Tate and the Walker Gallery replied in the same vein, but with courtesy; they made it clear they had heard of her, and Juliet was almost buoyed into confidence by the tone, even if nothing had come of it. Another week went by and Juliet, who had already dipped into her Premium Bond savings, drew up a list of options.

AirBnB the house.
Rent out half the house.
Sell some of the land.
Sell the house.

In the meantime the children returned with peeling noses, flushed with the success of the holiday; Elise and Isla were 'best friends', Tess had taken Bea shopping in Turin and they'd bought matching leather belts, and Sandy had spent the whole day in ski school, where he had apparently become friends with a llama – Juliet didn't really understand, two-year-olds not being the best reporters of their own lives. 'Dad was on great form, Mum,' Bea told Juliet, the first evening, as they sat on a faded rug playing Uno in front of the fire in the chilly sitting room, each edging as close to the flames as possible. 'I think he's much happier, if you don't mind me saying.'

'Of course I don't mind you saying. I'm really glad.' Juliet watched Sandy, toddling off to the lavatory, Isla proudly holding his hand.

Bea blinked hard, so her lids vanished, like she was making a wish. 'They both said the divorce should be smooth, Mum – it will be, won't it?'

'It's not your thing to worry about. It will be OK. I promise. All things pass, Bea, you have to remember that.'

'All things?'

'Eventually, yes. Well, they have to, don't they?'

The next day Sam Hamilton got in touch.

Our appointee has dropped out. Would you be able to come in for an interview? – Sam

Chapter Twenty-Six

There's a smell to art galleries, one Juliet could never quite identify. Perhaps it's linseed, or a special cleaning fluid, or new carpets. Something fresh and clean. She loved it, anyway.

It was pleasant, sitting in Sam Hamilton's white, clean office at the Fentiman Gallery, the Oxford traffic blocked out, the only sound that of birdsong. Dawnay's had smelled of musty old books and heavy perfume. She inhaled and looked out of the window which gave out over a small courtyard, where yellow winter flowering jasmine festooned itself over railings. Juliet had given herself a pep talk in the car. *Be calm. Don't talk for the sake of saying something. He's probably a nice person now. Don't mention Ginny.*

She repeated it again to herself now. *Be calm. He's probably nice* – as the door opened and Sam Hamilton came in, hand outstretched. 'Hi, Juliet. Good morning, thank you so much for coming in. Sorry to keep you waiting. An important call . . .' He shook her hand firmly. 'So it *is* you. Hey. You look exactly the same.'

Juliet stood up, shaking his hand, and stared at him as much as she could without showing her surprise for she, on the other hand, wouldn't have recognised him in the street. He had been a rangy Canadian grunge boy with a backpack who wore sandals and thick mountaineering socks, and had long hair hanging in curtains in front of his eyes. His hair was still dark brown, almost black, but it was short. He was very tall, dressed in a well-fitted dark suit and open-necked shirt.

Wrongfooted, she heard herself say, 'Yes, it's me. How many art historian Juliet Horners do you imagine there are?'

'I should imagine plenty, wouldn't you? Oh, of course. You think you have a particularly unusual name, I recall.' He sat down, gesturing for her to do the same, watching her with dancing eyes and she saw he was enjoying this. 'So, how are you, Juliet?'

'I'm well, thanks.' Juliet said, suddenly. 'I am – I don't remember you being this tall.'

He unscrewed a fountain pen, and scribbled something on a memo pad in front of him. 'Yeah. Well, it's fair to say at college I distracted myself from homesickness by channelling Brett Anderson as much as I could. That meant stooping a lot. Art college pop stars and Seattle guitarists don't tend to stand up straight.' He shrugged. She noticed he had a lock of hair at the front which occasionally fell into his eyes, almost a harking back to earlier grunge days.

'There was a lot of greasy hair around then,' Juliet said. 'Not yours, I'm sure. Then, or now.' She trailed off, astounded that despite her car pep talk she had still managed, within ninety seconds of greeting him, to say three embarrassing things. 'Thank you very much for meeting me.'

'But of course. There was some confusion in-house about the guy we appointed. It was set in motion before I joined and it went on for months. His references didn't check out, and no one had spotted this. I had to unpick it and it took a while . . .' He smiled somewhat cautiously across the desk at her. 'So. I'd have had you in anyway, if you hadn't emailed.'

'That's really kind of you.'

'I wasn't being kind. I'm only sorry for the to-ing and fro-ing. We'd be thrilled to have someone of your calibre.' He smiled again, then tapped his fountain pen on the desk. 'I don't remember you being this coy at Oxford.'

'I'm not being coy,' said Juliet, wishing the weird energy in the room would dissipate. Perhaps this had been a mistake.

Sam Hamilton was notorious amongst her friends for being literally the most superior person they'd ever come across. When he dumped her friend Ginny after four dates, he'd said it was because she was quite intelligent compared to him. 'Quite Intelligent' became their catchphrase for everything they wanted to damn with faint praise.

He'd come from Canada as a Rhodes scholar to her comparatively scruffy Oxford college and he had also been the only person she knew, apart from herself, who delighted in its high Victoriana: the Pugin-esque arches, purple stone, the Dalbeattie-inspired wooden interiors. Sam had also studied Art History and so, long after the famous dumping of Ginny and the calling her Quite Intelligent, to her annoyance Juliet found she kept being thrown together with him.

He seemed to want to let you *know* how clever he was, which in a place where everyone was there because they'd already proved they were clever was a big no-no. He was dark, intense, sarcastic, aping the art-school bands he loved. (Not Blur. She remembered him once, laughing bitterly at a guy in the bar who asked if he liked Blur.) Justine Frischmann was his ideal woman, as he kept telling everyone, and everyone else, who thought he was weird, would nod politely. He talked about himself too much. They used to mimic him to cheer Ginny up. 'I'm from Oddawah. It's got more PhDs per square mile than any other Canadian city.'

But at the same time he had a sardonic side, a way of smiling that pricked pomposities. She had seen him once pointing out to a Piers Gaveston-esque type – who had been loudly hectoring a porter about letting his girlfriend into college – that his boxer shorts were bunched up over his trousers, before quietly melting away, tucking his hair behind his ears with a self-satisfied flick. She often saw him with the porters, or down at the pubs in town where students didn't drink. Sometimes when Juliet took herself out for a walk away from her books, she'd bump into him coming across Christ Church Meadows, or lingering in backstreets, admiring the architecture of the vast Victorian villas at the edge of town. 'Oh, hi,' he'd say, Walkman headphones on, raising his hand and smiling at her in a curious way, then walking on with no further attempts at conversation.

It was as though he found all these British people mildly hilarious, straight out of central casting. Juliet alone felt she saw this, knew that he was laughing at them.

Only once had she seen him discomposed. She had asked him to move out of the way rather late at night at a Commemoration Ball – he was blocking her exit into the quad, where a young man was waiting for her. Sam had been at the ball she assumed for he was in black tie, the bow tie unfastened. He was leaning against the stone doorway. He'd nodded, expression unreadable in the dark, and then he'd said:

'*Dull sublunary lovers' love.*'

'What?' she'd screeched at him, as 'Boom! Shake the Room' echoed around the panelled corridor. 'Dull what?'

He seemed to hesitate. 'Oh. Well, I said dull—'

Juliet didn't want to waste time – she had been after Hugo for a term, and he was the kind of bloke who if you didn't pounce fast would simply wander off and nab someone else to snog. 'Oh God. You always have to be so superior, don't you?' she said, briskly. 'Could you just please get out of my way?'

'Right. Juliet.' He had stared at her, his dark eyes large, his face pale in the floodlit archway and for some reason this image of him had stayed with her afterwards. 'I'm so sorry. Yes. Of course.'

'Thank you,' she said, pushing past him.

When she'd reported this back to Ginny the next day, Ginny had raised her tangled head of hair above her duvet and said in a low croaking voice:

'Sam Ham's a rando. One of those guys who *thinks* he's better than you but also has to *tell* you he's better than you. He's a pratt. He was a great kisser though. I mean the best snog I've ever had. Which is annoying.'

Dull sublunary lovers' love. Juliet thought of this now with a smile. She wondered what had happened to Ginny. She'd gone off her when, in their final year they'd lived together and she'd turned out to be one of those people who minds about the washing up. She made Juliet pay extra for washing-up liquid because Juliet liked her tea really strong; Ginny said this left tannic stains around her mugs that were harder to clean. The last Juliet had heard of her she was a vicar of four different parishes in Yorkshire. She wondered how hard the water in Yorkshire was – and then, with a start, realised Sam Hamilton was talking again.

'. . . acquired the archive last month, in fact, at auction. I *say* auction, but we were the only bidders. He's not the star he once was, although I remember you like him too.'

Juliet took a wild guess. 'Dalbeattie? Yes, I'm – I love him.' She pulled herself together. 'Sorry. You've acquired his archive? I'd heard it was up for auction. That's thrilling.'

'Isn't it? I love the guy. I'm from Ottawa, that's where he ended up, you know.' It didn't sound funny any more. *Oddawah.* Maybe it never had been. Maybe she'd been a cow at college – Juliet shifted in her seat.

'Yes, I remember. So sad. Such a tragedy. I often wonder why he went there.'

'Why? Why shouldn't he?'

'Oh, because he should have had everything here, I think. Something obviously happened. Marvellous as Ottawa is.'

'Ha.' He laughed, lifting his eyes to hers. 'I can't wait to look through the archive. He kept notes on everything. Every last detail.'

'Oh yes. That's what I love about being at Nightingale House – the detail. He thought of everything. Hooks on the back of every door, hinged window seats in every room so there's storage for everyone, the bird boxes outside . . .'

'So you do live there now,' he said, and he leaned forward in his chair, hands clasped together. The light from the courtyard caught his right cheekbone, played in his dark hair. 'Juliet, that's wonderful.'

'Yes,' Juliet said, and she folded her arms. 'Yes, I was made – I left Dawnay's, as you probably heard. I inherited the house around the same time so we moved here in July.'

'How great for your family to grow up there.'

'Well I think so.' She was laughing.

'Why's it funny?'

'They're not so sure, not just yet. But I think it's great.'

'I came to Nightingale House once, you know.'

'Really? When?'

'At Oxford. My mom and dad had come over to see me and they were so excited. You know, my dad hadn't ever left Canada before.' His face split into a smile at the memory. 'Yeah. A very cross lady opened the door and when I asked if it was Dalbeattie's house she said yes it was and then slammed it in my face.'

Juliet laughed, despite feeling embarrassed. 'Oh, no. I'm so sorry. She didn't like Dalbeattie, for some reason.'

'My dad was quite impressed. He kept saying afterwards, "Well, she was a real old broad, wasn't she?"'

'That'd be my grandmother. Stella Horner.'

'Of course. The daughter who's not in the painting. I always forget her.' He nodded his head slightly.

'Well, she was born after my great-grandfather died,' said Juliet, inexplicably nettled by this. She thought of Stella's exercise book filled with instructions which Juliet kept by her bed, the large handwriting, the careful notes. 'Almost nine months to the day. They were very old – my great-grandmother would have been forty-four. She's not the lost daughter, she's just the – the surprise.'

'OK. Well. The archive arrived just after New Year. Kate Nadin, our archivist, hasn't got to it yet, she broke her ankle over Christmas and she's been off. I can't resist though, I keep going in and opening up boxes. She'll be furious with me.'

'Wow. How exciting.' Despite herself Juliet's eyes lit up. 'What's in there?'

'Oh, you'll have to come look. There are wonderful letters between Dalbeattie and Ned Horner. The hours he slaved over it, transforming the place for his friend, and Ned – well, he was quite a worrier, that guy. And Dalbeattie died pretty young, really. He just seemed like a wonderful man.'

His enthusiasm was infectious. 'He was. I think our house taught him a lot. And Ned, as well. He always said that the house inspired him as much as anything else.'

A swift half-smile crossed Sam's face. 'Oh. Of course. I'd forgotten.'

'Forgotten what?'

'You and your Horner thing.'

'What are you talking about?'

His eyes danced again. 'How do I put this, Juliet? You rather tended to namedrop Ned Horner.'

'No I didn't!'

'Oh, you did. Like he was more famous than Elvis, and no one cared, no one but me, and you ignored me for, like, the whole year!'

'We – we were talking about Horner, it's entirely relevant!' She looked at him, not sure if he was joking. 'Me ignore you? You – wow! You dumped my best friend.'

'She was a tightwad. And she snored.'

'You told her she was stupid.'

A shadow crossed his face; he put his hand swiftly to his forehead, then down on the desk again. He looked quite shaken. 'I'm sorry. That's not cool. Poor – what was her name?'

'Ginny. You can't even remember her name.'

'It was almost twenty years ago. Wow. Well, I'm sorry. What's she – what's she up to now?'

'Oh, you know,' said Juliet, vaguely. 'This. And . . .'

'That?'

'Yes, that.'

'You don't know where she is, and she's supposedly a great friend of yours. Well OK.'

'I do,' said Juliet, her subconscious suddenly snapping into action. 'Pickering.' She had no idea where this had come from, and knew it was right, but no idea why. 'She's – she lives in Pickering. She's a vicar.'

'I'm sorry,' said Sam, after a moment. 'This isn't a very professional way to conduct an interview. I apologise. I guess I was nervous, seeing you again.'

'No, no, I'm sorry,' said Juliet. 'Really, I'm being so rude. You're supposed to be interviewing *me*.'

'I just didn't really get that you'd moved here, that's all. Much less that you'd want a job with us.'

'I have three children and I'm getting divorced. I have to work. And besides' – she shook her head, and she could hear her voice breaking a little – 'I *want* to work.'

Sam Hamilton looked at her. 'Let me try and conduct an actual interview for a few minutes, shall I? I do actually have questions from the board that I'm supposed to ask potential employees.' He spoke in a monotone. 'What are you most proud of in your professional life?'

Juliet thought for a moment, and then smiled.

'What's so funny?'

'Nothing.' She'd been about to say: *potty-training Sandy.* 'I suppose it's finding a Millais sketch in an antiques shop in Banbury.'

'No way.'

'Yes way. It paid for our first car.'

He was watching her with that curious intensity of his, but now he leaned forward. 'I don't mean to be rude,' he said. 'Shouldn't it be relatively easy for someone like you to spot one of his sketches? You're Juliet Horner. I was reading yesterday how you paid for the cleaning of that murky landscape at the Tate out of your own pocket and it turned out to be a William Dyce.'

'I did. And you're right. But this—' She shook her head. 'We'd gone into the shop because my husband saw an old enamel Bialetti sign for sale in the window. We woke the kids up from the car, so they were truly horrifically grumpy. They were screaming in the background and – sorry. Do you have kids?'

He shook his head. 'No. I got divorced last year. I'd . . .' He trailed off. 'It didn't work out that way.'

'Oh,' said Juliet, wishing she'd never asked. 'It's just . . .' She cleared her throat.

'Just what?'

'Well,' she said, awkwardly. 'With kids, it's like Whack-a-Mole, you know? Keeping one down before the other one pops up again. And there were only two of them then. We were driving back in a hire car from Matt's old colleague's wedding and we'd had a huge row about –' her hands stole to her burning red cheeks – 'something else, so there's then a third tension about who's looking out for them, and I can tell you the husband never, *ever* looks out for them. Sorry,' she said, raising her hands at Sam.

'Don't apologise. The patriarchy hurts us all,' he said, nodding, half joking, half serious.

'Well thank you. So you're in an antiques shop piled high with crystal punch bowls and china shepherdesses with two tired hungry children and your husband thinks he can haggle with an antiques dealer who doesn't believe in haggling. And you keep seeing these sketches, on rough paper, in the corner of the shop stacked on top of a bureau, and there's just something about the top one – it's like a high-pitched buzz in your ear . . . Something special. So you spot an old girls' school annual and give it to the nine-year-old, and a wicker basket, and a teddy bear, and you tell the two-year-old she can put the teddy to bed with your scarf. You give them the scarf. That gives you about forty seconds, max, to flick through the drawings before they kick off again. And the first few sketches, they're lovely, but it's the fourth one you see, there's just something, *something* about the shading, the expression in the girl's eyes, the way the hands are treated . . . you get that prickling feeling, on the neck, and you're there, right there – and now your youngest child is yelling about Frozen and clinging to your leg and it's over.' She glanced at him. 'Honestly, you'd have been proud of discovering it, if it was you.' She shrugged.

Sam was nodding. 'Wow. Yep, I would.'

'It's not rocket science. Like you say, I should have known.'

'Well, you tell it well then,' he said. He stood up, and went to look out of the window, his arms folded. He didn't say anything for a moment. 'Can I say something? I said you look the same, but you're really quite different than you were at Oxford.'

'How so?'

'I don't know.' He shrugged. 'We all got each other wrong, perhaps. I wasn't very happy there actually. I was pretty lonely.'

'You seemed to know everything. You didn't seem like you wanted friends.'

'That's funny. I did. Desperately. I didn't fit in.'

'It's not a finishing school. I wasn't anyone interesting. I was from a North London comp and I went there.'

'You'd be surprised, though,' he said, and she nodded at the same time.

'You're right.' She curled back against the chair. 'I am sorry. If you didn't have a good time. I should have been more friendly. Especially like you say because we did actually have interests in common, as they say. I don't suppose I was that happy, either. I was convinced I was ugly and stupid and my parents moved to France literally the day after I went to university like they couldn't wait to be shot of parenting. I didn't have a home any more, so I'd stay with my grandmother in the holidays. And everyone else was so incredibly clever and posh, and I was sure I wouldn't get a job afterwards.'

'Wow. It doesn't matter. Hey, everyone's going through stuff, right?'

'They are. Always.'

'Listen, it's great to see you again, Juliet.' Sam leaned across, holding out his hand. 'We're lucky to have someone like you coming into the area. You know it. The board asked me to ask you if you'd take three days a week to start with, moving to five if we get the Arts Council funding we want for the extension.'

'I don't understand.'

'I'm offering you a job. Sorry. Was that not clear?'

'Of course it's not clear,' said Juliet, laughing. 'That's wonderful!'

'You're Juliet Horner,' he said, waggling his outstretched hand so she'd take it. 'We'd be mad not to hire you. It was a slam dunk.'

'What?'

'It was obvious.'

'I like this board.'

'So you should. They like you. We need your help. Aside from the extension and the Dalbeattie archive, we're mounting an exhibition of Horner's sketches in 2019—'

'Really?'

'Yes. We've asked Julius Irons to loan us *The Garden of Lost and Found* sketch.'

'My goodness. Do you think he will?'

'After the level of outcry about his taking it out of the country and stuffing it in some vault I think he'll have to say yes. I heard he's told people he overpaid for it. Early signs are encouraging, put it that way.'

'Sam!' Juliet's smile split her cheeks into apples. 'I – that's absolutely wonderful. That's – that's great! To have it hanging here . . . I accept. Don't care what the job is.' They grinned at each other.

'Reunited over Edwardian art.'

'Victorian. Summer 1900.'

'There you go again, showing off about your relative.' He stood up.

Juliet ignored this. 'Thank you for seeing me. And about the painting. It's wonderful news. When can I start?'

'February third would be great, actually.'

'Great. Thank you again – and Ham? Sam. Sam Ham? Oh, dear. I'm sorry again. And for making you sound like a Dr Seuss book.'

'It happens all the time back home. It's mainly why I moved over here. So let's have a clean slate, shall we?'

'I long for a clean slate. I dream of clean slates. Piles of 'em,' said Juliet. 'That sounds great.'

And for the second time, a little too enthusiastically, she shook his hand, smiling at him.

Chapter Twenty-Seven

February

Check the guttering in February, Juliet. The leaves have often turned to mulch, they block the old pipes. Do it three times. Once in November, once in January, once now. Three times. Any leaves you clear can be put on the soil, but make sure it's not too wet or it will freeze and harm your poor plants even more. Enjoy the bulbs you planted, the narcissi and the snowdrops. The evenings are lighter. I do not fear winter. I revel in its quietude, in the feeling the earth is sleeping.

Spring is coming. It's not here yet, but it's coming. There are secrets in the soil. Buried deep, waiting to burst up, out, into the open.

Juliet had always hated February – the sound of it, like a taunt. *Februareeeee*. But here, even now, when the branches were bare and the days still so short, she found joy in every day. The stark contrast of the black trees against the pale-blue sky; the small mists on the valley in the mornings, curling and hugging the undulating wold. And, everywhere, the feeling of waiting. Treacle-brown buds, almost ready to open, and the dark earth, rich, thick with dead leaves and worms and a winter's worth of clean rain.

She suppressed a yawn as she steered the car round a bend. Winter had sapped some of her energy. She'd been up at five-thirty, clearing the leaves from the guttering – she had done it twice, once in autumn, once before Christmas, and almost hadn't got up to do it that morning. But Grandi always said it needed to be done three times, and the plumbing at Nightingale House had proved to be so erratic that Juliet was terrified of angering it when it might be avoidable. She'd learned over the winter that if you put off small jobs, they had a habit of swiftly turning into big problems. The previous day she had slipped on the stones on the terrace.

Hi Ev can I ask you something else? What can I use to clean the terrace stones? They're slimy and green and disgusting and I slipped on them y'day. I can't use bleach can I?

Ju mate hi. Don't use bleach no way that will kill lichen / get into plant roots when rains. Jeyes fluid is OK.

Thanks hope you're good. X

I am. You can plant fruit trees now it's cold. Make sure the hole is deep & root ball has space. Plant a damson tree always wanted one of them ;) see you in summer

She was able to look back on winter, now it was on the way out: it had been wild, wet, too warm, not the crisp, glittering affair she had hoped for: she'd kept wrapping up in cosy knits and lighting the smoking, sputtering fire and would find she was hot, uncomfortable, wet. Always wet. The rain created new problems all the time. The french doors from the dining room and the study were swollen shut and wouldn't open, the stream at the bottom of the Wilderness had burst its banks, and the grass was waterlogged, the plants in the lower borders drowned in mud. Two apple trees had lost large branches which simply cracked clean away and were carried along by the water before jamming further downstream. Only last week a huge branch from an oak tree that shaded the house had torn off and crashed into the Birdsnest on the top floor, smashing one of Bea's bedroom windows – thankfully, while she was at school.

'I could have had a day off school if it hit me,' she'd said, grumpily. 'It's not *fair*.'

Juliet had laughed. 'Of all the things in life that aren't fair, you not being seriously injured by a fallen tree and thus having to go to school is not one of them.'

The tree looked wholly sad now, the custard-and-orange wood revealed beneath the missing bark a strange, unseemly contrast with all that black and green, and the grey graves now visible over the yew trees.

Every morning, new jobs to do, new crises fomented during the nights. When she thought of how she and Matt used to row over whose turn it was to replace a lightbulb and whether they should put Sellotape on the scart cable to help it stay in the TV she wanted to laugh.

Should she have made leaf mould? What *was* leaf mould? What did you do with all the browning apples you'd picked and neatly stored? How did you insulate a bedroom window that rattled so loudly at night it woke your child up? What were you supposed to do if you saw a hedgehog being rolled around the lawn by a fox? Would there ever not be mice?

You left me plenty of instructions, but it turns out not quite enough.

Juliet slowed down to let a horsebox pass, crushing her car against the hedgerow. When she'd first got here in those dog days of summer, she had been terrified of the narrow lanes, the heavy farm machinery that lumbered out at you around corners, of the mud-spattered Land Rovers, bashed about and rusting, dogs sitting in the back. She had never really cared about her car: in fact only that very day, walking away from the Fentiman, absorbed in conversation with Sam Ham about a new painting by Holman Hunt that had suddenly come on the market, she couldn't remember where she'd parked it.

'It's been over-restored – a huge pity, as I think the layers underneath would have revealed – what's wrong, Juliet?'

Juliet was patting her pockets, as if that would help. 'My car. I can't find my car.'

'Oh. I won't ask if you're sure you parked it here.'

'I really did. I saw you on the way in, remember?'

'Of course.' Sam turned to his two-seater sports car, nodded, then turned back, hand clasped to the back of his head, which she had learned was how he thought best. 'Could it be . . . the next road? They're very similar.'

'No, I remember this yellow front door. I'm already late for Bea,' she said, trying not to sound panicked. She had set in stone with her daughter a date every Friday, where they'd make supper and then pick a film for the four of them to watch. Today Bea was making spinach and chickpea casserole and Juliet had promised to bring back some smoked paprika. Cooking together was the only time of the week Bea ever told her anything. Juliet had mastered the art of extracting information: it was all about the long game. If her daughter had given too much away the previous week (anything from the fixable: 'Miss Wrexham says my long shore drift diagrams are way off and I need to practise them' to the unknowable from last week: 'A girl at school said she liked me and she's bi though I actually think that's just something she says to sound cool, and anyway when I was at Dad's last weekend Fin and I had a chat about being exclusive'), sometimes, though it killed her, Juliet wouldn't ask her anything the following week. So Bea never realised the whole operation was to get her to want to talk. And it was working: she'd got more out of Bea the last month than the previous year. Her daughter amazed her. Juliet chewed her lip, eyes darting up and back along the street. This was why the Friday cooking session was so important.

She stared up at Sam in dismay. 'Do you think someone's stolen it?'

'Perhaps.' Sam got out his phone. 'It's rife at the moment. Look, I'll call the police, then I'll call you a cab.'

'Thanks. Let me just walk up the road again.' They walked up and down the street. 'Why would they steal my car and not your Audi, that's what I want to know.' Juliet glanced up the road, pushing her hair out of her eyes. 'I – oh my God.'

'What?' Sam looked up in alarm. 'Do you see them?' He gripped her arm.

She spotted her silver Škoda with shock, seeing it for the first time as others must: windscreen covered in dead dried leaves and bird shit, scrapes wiggling like thin streamers along the metalwork from bonnet to boot, one wing mirror hanging on by a thread, the result of a close encounter with a tractor when she was racing to collect the children from Matt.

'No . . .' she said. 'I see it. Bad car,' she said, thumping the car crossly on the roof when she reached it. 'Naughty!' She turned to Sam. 'God, I'm so sorry.'

Sam raised his eyebrows, chewing the inside of his mouth. He seemed to do this often, as though he found her intensely alarming, or as though he were trying not to laugh at something. 'No harm, no foul.' He touched her arm, as she climbed into the car. 'It's all good. All good. Thank you for a great first week, Juliet.'

She was coming to the crossroads, where three old grain stores of the old Tooker Farm were being converted into luxury accommodation. A large truck with a smart logo on the side had got stuck in the entrance, unable to make the turn from the lane. In the opposite field, a farmer dressed in rubber dungarees was shaking food into one of the troughs, pushing the pigs that crowded round him away. Juliet wound down her window.

'What's it now?' she said.

'They're putting in the tiles for the swimming pool today,' said Tom, shaking out the last of the scraps. 'Mediterranean glaze. All the way from Italy.' He had a reddish face, a grizzled, balding head and sparkling blue eyes.

'Very nice,' said Juliet, solemnly, and they were both silent for a moment, gazing across at the construction site as the pigs behind him grunted and squealed, jostling for food.

'Isla's welcome to come back any time,' Tom said. 'Grace loved having her, she wants her to come for a sleepover,' Juliet nodded, pleased. 'Debs is taking Grace swimming tomorrow. Have a word with her about it then,' and he turned back to his animals, social niceties over.

'Thanks,' Juliet called, and drove on. At first she'd found it hard to know what to say to people who weren't just strangers but whose lives were completely different to hers. So she'd learned less was more. Everything at home in London had been so high-octane – this playdate, that friendship group, this party, that secondary school. Always pushing, always going for more. But she had gone to pick up Isla from Grace's house a few weeks ago, just after they'd gone back to school, and found another one of these trucks stuck in the lane again, this time bringing Carrara marble for the bathrooms.

Debs and the girls had appeared in the lane to tell her to back up and leave the car on a verge a hundred metres back.

'Sure.' Juliet had sniffed – she had a cold.

'Yes,' Debs had said, solemnly, and though Juliet's nose was totally blocked she could still smell the faint stench of pig and pig farm. 'Pigs are very clean animals, you know, but the smell of all that manure is disgusting. So's what they eat. Took me years to get used to it.'

'Can you smell it from the house?' Juliet had asked, as they'd walked up to the Tolleys' farmhouse together, Isla and Grace running behind them, dodging in and out behind the trees that lined the path, the family's collie jumping ahead of them with joy.

'Us? No, we're high up on the hill. The wind blows it down, away from us. Always has done. Why do you think they built the house up there all those years ago?'

Juliet looked down at the barns. 'What about those new houses, then? Won't they be exactly downwind of the smell of your pigs?'

'Yep,' said Tom, with a straight face. 'But the property chap who bought old Tooker Farm for a song, did he ever come to introduce himself, talk to us about it? Has he ever apologised for the noise and the traffic, and their SUVs blocking everything, and the people on their phones shouting and these guys from Oxford and London swarming everywhere in their smart suits? Have they thought of the fact there's twenty gallons of pig shit being produced every day less than twenty metres from where they want to have their luxury barns?'

And he started to grin, broadly and Debs smiled, and Juliet, too. 'Oh that's great,' she said. 'That's just bloody great.'

The new truck showed no signs of being able to remove itself, but Juliet was able to squeeze past and she did, the encounter with Tom leaving her with a warm glow inside despite the chill of the wind. Nearly home. In a few minutes the turnoff to Farmhouse: Space loomed on her left, and Juliet peered nosily in, just in case. There was always the chance you might spot some celebrity arriving, though more likely it was a cab dropping off some glossy-haired media people. It had opened in September, and was the talk of Godstow; who'd applied for membership, who had been spotted there.

Of course, George was a member – he would be, though Frederic refused to go, saying it wasn't his kind of place. George loved it; he'd asked Bea if she'd like to go there with him for a cocktail, and she would have gone, had Juliet not put a stop to it. 'She's fifteen, George. OK?'

'She could do with a night out.'

'With other fifteen-year-olds.'

George had rolled his eyes. 'Boring.'

Juliet had been to Farmhouse: Space once, before Christmas, for a drink with two mums from Bea's class – both London escapees whose husbands' business interests had taken a tumble and who needed to downsize. It was obvious this was an audition to see whether Juliet might become One of Them, but if so she had failed. She desperately coveted the style of the place, the casual yet studied boho chic – Moroccan wall hangings, faded turquoise tiles on the terrace, Bloomsbury-era fabrics on the cushions, the smell of jasmine and grapefruit everywhere – but it all felt totally unreal, and after five minutes she got fidgety, as the other two women droned on about house prices and how great it was to be out of London and whether the local school was good enough for Jagger and Bay and then one of the mums, the taller one with long, long

309

blond hair and a large-ish nose, had turned to her and said, in her London–LA drawl:

'So, is it a problem for anyone, Bea being gay? I don't have a problem with it of *course*.'

Juliet found herself staring at her clear, dewy skin. How did you get skin like that? 'Not that I know of. I've talked to her teachers. We've focused on making sure she believes her family loves her, it doesn't change anything else for us.'

'Right. So good. Because so many people down here aren't as enlightened as London. Different attitudes. And Bay-bay said Bea had had a difficult time settling in, wasn't making many friends yet. I just wondered if you'd had any comments about it from some of the parents.'

'Oh, yeah,' the other mother had chipped in, her face a rictus of concern.

'No, none at all.' Juliet could feel herself stiffening. 'She – it's been a tough year for her.'

'*I* don't have a problem with it,' said the other mum. 'I think it's *really* great.'

'Great?'

'That she's gay. I mean – you know. I totally get you. I'd find it really hard if it was Zalie, or Coco, *obviously*, but Bea doesn't really seem to care about being popular, does she? Which is great.'

'Oh. Well . . . she—'

'Oh my God. Did you hear about those Moo lodges, down towards Stroud? James says they're seriously incredible. He thinks we should go and look at one this weekend.' And with a wave of her hand the subject was over.

Juliet had made her excuses and left as soon as she could. Farmhouse: Space was not for her.

She'd got the paprika. The film she was going to suggest they all watched was *Lilo and Stitch*, though Bea always ignored Juliet's suggestions. Juliet turned into the lane, feeling a glow of anticipation. The rest of the weekend stretched out ahead of her: they were going to go swimming, then it was Sandy's third-birthday tea, and Juliet had invited three friends of his round from nursery: George, Charlotte and Arthur (Juliet noted with interest and amusement the fact that no one in London had children with the same names as the royal family, whereas in Godstow, down-from-Londoners aside, it was practically the law.) And spring was coming. It was.

In the lane above the house she saw a woman walking towards her. She waved, and pulled into a siding, winding the window down.

'Honor! Hello!'

'Hi, darling. I was just leaving you a note.'

'Oh. Come in for a cup of tea.'

'I won't, thanks,' said Honor, zipping her jacket up and plunging her hands into her pockets. She shook her ash-blonde crop, vigorously. 'I'm walking back. Bryan's making curry.'

Juliet got out of the car, and gave Honor a hug. 'Good weather for it.'

'Absolutely, only he insists on making it far too hot, and I can only eat two bites at a time . . . anyway.'

'Honor, you think carrots have too strong a flavour.'

'Well, carrots are awful,' said that lady now. 'Hideous. They're wet and crunchy at the same time. Listen, I had a nice chat with your lovely Bea. She was chopping up onions and weeping copiously, poor lamb. Haven't you got her well-trained. I couldn't have got Ev to cook at that age, not for all the tea in China.' She smiled at Juliet.

'How is he?' said Juliet. 'Have you heard from him?'

'He's planning to come for a visit, in June, after the job's finished.'

'Please, do tell him to come. We have to catch up properly. I want him to see the garden again. Tell me what to do with it.'

'That's why I came over actually. I was going to ask if you want me to pop back some time and we can walk through the whole plot, and work out what to plant.'

Grandi and Honor both maintained Ev had his love of gardens from Nightingale House, but his ability and flair came from his mother, who had created from a grassy field at the side of their converted barn a stunning formal garden hung around with hibiscus to remind Bryan of Jamaica. 'Oh wow, would you?' said Juliet. 'I'd be so grateful. I cleared a lot of dead wood, before Christmas, and I've been feeding the soil. The bulbs are starting to come up, but it's things like perennials and seedlings and what to grow in the veg garden and the greenhouse. And what's going to last. I don't want to re-create Grandi's garden. I can't.'

'Nor should you. That was based on Liddy's Victorian garden, and it was all roses and violets and rhododendrons. Lovely, but awfully blowsy. I'll come over this weekend, how about that?'

'It's Sandy's birthday,' Juliet said, grimacing, but she was glad, almost – proud of the melee of events. Birthdays, gardening, swimming, Friday night film nights . . . She reached out and grabbed Honor's hand. 'Come for some cake, will you? Bring Bryan. He hasn't met them all properly.'

'Oh I'd love that. So would he. Oh, you are clever.' Honor leaned on the window of the car. 'I'm so glad you're back. Your father – well, pshaw. But Stella would be *so* happy.'

'I feel at home here. Properly, totally at home, even though I'm not very happy a lot of the time. The two are separate, you know?' She stared at Honor almost wildly, wanting her to understand, desperately hoping she would. That someone would. 'I am just not sure . . . for the kids . . . that it was the right thing. And I don't know when someone rings the bell and says, "Ding ding! That was the correct route to take!"'

'Course it was,' said Honor, stoutly. 'You're doing what all women do. You're confusing what's best for you with what's best for your children. We'll come for cake, but how about next weekend for the gardening? Be prepared for me to be brutal.' Juliet gave a mock grimace.

'I can take it.'

'You can take anything. I think, darling, you underestimate yourself. I mean your father is my oldest friend but I do think he and your mother could have paid you a visit by now and shown you some support. I've told him so. Have a glass of wine this evening. Tell yourself you're bloody great.'

Juliet drove on, smiling, and turned into the driveway of the house, her mind running over things. *Divorce papers. Colin the caterpillar birthday cake. Socks. Tampons. Call back the window man.*

'Hi!' she called, as she let herself in. Annie, Mrs Beadle's grand-daughter, had picked up Isla and Sandy and was watching TV with them. Juliet sniffed, inhaling the welcome smell of onions and garlic.

'Hiiiii,' the two youngest children called back dully, not really paying attention. She could see them sprawled on the beanbag, glazed expressions fixed on the TV. Sandy was still in his coat. Juliet picked up the post and wandered through the dining room, noting it was still light, noting too the condensation on the windows, which meant some heat must be being kept in. She came into the kitchen.

'Here's your paprika. Um – how much TV is Annie letting them watch, Bea?' She looked up. 'Oh God, Bea! What's wrong, darling?' She dropped the post on the counter and went over to her daughter.

Bea was standing in the middle of the room, holding a wooden spatula, her face red with silent crying. Juliet folded her in her arms. 'Darling? Darling!'

Bea couldn't speak for a while. She juddered, and said quietly: 'M-Mum!'

'What's wrong? Tell me.'

'You said every-every thing w-w-would p-pass,' she said, even-tually. 'You said it would get b-better.'

Dismay, fear, filled Juliet, inflating inside her like a balloon. 'It does, darling. I believe that.' She kissed Bea's head. 'Promise. Is it Fin? What's happened?'

'Argh!' Bea pushed her away, and retreated to the back of the kitchen. A piece of the old fabric which acted as a door covering the pots got caught in the zip of her boot, and tore away from the counter. Bea looked down at it, crying even harder. 'This *stupid bloody house*! It's not Fin. You're always *saying* all this stuff, and it's rubbish.'

Juliet mechanically picked up a pair of kitchen scissors and began cutting off some gaffer tape. She held out the piece of tape, on one finger, and picked up the torn fabric. 'I'll fix it. What's happened? Please tell me, darling.'

'Do you know why Dad's pushing the divorce?'

'No, darling. W-why?'

'Tess. She's pregnant. She's having the b-baby in August.'

Juliet dropped the fabric, and the gaffer tape she was clutching flew up on to her hair, sticking grimly and twisting itself around. She pulled at it. 'What?'

'Tess. She and Dad are having a baby. It's due in the summer.' Bea had twined her hands together. 'I knew something was up last weekend. He was being really weird. He kept asking me stuff, about the divorce, and she was crying and she didn't eat anything. And – and I rang him . . . just now . . . he said . . . he said they'd both wanted it and he was going to t-t-t-tell you to tell us this weekend.' Her hair was in her face; she pushed it ineffectually away, then batted at it angrily when it fell back over her eyes. 'How – I – I just . . . I just want it to stop!'

'Oh my love.' Juliet pulled at her hair, her fingers clumsy. 'Well.' She took a deep breath. 'You're going to have a little sister or brother!'

'I don't *want* a little sister or brother . . . I want it to all be the same again, Mum . . .'

Juliet tugged at her hair again, then went over to her. 'Darling. Oh my love. It's OK. It's more than OK.'

It wasn't OK at all though. It was shit.

It was shit of Tess to get pregnant, shit of Matt to impregnate her, it was shit that Tess's own two kids had to deal with having a new baby in their life on top of everything else – her own children, too, who were more insulated from it, but still. Babies were a blessing, they said. But, as Juliet's mother had once darkly muttered, 'Of course that's what they tell you, because they need us all to believe it.' The tone in her voice was what Juliet remembered.

The house in Dulcie Street was too small for three children: she

314

knew that better than anyone. Robert, Tess's ex, was a bully and would use this against them – Juliet saw, with clarity now, why Matt had been after her for money, why he was pushing the divorce . . . And she saw, looking down the long years, the difficulty of another baby, the screaming, the tiredness and rows over division of chores, the fragility of this new relationship, Tess's brittle character, Matt's childishness, his need to be right. Saw it all, and understood what a disaster it was. This poor baby was the line drawn between the past and the future, not Juliet's leaving London. And she had to make it OK for the children – yes. Keep on keeping on.

'Dad said you'd be upset.'

'I'm really not.' She stopped pulling at the tape which was now a tacky ball in her hair, and smiled at her daughter. 'Darling, I think Tess is going to have her hands full. It's bloody great this baby's got a half-sister who is as kind and cool and wonderful as you.'

She reached out and picked up the pair of kitchen scissors, and cut off the tangled hair-tape ball. The tail-end, not caught up, dangled free, like a feather, and as she stared at it she saw, as though through a stranger's eyes, how faded her hair was. Once it had been a vivid red-gold. Now it was pale, sandy almost, all the glory in it gone. She threw it in the waste paper basket. Tomorrow she would get the rest of it cut, three or four inches.

Bea was staring at her in horror. 'Why did you do that?'

'It wouldn't have come off any other way,' said Juliet, simply, and she put the scissors down gently.

Chapter Twenty-Eight

__March,__ a month for:

cleaning the windows
sorting out the books
dusting, inside and out
wiping the wood down with a soft cloth
but most of all:
be wary of spring – it is dangerous, it creeps up on you and gives you
HOPE. Sometimes the days are like summer and the sun is hot and
you forget yourself, Juliet. You forget it's not summer yet. Be wary.

'What are you doing for Easter, Juliet?'

Juliet looked up vaguely from some papers. She twisted her hair into a bun before remembering for the hundredth time that day that it fell now just above her shoulders. 'Oh, hi, Sam.' She stared at him. 'What am I – oh yes. Well it's Good Friday tomorrow so strictly speaking we should be eating fish pie but we're having a sort of birthday slash early Easter egg hunt for Isla, it's her birthday. Secondly, I will be prising Sandy off my leg or off the floor, that's his default position at the moment.' She ticked each one off her fingers. 'Um – then I'm sorting out AirBnB stuff. And for the big finish, hopefully I'm getting divorced! Yay!' She frowned, and pushed the papers into her bag, rubbing the bridge of her nose. 'Pretty run of the mill. How about you?'

'I'm seeing friends.'

'Where?'

'They're coming to my house.'

'Oh.' Juliet kept her eyes fixed on the paper in front of her, an export request, and signed it carefully. 'That'll be nice.'

'What does that mean?' Sam demanded, suspiciously.

'That'll be nice!'

'Oh.' His shoulders slumped. 'I thought – well, after the Strategy Day some people said my house was – never mind.'

Juliet looked for another pen. 'No idea what you're talking about.'

Sam leaned against the door, and said: 'So you're one of them. I heard Priya and Briony in the kitchen last week, talking about someone who had armchairs that looked like they'd been found under a railway arch. I didn't know what they meant. But they meant me, didn't they?'

'Surely not,' she said, noncommittally.

A couple of weeks earlier Sam had had the whole team – twelve of them – over to his house in North Oxford to discuss strategy and the future direction of the museum. Juliet had been to days like this before: they usually took place in the windowless room of a London hotel, with expensive glass bottles of water and laminated folders. She was a little surprised it was at Sam's house. Though she saw him three times a week and knew he owned several actually quite well-cut suits, she still sort of thought of him as a student in an Elastica T-shirt, Birkenstocks and a backpack. If she'd thought about where he lived she'd have assumed his home was some grotty student flat peopled with other disgruntled grunge fans.

It was not. It was a large detached Arts and Crafts pile in a silent tree-lined street peppered with large cars and other signifiers of Oxford affluence (Dragon School concert posters up in the windows, Berry Bros delivery vans). Inside, it was a shell of taupe, beige and cork tiles, the previous occupants having lived there for forty years, raised their children and then downsized. Dusty rectangles on the walls marked where paintings and photographs had hung for decades. On the kitchen doorframe, pencil and biro markings of height: 'Luke, 1/4/1983. Emma, 17.5.1985.'

317

'It's got all its original features. I like the way they didn't muck about with the place,' said Sam, somewhat defensively as he showed them round.

'No, nor have you,' muttered someone – Kate the archivist, or Graham the Fundraising Director. Juliet had moved around the house, oddly touched by it, the ghosts of the previous family still so present.

'Have you just moved in?' she said.

He thought for a moment. 'Yes – oh, no. It's more than a year ago now.'

Poor Sam Ham. A packing-case was used as a side table in the sitting room and in the dining room was so much pine furniture they couldn't all get into the room at the same time. 'They had it going cheap at the charity shop. Table, six chairs, a nest of side tables, two chests of drawers. I had to get it,' he said, with enthusiasm. 'Only there's more of it than I imagined . . .'

'You've got no curtains,' Graham said, staring out of the bedroom window. 'Sam, mate, forget about buying nests. You need to get some curtains.'

Sam scratched his head. 'I haven't got round to it, yet. I ought to go to a store but work – you know. In the winter, I – look, there's this blanket. I tape it up in the bedroom.'

'Dear God,' Juliet had muttered.

The plates and mugs were a totally random assortment of charity shop purchases and slogans acquired over the years: Wayne Stock, royal weddings, Cézanne at the Tate, and some optometrist in Ottawa.

'But at least that's his stuff,' Kate, who was practical, had said.

'Barely!' Juliet held out a 'Bertams Removals' mug. 'Oh Sam. You need to work a little less and spend a weekend in John Lewis.'

'The dream,' Kate said.

'I love John Lewis,' he'd said. 'I just haven't gotten round to it. What's the point? I like coming to work.'

They'd all helped move the tangle of pine furniture out of the dining room and then they'd had a great morning, sitting around the dining table finalising strategies and throwing around ideas. It was a big, light room. There was an apple tree in the garden, a listing wooden swing.

At lunchtime, Sam had pulled a stew out of the oven and some baked potatoes and then an apple crumble with clotted cream, and they'd all had a glass of wine, and Graham had told a rather risqué story about the previous museum director and his mistress arriving out of the blue whilst they were holding a fundraising reception.

'You're a great cook,' Juliet said later in the kitchen, as they were clearing the plates away. Sam nodded.

'I'm OK. I love to cook but I don't do it so often any more. This house needs people in it.'

'It's rather huge.'

'I know. I shouldn't have rented it. But when the divorce came through I was determined to really make a go of it here. I think I saw myself living in bohemian splendour in North Oxford not – not . . .'

'Trapped in suburbia with too much pine furniture.'

'Exactly. As you can probably tell, I didn't get much stuff in the divorce.'

'Who needs stuff? You escaped with your sanity,' Juliet said. 'That's something.'

'Believe me,' he said, seriously. 'It's everything. I got out, and I don't hate her, and she doesn't hate me. That's why I don't care about the house so much.' He rinsed a plate under the tap, then plunged it into the hot water. 'You know what I mean. I don't need smart curtains or the right TV. I need to be on my own, with a good book and a glass of wine, for a while. This was obviously a happy home before me. I like sitting here and feeling that. I – I'm still getting myself together.'

She stared at him, not knowing what to say. He handed her a cloth. 'Any of that make sense?'

'All of it, Sam,' she said, and she took the plate out of the sink, shaking it off.

*

Now, Juliet said: 'These lucky guests coming for Easter, what will they be eating?'

'Twenty-four-hour marinated lamb. I found it in a Pashtu recipe book, believe it or not.'

'I do believe it. That sounds incredible.'

He gave a lopsided smile. 'I hope so. It'll be nice to have people over. Warm the place up.'

'How many?'

'Eight.'

'You'll need more dining chairs,' Juliet said seriously, biting her lip.

'I foresee a trip to the junk shop on the Cowley Road this afternoon.'

'I love that place. I bought a coat hook there of a carved wooden bird many years ago.'

'They do house clearances. People who've died, or are divorcing. You can pick up some amazing stuff.'

'I should come with you some time. I'm addicted to poking around places like that.'

'Well, that would be remarkable, were you to come. I – I'd love to take you. Not this weekend but—'

'Of course. I can't anyway – Easter . . .'

'Of course . . .' There was a pause. Juliet clicked on her email, and wrote a note to herself about calling a gallery in France. Sam coughed, and said, 'I actually came in to ask you a question.'

'Yes,' she said, gratefully. 'Is it about the Dalbeattie archive?'

'Oh! No, actually. Though while I think of it, Kate Nadin has started going through all the papers. She's found Dalbeattie's letters to Ned, about Nightingale House. I must show them to you. Some really interesting information about the materials they used. The willow was Scottish, that's a nice fact for you. There's a terrible letter of condolence he writes when Ned's daughter dies. It's strange, really. He apologises. He says, "I'm so sorry."'

'How do we have them?'

'I'm sorry? We bought them. Kate is . . .'

'No! Sorry, I mean, if Dalbeattie wrote them to Ned, wouldn't they have remained at the house? Why did Dalbeattie get them back?'

Sam said, slowly, 'Well, Horner returned them to him. All their letters. With a note that says "You may consider any correspondence between us at an end."'

Juliet drew her breath in with a hiss. 'Oh no.'

'The last one is dated 1914. He begs for information about someone called Mary. Do you have any idea . . . ?'

'Mary was my great-grandmother's sister. That's strange.' She sat up. 'You know, all my grandmother ever said about it was that her mother used to talk about Dalbeattie, but not Mary. She'd cry when she thought of her. I think the assumption was they were lovers.'

'Wow, really?'

Juliet nodded. 'But something happened, as you can see. Perhaps over the death of Eliza, because that's when the breach occurred. I don't know that Liddy and Mary ever really were close again, and obviously Dalbeattie and Ned weren't. Oh, how awful.'

'What happened to Mary, after Eliza died?'

'I don't know,' said Juliet. 'But she and Liddy were everything to each other. Once.' She looked at her watch. 'I'm so sorry . . .'

'Another time. Just before you go, did you get a chance to look at the programme for the conference?'

'I've emailed you some notes.' Juliet leaned over to turn off her computer, then picked her handbag off the floor. 'I think the running order is great, but I personally would like to see more on Leighton.'

'Yes.' He leaned his tall frame against the desk, one hand on the back of his head, watching her intently. 'Sure. Why?'

'It's a conference on how we became Edwardians. He's vital. How he changed the RA, some of the beliefs cemented during his tenure as President. And I was thinking perhaps we should ask Albertine McIntyre to do a paper on him. She's the Leighton expert.'

'Ahh.' Sam hesitated. 'Thank you, Juliet.'

Outside, the watery sun shone boldly through into her tiny pale-blue office. There was a magnolia tree just by her window, where a robin sat and watched them both. 'Have you heard of her?' she said, hesitating. 'Maybe it's a terrible suggestion?'

'No, it's great. It's just funny because she's coming to my house for Easter in fact.' Their eyes met as they laughed. 'She's divorced too.' Sam considered for a minute. 'I mean, everyone who's coming on Sunday is. It's been a long week. I'll suggest it to her this weekend.'

Just then Juliet's phone buzzed and she looked down, worried Matt was on at her again about the divorce paperwork.

Buy more butter. M Beadle

She smiled and picked up her cloth bag, inadvertently upside down so the papers slid out and over the desk onto the floor, a waterfall of text.

'Oh lord.' She bent down, but Sam had already gathered most of them up.

'Divorce papers. Sorry, I couldn't help . . .' He pushed them towards her. His grey, usually twinkling eyes were solemn. 'Sympathies.'

'Yep . . . yep. My husband wants to accelerate things. His girl-friend is having a baby.'

'Very modern,' Sam said mildly, and she laughed, shuffling the papers, receipts, forms, letters together again. 'Are they having a shotgun wedding for which they need you out of the way?'

'He has it in his head he can't be married to someone else when the baby's born. It's no contest.'

'That makes it simpler, doesn't it?'

'Thank goodness. Stuff about the kids . . . all that has been quite easy. He's just – on at me a lot.' She chewed her lip, determined not to complain. To say all the things she wanted. How he texted all the time. How Tess had started to make 'demands'. Isla mustn't say this to Elise. Sandy mustn't have muddy wellies next time.

Sam handed her another sheet from the floor. 'When I got divorced from Anna, I kept dreaming about our wedding. I had a cold. I couldn't remember any of it properly, because I felt so terrible. My mom and dad were there over from Canada and they didn't know anyone. It was a strange day, but who's into clichés, right? So I ignored why it felt strange and then afterwards it occurred to me that's because it was wrong.'

'Oh,' she said. 'Yes, that's it, exactly.'

Her cold, cold feet – why hadn't she worn tights? – in flimsy silk heels clattering on the marble of the church floor, her dress that was too tight, Matt's hand in hers, squeezing her bones, also too tight – she had just wanted it all to be over, all of it. The flowers were fake, and her parents' smiles stretched wide. Afterwards, as they stood awkwardly outside the gloomy Victorian church, Matt had scratched his head and said, 'Shall we go to the pub?' And so they had, but she had been more relieved than anything when her parents left early, and Matt's mother, Luisa, had pleaded a headache and gone to her hotel. The one person who said anything was Honor, Honor with her husky voice who had grasped Juliet's chin in one hand, the other hand holding Bryan's, and said, 'Oh, be happy, darling', and then Bryan had kissed her on the cheek and, in a low voice, said, 'Your grandmother wishes she could be here, love. You know she does.'

A shotgun wedding, for all the wrong reasons.

'Well, I think you're incredible, Juliet,' Sam said quietly. 'You never complain.'

'Ha! Oh, I do.'

'Not to me. It must be hard.'

'It's not that. It's that you know you've failed.'

'What?'

Juliet was staring at the floor. 'You should have been able to make it work. That's what you think to yourself, all the time.'

'I know.'

'Other people do, why couldn't you two just put your differences aside? Forgive and forget?' She looked up now. 'But I knew I couldn't. And it's with me, all the time, the failure of it. What it's done to the children, how it's marked them for life . . .'

'Oh, Juliet.' He shook his head. 'From what you say you didn't fail. You tried. He's the one who failed you, all of you.'

She shrugged. 'Well. But you blame yourself, don't you?'

'No. Stop it.'

'It's fine,' she said, wishing she'd never said anything.

'Hey, go easy on yourself. Look here – what you've done here, in only two, three months or so is quite remarkable. We're very lucky.'

'I am the lucky one,' she said, touched by his words and the kind way he said them. 'I really must go. Have a wonderful Easter. I'm sure the lamb will be amazing. Thanks, Sam Ham.' She smiled at him, hugging the cloth bag to her chest in the doorway.

And Sam put his hand on her wrist. She felt a jolt, at the unexpected physical contact, and looked down at his tanned hand, the strong fingers on hers. 'Listen – it'll be over soon and then it's done. You can move on. It's a cliché, but it's true. That's the thing to remember. Enjoy the weekend with your kids.'

'I will.' She wanted to hug him. To acknowledge the gratitude she felt for him, because he had sat her behind a desk and made her think about paintings again, and she loved it. She sometimes had to remind herself this was Sam Hamilton, her college nemesis, that the dark, scowling, know-it-all geek had grown into a dark, intense, know-it-all geek whose company she actually enjoyed. *The past is burnt and gone*, she thought to herself, as she left, with a wry smile.

Chapter Twenty-Nine

The Respondent is financially irresponsible, and has failed to maintain the Petitioner and their children. The Respondent has deserted the family home removing the Petitioner's children without informing him beforehand. The Petitioner is not to be liable for repairs to the Respondent's new house nor financially responsible for anything contained within the house and waives all rights to any future profit to be made from said house namely Nightingale House. The Petitioner will make some contribution of child support payment but wishes these above considerations to be considered by the court before finalising a monthly sum to be paid to the Respondent.

These little jabs, accusations of her ineptitude, as though he'd been supporting the family single-handedly for years, instead of it being a joint enterprise – if you defined 'joint' as Juliet working virtually full time and contributing more financially whilst also doing most of the childcare and all of the housework. Driving through the lanes, words and phrases from the divorce papers kept floating in front of her eyes and she felt dizzy with the lightheadedness that kept assailing her of late.

He'd proposed to her near here. That last time at the house, Grandi standing in the doorway, arm outstretched, finger pointing. 'Out!'

They'd driven away at full pelt, stopping so she could be sick in a hedgerow, Matt holding her hand, rubbing her back, comforting her. 'It doesn't matter, none of it. You loved her, but it's not your fault she's changed like this. Sad, and bitter.' He hadn't been all bad, she had to remember that. He'd been great sometimes. 'There, you see? A smile. That's good.' He'd rubbed her back. 'I don't care what she says. I love you now. I love the baby already. Let's get married.' So they were engaged in a hedge while she was being sick: the irony was it was the most romantic thing he ever did for her.

Juliet pulled into the driveway. I must help him now, a voice in her head said quite clearly. I must let him go as smoothly and quickly as possible. She sat on the stone bench outside the house and pulled out the divorce papers, and a pen. She could hear cries of excitement from inside. Birds were singing their evening chorus in the trees behind her, and she could feel the countryside around her humming, coming alive after winter. It was April. Next month it would be a year since she had lost her job and come back early to Dulcie Street. Four seasons had passed and she had marked every month within them. It was time to draw a line here. The final sticking point had been maintenance for Sandy to end if she married again – she let it go, and signed the papers. If she married anyone again she'd be so surprised she wouldn't notice the lack of maintenance: anyway, Matt's contribution was so paltry it made very little difference.

It was not enough – it turned out the job was not enough, either, to keep her afloat. She had only seen as far as the job and not the economics of working three days a week for a publicly funded institution whilst paying childcare on top. Last month alone the heating bill for Nightingale House had been almost four hundred pounds. She was supplementing her salary with the premium bonds left her by her other grandparents, Mum's mum and dad, shadowy figures who had died when she was young and who had lived in Hampstead Garden Suburb, in a house about which all she remembered was that there were knitted covers for the spare toilet rolls shaped like top hats with ribbons. Juliet, aged five, had thought this was utterly extraordinary. She could barely recall Gran and Granddad Wilson, but she thanked them daily now.

She stuck down the envelope, resolving to make this the weekend she tidied the house to take photos for the AirBnB listing. And, with renewed zeal, Juliet leaped up and back into the car, hoping to catch the post. She drove into Godstow again and dropped the papers into the letterbox. She bumped into Jo and said hi, then quickly dropped into Pascale and Co for a hug from Frederic, who called George down, the two of them clutching her tightly, Frederic's warm, large hand comfortingly on her back.

A hug makes everything better. She bought the butter and some firelighters, asked in hope rather than expectation for sumac for Bea's next Friday night recipe . . . all these things seemed like mundane activities after posting off your signed divorce papers, but deeply comforting ones. She felt giddy with some sort of release, though her head still ached, the way it would before a thunderstorm. So much so that, arriving home again and locking the car, she glanced up at the sky, expecting storm clouds.

'No, Sandy, no more crisps. Eat your omelette.'

'No!' Sandy cried, and pushed his plastic plate off the table, then held his small arms, rigidly outstretched, towards her. He was very clingy at the moment, whether because she'd started the job and Mrs Beadle, or Annie, was picking him up three times a week, or because he knew more than she assumed? Or simply because he was three years old – whatever the answer, every little thing was exhausting with him at the moment, mealtimes, bathtimes, bedtimes – it was a battle, and she felt sorry for him. He was furious all the time about *everything*.

'No, Sandy! You mustn't throw it on the floor,' said Juliet, for the tenth time. 'That's naughty. I'm cross with you.'

Sandy's huge grey eyes, swimming with misery, stared up at her, his flushed fat cheeks blobbed with tears.

'My? Naughty?' he repeated. Beside him, Isla munched away at her omelette, turning the pages of her book on Greek myths and humming quietly to herself. Bea was nowhere to be seen. Sandy picked up another piece of omelette and threw it on the floor. 'No omelette.'

Juliet felt bone-tired, and snappy. She gritted her teeth, thinking resentfully of Sam, alone in his huge, empty house with the lit windows blazing out on to the street, drinking a glass of wine, possibly listening to Pulp, and doing something like reading a thriller or making tarte tatin. What a life. She wiped a piece of banana off the table. 'No treats for Sandy when he throws food.'

Sandy responded by hurling himself on to the floor then tightly clutching her leg and wailing. 'Mamma! *Maaaammmmmaaaaaaa . . .*' As he gasped for breath, howling inconsolably, he rested his bouncing curls on her knee, patting her leg, forgiving her for this terrible wrong. '*Noooo, Mammmaaaaaaaaa,*' he bellowed into her knee.

'God,' said Bea from the doorway. 'Shut up, Sandy, stop being a drama queen.'

'You have no idea,' said Juliet, her heart leaping with joy at the sight of her. 'How are you, darling?'

'Good. I'm good, Mum. Listen. I know it's short notice, but is it OK if Eva comes to stay for Easter weekend?'

'Oh.' Juliet stepped back, before realising Sandy was still attached to her. Isla muttered something under her breath, and turned the page. 'Eva? Who's Eva?'

'A girlfriend of mine from school.'

'I thought Fin was your girlfriend.'

'Mum – it's not really any of your business?'

'It's my business if someone else is coming to stay.'

Bea sighed, as though Juliet were particularly slow. 'She's not my actual girlfriend. Her parents are away? And she has to be around to go to a party. I'm going with her?'

'Right,' said Juliet. She genuinely didn't know what to do. If she wasn't gay she'd let a girl stay in Bea's room with her, wouldn't she? But if it was a boyfriend or a girlfriend and they might have sex she wouldn't, not just yet, would she? But what if this girl was just a friend? She rubbed her eyes. 'Um . . . where will she stay?'

'In my room.' Bea folded her arms. 'Where else?'

'No, she won't, thanks.'

'Oh my God, Mum. It's not like that. You do have a problem with me being gay. I fucking knew it. Tess said—'

'Don't talk to me like that,' said Juliet, wearily. 'You're fifteen, I've never met Eva, I thought you were with someone else. And don't walk away – Bea!'

'You sad, pathetic lonely *loser*.' Bea had stalked off, opening the front door and stomping over to the Dovecote, flinging the door open. 'Just because you're unhappy and all on your own, don't take it out on *me*! I am *so sick of you*!' she yelled.

I'm sick of you too, Juliet wanted to shout. I'm sick of you always blaming me, and your father being an idiot, and your brother driving me up the wall, and your sister bursting into tears for no reason, which breaks my heart every time. I'm sick of the mildew and the mice and getting three children ready every morning and constantly forgetting to buy more cereal and socks and I'm sick of always being the one who shouts and chivvies and . . . I signed the divorce papers today and I'm sick of it all.

Isla, thankfully, was still completely absorbed in her book about the Greeks. Juliet followed after Bea, prising Sandy off her leg and then, when he slumped to the ground, picking him up and carrying him, though he made himself stiff and heavy, sliding down from her tightest grasp on to the ground. Juliet left him, and carried on. She threw the door of the Dovecote open with such force it banged back and she had to shove her foot in to stop it hitting her in the face. Behind her, Sandy toddled, crying louder than before. He reached her and she scooped him up again, but he would not be consoled.

'Make him be *quiet*,' said Bea, her face pinched, and she bit her lip.

'Yes,' said Juliet coolly, and she crouched down on the cool ground next to Sandy, and stroked his hair. She spoke in a soft voice. 'I will, but don't ever talk to me like that again. You are fifteen, I'm not having someone stay in your room with you till you're sixteen. It's not about whether you're gay or not and you know that. I know things are hard . . .' She took a deep breath. 'But there's a line between what is unfair and when you're trying your luck. Listen to me. Don't talk to me like that. And don't push your luck.'

She stroked Sandy's hair, hoping he'd stay quiet for a bit. He was babbling to himself, very quietly. One soft white hand patted the painting table, his fingers smearing the glass top.

'House!' he said suddenly, pointing up to the mezzanine-level shelving that ran around and above their heads. Juliet looked up. She had forgotten the doll's house had been moved here, as part of her January clear-out. Bea had wanted it in the Dovecote. She liked looking at it, almost like a talisman. Isla had never been into dolls and Sandy was too little to be trusted with the delicate fretwork of the banisters, the tiny table legs and scraps of material fastened on as curtains . . . But there was something rather sad about it there. She frowned. How tiny it looked, perched up on high. It was dusty.

'Yes, house,' she said. 'Look, darling.'

Bea shrugged her shoulders, calmer already. 'You don't ask me about it, not ever, you don't. Dad says you're in denial.'

'About what?'

'Me being gay. You said you accepted it, but we never talk about it.' Bea gave a great sniff, and pressed her face to her hands.

Juliet stood up. 'Bea! Come on. I've tried to talk to you about it umpteen times and you never want to. That's fine if you don't want to. But I can't keep asking the same things over and over again, because you get irritated and shout at me. That's fair enough, but you can't have a go at me for it. Perhaps I haven't supported you enough in ways I haven't realised, and if that's the case then I'm really sorry.'

'No, you have,' said Bea. 'I'm – you've been great.'

'What?' Juliet blinked, astonished at the vacillation of teenagers. Sandy was on the wooden steps that led to the mezzanine shelf. She lifted him gently off again.

'I don't know – Mum, it's so confusing. I like Eva. A lot. But Fin has been with me since school and we get each other and . . .' Bea shuddered a little. 'Mum, everything is so *hard*.'

Juliet almost laughed manically. She bit it back. 'Oh darling. That's being a teenager – don't shout at me, but it's like that.'

'House! See house!'

'Mum, can I ask you something?' Bea took a deep, ragged breath.

'If you could choose over again, would you move back here? Or would you take the money and run?'

Her eyes were fixed on her mother's. Juliet inhaled sharply. She paused, letting the idea wash over her for a moment. Money. None of this stress. 'I don't know,' she said, in a small voice. She looked up, around her. 'You know, I think I'd probably – Jesus. *Sandy!*'

Sandy's wild, golden curls shone high up in the darkness of the mezzanine, where the fig tree had already come into leaf, blocking the light. He stood triumphantly next to the doll's house, perched a little further on the narrow shelf, and pointed at it. 'House!' he said, simply. 'My house.'

'Sandy – Sandy,' said Juliet. 'Come down, darling.' She made for the steps, but Bea was already climbing up them.

'No. My house.'

'Sandy.' Juliet felt her knees turn to water. 'Sandy.' She locked her gaze on him, hoping to distract him from every other thought. 'Look at me, darling. Look at Mummy. Stay still.'

'My *house*,' said Sandy, and he took a step towards the doll's house – a step into air – his foot missing the edge of the shelf. For one second, a second that stretched into time, the other foot hovered over the edge, his balance falling between one side and the other, his little arms wavering, turning like windmills, and then he arched back with a surprised sob, trying to catch hold of the doll's house, but he could not reach it and fell, his head smacking against the edge of the stone shelf with a sickening thud. He plummeted on to the hard stone floor with a weak cry, and Juliet missed catching him by a split second.

One second later, the doll's house toppled over after him, landing on his small body with a thud and then on to the floor, with a loud, shattering crack. Pieces, people, fairies, furniture all tumbled out; the central chimney was smashed in two, the insides rolling on to the floor.

Next to it Sandy lay, utterly still, eyes closed. There was no blood. No sound except the whirr of an old coin, rolling in a semi-circle on the hard stone, back and forth.

Chapter Thirty

August 1914

Dear Ned and Liddy

Now that war is here permit me to write to ask you: is Mary well? I can find no trace of her though I have searched high and low. I think of her, and you, my dear friends, often.

Perhaps I still do not have the right, but I must ask about her. I'm sorry. I understand that I cannot ever hope to visit you. Know you are all, as always, at the centre of my thoughts. I follow your progress. Allow an old friend to say I think you can do better, forgive me for it. My dear man, you are a greater painter than these pictures.

Your friend Dalbeattie

P.S. dearest Liddy I am sure that I saw that rotten old nurse of yours. Bryanston? Brierley? Quite mad she looked, staring eyes the colour of steel. A most unpleasant female. I saw her coming out of the church, carrying lilies; she stared at me. Most weeks I walk on the Heath and always make sure to take a turn past your family home. It helps me to remember. We are old now, aren't we? So your father is dead, I'm sorry to hear it, and quite should have begun the letter with my condolences

– L.D.

'The impertinence of the letter!' Liddy put a finger to her temple, frowning. 'But how would I *know* he'd died, Ned dearest? I have not had a thing to do with him for ten years or more. He's not been in touch. Not since . . .'

She let the silence hang, but Ned was impervious to its meaning. 'Surely they'd have written to you, if he were dead?' He passed a hand over his forehead, leaving a streak of carmine red in a line, like a savage. 'You'd have heard, he was a legal man, there must be a will, executors.' He blinked, then turned back to the canvas. 'Damn Dalbeattie. How dare he say . . . This damned light—'

Liddy said patiently, 'The fig tree needs cutting, dearest. You will have no light until you cut it back, so that it doesn't climb over the glass roof. And the birds, too, their leavings all over it, Ned, it's easy to fix, I'll make sure Darling attends to it.'

'I'll clean my own studio, thank you. *"Allow an old friend"* – How dare he!'

Liddy shifted on her seat, flexing her cramped fingers. The heavy silk of her tea-rose pink dress clung to her in the stultifying atmosphere of the Dovecote. She had been sitting for Ned for a week now, every day from almost first light – he wanted to begin at 5 a.m. but she had refused, forcing him to settle for seven o'clock in the morning, when John was still fast asleep and only Nora, their new housemaid, up and about. It felt like old times, the two of them stealing away to the Dovecote together, hand in hand across the dew-sprinkled garden, the late, late-summer flowers a riot of collapsed decadence: listing hollyhocks, nodding sunflowers, fading, dying roses and blowsy bright dahlias, burnished by the sun. She had not been painted by him for so long now, not since *The Garden of Lost and Found*. She had forgotten what it was like: the tedium of it, mixed with the joy of watching him, the agonies he went through.

He was older now, almost forty-two, and his windswept hair was threaded with grey. He was fêted by younger artists, mocked by them too in equal measure. 'Old Horner, he knew his stuff before he took to painting children!' He had been knighted, and so she was Lady Horner; it meant nothing to Liddy, but he was thrilled by it, and by the encounter with the King, so much older and larger than Liddy had expected but also so very, very *charming*. Ned wore brocade silk waistcoats, and had a cane – Liddy teased him that he used it to seem older than he was, and he was very cross then, shouting and waving the cane about: 'Dammit! I do no such thing!'

The Garden of Lost and Found obsessed him. She knew it. It hung in the window of Galveston's gallery now, returned from its travels all over the world, in the fog after Eliza died. Afterwards Liddy could see that three or more years had passed since the loss of Eliza and she remembered nothing of that time. Nothing at all. As if she, too, were in the ground, next to her daughter. She was still never quite sure what places it had visited, how many millions had gazed upon it, only that it made money, for Galveston kept telling them. When they went to London, they always found a way to walk past it, but never stopped. Liddy knew however that Ned would go back to look at it. Galveston's wife had told her. 'He stands for hours, just staring.'

The work he was making now was to be called *The Lilac Hours: Reflections of England, 1914*. It showed Liddy pressing her face delicately to a bough of lilac. The lilac had long since died back and Liddy did not see how her smelling some withering purple flowers reflected the state of the nation, but she had never interfered with Ned's vision. Privately, she hoped he would stop returning to the theme of England and the Empire in his work. Lately it had become something of an obsession, though she seemed to be the only one who thought so. *We Built Nineveh,* his last painting, had been a fairly poorly disguised metaphor for the strength of Empire, a lot of muscular young men and women posing on the steps by the Albert Memorial. To Liddy it was almost an inversion of *A Meeting,* the painting that made his name. There, the young were individuals, idealistic. Even in *The Spirit of the Age*, the panorama of workers on the Strand, which was Ned's representation of British industry, had worn its symbolism with a jolly, celebratory grace. In *We Built Nineveh* they were ciphers. 'INDUSTRY. ART. UNDERSTANDING BETWEEN NATIONS.' The girl representing 'Love of Outdoors' seemed to have a sort of oak tree growing out of her back. 'One wonders if she's wearing it as a sort of umbrella or carrying it, perhaps it's a present for a friend,' John had whispered wickedly to his mother at the Summer Exhibition, and been swiftly hushed by her.

Liddy bolstered her coil of hair, sliding the comb at the base of the neck in more firmly. 'Dearest, can I put the paintbrush down, just for a moment?' she asked. The letter from Dalbeattie had been waiting at the house when she went up for lunch. 'I must write to our old home. Or write to Mary – perhaps she has heard. Or I should go up to London, to see—'

'He's using you to flush Mary out,' Ned said, roughly. 'Your father's not dead, Liddy, don't you understand?'

She gazed at him and said with a helpless laugh: 'Oh my love, I fear he must be, for—'

'Don't, whatever you do, go back to your old home, Liddy! That woman will be there, she'll get you in some way, damn her. Besides, London's not safe at the moment, with all the troops.'

'I think I have to. It's been such a long time since I heard anything from them now, thirteen years.' She put her hands down.

He nodded and she knew he understood. 'Let me finish *The Lilac Hours*,' he begged. 'I'll take you to London, we'll do it in style, my love. I'll drive you up to Highgate myself.' A curious expression crossed his face. 'We don't need his money. We have money. Too much money.'

She gazed at him with tenderness. 'Oh, Ned. Of course I don't care if he's left money. I'm sure there was none left. I want – I simply want to know, he's my father, after all. And Mary might—' She swallowed, for she missed her sister so much still, fourteen years after her child's death, that it was a physical pain in her chest. Oftentimes Liddy would wake up talking to her, knowing she had been there, by her side – a new coat she'd bought, a most interesting book, that funny saying of Hannah's . . . Mary sat beside her, in her dreams, her small heart-shaped face alight with laughter, the two of them, heads bent over a drawing, or a flower . . .

And then would come the memory of Mary's head, bent now and hanging with shame, of Zipporah's broken cries when she finally came into Liddy's room two weeks afterwards, eyes red, lids raw from crying – 'I saw him coming out of her room, that time, all those times, I never breathed a word.' Of Eliza's eyes now, fixed in horror on her mother as she tried to breathe, and Liddy's heart would harden again. Then, the years did not bring any diminishment of pain.

'Of course, my Liddy,' he said. 'I will take you, when I can. Now, may I begin again?'

Several minutes later, in the doorway of the studio, a voice said quietly, 'Mama?'

'Hello darling,' said Liddy. Ned was bent over the canvas, an inch away from his nose, scraping furiously at it with a knife, muttering to himelf, and Liddy knew they could invite a marching band in and he would not pay any attention.

'I won't disturb your pose,' John said, coming towards her, cool, golden-blond, fresh as a daisy. He took off his boater and, with a gentle rolling twirl, laid it on the stone shelf next to her. She regarded him fondly as he sniffed the paintbrush solemnly. 'This is standing in for the lilac, is it?'

'Yes, this is my lovely fragrant bloom.'

'You are good, and patient, Mama. I'm sure that's why he never painted us again.' He turned to her, his eyes smiling. 'Do you remember Eliza threw those wings into the stream afterwards?'

'I've never been so *townfumftable* in all my days,' Liddy said, quickly squeezing her son's fingers back and smiling into his sweet, open face. Behind them, Ned cursed under his breath.

'*Townfumftable?*' John said.

'Yes, that's what she told me it was! As *townfumftable* as being in town.'

John gave a small laugh. 'Oh, that's her, to the life! Yes, I can't see her like Jessica or Charlotte Coote, doing a season in London, can you? She'd have hated it. She was a true country girl.'

She loved many things about her sweet-natured, kind son, but perhaps most of all was his easy manner, and the way he spoke to her freely of Eliza. No one else mentioned her daughter. Death swallowed the loved one up: memorials, portraits and gravestones took the place of the dead. But John remembered his big sister,

336

often better than Liddy, who sometimes found she could not recall a certain feature of hers; cruel time was stripping away her memories of her golden-haired, loose-limbed, laughing girl. So John knew she had loved *The Arabian Nights* stories, especially Aladdin and the naughty genie, that her favourite flower was the iris, that she had adored cats, while he, of course, had longed for a puppy, implored, beseeched his parents for one, until Eliza died, when a puppy was never, ever mentioned again.

Ned did not speak his daughter's name after she died. When Liddy thought about it, the fact of it catching her unawares, it made her angry. Sometimes she felt she might strike him, to see how he reacted. His daughter whom he had borne down the garden on his shoulders to pick apples, whom he had sketched over and over again, capturing her smooth unlined feet and fat toes, and each perfect curl, who had held his heart in her tiny plump hand. But then, so many things made her angry now that it was simpler to say nothing. *We go on.*

She tried not to think about Eliza too often, but it was very hard pushing the grief and the questions down, down. They kept coming back up into her mind. What she would be doing, now. Would she have enjoyed tennis, like John? Would she have been a reader? A good dancer? As bright at her lessons as she seemed? She would be a young woman now; Liddy could picture exactly how she would have turned out. Beautiful, spirited, fierce.

She shook her head now and smiled into her son's eyes. The letter from Dalbeattie was on the stone shelf behind Ned, but she would not show it to him. 'So, my darling boy,' she said. 'What news?'

John had tucked something in his hand but now he unfurled it. 'I thought I'd better tell you myself, since you won't like it.'

She was still smiling, and she looked down at his open hand, at a piece of paper.

'Fight alongside your friends,' he said.

Scrape, scrape, scrape . . . the knife scratched, and Ned grunted, behind the easel. She could see the palette occasionally, the finger hooked around it, as though it were part of him.

'What?' Liddy did not really hear him properly. 'What's this? Another game? Shall we play after tea?'

'Jack Barnaby, Tom Peck, Coote and a few others – we are going to the recruiting office tomorrow.'

Liddy looked properly at him. She saw now his skin was slick with sweat, his face pale. She blinked.

'What do you mean?'

He cleared his throat. 'We're signing up, Mama. Your King and Country need You.'

'No,' Liddy heard herself say quietly. '*No.*'

'Mama!' John laughed, as though it were funny. 'We must all do our part. The Godstow Pals – we're all going off together. We'll be—'

'You will not!' she shouted. 'Ned! Ned, listen to this. *Ned!*'

His voice was faint behind the easel. 'One moment, Liddy, then I am entirely yours.'

Liddy dropped the paintbrush to the floor and stood up. 'John, my darling, they won't make you go. You can't go.'

John gave a ghastly smile. 'Jack and I had a bet, and—'

Ned looked up, suddenly alert. 'What's this? You and that farmer's boy?' He nodded at his son. 'What devilry now, what are you planning?' He jabbed the easel at him. 'What's it now, Liddy?'

'He's going to the recruiting office tomorrow,' said Liddy, hearing her own voice say the words, and it was ghastly. 'John is joining up.' She covered her face with her hands for a moment and when she looked up again Ned was staring, frozen, at his son.

'If we go together, we'll all be in the same battalion,' John said. 'It's a great show, Mama, they have a brass band over at Godstow and the village is cheering each man as he goes into the office . . . The Pals' Brigade they call it. It was Jack's idea . . . He loves a scrap. I know I'm not a fighting man—' He cleared his throat, said hoarsely, 'But everyone's going, Mama. I can't be the only one at home.'

'Yes, you can,' said Liddy. 'Ramsay MacDonald—'

'Ramsay MacDonald is a traitor and a liar!' said Ned, almost shouting. 'My love! At this moment, of national crisis, when our country is beset by forces who would threaten everything we hold dear about the Empire! I beg of you not to speak the man's name.'

Liddy's eyes were blazing, but she kept her voice light: 'Oh, Ned. Where is the boy who disdained organised religion, and used to say the Empire was too powerful? Our son, dearest, our son is saying he is leaving us, that he wishes to join up.'

'You think we should abandon France to the Germans?'

'I do not. I merely think . . .' She shook her head. 'I have a distaste for war, this war especially, which is apparently shared by very few. John, my love, I say again that I wish that you would not go.'

'No. He's quite right. He must go.' Ned put down the palette, went over and put the boater back on his son's head. He straightened his collar. 'My boy. . . so.' His face formed into a small half-smile. 'I'd say it's the thing to do. Quite right.' He patted John's smooth cheek. 'Put hairs on your chin, John. Make you into a man.'

They had fought often about John. There was the time he had been sent away to school against Liddy's will and had written such heartbreaking letters home, and eventually they had found out about the schoolmaster who did such terrible things to him, beating him with a branch John had had to select himself and making him walk through the school grounds holding a sign: 'COWARD'.

It was Nurse Bryant all over again, Liddy had screamed, when Ned had uneasily said he supposed that was what happened at good public schools. But she had won that argument, though it had cost her dear and it had forever altered Ned's relationship with his son. He could not understand how his own boy who, but for his golden colouring, looked so very like him, could be so utterly at odds with his father. John let every bluebottle and daddy-long-legs out of the casement windows and refused to eat meat after he turned sixteen. He grew tall like a tree, his muscles huge and supple, and worked the land at harvest-time, helping the Burnabys bring in the corn, tossing bales of hay high into the sky with the flick of a pitchfork. He went to a local boys' day school over in the nearby market town of Walbrook, not the great public school future his father had wanted for his only son. He would walk home every day come winter or summer, though it was an hour or more. He said he liked the hedgerows, and the people one met. He wanted to be a teacher – an art teacher! He was a fine artist, and drew sketches of everyone he met in the notebook he kept in his knapsack. The loss of his sister had turned him from a little brother into an only child. The house was never quite the same again. Happiness was gone. But John was kind, calm, conviction shining through everything he did – Liddy often thought of him as a tree: strong, solid, unbreakable. She wished Ned could see how very like him his son was.

John did not reply to his father, at first. He turned to his mother and said with his gentle, slightly lopsided smile, 'It'll be a great show. And, Mama, you wouldn't think much of me if I didn't.'

'Oh, John. It is not you speaking now, my love,' she said, very softly, watching him intently. Nausea kneaded her stomach.

'God Save the King!' said Ned smartly, jumping to attention. After a momentary pause John saluted smartly, echoing his father, in a clear, steady voice.

Liddy, weakly, mimicked them as they stood to attention in the sweltering room, and knew it was over at that point. What could she say now? How could she stop him?

'I must draw you, my boy,' Ned said, picking up his palette and knife again. He stared curiously at his son, as though seeing him for the first time. 'When you're in uniform. Do you get the uniform, before you go?'

'I believe so.'

Ned had turned towards the easel, gazing at the unfinished painting through narrowed eyes, a vein ticking in his cheek.

'There,' he muttered, jabbing softly at the canvas with a soft hogshead brush. 'Yes – yes, of course. That's why. That's why. There. It must be there.' He waved the palette at his son, and for a second the old light was there in his eyes. 'You must hurry. Or perhaps my father's old military jacket would do. It was his father's, he was in the Crimea. I must draw you. That's why it's been impossible to finish, I understand it now. *Reflections of England*, you see? There.' He nodded at his son.

'I'll find a jacket, Father,' John said, as though that was the thing, not his leaving for war.

'*God save the King*,' Liddy said softly and then, crumpling the letter from Dalbeattie in her hand and letting it fall to the floor, she dashed from the studio. She met Zipporah on the path back up to the house. The older woman clasped her hands, and fixed her pale-blue eyes on Liddy. All she said was:

'He's getting ready to go, isn't he? I knew he would. Our John.'

There was pride in her voice. Liddy pushed her aside, and went to her room, where she vomited into the china bowl on her washstand, heaving over and over. The smell of the decaying lilac, too rich, an edge of rotten mulch behind the rich scent, would forever remind her of that awful day.

She knew then.

Chapter Thirty-One

1916

It all started with a rug.

There was a horse chestnut tree beside Mary's room, overlooking the river. Every year the cycle of its frothy blossom, its budding leaves, the slow fading of its greenery to yellow and then dazzling orange and red, and the conkers which bounced down almost comically on to the passers-by below, pleased Mary. It stood in the lawned gardens stretching from her building across to the Dove public house and the dark, dank passageway that led towards Hammersmith. The glossy brown conkers were scooped up with great joy by teams of jostling boys, and from her window seat above the path Mary could look down at them and wonder how many would be called up to fight – how soon they would come for them. Some looked to be fifteen or sixteen – only boys, the pleasure they took in those conker fights, the ferocity of the swing and the – to her – sickening sound, like crunching bone, of the conker when it was cracked open. And then they would disappear, laughing and calling rudely to one another through the passageway. Games, games. It was all games.

The noise those boys made reminded her of the way the crows used to call in the yew trees behind Nightingale House, blithely oblivious to anyone or anything. She would lie there in the early mornings, listening to their billowing, grumbling *caw*-ing.

Once, long ago in that house, Dalbeattie had got up, gone to her window and thrown a stone from his pocket into the yew trees. The protesting noises they made were unbelieveably loud.

'Now,' he'd said, returning to the bed and climbing into it, pushing her unprotesting white legs apart, his long face wolfish, voice husky with passion. 'No more disturbances, my angel—'

Sometimes the memory of it came to her, the tingling, swirling warmth of ecstasy, and she would feel liquid, magnetic, as though being dragged to the floor, red, red blood staining her cheeks. His large long hands on her waist, on her thighs, how he handled her – as though she were material, something to be touched and worked and caressed into sympathetic agreement with him. How afraid she always was when he came to her room, how every time she would tell herself – I am not the girls who came to Pertwee, or the ones he visited. I am different. And then it would begin – a touch, a sigh, a word from either one and she could not stop herself, did not know how to – and it was, of course, extraordinary.

Yet the pleasure of it was inextricably tangled with the sight of Eliza's coffin, the beginnings of her suffocation, her little feet in laced boots stumbling back from the farm. Falling to the floor, legs tangled in her muddied white lace petticoat and smock, the first indication something was wrong – 'I don't feel well, Auntie Em. My throat . . .'

In the fifteen years since her niece's death Mary had lived in the shadows. She had found rooms in London, selling her mother's cameo brooch at first and then taking in sewing. She knew she was sliding slowly, incrementally towards poverty and the workhouse, but she had long decided that she would find her grave in the Thames outside her window rather than enter the workhouse or whatever version of it might exist when the war was over. She had it planned out to the last notion – arsenic procured from the chemist under the pretence of getting rid of rats, a skirt and jacket weighted down with stones sewn carefully into the lining – no one sewed more carefully than she – one jump late at night from the Hammersmith Bridge. A smooth, relatively pain-free death, or so she hoped. It was more than she deserved.

War had changed very little in Mary's life, only that she was slightly busier, because people were mending more, and buying less new clothing, despite the exhortations in the papers that one should support the Empire by shopping. She took in alterations and made curtains and cushions and did embroidery – she could turn her hand to anything. She deserved nothing, and thus it was not a bad life, she told herself; she often thought she should suffer more than she did. She had one room, and the light from the river helped her with her sewing. She had a small rocking chair, a bed, a little mahogany trunk, and a chest of drawers, all (save the mahogany trunk which she had taken to Aunt Charlotte's all those years ago) purchased from a shop nearby in Hammersmith under the new railway arches. Mrs MacReady, her landlady, made her breakfast and supper and brought it up, though frequently it was nothing more than hot water with a single potato and a piece of gristle floating in it.

She had everything arranged just so. But –

There was a space on the varnished wooden floor for a rug, and this is where the trouble started.

Mary told herself she deserved nothing more, but she wanted a rug. Every day she sat by the window and sewed until the light began to fail, and often she met with her fellow suffragists, in Hammersmith, at the WSPU meetings and rallies. And if there was no gathering or call to action, every evening alone she rocked back and forth in her chair and stared at the empty square on the floor where a rug should be. It was all she wanted, a rug like the one she'd had in St Michael's House. It was dark red and ochre orange, studded with interlinked roses, and it had been in her room from birth, save for the night she had tried, in her innocence, to give it to Liddy, before Miss Bryant had returned it. Every night Mary had fallen asleep, looking at it. It was the first thing her bare feet touched every morning. Her mother had owned it as a child, and it was the last link Mary now had with that old life, her mother, the happy family they might have been had she lived, if a woman hadn't taken a walk with her sick nursemaid one afternoon. If Bryant hadn't seen the situations vacant column in *The Times* one particular morning. If Liddy hadn't got up out of bed and dared to leave the house. And she thought about that rug.

So one Sunday in October 1916, two years after the Great War began without really understanding why she did so, Mary walked to the Tube station and, travelling across town all the way to Highgate, found herself standing outside the old family home again, peering through the gate.

It had been twenty-five years since she'd last been there, and she had no real idea about what she should do next, or what she'd say, or even what she'd find. She had heard nothing from anyone in her family for over a decade – they did not know where she was; she was content with it that way.

She pulled her frayed and faded Paisley shawl more tightly around her, and slipped her hands into the pockets of the midnight-blue jacket she had made for herself. In the front window, which had been her father's study, a gas lamp burned steadily. Mary pushed open the gate.

The first sign something was different was the black paint which came away in her gloved hand, revealing a layer of scaly ochre-coloured rust. The gate creaked, a high-pitched, jagged wail. It had not been oiled for some time. Dead ivy clung to the crumbling bricks of the walls protecting the house.

Mary walked unsteadily up the uneven garden path. It was a cold, cloudy autumn morning. She looked around for the final roses but everything was gone. The box hedging, she also saw now, was dead: leaves yellowed, black roots. She knocked on the door smartly, though her hand trembled.

There was no answer. After a minute or two, Mary knocked again. The hall lamp behind the swirled glass of the door was suddenly extinguished. Intrigued now, and realising she was not scared, Mary knocked again, louder.

'Hello? Father?' she called, through the door. 'Is anyone at home?'

She blinked, when she thought she heard the rustle of skirts – it had always been Hannah, smoothly moving around the house, answering the door if Gumball was not there. Gumball was long gone. And Hannah was dead, buried in the same churchyard as little Eliza.

Mary paused, leaning against the door, and feeling a little faint.

She was hungrier than usual that morning, for Mrs MacReady had refused to give her breakfast until she paid her rent, and she had not eaten since lunchtime the previous day.

'*Father!*' she called, loudly, ear pressed to the door, and she distinctly heard the sound of someone, moving through the house, a creaking floorboard or hinge, but still no one came, and Mary, tired and hungry, found she was angry.

'Nurse Bryant!' She did not care that she was shouting, now. 'Bryant, do you hear me? Is my father there?' She moved to the side window and peered into her father's study. She kept waiting to feel fear, but it didn't come.

There was nothing in the room at all, compared to before. Gone were the great mahogany desk, the vast bureau against the wall, the glass-fronted cabinets filled with papers and ephemera and cases of curiosities, evidence of her father's profligacy. There was, in point of fact, a small school desk, upon which rested a gleaming gas lamp, and a chair. Everything was scrubbed clean, the stench of carbolic and Pears overwhelming even through the rotting window. A small pile of papers rested on the desk; nothing else. As Mary stared hungrily in at her childhood home, her eye was distracted by a movement through the open door of the study into the hallway. She saw the edge of a figure, standing against the main staircase.

Nurse Bryant. She had not realised Mary had moved to the side and was standing stock still in the hallway, staring ahead of her in terror, at the door. Her greasy hair was completely white, pinned up ineffectively in oily loops around her head and over her ears. Everything else was spotless, gleaming, terrifying in its barren cleanliness, but she? She was filthy – her black dress marked and torn, her boots battered, one missing a heel. Her teeth had gone: she munched and mumbled on her gums, fingers periodically plucking at her lip. The same fingers that had pulled Liddy's hair into agonising tight plaits, which had slapped and scratched and dug and clawed, tied the children to chairs, pinched their skin, drawn blood. Now they were claws themselves, working away at the lip then moving to the dirty black stuff dress to pluck at that, too. Mary could see the material was rough and torn where Nurse Bryant scratched at it, mechanically, like a bird pecking at the ground. And she could hear her, muttering.

'Let me out. Let me out. Let me out. Let me out. Let me out. Please. Let me out.'

Mary moved to the other side of the front door, to look into the parlour, where in happier days she had spent Christmas mornings, Sunday afternoons, teatimes, where the chaise longue beside the fire was the place to be when one had earache, where shelves of gold-tooled books ran from top to bottom . . .

But it was all gone. Not a wrack left behind.

Everything in the house had gone. First her mother, then she and her siblings, the servants, then her father, then the contents, bit by bit, scrubbed clean. And still, in the hallway, almost hidden from view by the staircase, stood Miss Bryant.

Mary could see the look on her face now: entirely absent, staring at something not there. The rheumy old eyes were terrifying, the fear in them palpable. And she saw it then, that Bryant did not even know she was there. *She's mad.*

She did not know anyone or anything, only that she was trapped in a prison again. The Fleet: Mary remembered it, wisps of memory wrapping around her like mist. She'd had to cut off her hair to pay for food, she had told Mary once, whilst she was combing her hair and Mary was crying. She couldn't remember why – was she sad, or in pain?

And still the small, whispering voice.

'Let me out. Let me out. Please, let me out.'

Mary realised there was no point in staying. Mother's rug would not be there. She didn't need it. Backing away, staring at the huge house, she wondered where everything had gone. What on earth had Bryant done with it all, with all the money she must have raised from selling everything? Given it to her strange church. Or spent it, on what they'd never know. They would never know.

She took one last look at the tiny black figure frozen in the hallway. The architect of our family's ruin, she thought, is this broken, pathetic creature. And, staring at her and out into the dining room beyond she could still make out the trees of Highgate Cemetery behind the house. Mother was there, and Pertwee, and now, presumably, Father too. Mary pressed her small, nailbitten fingers to her mouth, tears falling freely from her eyes on to her soft dark jacket. They glistened, small crystal globes in the midday sun. Only she and Liddy were left now.

Mary forced herself to walk away. Oh, the gift she realised she had now, which was freedom. She was free, truly free. It was all gone – all in the past – she opened the gate, stepping out on to the street once again.

'It cannot be – Mary?'

A hoarse, quiet voice from a figure on the pavement, a hand on her shoulder: Mary jumped, half out of her skin. 'I am so sorry, my dear –'

Mary turned, as though in a dream, and found herself face to face with him.

Her hand flew to her cheek, head swimming. '*You.*' He was older – of course – more lines, his hairline further back on his head, but the dancing eyes were the same, the eager face. He was as slim as ever, not run to fat like so many of the middle-aged men whose wives paid her to let out their waistcoats. He stooped still and removed his hat, his gaze never once leaving her.

'Why are you here?' she whispered, looking around wildly, as if it were a trap.

'I walk on the Heath on Sundays. I begin in Hampstead, and end here.'

'You come here? Every Sunday?'

He said simply: 'It is my last connection to you, and Liddy, and Ned, other than Nightingale House.'

Mary found she could not speak, but stared at him. His fine cheekbones, hooded eyes, the pleasing scroll of his ear. His broad shoulders, the large hands, nothing dainty about him, she who worked in tiny stitches, making the visible invisible. She remembered him in his embroidered dressing gown, majestic like an ancient king, and how vulnerable he was, naked, inside her; how frightened he had sometimes seemed, how sad . . .

He reached out then, took her hand and folded it in his. 'My dearest.' The faint hint of a Scots burr at the edge of the warm, low voice. 'You are as young and serious and sweet as ever. I cannot—' He touched a ribbon on her jacket. 'What is this?'

Mary looked down, and found her voice. 'Violet, green and white – universal suffrage,' she said. She held up the ribbon, proudly. 'I've been arrested, you know.'

'My Mary,' he said. 'I'm sure you have. You are a constant. The world changes to keep up with you.'

There, in front of the house, he bent down, and kissed the ribbon. His mouth was warm on her shirt; she could feel the press of his cheek on her breast. There was a rushing, whooshing sensation in front of her eyes. Dalbeattie stood up again and then caught sight of her face. 'I say – are you all right?'

'I haven't had any breakfast,' Mary said, and she felt herself floating, speaking to him as though from a long way away, and the earth started revolving, slowly, then falling towards her. 'I think I'm going to—'

When she came to she was in a carriage, travelling down the hill into town, Dalbeattie beside her, but she was too weary and weak to say much, and the motion of the cab made her feel sick, so she found that, if she closed her eyes again, she could sink back into an unconsciousness, which she did. When she came to again, she was being lifted by him into bed.

She woke later that afternoon in a strange room. A merry fire was burning in a grate. Outside it was raining, she could hear the patter of water on a strange roof. The heavy curtains were richly embroidered. Mary lay in bed, surrounded by plump, soft cushions, feeling very sleepy, but content. There was a faint smell of cigar smoke – she knew Dalbeattie's particular brand of old, a comforting, spiced scent and she breathed it in, happily, wiggling her toes.

The door opened, and he came in, carrying a plate on a tray. Bread and butter, thick slices of golden cheese, thin curling slices of ham and an apple, delicately cut so it fanned across the plate. And there was tea, which he poured for her, spiced with orange and bergamot. He fed her until she took the food from him, and ate it all. He held the cup up to her mouth, saying nothing, watching her, as she drank.

Then he left her again, and she slept again.

Later, when it was growing dark outside, and still raining, he came in to put more logs upon the fire.

She observed him from under the blankets, and said, 'Where are we?'

'In Bloomsbury. In fact, you will be glad to know Mrs Pankhurst is around the corner. They put up quite a fight, those ladies. When she's released from hunger strike and taken home again you can hear 'em screaming as the police knock them down and cart them off.'

'I have been here,' she said, wondering. 'I was one of them.' All these years, and she had never known. 'It is yours, this house?'

'I bought it ten years ago. When I was the great hope of those looking for a new Webb, or Pugin, before Lutyens came along. Now I shall probably have to sell it, if my fortunes do not improve.' He laughed ruefully.

'Even I hear your name spoken in tones of great reverence, Lucius. I do not believe that.'

'War has put a stop to it all. People don't want large family houses, or churches, or concert halls. Or they do, but they say they'll wait, and I have so many ideas, and I can't wait.' He poked at the fire expertly, flipping one log over and Mary felt soft heat reach her. She pulled the sheets and eiderdown around her, gratefully warm. 'I am entering a competition to design the Canadian parliament buildings. Four in all. If I were to get it, it would set me up again, most successfully. If not, I'll have to make some alterations in my living arrangements.' He saw her face. 'I am comfortable. But I must find more work. And this house . . .' he trailed off. 'It is too big for one person.'

'Did your wife never live here?' He paused, rubbing his face and looking at her with a grave expression. 'Dalbeattie . . . ? Will you not speak to me of her?'

'Forgive me. My wife has not been back to London since I bought the place. I had hoped at first it would be a family home. But it was not to be, as you may remember.' He spread out his long, strong hands.

'The fork . . . I do.' Their eyes met. Old friends, who knew the other's stories. When was I last so at ease with another person, she thought. Not for years. Not since — and she glanced around at the dark, warm room. 'Have you remodelled this place, like Nightingale House?'

Silence fell between them, and then he said sharply, 'I will never do that again. I will build myself or live in another's home. It's bad luck, to combine the two.'

She thought of the children's cupboards on the top floor, of the wooden window seats in the sitting room for small people to put their toys in. Eliza's head, bent over one, throwing wooden blocks and books and toys out behind her with glee. She thought of her room in the long afternoons, the sense of him upon her, pressing down on her, the two of them, melding into one . . . She nodded.

'Do you have any servants?'

'They're not here.'

'Come here,' she said, and he sat down on the bed, spreading his long hands over the oyster-coloured silk of the eiderdown. He lifted the empty plate gently on to the side table.

'When was the last time you ate?' he said.

'Yesterday lunchtime.'

'Before that?'

'Oh, the day before. I had tea at a friend's house. She gave me food. She knows my situation.'

He was silent, and then said, quickly, 'Tell me, Mary dear. Has he gone? John? Horner's boy, has he gone to war?'

She shook her head, miserably. 'I don't know, Lucius. I don't know anything of them. I write, but . . . I understand.'

She could feel his leg against her knee through the sheets as he sat facing her. 'Do you see anyone from the old life now?'

'I am often with my new sisters now. Organising meetings, planning demonstrations . . . we support one another. None of us have much. We are mostly spinsters.'

'Is that so?'

'It's hard to believe, isn't it? An old man spat on me last month. Told me I was a dried-up old busybody *and* that I was lost to sin. I told him it was quite something to be both.'

He smiled, the warm, anxious, quizzical smile and she felt that liquid feeling of certainty, of pleasure. 'And are you?'

She could feel his leg, pressing more firmly against hers, and he leaned towards her. It was quiet again, no carriages or motor cars, only the distant sound of a dog, howling somewhere, and the rain.

'Am I what?'

'Lost to sin?'

Her eyes raked him over; a pulse throbbed at the base of her throat. Her face was warm with anticipation. 'Yes. I think I always was, Lucius.'

He took her in his arms and kissed her, and Mary, after a decade or more of no physical contact more than either the rough hands of a policeman or a friend's warm handshake, moved against him. His mouth on hers, her skin on his . . . He was saying something to her, something in her ear:

'I did not bring you here . . .'

She stopped him. 'I know. Goodness, Lucius. Of course.'

'My dear — are you sure?'

She made him leave the room. He had taken off only her jacket when he laid her in the bed. Carefully, she now removed her much-mended long tweed skirt, her blouse of fine cambric French lawn, near to where the fighting was right now, she knew. Then her petticoats, her stockings, so she was only in her camisole. She let down her dark hair, so that it brushed her shoulders. She was alert, erect, her body almost twitching with desire. Unbidden, came the thought of his wife – of her own sister – of all the many dreadful wrongs caused by their previous affair.

I am already so far lost that it makes no difference if he takes me now, she told herself. And, dear God, I want him.

'You may come in,' she called, and he opened the door, and his eyes glazed as he saw her again, and she saw his nostrils as he inhaled.

'My dear Mary,' was all he said. 'I have been half alive without you, all these years.'

She met his gaze. 'And I you, my love.'

She was his mistress from that night, and as they came together in the high-ceilinged room with the rain cascading down against the shutters, thundering on the front steps, pounding on the pavements below and gushing down the drains, all Mary could think of was of becoming clean again. As she moved against him, half frantic, half caressing, sure of herself, she realised that with age came a comforting kind of certainty. She fell asleep against him. The crisp clean sheets smelled of starch. She had not smelled starch for many years.

Chapter Thirty-Two

November 1917

Dearest Liddy

I think of you so often. I know that John is in France but I do not know how he fares. Was he at the Somme? Have you seen him this past year? May God keep him safe. Dalbeattie saw La Touche at dinner who told him John had gone to war and that is how I know.

Darling Liddy, I am Dalbeattie's mistress. We are in love and live for each other. His wife is in Scotland and does not travel to London. Divorce is out of the question for not only would she not consider it, his reputation must not suffer; fortunately, my reputation concerns no one. I have picked up my pen to write to you so many times and cannot find a way to set down the words but now I must do so.

I have never quite fitted anywhere else. I do believe that this is what I was made for: to love him. I miss you, Liddy, I love you, I miss dear Ned, and John. I know I can never atone for what I did; I have learned that now, and that like you I won't ever really know happiness, nor even that I should seek it. I wrestle with that every day. I have found him again; we love one another; we are as content as we might be; but I do not think I deserve to have these rewards. So perhaps one day to pay for it I will simply have to set him free.

The Times yesterday had news of your stay in London and that you were residing at the Galvestons'. Has Ned another painting like The Lilac Hours? *He is a grand old patriot now, isn't he, Liddy? Times change us all.*

Liddy, I shall be beside the Albert Memorial on 28th November, that is two days' time, at noon. I write to ask you if you will meet me there? My love, I am certain I am with child and am to be confined,

354

perhaps in June. I long to see you. One more time. We are the only two
left. I will understand if you are not able to do so, but I will be there
and very much hope to see you, dearest.

Your loving sister
Mary Helena Dysart

'She uses her own name still!' Liddy had said, waving the letter at
Ned, who was pulling his black tie from his neck. She bit her nail,
staring out at the frozen street through a tiny chink in the heavy
silk brocade curtains. 'A *child*. You don't – you haven't heard from
Dalbeattie, have you?'

Ned shrugged out of his waistcoat. 'I've heard nothing since
that last letter when I wrote to tell him to send no more, my love.
Will you meet her?'

Liddy looked down. 'I don't know that I can. I want to return
to Nightingale House as soon as I may,' she said, sliding a comb
from her hair and laying it on the dressing table. 'You know John
may be back on leave, at any time. To miss him—'

'She asks nothing of you other than one meeting.' Ned dropped
a kiss on to her loosened tresses.

'You don't understand. I –' Her heart ached; it was tired, she
thought, tired of all this.

'My dearest.' Ned stood in front of her and took her hand. 'You
should meet her. She is your sister, after all. When you think what
we endured, all of us . . .'

Liddy closed her eyes. 'She is the only one alive now who knew
how I suffered as a child. She is the one person who understood.
I cannot escape the conviction she betrayed me. I know it is foolish,
but it is a conviction.' She bowed her head, overwhelmed. 'I must
get home, tomorrow, anyway.'

'This is your first trip from home for – what is it? For three
years. You must learn to enjoy yourself, just a little, Liddy darling.
I want you to stay tomorrow, for a special reason.' His smiling eyes
danced; he caught hold of the iron bedstead and rocked backwards

and forwards, with excitement. It was infectious: she leaned into him, and suddenly they were teenagers again, twining towards each other. He said, 'John wouldn't want you to be chewing your nails and sitting anxiously by the door, waiting for him to come back, would he?'

'No . . . Perhaps you're right,' she said. 'My love.'

'Oh, Liddy. How lovely you are tonight,' he said softly in her ear, and she took his head in her hands and looked up into his face, warm in the gaslight. She could see every wrinkle and line, and, about the eyes, a spark. He had, since their arrival in London, been on edge, twitchy; she was glad the dinner had gone well, that he seemed more content than he had been for a while.

The war had been good for Ned. *The Lilac Hours* had been greeted with enormous enthusiasm. He had not received the same amount for the painting as he had for *The Garden of Lost and Found*, but thousands had come to see it, first at the Royal Academy, for the first wartime Summer Exhibition, then at Galveston's gallery. The soldier, added at the last minute, was a shadowy, noble symbol in the doorway bidding the central female figure goodbye, the black outline of his officer's cap and rifle throwing into relief the soft, anguished, yet stoical smile on the woman's face. The hint through the open door of an English garden in full beauty, the ideal for which the boys at the Front were fighting – all these artful details meant the painting was an unqualified success, his first in years. It was not to everyone's taste, but it was a beautiful piece of work. And he had done a panel series too – four paintings, shown in sequence, called *Tommy Atkins is Off.*

Tommy Atkins is Off was the story of a young soldier. In reality he had been modelled by a grumbling and arthritic Darling, dressed in the garb of a young private on leave. *The Graphic* magazine had bought the copyright and printed a different episode each week, designed to be clipped from the paper; later they produced high-quality reproductions which they gave away during the first two Christmases of the war: thousands, perhaps millions, of homes now had a *Tommy* on their wall: Tommy and his friends in a cheery group walking towards the recruiting office; Tommy bidding goodbye to his sweetheart, chastely, over a cottage garden wall, their hands touching, kitbag slung over his shoulder; Tommy now one of hundreds of men aboard a great train bound for the coast filled with excited, freshly minted soldiers, and finally Tommy in uniform, walking along a country lane towards – what? It wasn't made clear, but his jaunty step left one in no doubt Tommy would be home shortly, victory achieved.

Privately, Liddy disliked the jingoism of it, and thought Tommy Atkins would be, in real life, the most tedious type of rascal. Liddy wondered if she was the only one who looked quizzically at him, at the role he – and by extension Ned – was playing in convincing the nation this war was to the good. But of this, as with so much else, she had said nothing to Ned and so, despite her constant fear John would be given leave and go to Nightingale House only to find them absent, they had come to town this glittering, ice-cold November for a dinner Galveston and the critic la Touche were hosting together in Ned's honour.

Though she had tried to plead for her absence, once she was in London again Liddy had enjoyed herself at first. There were old, and dear, friends who exclaimed over her, said that they never saw her. She was dressed in black chiffon trimmed with cream lace, her shoulders bare, wearing the diamond earrings Ned had given her when she gave him their son. Her hair had been dressed by Laura Galveston's lady's maid, and Liddy knew, as she descended the stairs, that she was quite elegant, still, despite being now a lady of forty-two and quite, she assumed, beyond the gaze of men. Galveston had seated himself next to her at supper. La Touche had whispered across the table to her that she was still a great beauty, and Sir Augustus Carnforth, the great industrialist who had bought so many of Ned's paintings over the years, had calmed her fears greatly over John, and the current situation.

'I have it on good authority from a dear friend of mine, a major, you see. It's a great fight. The boys love the "scrapping", they call it, Mrs Horner. It's an adventure, out there. Your boy is with . . .?'

'The Worcestershire Regiment. Fourth Battalion.' Liddy looked over at Ned, who was standing in a corner, whispering with Galveston. Some new plan afoot, she knew it; Ned was wild-eyed at the moment, particularly on edge.

'Ah.' A slight pause, and incline of the head. 'A good regiment. He'll be having a terrific go, you'll see. Not that he'll tell his mama about it! Hah!' He had raised his glass to her.

He tells me everything, she had wanted to say, but he was being kind and she did not want to be rude. *And what he doesn't tell me, I know, oh, I know it very well. Even if he doesn't suspect I know it.*

'He was at the Somme,' she said and she could not but help let pride creep into her voice for the news of the eventual victory there and the huge, catastrophic casualties sustained by the French and British had lately been received back in London. 'He was very lucky. He was involved in capturing—'

Panic gripped her, as so often when she thought of him, and she could not remember the name of the village. And she didn't want to be here, suddenly. She wanted to be back at Nightingale House, near Eliza, and waiting for sweet gentle John, alone with her own unhappiness, for the truth, real truth, was she could only tolerate company for a short time now. The words of John's last letter swam before her eyes:

I should be getting leave soon – please don't go too far from Nightingale House in case I can come home – please do write as often as you can. Please do. It is sometimes very hard here. I am awfully well but I have seen some rather upsetting things and letters do make a difference. Tell me about home. Tell me what is on the trees and whether the apples were good this autumn and who Zipporah is going to marry this week and what you found on the roof. Please do write, Mama, as often as you can.

It was a slow agony that ate away at you, every day, this business. Knowing your one surviving child was suffering, was crying out for you, that he was far away and you could not help him . . .

Sometimes, the words of his letters would burn into her memory and it was all she could see. *Please do write, as often as you can.*

After she had combed her hair, Liddy climbed into bed. Ned was already asleep, lying on his back, snoring. She shook him a little, very gently, for she would not disturb him. She picked up Mary's letter again, her eyes scanning the words, looking for a sign and then, unable to read properly in the dim light, turned down her lamp. The heavy curtains utterly blocked out the street lamps and she lay blinking in the inky blackness. Thoughts scrabbled in her head. John's face. Mary's handwriting. Ned's hand, writing something on Galveston's gold and marble Heppelwhite side table that evening, watched by Galveston. And the pulsing beat of her conscience, what she knew to be true.

If you had been there . . . you would have taken them to see Hannah, too. They would always have been at risk. She would always have given diphtheria to one of them. It was ordained.

'Oh—' she cried out softly, pushing her hands into her eye sockets. Ned muttered in his sleep, and was silent again, but Liddy did not sleep.

The following morning, she sat in the great liver-and-white-marbled breakfast room, pushing a plate of uneaten kidneys and toast around her plate and staring out of the window. It was deliciously, luxuriantly warm inside, but outside it was a cold, clear day, the sky a piercing royal-blue. Liddy longed to open the french windows, to inhale the fresh air, feel its bite in her lungs. She realised she hated London, and now only wanted to go home.

Out in the hall of this great, echoing house someone was delivering something, and the doors were being opened, men shouting to each other. Liddy swallowed some coffee, her stomach churning. She had not slept. Mary was somewhere – how? Where? What was she doing? Was she well? Mary was small, like Liddy, but not tough;

359

she had been so ill as a child. She should not be having a child herself.

I will go to meet her. Yes. Liddy speared a kidney, then put it down. She felt sick. *I can't.*

She thought of brisk, bustling, glamorous Laura Galveston, who had casually revealed yesterday after dinner that she had cut ties with all her family for many years now. 'It became too hard to maintain relations with them. There were difficulties about expectations, money, unfortunate incidents of a kind we could not find acceptable . . . I found it easier to slice the trouble out, root ball and all.'

As if one were dismissing a servant, or cutting down a diseased climber. She bowed her head, alone in the room, thoughts jostling for space, just as the door opened and Ned came in, tugging at his waistcoat.

'Ah. My love,' he said. 'I have a surprise for you.'

Liddy looked up, in a daze. 'What's that, dearest?'

'Come with me,' he said, taking her hand, and with the other smoothing a finger across her forehead. 'This will take your sadness away. Yes! I promise you it will,' he said, laughing at her querying face. 'Come!'

He pulled her into the hallway, lined with its cabinets and sideboards and ormolu vases. There was a Rococo mirror from a king's palace in France; Liddy knew because Laura had told her this yesterday, as well as what it cost. Her heart was beating – what surprise could it be?

Galveston was standing in the vast hall, next to a painting on a wooden stand. He was rubbing his hands. 'Good morning, my dear Liddy,' he said. 'Your husband has, yet again, made a gesture of ridiculous generosity towards you – I tried to stop him – he wouldn't hear of it!' He raised his hands now, disclaiming involvement, eyes twinkling.

'I wanted you to have it back,' said Ned, almost shyly, in her ear. 'I – look, here it is.'

Liddy didn't understand. He led her around to the other side of the easel. She gazed at the painting before her. She had not set eyes on it since they had left London on that dreadful day sixteen years earlier.

There were the children, running into the garden; there were Eliza's wings. Eliza's strong, slender foot. Her golden hair. The window up above Liddy's study open; a creeper twining towards it. The glinting stars on the ceiling in the Birdsnest. She had never noticed that detail before.

Liddy stared at herself, a hazy small figure, straight-backed and calm, precisely at the very centre of the painting, and of that world. She had never really noticed that before, either.

'Ned,' she said, slowly. 'What have you done?'

'I've bought it from Galveston,' he said, softly, as if they were alone. 'Got a fair price, I promise you. I wanted him to stop making reproductions of it, selling it everywhere. I wanted it at home again.'

'No,' Liddy said again. She tore her eyes from the painting. 'I *don't* want it, Ned. I don't ever want to see it again.'

He gave her a small, mechanical smile, as if she were a cross child. 'But it's ours, dearest. I leave at lunchtime, I'm taking it back to the house again. I thought we could hang it in the hall—'

'*No!*' Liddy said, raising her voice. She turned away from Galveston towards her husband. 'Ned, how much did you pay for it?'

Ned glanced at Galveston, whose expression was more fixed than ever.

'I'll leave you, dear Liddy, to discuss this with your husband. Excuse me,' he said, melting away and she saw him folding a piece of paper smoothly into his waistcoat, like a magician.

They were alone. Around them, the sounds of the house in the morning: tradesmen on the street, a maid banging a carpet somewhere, Laura Galveston talking upstairs. Liddy turned to Ned and in a low voice hissed:

'Tell me, Ned, damn you. How much was it?'

He looked at her, utterly surprised; she'd never spoken to him like that before.

'Well – five thousand guineas, my love. It's a lot, I know, but with *The Lilac Hours* and *Tommy Atkins* and my work now—'

'Five *thousand guineas*!' Liddy's hand flew to the tight lace collar at her throat. 'He let you – how *could* he?'

'It's a good price – dear, I wanted you to—'

'You've paid five thousand guineas to buy back something you painted, you painted with love . . .' Her mouth was full of bile. She swallowed. 'Ned, dearest – we do not have that money.'

He looked around, furiously. 'Don't discuss our finances in the damned hallway of our host,' he said, pulling her back into the breakfast room, glancing at the painting, standing alone in the hall. 'Liddy, I thought you'd be as pleased as I am.'

She shut the door, breathing fast. 'I don't understand how you could do this. Don't you see? How – how can you ask me to look at this painting every day? How can you!'

'We were happy! We – we are still, of sorts, are we not?'

She took his hand. 'You won't ever speak of her. You don't ever let me mention her – her name. Eliza.'

He turned his head, closing one eye, wincing. 'I – do. I can.'

'Her name was Eliza, and she was seven.'

'I say – don't.'

'*Eliza!*' Liddy heard herself shout. 'That was her name! It is inconceivable to me that you won't name her! She was our daughter, and you—'

He cut in.

'It was inconceivable to me that you wouldn't let Carritt perform the operation,' he said quietly, and he lifted his eyes to hers, and she saw the coldness in them. 'It might have saved her.'

She stared at him. 'You blame me, then, for what happened?'

'I do not.'

But she didn't believe him. Liddy's throat hurt, as it always did when she thought of Eliza. 'Then that at least is why you think I am wrong to be angry with Mary.'

He pulled his hands away from her. There was something desolate in the way he said, 'I don't care any more, Liddy, dearest. I did it to try and make something right again. I wanted it to make you happy.'

'*Happy!*' She gazed around her. 'Happy . . . oh, Ned. Do you not understand? When I walked behind her coffin I saw the rest of my life, my dear. I saw it stretching ahead of me: I knew I could never be happy again. It's not something you can bandage up, make better, dearest. We lost her. She—' She shook her head, and whispered, 'How can you have believed that I would have wanted you to spend our money on this? It will ruin us.'

'It's my money,' he said, flatly, and she stared at him, teeth gritted. 'I wanted to do it, Liddy, to remind us both, we had it, we had this life, we are these people! I think we've forgotten it, over the years, with everything that's happened. But we were awfully happy, and we did . . . the children . . .' He trailed off. 'I love you so very much, my dearest. I—'

She knew, then, of course, that his very reasons for doing it and hers for hating the gesture were the same, but the breach was too wide.

'Can you tell Galveston to sell it to a museum, instead?'

'The deal is done,' said Ned, drawing himself up. 'I wouldn't try to go back on it. I will take the painting home, today. Will you join me?'

She could not stand to look at him, suddenly. To be near him. Rage suffused her.

'No,' said Liddy, her jaw set. 'I will not. I will come tomorrow.'

As if they were discussing the weather he said, 'Will you meet Mary?'

'I don't know yet. I – I don't know.' She pressed her fingers to her mouth, wanting to be sick, wanting to get away from him. 'But I won't come with you today.'

Mary unwound her scarf from around her red, frozen fingers; she had no gloves and had left her muffler in Bloomsbury. Shaking, she pulled at the door pull.

'*Is that you? Oh, it's you, isn't it! Hooray!*'

She could hear his lanky legs, tumbling down the stairs from the top floor. Behind her, the traffic on the road thrummed in her tired ears – horse and cart, carriage, motor cars, bicycles. He flung open the door, clasping her cheeks in his warm hands.

'Hello, my darling,' he said. 'How wonderful to have you at the studio. Come into the warmth.' And he kissed her.

'The warmth,' Mary said, leaning into him. 'I am mostly ice. Feel.' Dalbeattie took her hand in his, and shook his head gravely. He led her upstairs.

Dalbeattie's studio in Barons Court looked out over the busy Cromwell Road. The top floor was a vast room flooded with light through a large curved and leaded window. He had had the place for years; once, long ago, he and Ned had worked there together.

It was cosy, a fire burning in the grate and the smell of his cigars hanging in the air; a draughtsman's board by the window, and two chairs beside the fire. Dalbeattie sat her down carefully on one of them, chafing her hands all the time, and scolding her. 'What am I to do about you if you go out without a muffler or gloves, Miss Dysart?' He set about making her some tea; a kettle, hanging over the fire in the huge hearth, was put on at once to boil.

Her velvet cap, which had been next to a wet umbrella and thus damp when she left his house that morning, had actually frozen in the hour she had spent waiting beside the Albert Memorial and then in the subsequent walk to Barons Court. She removed it and it began to melt in the warm room, moisture dripping on to the floor.

She watched him, thawing herself, her chin in her hands, unable to stop herself smiling despite the day. The sight of him was so very comforting. His long arms reached fluidly around the room, gathering this, putting down that. He was efficient, capacious, eccentric, brilliant. He filled every room with his warmth; you were always waiting for him to come back in when he left.

I love him so much, she thought simply. That is all there is to it.

Blinking, Mary stood up, to look at the drawings on Dalbeattie's board.

'What are these, my darling? More sketches for the Canada competition?'

'No . . .' He hesitated. 'It's a house.'

She turned, surprised. 'I thought there was still very little interest in houses.'

'Well . . . you see. My lovely Mary.' He came towards her, with a plate of sardines, and toast. 'It is a house for us. To live in.'

Dalbeattie set down the food and, standing behind her, wrapped his arms around her. She could feel his voice reverberating against her as, with one hand, he gestured to the drawings. 'Here's the front door. Right in the middle. Yes, rather revolutionary of me, I know. Off to one side, that's the drawing room. The other side, there's the dining room and the kitchen's behind it. Now upstairs, there are three bedrooms.'

'Three?'

'For whoever needs them! We shall have everyone to stay. All our friends shall come. And, look, there is a skylight here, with milky glass which lets in light all year round. And down there is a chute, so all the laundry disappears into the room at the bottom of the house and you and I will never be troubled with untidiness.'

Mary gave a great laugh, for order and precision, except on the draughtman's board, were not Dalbeattie's strongest suits. 'That is a masterly idea. You are . . .' She nestled against him, inhaling his lovely, warm, spiced smell. 'You are very clever, Dalbeattie.'

His warm lips kissed her neck, his arms held her tight to him. 'There's a seat by the fireplace, next to it, for you to sit in when it's cold as today. So you are always warm. There's a little garden at the back and at the front, I think it's so pleasant to have something at the front. And there will be an apple tree, for my Mary to put a swing in, and lie under its branches on hot days.'

Gently, she touched the plans. 'When will you build it?'

'Well, alas, not soon. My lovely girl, look at me.' He pulled away from her, and turned her so they were facing, then he shuffled towards the fire. 'There. I have to tell you that I found out today they have taken me on for the Canadian parliament commission.' His face split into a smile. 'I can't say anything, but to you I must of course. They want me to come over as soon as I can – you will come too, of course. We will make it all right—'

'Oh, darling. At last. I'm so very happy for you.' She stood on tiptoe, head spinning, to kiss him, and felt the hardness of her stomach, pressing against his waistband. Soon he would notice. Wouldn't he? Didn't he ever wonder how she dealt with such matters?

'The Canadian fellow who's appointed to lead the competition is awfully nice. They *all* seem awfully nice. Perhaps we should – I think we could consider starting again over there. You and I – I could build that house . . .'

'What of your wife, my love? If they were to discover that – we'd be going into it with a lie,' she said. She wanted to sit down, suddenly. But, with ice-cold clarity, she saw now that their days together were numbered and she clung to him.

'We'll make it all right,' he said, looking at her rather strangely. He moved away from her, and took a sardine, wiping his fingers carefully on a napkin. He offered her one; she shook her head, suddenly dizzy with nausea, but smiled through it. He mustn't know now. Not now. Her plans must be in place. 'They – I won't mention it to them, but if you were to come with me and say you were my wife . . .'

'But if they discovered that were not the case, which, my darling, they easily would? And her father is already angry enough with you, for staying away so long, even though it is at her bidding . . . It would come out, and we have never dealt in subterfuge. We have lived quietly, but never lied.' She smiled, to hide the rising panic she felt. 'My darling.' She stared at him, their dark eyes locked into each other. 'You *must* go. Do you understand?'

'But I want you to come—'

'Yes, and I will join you, later.'

He was silent for some time. 'Perhaps you are right. I – I cannot betray Rose, more than she has been betrayed.' He gave a deep, sad sigh. 'I'll leave you money—'

'Thank you. I will be with you, darling. You see, don't you?'

'Yes,' he said, nodding, and the relief on his face was palpable, and Mary understood then that he had realised she couldn't go, but

366

hadn't known how to say it. She knew him: his only weakness was wanting to please all the time. He had always been so; kindness leaked out of him. 'Now, my love. I will make you some tea, and we shall sit and be warm, and then I shall convey you back to our den of sin in fashionable Bloomsbury, will that suit you?'

'It will.'

Having handed her a cup of tea, Dalbeattie stuck some bread on to a toasting fork and plunged it into the fire. Mary stared at it, wiggling her toes, almost warm again. The enormity of all the decisions to be made closed in on her then seemed to bounce off her, as if they were so great they couldn't stick to her, but must move away, like clouds. She shook her head, blinking. What am I to do?

With a great start Dalbeattie dropped the fork. 'My love, I haven't asked you how it was today. How selfish I am!'

Mary had to drag herself back to the present moment. 'What's that?'

'Did you see Liddy?' He smote himself on the forehead. 'Your meeting — how could I have forgotten to ask you! How was she?'

Mary wrapped her hands around the warm teacup. She smiled up at him, swiftly. 'She didn't come. It's of no matter. I was certain she wouldn't.'

'Oh — my love. I'm sorry . . .'

'Let's talk of other things.' She sipped the tea. 'Of what you know of Canada, and your plans.'

'In a moment. But will you write to your sister again?' His kind, dear face stared at her. How many more hours were left to them? How many more moments like this?

And so it begins, Mary thought. *Now, now I must pay for my sins, and for dreaming of happiness.*

'I miss her most dreadfully, every day,' she said, staring at the black kettle, swinging on its hook from the heat of the fire. 'But I don't think we are sisters any more.'

Chapter Thirty-Three

The telegram was waiting for Liddy when she finally returned to the Galvestons' that evening. She had been out all day with Laura Galveston, hours of walking through Knightsbridge, looking at cloth for curtains in Harrods, stuff for the chairs, visiting a silk emporium off Piccadilly, and they had taken tea at Fortnum's. Ned had left at lunchtime, with the picture, and as midday came and went Liddy was glad of the company of the garrulous older woman, who asked no questions of her guest and ignored Liddy's red eyes, shaking hands and distracted manner.

Several times Liddy almost said, 'I have remembered a prior engagement. Would you excuse me?' She could right this wrong – as she sat there with Mrs Galveston, refusing tiny delicate pastries pressed upon her at frequent intervals, she began to see she had made a mistake. She could, still, meet Mary. They were in Piccadilly; she was so near the Albert Memorial. She could almost run there now. She could see her sister . . . hold her, kiss her . . . look into Mary's sweet, dark eyes, hold the hand that had soothed her all those years. . .

And yet, of course, she didn't.

The telegram lay on a bowl in the marble hallway. Liddy, divested of her cloak, caught sight of it, and found herself feeling faint. 'Oh, dear God.'

She snatched it up, fingers trembling, scanning the spidery pencilmarks. *Not 'Regret to inform you'. Please, please, anything but –*

'What does it say, my dear?' Mrs Galveston whispered.

John here unexpectedly home on leave stop must
return Friday stop come back as soon as you can
Horner

Galveston had taken their new motor car to visit a client. Laura
Galveston said, vaguely, that she was sure she could try and find
someone who could drive Liddy back . . . 'But, dear, it's rather late,
they'll think it all rather . . . odd. Oh, this is the end, we must have
a telephone installed, I swear we're the last people to have one. My
dear, I'm so sorry, what else can I do to help?'

She wouldn't help her, Liddy knew it. These people weren't her
friends, they had profited from Ned his entire life, but now, when
help was needed, did nothing.

There were no more trains that night, so she caught the first
one the following morning, not reaching home until well after
lunchtime. Old Darling picked her up in the car from the station.
She had not slept, nor eaten, and as Liddy slammed the car door
shut, fingers frantically fussing with her bun, she said urgently:

'How is he, Darling? How does he seem? Oh, do hurry, please
do.'

'He's different, ma'am,' is all Darling would say.

The torture of the slow lanes, of the car stalling and having to
be restarted, of Darling jumping on to the running board, of the
freezing ice that meant they had to travel slowly – all her life, all
of it, Liddy would remember the agony of the journey, of being
utterly powerless.

At last, just after two, they turned into the driveway. A Daimler,
with chauffeur, stood in front of the house. Liddy leaped out, barely
noticing it as she rushed to the front door.

'Where is he?' she called, wildly, hammering to be let in. 'Where's
John? Darling – John boy, where are you?'

The front door opened. John stood there, smiling at her. She
flung herself into his arms. He hugged her, stiffly.

He was very thin, and smelled of tobacco, and strong disinfectant
soap, and something else – a metallic smell, earthy, outdoors. The

369

shoulder straps and hard brass buttons of his uniform chafed her cheek and shoulder as she held him tight, muttering his name.

'John, John. My darling boy . . . John . . . darling . . . I'm so sorry – Why on earth didn't you tell us? But you didn't have any notice, I expect? When did you get here?'

'Two days ago, but I needed to sleep. I wasn't – I couldn't – I needed to sleep.' He gripped her shoulders and she looked at him again, properly. His eyes seemed to stare past her, not at her.

Liddy caught his hands, panicking at the blankness in his eyes.

'You're thin, and you've grown a moustache – it's very handsome, Johnny. But why—' She fingered the brass buttons on his army coat. 'Why are you dressed like that?'

'I've to leave, now,' he said. 'There's a mistake.' He gestured at the waiting car. 'Major Coote very kindly agreed to take me back with him. We ship out again tomorrow.'

She had the feeling she had dreamed this but now it was like a nightmare, playing out in real time. She turned, an ache in her neck, and saw a figure inside: little Alfred Coote, Alfred Coote who had played with John, tormented him rather, when they were boys. He was a man now, wearing a captain's peaked hat, winged stripes on his shoulders, moustache covering his lip. He touched his brim, formally.

'Good afternoon, Lady Horner,' he said, over the juddering engine's noise.

'But can't you go back tomorrow . . .?' she asked, and as she did the words died on her lips. There was no point.

'Come inside with me,' she said, tugging on his arm. 'Just for a moment.'

He nodded at the car, and turned back, inside the house.

'Where's Dad?' she said, as she led him into the sitting room. A roaring fire leaped in the grate; the old sofas, worn and comfortable, the books so dear. She felt she had been away for months, not days, that she was seeing the old house through John's eyes. The agony of his departure hit her again.

'We have said our goodbyes. He's working.'

He was shivering. She looked at him, not knowing where to start. 'John, darling, are you well? Do you have enough – enough to eat?'

Again, the thousand-yard stare, behind her, into nothing. She pulled him down, on to the sofa. He rested his head on her breast, and inhaled deeply; she stroked the scratchy wool of his uniform, then his hair. It was shorter than it had ever been, and uneven; shorn by some unknown hand. His hands were different too: the fingers bursting over the nails, tiny rectangles bitten to the quick. Two of them were missing. She stroked one finger; he pulled the hand away.

'Flung about a bit during a shell.'

She pressed his head tightly to her, hearing his breathing. 'Oh, my dear. Is it – is it very bad? Please tell me. Tell me the truth, dearest.'

John leaned back, his kind eyes searching her face. 'I won't, Mama, if you don't mind, very much.' He buried his head against her shoulder again, as the fire crackled. 'I can't really bear to talk about it. I don't want you to know how awful it is, to have it in your mind, too. Honestly. Some chaps rather like it. I'm afraid I'm not one of them. Let me just enjoy this, this last moment, will you? Talk to me about something. About something lovely.'

'Something lovely.'

'Yes, Mama. When we were happy, here. Tell me something.'

A silence fell in the room, apart from the fire, and the sound of the engine outside, throbbing ominously. Liddy swallowed, and then told him again, for the final time, the story of the *The Garden of Lost and Found*, and how they were painted by Ned that summer's day.

And what did Eliza do?

She tore off the wings and threw them away.

And what did I do?

You were so hungry you ate leaves and were sick. And in the end I had to tell your father you were both rebelling. And you were allowed to pick what you wanted, and you both had Welsh rarebit for tea. And honey in your milk.

When she looked up she could see the garden out of the large old windows, the sloping land, the bare branches of the Wilderness hung with the first frost and the fading autumn light, deep gold and silver. After a while she finished the story, and was silent, and nothing else was said. They clung to each other and Liddy knew then. There was a sense of calm acceptance and of destiny, and perfect understanding between her and her son. There always had been.

John stood up. 'This is bloody,' he said, and he picked up his kit bag and coat, and slung it over his shoulder. 'Goodbye, darling.' He paused in the doorway, beside the coat hooks, and put one hand on the front door. She watched him, for the final time; his handsome kind face – he was still a boy. He should not be going.

'My lovely one.' Liddy got to her feet. 'Please – please take care of yourself. Come back to me.'

He winced, and shook his head.

'I have already gone, Mama,' he said, in a toneless voice. 'You know that, don't you?'

And he closed the door behind him.

Part Four

Chapter Thirty-Four

Here are a few first aid remedies for one's children, Juliet. These herbs all grow in the little kitchen garden.

Mint leaves can be rubbed on the tongue for an ulcer and to heal aches and pains and bruises.

Dock leaves can be picked and applied to nettle stings, they grow nearby, their roots are red. You know this! The roots, when boiled in vinegar, help rashes and itches from coming.

Use thyme in hot water for an upset stomach.

March 2015

What things you must see as the barista on the night shift at the Costa Coffee shop in Walbrook district hospital. Juliet watched the woman taking her order. She herself couldn't stop shivering, she was filthy, bedraggled. Her trousers had caught on a twig on the fig tree as she'd run up to the house and were torn up to the knee, and she had tripped over into the mud, scraping her arm, tattooing it with little dots of embedded gravel that would not come out. She thought the woman must surely comment, make polite conversation. 'I hope you're OK.' But she barely made eye contact, just took the order with a nod then turned to make the coffee.

It was 5 a.m. Juliet wished she'd found the coffee shop earlier. It hadn't occurred to her that they'd have them in hospitals. How lucky she had been, all these years, to avoid hospitals, apart from the in-and-out births of her children and the occasional trip to A&E because of a viral infection or a cut: all seemed so silly, such overreactions now. How damn lucky she had been all her life. She saw it now. But here were all these people, with stories like hers, some disaster befalling them. Broken-down old women, bent backs, collapsed faces, heavily lined and blank. Normal-looking men: were they husbands? Sons? Fiddling on their phones as they waited. And the doctors and nurses, trying to pretend this was any other coffee queue in any normal coffee shop, like the Pret on Piccadilly where Juliet used to get her morning coffee, where the Italian barista sang to you and the whole place was thrumming, a stage, alive with the beginning of another London day. Here, you were queuing because something catastrophic had happened. An illness, growing, spreading inside you, whatever form. Or a swift brushstroke, a moment, one that could so easily have been avoided.

She had not left Sandy since they arrived at the hospital ten or so hours ago, except when the doctor had called her into the side room and explained how serious it was, as if she didn't know already. The room was decorated with soothing photographs of Greek monuments, and there were fake, dusty flowers, pink-tinged lilies, in a gel-filled vase on the shelf next to her. Bleeding on the brain. A broken arm and tibia. Condition grave. Brain scan. Intensive care. All these words, which she had to convey to Matt when he arrived, as accurately as possible, and she found when she repeated them to him they didn't make sense. She didn't know exactly what a tibia was but she hadn't asked – what question to ask, when there were so many?

Matt arrived at ten, and the girls cried. Juliet could not cry, she found. She did not know what to do beyond the sense that she must be happy and smiling when Sandy woke up. He had until recently been such a happy, smiling boy: it would distress him to see her unable to cope, keening, sobbing. And until she knew more about how he would be, that was her reasoning.

Matt couldn't drive the girls home, not yet, he said. He wanted to stay at the hospital, and neither of them wanted to leave.

At midnight Juliet realised she could actually ask for help, that this was a time to reach out to other people, say what she needed. So she called Honor's landline as she had no mobile signal at the barn, but there was no answer. She left a message, telling her what had happened, asking if someone could come and take the girls home, then she called Frederic, and said the same. But there was no answer there, too – of course not. Everyone was asleep.

They had put Sandy back into a medically induced coma, to allow the brain to rest and not over-exert itself, to minimise tissue damage. The girls were allowed in once. It was absolutely freezing in the intensive care ward, and Juliet did not realise how cold she was until she left to get the coffee and once in the warm lift, began to shake. The lift to intensive care took you straight up, missing out all the other floors, that was when you knew it was serious, too.

Sandy's little plump hand, with the dimples where knuckles should be, was awfully cold. The other hand was bandaged, so this was the one bit of him she could touch. She kept telling them that. 'Isn't he freezing? It can't be good for him, being that cold.' But they didn't care, or they pretended to, the nice nurse who was assigned solely to him. 'Don't worry about it.' Don't worry about it.

This was what life really was, pain and loss and endless suffering; she couldn't believe she hadn't seen it for so long. Most people denied it too, she supposed, until they were confronted with it. They lived their lives in the sunshine, ignoring the shadows that hovered around the edge . . .

'Ju?' A soft tap on the shoulder made her jump. 'Ju? Can you hear me?'

She turned in the queue and blinked at the figure next to her. 'George. Hello.'

George, in a hoodie, five o'clock shadow grazing his face, hugged her awkwardly. 'I heard the phone then I went back to sleep instead of listening to the message. I'm so sorry, Ju. This is awful. How is he?'

She leaned against him. 'I don't know. They say he's had a large bleed to the brain. He's broken some bones but it's the blow to the head they're most worried about. He banged it on the stone shelf when he fell then on the floor of the studio and I—' Her voice broke but she cleared her throat. No. 'It's my fault. I was rowing with Bea – with Bea!' She winced, as sharp tears pricked her eyes. George looked at her, his face an agony of sympathy, and rubbed her arm, then looked down at her scraped skin, dotted with gravel, and winced, but she shook her head. 'You take your eyes off them for two seconds . . . They always say that . . . Oh *God* . . .' She rubbed her eyes. 'What if he dies? Or what if . . . What was I *doing*?'

George didn't tell her what to do, or try and give false bluster. He patted her shoulder and said, 'I'm so sorry. It's not your fault, you know, Ju. Now, what can I do?'

'Can you take Bea and Isla home, stay with them?'

'Yes,' he said.

'Put Isla to bed, make sure Bea's OK. If they want to go to school, it'd be good for them to carry on as normal until we . . .' She trailed off.

'I'll do that,' said George. Someone else tapped her arm – it was the blank-faced barista.

'Please collect your coffee, madam.'

'I won't go,' said Bea. 'I want to stay here.' She glanced from Juliet to Matt and then awkwardly at George. 'I don't want to – please.'

'You don't have to go to school,' said Juliet. Isla, asleep in Matt's arms, shifted slightly, as though she had heard this. 'But, Bea, I need you at home, not here, my love. George will stay with you. I promise.'

'I'm not going into the Dovecote. I can't.'

'That's OK.'

'The doll's house – it's broken, all over the floor, I don't . . .' She folded her arms and looked down, her slim shoulders shaking, hair falling over her face. 'I said he couldn't play with it.'

Matt carefully handed Isla over to George, who hitched her on to his slight frame. She murmured something. Matt took Bea in his arms, and hugged her. 'Hey . . . sweetheart. This isn't your fault. Don't worry about the doll's house, about any of that,' he said. 'Mum will sort it all out. But I think you should go home. Let George take you and I'll be over later. We'll have news then. Good news, I know it, Bea, darling. It's a bad bump, that's all. They're very cautious with children, they have to be. OK? Promise. You mustn't worry.'

And he kissed the top of her head like he always had done and Bea nodded, and walked down the corridor, without another word, George following behind, carrying Isla, and Juliet and Matt were alone in the waiting room again.

'Shall we go back in again?' said Juliet, taking a sip of coffee.

'Sure. Juliet—'

The door banged open again and Juliet looked around to see what had been left behind, but it was the young doctor again. He shut the door, carefully. Juliet felt bile rising in her throat.

'Hello,' he said, looking down at his notes. 'Now, are you Sandro Taylor's dad?'

Matt held his hand out, eyes wide, terrified into formality. 'Yes, I'm his father. What's the latest?'

'Look, we are fairly concerned at this stage, I have to be honest. There are signs of contusions on the brain, and his blood pressure is very low, which indicates there may be increased intracranial pressure. That's when the brain tissue swells. We're worried about the neurochemical function, too. He's not responding well, he's very confused . . . His skull is cracked, that's part of the—'

There was a loud beeping noise, and the doctor looked at the beeper on his belt. 'Ah. Excuse me.' He stood up.

'Is that Sandy? What's happened?'

'Nothing to worry about, I'm sure,' he said, as though their son wasn't in intensive care with a head injury. As though it was something mundane, a lost toy, a scraped knee. And he opened the door. Juliet followed him out, Matt behind her. They reached the swing doors, the blast of cold air hitting them. 'Excuse me,' said the young doctor. 'Could you please just stay here?'

'Is it him? Or is it someone else?' Juliet called, but he'd disappeared, the door banging behind him.

'There's a—' she heard the nurse say, and some machine sounded, even louder.

Matt's arm went around hers. 'We can't stay here. Let's go and sit back down in that room.'

'Yes we can,' Juliet said, quietly. Her voice was thick in her throat. 'We'll just stay here, until they come out and tell us something.'

She knew then that he might die. That this was it. That close shaves and recoveries didn't happen in real life. He was so small, that was all, and he still had his fluffy, twining-floss baby hair, and the chubby arms and legs of a baby. He had direct blue eyes and a perfectly round head and he loved cheese. And Octonauts, and tigers. Loved tigers. And Bim, his teddy – Juliet shuddered at the thought that Bim was at home. Bim should be here. Sandy was so small but so strong and vital, it was so strange to think he might die. The violence required to snuff a life like his out, when he was not frail, failing. She swallowed, kept swallowing, because she might be sick.

They stood leaning against the wall, in silence, as the beeping continued.

How long they were there for Juliet didn't really know. But a face appeared on the other side of the door that led out to the lifts and she stared at it. Then it appeared again. Juliet went out and opened the door.

'George,' she said.

'Honor's at home with the kids.' His thin face was hollow. 'I just came back to give you something and to say – look, the thing is, I know I don't know you as well as Frederic but . . . my mum died when I was fourteen and I remember—' he broke off. 'God, that's not the right thing to say. I brought you this. I forgot to give them to you before.' He thrust a paper bag into her hands. 'It's sandwiches. And Lucozade. And some other snacks. And a thermos of coffee. And some magazines. Some of them are Frederic's antiques ones and a bit dry but you're into that stuff.'

Juliet looked in the bag, then back at Matt, who was staring curiously down the corridor at them. She looked back at George. He pursed his mouth up and shrugged.

'What I meant about my mum is, she was in hospital and I didn't eat anything for ages and it was bad. You need to eat. You'll fall over.'

'George—' she began, and he leaned forward, and gave a huge hug. He was bony, and his elbows dug into her too tightly, but he was steady, and firm. She buried her head against him, and he patted her hair.

'Juliet . . .' Matt was calling her. 'Juliet . . . They're taking him somewhere . . . We have to go.' He was standing by the door, gesturing with his hand.

'Go,' said George, instantly breaking away from her. 'Before I forget,' he said, sniffing loudly and smiling, 'Frederic's downstairs in reception. He came with me. He's got his car and he'll wait in case you need someone. Don't worry about him. We love you. Bye then.'

He turned away, as did Juliet, to see the doctor was in the doorway of the ward talking to Matt, beckoning her, fast. She ran towards them.

'Mrs Taylor,' he was saying, and she didn't understand, because that wasn't her, not any more. 'I have to tell you . . .'

Chapter Thirty-Five

'His manner is atrocious. They should send them on a course.'

'I think they do.' Juliet was stroking the cool softness of Sandy's cheek.

'Idiot.'

'If he hadn't recognised the severity of the bleed and operated it might have been different,' Juliet said, trying not to sound snappy. 'He's clearly not an idiot.'

'I'm going to have a word with him, anyway. The way he treated us, as if he'd died—'

'He nearly did die—' Juliet broke off. 'Don't Matt, please. Can you shush, just for once. What's that?' She turned away from him as Matt stared at her, open-mouthed. 'What did Sandy say?'

'I don't think it's anything, just dreaming,' the nurse said, coming over and looking at the vast computer screens which tracked Sandy's pulse and pressure and oxygen levels. 'Now that Mr Mirzoyan has operated and his blood pressure and neuro-function are improving he's more stable and hopefully becoming more alert. So he may sound very confused when he comes out of this. We're really very fortunate the doctor realised that was the problem.' Juliet blinked, then rubbed her face. The nurse said, kindly, 'Look. He's out of immediate danger now, we just have to wait to see what the long-term damage is.'

Juliet kept staring at her broken, bruised little boy, his face puffy with steroids and bruising from the emergency operation to relieve the pressure on his brain. One chubby arm was swept out to his side, bandages over his head.

'Mmm,' Sandy said, trying to move in his sleep. 'Mimmmm.'

'He's saying *Mum*,' said the nurse, pleased.

'He's not.' Juliet knew it wasn't that. 'He still calls me Mama, not Mum. He's saying something else.'

'I do think it's *Mum, mum*,' said the nurse, firmly, and Juliet gave up and turned to Matt.

'Do you feel like going to get some more coffee?'

They had eaten all of George's sandwiches, which were absolutely delicious – egg mayo and cress, and chicken and ham, the egg from the local chickens which gave beautiful bright orange yolks, well seasoned with pepper and cress and butter. The chicken and ham was delicious, thinly sliced, the chicken lightly flavoured with fennel and garlic, in a soft mustardy mayo, both fillings between George's sourdough bread. There had been crisps, and the first strawberries, sweet and plump. Of all the strange, terrible things about that night, for the rest of her life, Juliet would remember the taste of those sandwiches, after the longest, darkest night imaginable, and the kindness of friends.

'Frederic!' she said suddenly, with a start. 'He's still downstairs, poor old boy. I wonder if he's given up the ghost and gone home.'

'Who?'

'George's boyfriend. My grandmother's old friend, you know . . .' Juliet trailed off: Matt's tired eyes had glazed over. 'Don't worry. I'll call him – or maybe I should just pop down . . .'

'Mimmmmm,' said Sandy, suddenly, from his bed, and she jumped. 'Mimmmm. Mama. *Mama*.'

He started crying, a thin, wailing creak. Juliet stroked his forehead, very gently. 'Darling,' she said, as the nurse sprang towards her charge. 'Sandy, darling, you fell over. You're in hospital. You banged your head and hurt your arm and leg so all of them will hurt for a bit, sweetie. OK? But you're going to be fine.'

He stared past her, blankly.

'Do you know who I am?' she said, fear worming across her gut.

'Mama.' He blinked, and looked past her. 'Mama.'

He wasn't looking at her, but at a point on the ceiling. 'Can he see me?' she asked the nurse. She peered at her name badge. 'I'm sorry. Gabriella. Can he see me?'

'That's what I'm trying to check,' Gabriella said. 'I'll ask the doctor.'

'Mama,' said Sandy again. 'My mama.' Then he began to cry again, as Matt leaned over.

'Mate!' he said. 'Little mate. It's OK.'

'Mimm,' said Sandy. 'My want Mimm.'

'Bim?' She nodded. 'Bim, darling?'

'Mmmmm.'

He gave the softest, saddest cry, reached out with his one small hand for Juliet's fingers and he closed his eyes again, and in a minute was fast asleep.

'I'll go and get Bim, make sure everything's OK at home,' Juliet whispered, half an hour later to Matt, who looked up from his phone.

'What? You're leaving him?'

'I'll go home and get Bim. And some clothes, and books. I think it might help him to have some things around. And I want to make sure Isla and Bea are OK, the house . . .'

'You and that bloody house!' Matt was smiling. 'It's a joke. Are you seriously leaving your son to go back home?'

She stared at him. 'I just told you. I'm going to go and get Bim. They don't want Sandy getting agitated. If there are toys and clothes from home that make him feel secure so much the better. I'll have to go home at some point. It's a twenty-minute drive. I'll be back in an hour or so. I will have a shower, kiss the girls, grab an apple—'

'Say hi to your best friend George—'

'Jesus, Matt.' Juliet ground her jaw, and then closed her eyes, briefly. 'Honestly, let's not fight. We're really tired. I'll bring back some snacks. Maybe you could call the nursery again, explain—'

'Do you have the number?' Matt slid his phone out of his jeans pocket.

'I do but actually I've emailed and texted it to you loads of times as you're the second emergency contact. If you look on your phone you'll find it.' She stood over him, hoisting her bag on to her shoulder. 'Is that OK?'

'Sure.'

'Great. Thanks.'

When Juliet descended to the ground floor of the hospital again she felt as if she had lived eight more lives in succession. And there, in the middle of the row of mauve chairs, the morning sunshine dappling his nodding pate, sat a dozing Frederic, his wrinkled hands placed neatly palms down on his spotless twill trousers. Affection for him swelled within her – here he was, waiting for her.

She sat beside him and, just for a few seconds, allowed herself to feel the sunshine on her arms, to stretch out her tired legs and feet. Her neck crunched as she rolled her head around. She felt dizzy with exhaustion.

He snorted suddenly and jerked upright, wide awake, and stared at her.

'My dear.' He blinked, rapidly. 'What news? How is he?'

'He's conscious. We don't know if he's suffered brain damage. But they've relieved the pressure on the bleed. We have to wait and see. He's calling for me and he wants Bim. I thought I'd pop back to the house and get some of his things and have a shower, check on the girls.' She stood up. 'Will you drive me?'

'But of course,' said Frederic, and he offered her his arm, and they walked out into the sunshine to the car park. He helped her into the warm car, as though she were the child. Juliet dozed on the drive back to Nightingale House, waking with a gasping start as her phone buzzed. 'Jesus.' She shook her head. 'I – sorry.'

'Don't be sorry,' said Frederic. 'Don't be sorry for anything.'

They were five minutes from home. Juliet looked down at her phone.

Taken Bea to get some fresh air and to pick up Isla. Isla went off to school OK but I expect she's pretty tired now. I've swallowed my resistance to carrots as she wanted some. A magnificent frozen

shepherd's pie and lasagne have been left on the doorstep in a
freezer bag. I've cooked the shepherd's pie and left it to cool in
the fridge. Planted some lupins and foxgloves by the way.
Love to Sandy. Take care of yourself darling. Honor

I'm so very very sorry to hear about Sandy, Juliet. I've sent
some food over to your house so you're not worrying about
cooking. Thinking of you constantly. Please let me know if
there's anything I can do. Sam

Hey Ju mum told me about your kid. I'm so sorry. T
ake care mate. See you soon Ev x

He's still sleeping. Sorry for being a bellend. Take your time. M x

Just one more thing – solicitor just phoned. Stupid timing
but did you post back the divorce papers? Tess could drop
them off with Steve if so. M x

And Juliet found she was laughing though nothing was funny
but she couldn't stop. A seam she couldn't close. Eventually Frederic
pulled over in a lay-by. He patted her knee, as she laughed and
laughed, and waited for it to subside. Wordlessly, Juliet showed him
the messages.

'Who's Sam?' he said.

'My new boss.'

'Ah. This Matt – he really does want *un divorce*, does he not? Most
unfortunate.'

'It would seem so.' Juliet was too tired to be angry, or to feel
anything.

Frederic steered them past the church and into the driveway. He
patted her knee. 'Come on, let's go inside.'

She stared up at the house, suddenly terrified. 'I don't want to.'

'Nonsense,' said Frederic, sharply. 'You must.' Juliet set her teeth,
and nodded.

The house was eerily empty, abandoned shoes in the corridor, Juliet's jumper dropped where she had discarded it in the hall, cereal bowls on the dining room table. Together, they climbed the stairs. She went into Sandy's room, looking out over the Wilderness. The Dovecote caught her eye, the door still open from the dreadful events of the previous day.

'George is wonderful,' she said, for something to say.

'He is.'

Juliet was picking up books – *Oh No, George!*, *Alfie Gets in First*, *Peepo* – mechanically dumping them into a bag. She took two pairs of pyjamas out of the old chest of drawers.

'I thought he was a bit prickly at first. You know? Stupid of me.'

'I do know. When I was young, my first lover was an older man twenty years older than me.'

'At home?'

'Yes, in Dinard. He taught me so much about how to be. How to exist, to be calm, to listen to the voices of others around me. George tells me I do the same for him. I like the idea it has been passed on.'

Bim was on the floor, next to the Duplo – she picked him up, inhaling his soft fur, the scent of Sandy. Then she stopped.

'I didn't know you came from Dinard. The same Dinard Mum and Dad moved to?'

'Yes, of course, since I see them there every year as you know,' said Frederic, looking out of the window.

'I just hadn't put the two together. Did you know them when they started going there on holiday? All those years ago?' She counted in her head. 'Thirty – nearly thirty-five years ago I suppose?'

'I did know them, yes. They helped me very much. They, and Franc.'

'Franc?'

He bowed his head. 'Franc Thorbois. My first lover.'

'Oh, sorry. I see. They knew him too?'

'Yes, of course they did,' said Frederic, and he said something under his breath, and Juliet did not follow, was not really listening.

'I'll just grab some food,' she said, and ran downstairs, to the kitchen, where chaos reigned, Honor not being the tidiest of people. The shepherd's pie was delicious; she shovelled spoonfuls of it into her mouth, suddenly ravenous. She gathered up more food, little packets of raisins, a whole bunch of bananas – Sandy loved bananas, she'd feed them to him, as many as he wanted . . .

Suddenly despair crackled through her, as though she'd been struck by lightning, and she clutched her stomach, indigestion, a stitch convulsing her side. What if . . . what if even now he was waking up, and couldn't see, couldn't walk, was paralysed somewhere? *One damn second – if I'd only stopped him that third time from climbing the steps. I let my guard down for three seconds or so* . . . Her head spun. She clutched hold of the old wooden dresser, and it rattled. And she said to herself: *keep on moving, don't look down.* She thought of Grandi, and smiled.

Frederic appeared in the doorway. Juliet swallowed and stood upright. 'Let's go very quickly and look at the doll's house. Make sure the foxes haven't got in. I don't know what we'll do with it, but I should fasten the door properly anyway. Then let's get back to the hospital.'

She was glad to be going in there for the first time with someone, to get it over with. The afternoon sun shone through the fig leaves above on the scene of devastation on the floor. She was right: some creature, a fox? A mole? Badger? had shuffled the broken pieces around even more, knocked over Bea's chair, scattering Bea's home-work, her journals and books to the floor.

Juliet crouched down and looked at it all, then rubbed her face. It was colder than outside, the cool smell of must and earth. She stepped to the side, avoiding the house, still on its side, the middle hinge of the great chimney cracked in two.

'What am I going to do,' she said, in a small voice. 'It's a bit too much, at the moment.'

'May I say something, now?' said Frederic. 'Something that will not please you.'

'As if – of course.'

'I have telephoned your parents. They are coming back tonight. They will stay, and help you. Don't worry about this now.'

'You phoned Mum and Dad?' Juliet stood up again, and looked at him, quizzically. 'They won't – oh, it's very kind of you, but they're no earthly good, Frederic.'

'Why?'

'Well, they're never bloody here, for starters.'

'They are coming now.'

'They don't care about the house, haven't been here once since I moved back. It's OK – it really is. But we're not that close. I just don't think . . .' She trailed off.

'You need them.'

'I don't—'

'Juliet . . .' He laid his hand on her arm. 'I think you have lived so long in crisis mode, as they call it, you cannot see when a real crisis is upon you. Your son lies mortally ill, and you are the mother of two other children, living in the middle of nowhere, divorcing a man who is also a child. Forgive me, but it is fine now to ask for help.'

She shook her head, eyes closed, holding herself tightly, and then looked up and smiled at him. 'You're very kind. But they don't like it here – I don't ask them over because I'm tired of them making excuses, it's been nearly a year now and . . .' She ran her hands through her tangled hair, twisting it out of the way, and pushed at the central broken column of the doll's house with her foot. 'Sorry. I'm awfully ungrateful—'

Something on the ground caught her eye. She stopped, and crouched down.

'They want to come,' said Frederic, lowering himself slowly down on to a chair next to her. 'And they will help, they're good at getting on with things, as you know. It is time they came. You know, Juliet – I wasn't entirely honest earlier, when I was telling you about Franc. You see, your parents—'

But Juliet wasn't listening. In a strange voice, she said, 'Frederic – look.'

She had reached into the chimney hinge of the doll's house. The different floors had smashed apart, and half the roof had cracked off, and the chimney was torn in two, exposing the interior.

'It's a hiding place,' Frederic said, slowly.

The chimney was the width of a clenched fist, maybe less, and there was something inside the broken wooden stack. A rag, rolled into a cylinder. Stuffing, or something. She slid it out of the cracked cylinder.

Something was drumming in her brain. Tapping, trying to get out. *'It's a place to keep things.'* Who had told her that? Sitting here, on the floor with her . . . Juliet held the heavy fabric in her hands, weighing it.

It was a length of material about two feet long, rolled up. Her first thought was that it was insulation – and she smiled, at the idea the doll's house might have better insulation than the real house.

'What am I thinking of?' she said, quietly, and she sat back, jabbing her scraped and bruised arm on a small wooden lamp. She moved the lamp carefully to the side. The material was heavy, fastened with string, and Juliet pulled at the string which was tied in a bow around it, untying it.

'What is that, Juliet?'

Juliet's heart was hammering at the base of her throat. 'I thought it might be something. But it can't be.' Clumsily, she clasped the edge of the roll and slowly the canvas unravelled.

Rough, furzy-sparkling paintwork, darkening to green foliage studded with flowers of different colours – a house, the edge of a house . . . Her skin prickled, as she carried on unrolling.

'My God,' she heard Frederic say.

Juliet could not speak: she held her breath. The painting rolled away from her and was still, flat on the ground, as though possessed of its own magic.

There it was. The garden, and the fairies. The steps up to the house, glowing gold. The birds on the roof, the open window. Two small figures – ah, the skill of it, the way they were painted by a man who knew them so well! The central figure writing through the windows, the haze of late-afternoon sunshine . . .

She could hear Frederic, breathing heavily. Juliet clutched her chest, as though her heart might stop.

'I don't believe it,' she said, slowly.

'*The Garden of Lost and Found*,' said Frederic, and he gave a small, low exhalation. '*Mon dieu.*'

'Why on earth was it here?' Juliet blinked, looking at the smashed pieces of the ruined house.

'Someone wanted to hide it,' said Frederic. He touched her hand gently, and she looked up to find his eyes filled with tears. One dropped on the painting, and he stepped back, hastily. 'It's not that big, after all, is it?' he said. 'Two feet by three, yes. And it is perfect – as they always said it was. Look at the nightingales.'

'Look at the light on Eliza's wings.'

'And the woman – she's there, but she's not there, almost as if she is a ghost.' He sighed, and turned to her, eyes alight. 'Good God, Juliet, but who put it here? Who saved it from the flames?'

'They're two separate questions, I think. Ned must have bottled it at the last minute,' said Juliet. She lifted the canvas up, gingerly. 'I never believed he could do it, you know. As for who put it here . . . Don't ask me.' The force of the memory trying to burst out of whatever lost corner it was in was so strong she wanted to scream. But she couldn't quite get there . . . couldn't recall why she was sure she'd seen it before . . . 'The condition is perfect, the colours – oh, Frederic, it's exquisite. I suppose because it's been hidden away all these years, it looks better than if it had been on display in a gallery or someone's home . . .' She gave a shaky laugh. 'We should be jumping up and down and screaming for joy, shouldn't we?'

'I can do that for you,' said Frederic, and his voice was grave. 'Do you know who owned the painting, when it was burned?'

'I do,' she said, and her heart welled with joy, just for a second, as she looked at it again, this piece she had dreamed of for so long. The hours she'd spent at Dawnay's staring at the oil sketch, raking it over for clues as to the original, and this – her exhausted brain was depleted, not really quite able to believe it, any of it. 'He'd bought it back. From Galveston. For five thousand guineas . . . It bankrupted him. Liddy was furious. But he said at least now it was his to do with as he wished.'

'And now it is yours,' said Frederic, very seriously. 'You realise this is probably the most important piece of British art to be discovered again, well – well, yes, I'd say ever? This is extraordinary. You will be a very rich woman.'

'I don't care,' said Juliet, rocking back on her heels. 'I really don't.'

'Of course, not now. But you will care, depending on what happens at the hospital. You will care very much. And I must ask you another question. Your husband will be entitled to half of this, my dear. Unless – are you divorced yet? At least, have you signed the papers?'

For the first time in twenty-four hours Juliet smiled, genuinely smiled. 'Yes,' she said slowly. 'I damn well have signed the papers. But it doesn't matter – oh, none of it matters . . .' She looked again at the painting, the soft, textured colours hazy in the afternoon light. 'How funny,' she said, only half aware she was speaking aloud. 'As I thought: the shooting star isn't there.'

'What?'

'Nothing. A little extra on the sketch: a star falling to earth. It was yours all those years, do you remember?'

'I do. How strange, he must have left it out . . .' He touched her arm again, shaking his head in wonder. 'Really, Juliet. Look at it. I – just look at it.'

And they were silent again, as Juliet hitched the bag with Sandy's most treasured possessions in it over her shoulder, both of them staring at *The Garden of Lost and Found*, still slightly unable to quite believe what they were seeing.

Chapter Thirty-Six

June

You never knew your grandfather, Juliet. Michael never knew him either. He died during D-Day and I think of him at this time of year. It was all very convenient, the story one can tell a child. 'Daddy died a hero.' He was among the first boats to land and be greeted by the Germans. Strafed with bullets. He was killed immediately, they told me.

Possession is a funny word, for it implies the object is owned and embraced by the possessor, not that she is degraded and abused and humiliated by them. Andrew possessed me and – until he went away to war again – made my life a misery. The result is I couldn't love my son for years. Perhaps I never did, not in the way I should. Your dear father wasn't ever really <u>here</u>. He wasn't of the earth and sky and trees. He was, and still is I expect, rooted in his own little patch of earth, in his case with your mother in their little courtyard in France looking out over the pine trees and the rocky coastline. It is not that far really from where his father was killed.

Andrew is dead, and I have my name back, which I then gave to my son, but the facts can't be expunged. It is there in the church records, our signatures in black and white. I lived here with Mum so happily all those years and then he came. He invaded us. I let him, that's the thing. What a fool I was. He always wore boots and he used to put them on the coffee table in Mum's study. A tiny flaw – I know it is – but as so often with tiny flaws they collect together, all these little things that aren't right – the way the person speaks to the old idiot in the village who does no one any harm, the way they are with animals, how they thank you for something, where they leave their clothes at night –

393

whirling faster and faster, till they are not tiny but part of a whole, twisting cyclone that drags you off your feet and into the air and dumps you down again, broken and bruised.

I have expunged him from the history of the house. There was no body so he is not buried in the churchyard. He might as well have not existed, poor Andrew, but for the fact that Michael and you come from him only, oh – I choose to believe you don't. You're from the house, not from them. Genes, genes, they don't really matter, do they?

You thought I was angry with you when you became engaged, because I wanted you to marry Ev instead. I did not. I know Ev, better than my own son in many ways. He is a good, kind, sweet child but he would have made you very unhappy. Or perhaps the other way round. I did not want you to marry at all. Not then. Marry in haste, repent at leisure: marriages fail, people change – I did not want you with either of them, but there we have it. Girls are brought up to assume they must be with someone. It's a great lie, really.

Please come home here after I am gone. Please. I miss you so very much, Juliet. I am too sad to tell you the truth, but you will find it out one day. I am too old to pick up the telephone and call you and I really do dislike your husband most intensely. So here we are. I do not want to live any longer: I very much hope to die soon and you know, my will is strong. I expect that before too long, I shall go from here and be with Mum again.

'Build for yourself a house in Jerusalem and live there, and do not go out from there to any place.' I Kings 2:36

Days took on a monotony, something to be got through rather than enjoyed, and all the time this dragging sense of menace lurking, that Sandy might not, after all, be OK. Matt went back down to London, coming back up every other day or so, and his arrival often precipitated a crisis. He was absolutely brilliant with Sandy, knowing how to cheer him up and make him laugh, but it often meant Sandy got so excited to see him that afterwards he'd go downhill; he would have a temperature, and sob hysterically. Matt would also shout at the doctors – one of them, Dr MacIntosh, was patronising and talked in jargon and quite obviously thought he shouldn't ever be asked any questions, so Juliet quite liked it when Matt jumped up and down on the spot and yelled at him, 'You're not making any sense, man!' But, otherwise, she wished he'd be a bit calmer, though how could he? How could either of them?

Sandy's sight in one eye had not come back, and the doctors were not sure it ever would, but he was still so little they could not say for certainty either way at that point. Juliet, being practical and minded to gloominess, tried to accept that it would not; Matt insisted they could 'do something about it'. His pushing, relentless quest to make things better was infectious: she'd forgotten that about him. He'd ask for them to be moved to the better table at the restaurant, switch paint colours at the last minute, scrap the complicated meal he was cooking and start again if it didn't go to plan. It was admirable, she could see now. But how exhausting, being that person. And being with that person.

In addition Sandy's tibia was broken quite badly, and would require another operation on his leg when he was older. The scar on his skull was healing and in all other respects he was doing well, only it annoyed him so much to stay in bed all the time. That was the next challenge, stopping him from going crazy with frustration when he came home. Matt already had plans. 'We'll make him a mini-gym. I'll get Gav to knock something up in his workshop. It doesn't need to cost much, Juliet. Promise. It'll have levels, we can get that elastic stretchy stuff from Amazon, maybe some weights. I've drawn Gav a sketch.'

Juliet ate meals at weird times, wore odd clothes pulled from the wardrobe, slept when she could, but never at night-time, when she would lie clutching an old cushion staring up at the ceiling, waiting until she could go into the garden and weed, hoe, edge, trim, stake, feed, water. To take care, to have control, and every day, in small ways – a scented jasmine bush springing into life, or a sudden profusion of tomato and pea seedlings in the greenhouse – the garden seemed to thank her.

Sam Ham had taken *The Garden of Lost and Found* away – she had called him immediately, and he had come to the house the next day with a special glass frame to transport the canvas back to the Fentiman, where in great secrecy he had called in three independent experts individually to verify it, which they did. In the still watches of the night and when she was not worrying about Sandy, Juliet would worry someone might have tapped the phones and found out about the painting, could come here while Bea and Isla were in bed, to try and steal it. Proper criminals, the ones who broke into safes, stole watches and art from Mayfair galleries, who knew how to use glass cutters, lasers, gun silencers.

One afternoon about three weeks after the accident, Juliet arrived at the hospital to find Sandy fast asleep, puffed violet shadows under his eyes, limbs flung out, halo of golden hair spread on the pillow and she didn't have the heart to wake him. Isla had been in to visit the previous day, and they had sat up in his bed together (strictly forbidden by the hospital for fear of infection but Juliet had pretended to forget this) and watched the *Tigger Movie*, Isla with her small arm round her little brother's, patting the hospital blanket and sheets over him, making sure he had Bim. Juliet had taken photos, emailed them to Matt. Then afterwards, Isla had pretended to be Tigger, bouncing around Sandy's bed so loudly he got over-wrought and kept screeching and hiccuping with laughter – repressed release of so many things, she suspected. One of the nurses, Ali, had poked her head round the door.

'You're a very good big sister, Isla, you should be a doctor one day. I haven't seen him this happy since he came here.'

Isla had stuck her chin out. 'I might be a doctor actually, but of guinea pigs and chinchillas. Mummy says we're getting chinchillas in the autumn, one each.'

'Chinchillas? They'll eat you out of house and home.'

'Really?'

'Really, young lady. I hope you're mum's got a fortune stashed away somewhere to pay for all that feed,' said Ali, and Juliet laughed, way too loudly.

Staring down at Sandy's utterly still sleeping face, the scar from his operation puckering the skull underneath all that hair like an angry pink-and-black caterpillar, Juliet gently stroked his smooth cheek, and breathed in to smell him. She felt a sense of calm for the first time in weeks.

She left him to sleep. Back in the car she drove on, to Oxford. Spring was fully here now, fading from April freshness to the full blaze of May glory. The hedges were riotously green, bursting with cow parsley and blossom of all kinds – hawthorn, elderflower, bullace, blackthorn – the sky a clean, deep blue. Orange-tip butterflies darted alongside the car in and out of the lanes, keeping her company. She had not noticed any of it until now, she realised, the countryside coming alive again after winter. She had been sleep-walking for so long.

'I didn't plan to come today. I just wanted to look at it. Is that OK?' she said to Sam, after he had ushered her into his office.

'Of course,' he said. 'Follow me. Oh. Can I get you a cup of tea first?'

She had stood up, but at this she sat down again, laughing. 'Do I look that awful?'

'Never.' He pulled something out of his desk, and turned away from her, picking a book off the shelf behind him. 'Never, Juliet. But you do look like someone who might like a cup of sweet tea. See how British I'm becoming? Have a look at this while I'm gone.' He slid a book over towards her. 'Kate and I unearthed it yesterday.'

'Do I need gloves?'

'No, not this once.' It was a large book with a slim spine bound in midnight-blue cloth. And he disappeared, leaving her alone in the eighteenth-century office with the powder-blue paint and the white cornicing. It was very calm and quiet in there, the smell of wood polish and something spicy: bay, or fig. Outside, the magnolia had lost most of its blossom, but the glossy leaves shone in the morning sunshine. She opened the book.

DEEDS, PLANS, DRAWINGS & IDEAS FOR THE IDEAL
FAMILY HOME, BASED ON NIGHTINGALE HOUSE IN
THE COUNTY OF —SHIRE
LUCIUS G DALBEATTIE OM, PRA, FRIBA

When Sam returned, he was bearing a just-hot-enough cup of
tea, served in a blue-and-white china cup and saucer with a Jaffa
Cake on the side. She looked up at him, eyes wide with amazement.

'I've never seen this before. This is incredible.'

'He had it privately printed, when he settled in Ottawa. It was
to be his dream house, only he never built it. And it would have
been very like Nightingale House.' He crouched down beside her,
his long frame folding up and his slim fingers flicking through the
pages. 'This idea, for the children's bedrooms, the built-in cupboards
under the eaves and the use of the turret in the corner, closed off
to be used as a miniature castle or fort. The cupboards in the
kitchen, and next to the sink – really, it's the first fitted kitchen.
No one was doing that at the time. The sustainable wood, the same
coat hooks in the hall as at your hall. Really extraordinary.'

'"*I have spent my life trying to build the perfect house . . . circumstance,
and cruel fate, has rendered my efforts worthless, but I leave this plan in case
another should take it up. October 1919.*"' Something about the words
was heart-rending. She ran her fingertips over the depressions of
the words on the page. 'I always liked the sound of him, so much.
So he never built the house.'

'He died coming back to England, the month afterwards. His
boat sank, in a storm.'

'Is that it?' Juliet's hands fell into her lap and a tear dropped on
to them as she bowed her head and began to cry. 'I'm sorry,' she
said, pushing her fingers into her eyes, pushing her hair out of the
way. 'I cry at everything at the moment.'

He lifted her hair away, tucking it behind one ear, so he could
see her. 'Don't be. I'm sorry, I shouldn't have shown it to you.' His
strong, warm hand took hers, held it tightly. 'I'm sorry, Juliet.'

'No, honestly, Sam. It's wonderful.' She wiped her eyes. 'It makes

me think of our house, and . . . all of it. Grandi, how sad she was
. . . who left the painting there. I wish I knew. I know some of it
and still . . .'

'Well.' He released her hands, and went back to his desk. 'Kate
Nadin's working her way through the archive very methodically, but
it's in a terrible state, all out of order. She just found a letter I thought
I should show you, too. From Liddy's sister, Mary, wasn't it?'

'Yes, what's it about?'

'I can read it to you.' He held up a thin sheet of writing paper.
'"*My dearest. I have been up all night thinking of darling John and trying
to write to Liddy. Do you remember his dark blue eyes under the flopping
blonde hair, the strength of his long face, even at that age? What a darling
boy he was. . . oh dear God, Dalbeattie, where will it end?*" It's with a bill
for a new dressing gown in February 1918 and I think we can date
it – oh, are you all right?'

'I'm fine,' she said. 'John was, as I'm sure you know, their second
child. He went missing at Cambrai, December 1917. They never
found his body. Poor Liddy. Poor Ned. Go on.'

Sam's gentle voice, rising and swooping, seemed to hum in the
large, echoing room as he read. She listened, transfixed.

'"*Darling one, I am writing to wish you the greatest luck with your
Canadians. I am in no doubt that you will find them as enamoured of
you as so many others have been. Be in no doubt yourself. Be YOU,
brave, brilliant, kind. You make me proud to know you and to love
you. I will join you as soon as I may. We will build the house. We will
fill it with children. Keep the plans safe, Dalbeattie. It is wretched to
wish another woman to die before a situation like ours can be regularised.
It is a wretched world, and the idea of peace is perhaps as terrifying as
war for one will have to accept that everything now must be changed,
and the long years stretch out ahead of us all.*

*You have been my life these last three years. You have made me
absolutely happy, Dalbeattie. Know that, my darling. I will see you one
day soon. We will be together then. My love, Mary.*"'

He put the letter down.

'My goodness.' Juliet chewed her thumb, thinking, the cloth-bound book still on her lap. 'And she didn't go to Canada? Or did she?'

'We don't know. Yet.'

'Was there a child, then?' She stared at him and smiled. 'You're not their descendant, are you?'

'Dear God, no.' He looked horrified.

'It's not that awful an idea, is it?'

'Well, then we'd be cousins, and Juliet, that would be – quite wrong.'

'Only quite?'

'Quite as in very wrong. Not fairly wrong. The British use "quite" incorrectly . . . What's so hilarious about that?' he said, leaning on the desk, arms folded.

Juliet hugged herself. 'Ancient history. You dumped Ginny because she was quite intelligent. We used to joke about it.'

'Ginny – oh, your best friend Ginny whom you haven't seen for over two decades! She was a brainiac, for sure.'

'We thought it was because you meant she was quite intelligent as in "a bit, not very much".'

'She got a First in PPE.'

'Well, exactly. This is why we thought you were an arrogant . . .' She trailed off.

Sam leaned towards her, a lock of hair falling across his forehead. 'So let me get this straight. You've been harbouring this ill-will toward me for twenty years because you don't know the correct meaning of "quite".' He laughed, gently, then Juliet laughed too. Then the more she thought about it, the more ridiculous it seemed, and the more both of them laughed, so much so that Graham, head of fundraising, and Briony, the admin support, both pushed their chairs back in the outside office to see what was going on, then nodded significantly at each other, before going back to work.

'God, I'm really sorry,' said Juliet eventually. 'Perhaps this is the spur I need to get in touch with Ginny again. Set the record straight.'

'I thought we'd covered that. She wasn't very nice. You were nice.'

'I wasn't.'

'You were. You were young. We all were,' he said, gently, and smiled at her. 'Look, can we just finish the business with Dalbeattie, because I really don't want there to be any doubt about this. I'm not your second cousin or whatever it is. As with most North Americans my parents each have a much-thumbed white ringbinder detailing every last mad aunt and supposedly interesting historical nuggets, like the time my grandmother Simone shook Jean Chrétien's hand. He was Prime Minister,' he added, as Juliet looked blank. 'Very important in Canada – nothing? OK. Well, I know my father's Hamilton relatives, because we hear a lot about them and I own the kilt.'

'You own a kilt?' said Juliet, musing.

'I do, it's quite natty. Yes, I said it. And my mother's family emigrated from France after the war. Believe me, I'd know if I was descended from Lucius Dalbeattie.'

'Are the government buildings still used?'

'Well, two of them were destroyed by fire in the thirties. But there's a Great Hall left over, near the Parliament. It's a wonderful thing. They have ceremonies – I went to one, for the Rhodes scholarship. The language is classical, but it's very Arts and Crafts, you feel at home there. There are seats around the edge and the carvings have extendable wooden hooks, so you can hang up a coat while you're chatting.' He smiled at her. 'Now, you see, I mentioned the Rhodes scholarship and you weren't rude. I think that's a real breakthrough.'

Juliet was still staring at the letter, but she looked up and smiled. 'It's a breakthrough all right. Perhaps you're not so bad after all.'

'I made up my mind about you years ago, Juliet.' Before she could answer, he stood up. 'I think Kate will ask that you leave the letter here, but do borrow the book, if you like. Now. Shall we go and see the *The Garden of Lost and Found*?'

She felt dizzy, more tired than ever, and he seemed to understand, steering her through the maze of offices at the back of the museum, both heads down, not making eye contact with colleagues, until they came to the room where the most delicate restoration and reframing projects were done. There was a huge turning lock with combination safe on the door, and a man, standing next to it, in black. Julia looked at him suspiciously. Was this the high-level thief she dreamed of, waiting to spring them?

'That's Olly,' said Sam, as he opened the door. 'Security.'

'You hired a security guard?'

He shut the door leaving the two of them inside. Olly moved back into position, in front of the door.

Sam's friendly drawl echoed behind her. 'Juliet, do you know how much this painting will fetch, if it goes for auction?'

Juliet shook her head, impatiently. 'Of course. Of course I do. But I can't think about it right now.'

'Forgive me,' he said. 'But I think you should.'

They were standing in front of the painting. No frame, nothing, just the two sheets of glass in which Sam had removed it, two days after Sandy's accident. A soft light above shone on it, illuminating it but not covering it with glare. She stared at the two children. It wasn't the beauty that seduced her every time with Ned's paintings. It was the expertise, the absolute confidence of the capturing of one specific moment in time. The paint was alive, the figures, the setting. You believed it, you believed they were serenely, joyously happy.

'Yes,' she said, breathing out, and she realised she was leaning against him, very slightly, and she moved away. 'Oh, I just want to keep it. To have it at the end of my bed, Ned's room. To wake up and look at it every morning.'

'You can do that.'

'I could. But I can't.'

'Please know I will help you, whatever you decide. Only don't make like your great-grandfather or whoever he was and to burn it.'

'Whoever he was.' Juliet said, smiling. And then she stopped. 'He was.'

'He was what?'

She said, 'What was the date of the letter?'

402

'Mary's letter to Dalbeattie? Oh. February 1918. Probably.'

Juliet nodded. 'OK. OK.'

'What's up?'

'Just some things that are rolling around in my mind. Probably nothing.' She was staring in at the painting as Olly locked the door behind them and they walked to the exit. 'There was an old ha'penny piece in the chimney when it broke,' she said, for no reason. 'It rolled out on to the floor. I remember. Someone dropped it in there.'

'I'd love to see the doll's house.'

'It's still being mended, but it should be back soon. Look, they've started to talk about Sandy coming home in a few weeks. So you should come before then; it'll be mayhem afterwards.'

Sam paused on the steps of the museum, as Juliet fiddled in her bag for her keys. 'I'll wait for you to invite me.'

Juliet looked up at the low, long white stone building, shining in the spring sun. 'You can just drop by.'

'Juliet, I'm British now. I live here. I'd no more drop by than I would say, "Excuse me" without really meaning "Move out of my way now or I'll kill you." Even leaving those dishes on the doorstep was nervewracking.'

She laughed and turned to go, unlocking her car. 'He learns so fast. In fact . . .' She chewed a nail. 'My parents are staying. I really wouldn't visit while they're there, either.'

'I thought your parents were never here.'

'Well, they've come to help. They keep standing over me and starting to say things then trailing off. And they manage to cook only food my children won't eat. It's extremely relaxing.'

'Sympathies. My mom came to stay last year when I moved over. After three days I was taking daily trips to the dump, just for something to do. I almost started buying things in Oxfam just to have new stuff to recycle.'

'Which explains the excess furniture in your house. The dump. That's a good tip,' said Juliet. 'Look, see you soon – and thanks.'

'Thank you,' he said, nodding at her seriously. 'That was quite nice.'

As she drove away, into the tangle of traffic, she was smiling.

Chapter Thirty-Seven

When Juliet got back from the hospital that evening, her father was standing in the vegetable patch, scratching his head.

'Look,' he said, nudging some uncovered earth with his brogue. 'I know onions should be big at this time of year, but these are amazing. I've nothing like that in Dinard. It's the soil here. Lovely, rich clay.' He leaned on his hoe, and smiled at her. 'How's Sandy today?'

'Better, they had him sitting up.' He had been crochety after his long sleep, and wouldn't do his exercises the nice physical therapist had given him to keep the muscles in his unharmed leg and arm strong, but Juliet found her parents weren't able to process any setback, it threw them completely.

'He has to keep moving around,' the therapist had told Juliet. 'I know it's hard for him, poor little mite. Sandy? How's about you and me go and look for Bim, huh? He's gone off somewhere, and I know he wants you to find him. Shall Mama come with us?'

'Yes,' Sandy had said, allowing himself to be lifted gently off the bed, as Janine supported his back and Juliet took his good hand. The endless, boundless kindness of people: Janine's patience, Ali, the nurse who looked after him at night-time when he woke crying for Juliet and she sometimes wasn't there, of his doctor, Dr Mulligan, who brought in a special video of her children and their puppy to show Sandy because he had told her he liked dogs.

'We'll go in and see him tomorrow, Grandma Elvie and I,' said her father, turning back to his hoeing. 'She's inside now, making an omelette for tea.'

'Oh,' said Juliet. 'Great.'

When she opened the door she could hear singing, and the smell of cooking. She took a deep breath, and went through the dining room into the kitchen. 'Hello, darlings!' she called, aware her voice was slightly higher than usual. 'Hi, Fin, great to see you! Hi, Bea, my love, hello, darling Isla, how was school?'

'Hi, Mum,' said Bea, looking up from her phone.

'Hi, Juliet,' said Fin. She put down the T-shirt, on to which she was sewing an embroidered patch emblazoned with 'Mother of Dragons'. 'How was Sandy today?'

Isla crossed her arms and stared at her mother, mutinously. 'It's got green stuff in it,' she said, glaring at the plate in front of her.

'Mum! What a lovely smell!' she called.

Her mother was standing at the Aga, spatula in hand, wiping her forehead, hair sticking up at the front into a tuft. 'Omelette *aux fines herbes*,' she said, shortly, taking a large swig from a mug.

'It. Has. Got green stuff in it!' Isla called again from the dining room. 'LOADS OF GREEN STUFF, MUM.'

'Isla,' Juliet hissed. 'Don't be rude, please. Thank you. Eat your omelette.'

'But the green stuff IS GREEN—'

'I don't care, don't be rude.'

'Your children have an extraordinary attitude to anything that might be good for them, darling!' her mother called out semi-hysterically.

'Yes, well. I brought them up on chicken nuggets washed down with Fruit Shoots so no wonder.' Juliet put her bag on the table and took a mug from the cupboard.

'What?'

'Nothing. Thanks for looking after them today.'

'It's my pleasure! We've had so much fun . . .' Elvie trailed off. 'I wanted to walk along the river into the village but the tow path is all overgrown. That awful messy old tree that's half come away in the winter – can't you cut it down?'

'The mulberry? You can't just hack away at it, alas. It needs a tree surgeon, it's three hundred years old. It was here when they built the house.'

'Well it's such a shame. If you trimmed it it'd open the path up. Back in Dinard, they dock the trees every other year. It's really very efficient. Keeps everything nice and neat—'

Her father had come into the kitchen. 'Tea?' he exclaimed, in wonder. 'Oh Elvie, you are amazing. A cup of tea is exactly what I was in the mood for. How did you know!'

Her mother smiled and handed him Juliet's cup of tea. 'Sixth sense, my darling.'

'You angel! What a treat.'

Juliet watched them, in wonderment that they could still, after all these years, derive so much pleasure from setting up and then rewarding themselves for the simplest tasks. I am a bad person, and that is why my marriage failed, she thought. I'd no more congratulate Matt on making a cup of tea beyond thanking him than he would. She gave a small smile at the thought of her almost-ex husband clapping his hands together in joy at a pot of tea. He used to find this aspect of her parents infuriating, she knew, though he never said so. He just got on with it. She remembered, when they'd first met that New Year's Eve, being so impressed at the way the following day he'd asked for her phone number, and then called her. No messing around. No mind games, like her university boyfriends, no ethereal vagueness, like Ev.

Back soon now Ju, just wanted to say you need to keep weeding this time of year, it's mad. I'll come and help you. Can't wait to look round it, some great trails round there too, must bring my bike. Hope your kid is doing OK. Ev x

Cups poured, she and her parents retreated into the dining room to join the children. Juliet slid a plate of biscuits towards her parents. 'Here.'

'Thanks, darling,' said her mum. 'Ooh, Juliet, ginger nuts! Aren't you clever. My favourites.'

Juliet smiled, to herself, looking down, as Isla appeared in the doorway.

'Grandma Elvie, can I ask you something?'

'Yes, my love!' Elvie put on her special bright 'Grandma' voice.

'Why do you say things are interesting all the time when they're not?'

'*Isla!*'

'Sometimes they are, Isla!'

'How?' said Isla. 'Would you be very kind and give me an e.g.?'

Elvie appeared to consider this for a long time, as Juliet and her father exchanged looks. 'Well . . . do you know, I did a special job for many years, Isla. Do you know what that job was?'

'Astronaut,' breathed Isla.

'No. I'll give you a clue. Some say I was a dreamcatcher, of children's dreams.'

'Eh?' said Juliet, involuntarily.

'Lovely,' her father breathed.

'Um . . .' said Isla, nonplussed. 'So . . . were you a monster out of *Monsters Inc*, the ones that try to scare children to make them scream, not the ones who look after the office?'

'No, Isla. My very special job was that I was . . . a . . . *teacher.*'

'I've come to ask very kindly can I get down please,' said Isla immediately, looking at her mother, as Bea and Fin both struggled to keep a straight face. 'I want to write a new part of my story for Sandy tomorrow. Thank you for the lovely omelette with bits in, Grandma Elvie. It was delicious. I shall take it into the kitchen now. Thank you again.'

'You can go too,' said Juliet to Bea and Fin. Fin turned to Juliet, fiddling with her nose-ring.

'Thank you,' she said, her round face breaking into a smile which showed the gap in her front teeth. 'Um, hope it's alright to say it but I'm glad Sandy's doing OK.'

Juliet caught her hand, and squeezed it. 'Oh, thanks, Fin.'

'See you later, Mum, we're going upstairs. Oh, and later, can you give us a lift to Godstow? Ben and some other people are hanging out in the café, I said me and Fin would join them.' She glanced at her grandmother. 'Fin and I.'

'Thank you, Bea,' said Juliet's mother, smiling.

'Sure you can go. Fin, remember your epi-pen.'

'Oh! I will, thank you, Juliet.' Fin bit off the thread from the needle and held up the T-shirt. 'Dracarys!' she said, and Bea laughed. Juliet looked blank.

'*Game of Thrones*,' said Fin, politely. 'Is it a matriarchy? It's a real question. Does even George know the answer to that? Who knows?'

'George? I doubt it.' Aware she had literally no idea what they meant, but not minding, in fact joyfully happy that Bea's world was unknown to her now and that was a good thing, Juliet turned back to her parents, who were whispering to each other.

It *was* lovely to have them here, even if at this time of day she really just wanted to kick off her shoes and curl up in an armchair and stare out of the window instead of making polite conversation. And there were, still, so many things she didn't understand about them. Did they really have to disinfect their toothbrushes with a special French toothhead cleaning tablet morning and night? And were they really so worried about digestion that they had to drink nettle tea twice a day? And the business with windows having to be closed all the time . . .

'Fin is nice, isn't she?' said Juliet's mum bracingly, as two pairs of boots disappeared around the bend in the stairs. 'Very polite.'

Juliet did think Fin was nice. Privately she thought she was slightly too introverted for Bea, who would march for peace when she was older and kick at the system and get things done, she was that kind of girl. But Bea was fifteen. This was all new territory, like everything else.

'She's a very kind person. That's the most you can ask, isn't it? Someone kind.'

'So you spent all day at the hospital,' said her dad, his kind face turned towards her. 'I'm glad Sandy was better. A little better every day. Every day—'

'I wasn't there all day. I went to see the painting. Sam, my boss, and I were discussing what to do next.' She had told her parents about the discovery of *The Garden of Lost and Found*. 'Dad . . .' She cleared her throat, not sure of quite how she'd say what she wanted to but knowing now was the best time to talk to her parents. Sam's voice, reading the letter from Mary to Dalbeattie, seemed to echo in her head. *You have been my life.*

'The night of Sandy's accident, Frederic said something rather strange – I never knew he was from Dinard, too, did you? But you had to, because you knew him from the village, before he came to England.' Her parents, side by side, exchanged swift glances. 'And something Sam said today. I was thinking about Grandi.' She swallowed, her mouth dry. 'I was thinking how she was the only child here for most of the time. She never knew her family, did she?'

Her father was still staring down into the teacup.

'Dad?'

'Yes, darling,' her father said, very quietly. 'So she always said.'

'Ev texted me a few weeks ago about the Royal Wedding. It was a funny day, wasn't it?'

'Such a boring girl—' Elvie began eagerly. 'Oh, *that* Royal Wedding. The first one. Poor Diana –' She stopped.

Juliet looked from one to the other of them. 'Grandi wasn't the same afterwards, was she? She got so upset. There was a man, wasn't there? And you two, you're never here. And there's this other thing, about brown eyes. Bea has brown eyes.' She was speaking fast. 'All of this together – well, it keeps rolling round and round like the coin on the floor.'

'What coin?'

'Nothing,' she said, impatiently. 'Just that something doesn't make sense.' Her voice was shaking.

Her father sank back against the chair, and put his hands over his eyes, shielding himself from her gaze.

'Juliet—' He stopped, one hand up.

'Michael, darling, it's all right,' said Juliet's mum, swiftly. 'It's all right. Honestly.'

Juliet reached for a glass of water, suddenly scared. She swallowed, and said, 'What happened, the day of the Royal Wedding? Who was that man?'

'My uncle,' Michael whispered, his head in his hands, and Elvie put her hands up to his, her face a rictus of pain at her husband's distress. 'My Uncle John, darling. He was a very dear man.'

The room was deathly silent; no sounds from the garden or the rest of the house. Juliet said: 'What?'

Her dad's lip twisted; he rubbed at his eyes. 'We never told you. We *couldn't* tell you. It was a choice – her or him, and – God help me! We chose him. He had no one. All those years. But you were the collateral damage, do you see?' And he looked up at the sky, blinking. 'I'm not a religious man, but I pray we did the right thing. You were so happy here. It was what she lived for, really. This house, the idea of it.' He gave a despairing, small shrug. 'How could we take that away from you? So we gave her to you.'

'Darling,' her mother said, her voice firm.

'What?' Juliet's voice was shaking. 'Gave who to me?'

'I'll tell you. I'll explain it all,' her father said.

Chapter Thirty-Eight

July 1918

'John John, the painter's son, Stole a cake and away he rund.'

It was easier, sometimes, to steal a cake than to beg. Because you might be questioned, or worse still recognised – less danger in London, than here, coming towards home. But once, on Piccadilly Circus, smelling the scent of fresh bread from some oven close by, the growling pains of hunger had become too much to bear and he had thrust his cap into a man's abdomen. 'Pennies for a poor wounded soldier?' he'd said, and the man – well-dressed, top hat, a smart jacket of soft black wool, a plump mustard-coloured cravat – had looked down at him, in alarm, and with some repulsion – he had not bathed for weeks now, not since the stream in Brittany.

'No – no, sir, I thank you,' the man had replied in horror and, firmly grasping his elbows, had moved him out of his path. As though John was nothing to do with him. The bewilderment on his face, that was the note that stuck. This broken young penniless soldier, on the street, asking for money – what had that to do with *him*? Up and down Regent's Street there were banners, poems in shop windows, tributes to our glorious dead. 'Hang high their swords in churches across the land' – the dead were heroes. The war was still being fought but the living, the shuffling, beaten-down living were as dirt under the feet, to be ignored.

John ducked out of sight, back into the crowds, up Glasshouse Street and into the murky depths of Soho once more.

As spring had come, and the days were longer and lighter, he grew bolder, walking west, out of the city, begging a loaf here and there, stealing when he had to and only when he knew it would not be missed – a tray of Eccles cakes, fresh from the oven, left on the windowsill of a cottage in Bayswater, frosted sugar glinting like diamonds in the morning sunshine. A few slices of ham, from a butcher's in Middlesex when the back door had been left open. He was adept at spotting water fountains, and drank greedily from them, remembering the old army advice that often thirst felt like hunger. Nor was this the brackish rainwater oily and brown with human waste and dead rats and flies and tobacco such as he had drunk in Northern France for weeks at a time, and it was not leaves, or grass, or raw eggs snatched from underneath the hen, cracked open and slung hastily down the gullet before a furious, emaciated farmer appeared. 'Get off my land, you English brute!' He swiped a shirt from a washing line, burying his army shirt in a field. The jacket he had to keep, for warmth.

He was alive, that much he had. He was back in England, thanks to a friendly passage he had secured in Boulogne, doing things to the captain in the lean-to outbuilding of the harbourmaster's head-quarters facing out across the fields. Things that he didn't mind doing anyway: he'd seen far worse, been asked much worse. All he understood now was that he must keep moving forward, or else lie down and die.

In late June he caught the flu and was quite unwell, crawling from roadside verges into a disused barn where he lay for the best part of a week unable to scavenge for food or to beg. He had heard whispers, in pubs and on newspaper hoardings, that the Spanish flu that was killing thousands of men back in France had arrived here. For a day or two he thought he might die too, and hoped he would. He wanted it to be over. He wanted to end it, but he'd been too cowardly to do it. But, for whatever reason, he lived. He told himself he was lucky, though he didn't feel lucky.

He lost even more weight, and being sick made him sicker, of course. By this point he was somewhere on the Bath Road, west of Reading. His progress slowed, though he knew he must find his way home. He must see Liddy, for the last time.

John was well aware how many deserters from the war had been court-martialled, how they were still being rounded up. The 2nd

Battalion had been charged with executing five of them, before Cambrai; they did it, he knew, to stiffen resolve. If he was caught he'd be shot. He understood his old life was over, that he could never really go home again – it would put his father and his mother at risk of being accused of harbouring a deserter, to say nothing of the shame it would bring on them. He merely wanted to see his mother once more.

To smell her lily-of-the-valley scent, to touch her hair. To walk in the garden in summer, to spend – perhaps? – one night in the house, in his bedroom with the smooth floorboards, the turreted window. To hear the nightingales sing in the trees, now it was June, to relive, one more time, the perfection of Nightingale House in summer and the love that, once, they had all held for each other. To have a memory from after the war that wasn't wholly bad. Something to build a new future upon. His desire to live, he had started to realise, was strong.

So when he was better, though his boots had worn through and flea bites troubled him greatly, though the wound in his side was painful and his skin was easily sunburned and his guts torn to shreds from the mustard gas, and though every step grew harder, John kept on walking.

He had pictured, so many times, the lane along to the house, so that when he reached it finally it seemed unreal. Then he heard the birdsong – first the crows, croaking in the yew trees behind the house, keeping watch over the graves. Pushing aside the worn metal bars cut into the wall, John crept into the churchyard. He could not, now, remember what way was widdershins. Mama's arm, pinching his to go the right way towards the grave . . . 'This way little one, she's over here.'

He picked his way towards the new graves, fifteen or more of them, a village decimated. His heart hammered as he steeled himself to read the name on each fresh headstone. The Hoyle boy, and Lord Alfred Coote. A fine fellow he had been, he'd driven John back to the train that last, awful time he'd come home on leave, not said a word on the journey as beside him John had shuddered and vomited and then sobbed, brokenly. A good man, Major Coote, damn it. 'Cambrai, 1918'. So he had died only a few weeks after John had deserted . . . John touched the grave, repulsion at himself for his cowardice sluicing him like nausea once again. *I am here, and he is gone. A dear boy. The scion of the family, gone.*

That hazy summer morning when they'd all set off for Walbrook together . . . The Godstow Pals! And most of them gone now . . . One more name – oh dash it! A sob burst from John's mouth as he read the name: Jack Burnaby.

He and Jack used to fool about together in the barn over the hill as the pigs snuffled and snouted, wrestling and playfighting and it was there, one hot summer afternoon as the rest of the village celebrated Empire Day, that he had felt himself rising with uncontained excitement for the first time – and it was Jack who had known what to do, who had shown him what was happening. Dear Jack, whose gentle hands made him gasp, as he laid him back on the scratchy hay who had pulled and pressed at him till John exploded with joy. It had taken a while for John to understand what they had done was not merely illegal but reviled by almost everyone in the land. It wasn't a little bit against the law, like driving a motor car at 21mph. It was a disgusting act . . . and yet the memory of dear Jack, his lock of blond hair falling into his eyes . . . *That time, o' times.*

At the north side of the church she was there. He had been picking flowers, as was his wont, and now he scattered them at her graveside. It was overgrown with summer's long grasses and John pushed them back, and the ivy too, creeping towards the grave from the hedgerows behind.

Eliza Helena Horner
Born 1893 – Died 1901
She flew away too soon
And her brother
John Dysart Horner
1895 – 1917
Missing in action whilst fighting for his country
God bless our house · We loved them so

John stood very still, blinking, inhaling the scent of freshly mown grass. It is something to see your own gravestone with the supposed dates of your life carved upon it. He kneeled down, and kissed the soft, mossy earth, beneath which lay Eliza's remains. He could see her, dancing away from him in the garden, the image stronger than ever. She was not really there, he told himself. She is in here, with me.

Then he crossed through the churchyard down the lane behind the house, weaving slightly now, dizzy with fatigue and hunger, through the dark dead leaves left over from winter which crackled underfoot. At the bottom of the path John stopped and, looking up at the rose-red roof in the afternoon sun, rubbed his eyes. He was home.

John walked carefully past the front door and the stone chair for weary travellers, and paused. He realised he could not pull the bell and implicate anyone who didn't need to know he'd been there. Zipporah, or Darling the gardener, Nora the new housemaid – not so new, it had been four years since she'd come. She had had red-raw elbows, and fingers, and hair always escaping from its cap, and she was terrified of everything. She would be terrified . . . John rubbed his eyes, unsure what to do. Then he heard the old familiar sound, a palette knife on painted canvas.

Scrape, scrape, scrape.

John straightened up, and proceeded slowly towards the Dovecote. The old familiar smell of the fig almost knocked him sideways – sweet, musty, dark. He peered in. The fig had covered the glass roof – did his father not notice how much darker it was now, inside? There was his father, bent over the old easel, priming a canvas himself. He was shorter than before; John caught the side of his face. *He's old.*

On another easel, to the side of the studio, stood another painting, facing away from him. John coughed, and said, slowly:

'Father?'

His voice was rusty from misuse and the word croaked out,

rasping. Ned swung round, on one foot, paintbrush in one hand, palette in the other and saw his son.

The paintbrush fell from his hand but he said nothing at all.

John noticed, with some alarm, how pale he was, how thin. 'Father . . .' he said, again. 'I – I thought I'd come back and pay you a visit.'

Ned really was like a little gnome. Rumpelstiltskin. He stamped one foot, and cleared his throat.

'You,' he said, slowly, and he ran to the door, past his son, peering out, then he shut the door, pulling it hard, and turned to face him. 'So I was right. I knew you'd deserted. I knew you weren't dead.' A terrible smile twisted across his father's face.

'You did?'

'I know you, my boy. I never said a word of it to your mother, but I know what you're like. Who you are. You can't stay here,' he said suddenly. 'You understand, don't you?'

John nodded. 'Yes. Of course.'

'So why'd you come?' He passed a hand over his forehead: he was blinking, as though he wasn't sure where he was, what to do. 'Oh John, my boy. Why'd you come?'

John's legs shook – he was a child again, caught in the glare of his father's attention, his disappointment in his only son almost palpable, for it was also displaced rage at the loss of Eliza, who had been so very, very like him.

'Father, I wanted to see you and Mama again, one last time.' He took a step forward and put his hand on the paint table, to steady himself. 'I'm – I'm very thirsty, Father. I've been walking for a while, do you have any water?'

'Here.' Ned thrust a glass bottle at him and John drank his fill, all the while aware of his father's eyes on him.

'Thank you,' he said, wiping his mouth and setting the bottle down again.

'You can't stay,' said Ned. Again, that impassive, unsettling stare. 'We've Lord and Lady Coote coming for supper this evening.'

'Alfred's people—'

'Yes. They have no one now. The girls cannot inherit. But they mourn him with pride. They know he died holding his line. We'll win the war because of men like him. He was a hero.'

'He – he was.'

His father was staring at him. 'John. They'll shoot you if they find you. You understand, don't you? You must go now.'

John could hear the desperation in his own voice. 'I know. I only want to see Mama, one more time. I simply want to kiss her and tell her how very sorry I am but that I am well and won't disturb her again. I won't ever come back.' John had rehearsed the speech, but now, shoehorning it in like this, it sounded all wrong. This was *all* wrong. 'Father – I'm back, though. Are you not glad to see me?'

His father pressed his hands to his face, blocking him out. A small, muffled sound came from him; he didn't move. He looked up, his mouth set, his kind blue eyes hard.

'You must understand. Your mother believes you are dead, John. She thought you died in December. She has buried your letters to her from the Front. We added your name to the gravestone, last month.' Ned coughed. 'What was I to do? I was there as we said prayers over the grave. "What vengeance shall the Lord wreak on me for my lies when the Day of Judgement calls, John?" His voice rose. 'I-I knew you were a coward, a prancing, gambolling, mincing defective coward—' His voice broke and he looked down. 'I don't feel well,' he muttered. 'Not well, not well.'

John looked at him, with an appraising stare. 'You are pale, Father. Have you taken a chill?'

'This flu,' Ned muttered. 'I think I'm sickening for something, and the devil of it is there's this influenza, they say there's three dead of it in Walbrook hospital. The Germans, you see. They've organised it to finish us off. And I must work, I must keep on working.'

'Father . . .' John leaned against the shelf, wiping his forehead, drinking more water. This man was not his father. 'I think you should rest, not work. Can't I—'

'*No!*' He tapped the corner of the golden frame beside him. 'She's still worried about money. Worry, worry, worry. Why, what's it all for, now, anyway?' Like a sly child with a secret he tapped a frame, then turned it around on its stand. John gaped at what he saw. 'Look. I've bought it back, y'see. Bought you children back to keep you close by.'

Then John understood, the frantic air about him, the almost palpable desperation. 'You bought back *The Garden of Lost and Found?*'

'I wanted you close by! I said so! Damn you, don't you hear me?'

John swallowed, to prevent his throat closing up. He must keep him talking. 'That must have near about wiped you out, Father.'

'No. No!' He stamped his foot. 'It had to be here again. So we remember.' His stare was glassy again. 'I must work. I must paint. More paintings.' He gestured to the gleaming white, blank canvas. 'Now go, get out of here, John, leave me be. If you're a ghost, you're a damned good one.'

'Father—' John could feel the fear building inside him again. 'Please, let me see her. Just once more. You must.'

He stared at him blankly. 'See who?'

'Mama.' John's mouth was dry. 'For five minutes or so, that's all I ask.'

'I'll not. You cannot. Don't you understand? She has believed you dead for eight months. It has nearly killed her. She has lived in hell, John. She has just started now, only now, to remake her world. She was so proud of you! When we had so many worries about you she was able to tell the world you died a hero. You can't creep back on your belly for one afternoon and tell her you're a damned deserter, so you can hang about her neck and snivel for an hour then creep off again. Can't you see that?' His finger was jabbing John. 'It'd kill her.' He glanced around. 'Here. Here! Take this.'

He plucked a folded piece of paper from his pocket book and gave it to John, who took it. Their shaking fingers touched. Ned sprang away. 'You're afraid of me, aren't you?'

'No, Father, of course not.'

'Here's this too—' he was wrenching his pocket watch from his waistcoat. 'Take it, it's gold, it'll sell well. Five pounds and a pocket watch, that's your father's lot. I loved you, my son, but it's all over, you might as well understand now. You do, don't you?'

His white face, his terrible, hooded expression: John wheeled round, glancing outside, just in case she was coming towards him, or peering out of a window. But outside it was glorious sunshine, the garden undisturbed.

'Where is she?' he said, trying not to weep.

'I – well, I don't know where she is. She's not here.'

John did not believe him. She was in the house, he was certain, yards away from him now. It was unbearable, and yet what could he do? Would he disobey his father, run inside? Risk it all, risk them all? *She was able to tell the world you died a hero. You can't tell her you were a deserter. You were her world, my boy. It will kill her.*

He took the money, and the watch, placing them carefully in the pocket inside his jacket.

'Where'd you get the papers to come back home?' his father said, quickly.

'I stole them from a dead man,' said John, not caring any more. 'I found him as I was running away – his head had been blown off – I couldn't see whether it was from a gun or a shell. I swapped his papers with mine.' He picked up a crust of bread from the table nearby, and bit into it. It was fresh, springy, delicious. 'I'm Frank Thorboys. Don't worry, Father. There's nothing that could possibly link you to me.'

He had to go, he knew that. He couldn't stay any longer. If he was to be somewhere by nightfall he ought to push on. He took the rest of the hunk of bread and the slices of ham and cheese and tipped them into his pocket too.

'I won't ever come back. Don't worry. She'll never know.'

He turned in the doorway.

'It was all for nothing, wasn't it? All your striving.'

And he walked up the driveway, skirting along the edge of the yew trees, in the shadows. He felt that was what he was now, a shadow. At the lane he stopped, leaning to one side, his near-empty stomach churning with acid as it attacked the bread. And should he now go left, back towards the town, the church? Or right, out up on the wold. He could walk to Bristol, and thence find passage to France. Left? Or right?

The morning after the final assault at Cambrai John had found his friend David Cooper, drowned in mud, his horse too. He had wiped the mud from David's face, and had crouched down, unable to cry, but with his eyes closed, and opened them again fifteen seconds or so later to find a rat gnawing on David's eye socket. Tanks were rumbling away from the conflict in the distance . . . the earth seemed to shake, to its very core.

John had walked away, tripping on boots sucked into the bubbling grey mud, stumbling on dead trees and dead men. He had hidden in the barn he had staked out in on manoeuvres the previous week. He had stayed there without moving, wetting and soiling himself, until nightfall. He did not move; in fact, he found he could not move.

When he walked away, when he escaped, he had no plan, no strategy. He simply walked away from it all, back towards home.

The following day, he found Frank Thorboys's body, and took his papers and helmet, and gave him a burial in the sea of mud that seemed now to cover most of Northern France. He was operating with a plan now. He did not realise that every step he took away also meant forfeiting the right to go home. It was not a desperate flight, either, it was the slow creep of a broken thing. I am not made for fighting, he'd told the drill officer at training camp in Worcester, very early on. Too late, sonny. We'll make a fighter out of you yet.

The shells. The sound of it, cracking open your head. The smell and sight of mustard gas, what it did to your skin, your stomach, your eyes: blocking up your nose and throat with blisters, so some men suffocated with it. He'd seen them dying, just as Eliza had died. Over and over again. He'd watched men fighting for breath like he'd watched his sister through the crack in the door, watched the green cloud moving slowly towards them on the ground, only they were below the ground, trapped in maze-like trenches from which there was no escape, mud like liquid glue sticking them to the spot.

The screams, day and night. The cries of dying horses, they took so long to go and there was no ammunition to waste on finishing them off. The stench of decaying corpses, of death, that hung around you all the time. But to John the worst was the rats, grown vast with feasting on dead men and horses. They were the size of rabbits. They would wait, wait, wait till you were in the deepest stage of sleep and nibble on your ears. John's sergeant had had his ear lobe bitten clean off. When it was quiet at night, the nibbling, scratching, scurrying sounds they made that bore into your head so all you could hear was rustling, driving deeper into your skull so sometimes you found you were praying for a loud noise, a gun, a yell, just to mask the sound of them feeding, growing, breeding . . . When he dreamed, it was not of war, it was of rats, rats taking over the world, eating everyone up, nibbling at a child's fat fingers, a woman's soft arm, his face while he slept . . .

John blinked, becoming aware of his surroundings once more. He was back in a quiet, verdant English lane, staring into a hedgerow, tangled with pink dog roses. Behind him was home.

Left? Or right? He had to take the first step on the road away from Nightingale House – then another, then another – he went right, striding down the lane, ignoring the gnawing feeling of nausea in his stomach, the knot in his throat that would not let him cry.

'John!' came a faint, high voice.

He turned back, hope blossoming, that it was she whom he most wanted to see. But it was his father, barrelling down the road towards him, waving something. He limped; he was worn out, John realised.

Ned drew to a halt and dug his hands, bloodied red with carmine and streaked with vivid emerald green, into his smock pockets. He withdrew them, then pressed a wooden cylinder into his son's hand. Sweat drenched his face, his clothes.

'Have it,' he said, breathing heavily. 'It's worthless now. Have it. Goodbye, sweet John. Goodbye to you.'

John slid the rolled-up painting out of its wooden cylinder. He blinked, stared. 'What's this?'

His father said hoarsely: 'I've cut it out. There you are. And your sister. All gone. Have it, take it with you. Take with you the memory of the love we had for you. Remember us, remember what we were. I did love you, my son. I do love you. Take it with you.' Tears rolled down his cheeks. 'It's all gone.'

John looked down at the painting, neatly sliced from its frame. The newly raw edges had had no time to fray. He shook his head in horror. 'No, Father. I don't want it.'

'*Take it.* Damn you. I can't have you back in the house, I can't – you know that. You mustn't come back. But we loved you. Look at this sometimes and remember that.' Tears ran down his face, streaking the paint marks. 'I'm on the way out, my boy. These new boys painting something blue made of squares . . . My God, these chains.' He tugged at his shirt. 'It'll be worthless in a few years, except as a keepsake of the love we all bore each other. So take it.' Ned stared at the painting. '"*The past is burnt and gone.*" I shall burn the frame, and my new canvas so there's nothing left, you see. You used to love bonfires, when you were a lad. You'd help me – do you remember?'

'N-no. Father—'

'Yes. You'd come with me down there, down past the vegetables, collecting up your sticks, and you'd help me strike the flint. You were ever so good at it. I loved autumn because of it, collecting the leaves together, piling them on the fire. You were my boy, Johnny – I'm sorry. Farewell, my boy. Farewell—'

He rubbed his eyes like a small child, blinking furiously. Then he turned back, hurrying home: John could just make out the bird finials atop the house, golden in the falling sun. Once, his father stopped, looked down at the dirt track beneath him, and then he turned into the driveway and was gone.

John rolled the painting up again, fastening it tightly, and he went on his way. He did not look at it, not for many days. That night he lay down in a hedgerow, and feasted on the ham and bread from his father's studio. In the morning, he carried on walking, and but for a few hours' snatched sleep each night he didn't stop until, several days later, he reached Bristol.

After many years in Brittany, in his small stone house behind a cobbled courtyard on the edge of the green hill that sloped down to the black rocks and the churning sea, John Horner felt safe enough to allow himself a little luxury, only when he was alone, or perhaps after a *digestif* or two. He would sometimes go to the bookshelf in his bedroom, hidden behind a curtain. Pulling back the fine embroidered French linen, he would remove a particular pile of books, stacked sideways, sticking out a couple of inches more than the other books on the same shelf. Behind them was a cylinder, and inside was the painting.

He would unfurl it slowly, his eyes darting over the English country scene – the briar roses, the wild informality of the garden, the golden stone that was particular to that part of the world only. He would stare at himself, in his teal-blue knickerbockers and white ruffled shirt. Bare feet, head crooked on one side. He could still remember the feel of the parched July grass under his toes, scratchy, dry. He could still hear Eliza's voice. 'I'm so tired, Papa! Can't we *play* now?' The wings, which Mama had made by stretching material over wire. He could hear her, telling him all about it, now.

As John grew older and his eyesight faded, he could not see the details of the painting at night, so he took to removing it from its cylinder during the day. But footsteps in the quay behind the house alarmed him – his hearing was not what it had been, someone might come in while he was staring intently at it, and in his mind he had it that everything would unravel if he was found out.

He knew his father had died days after their final meeting, for he had seen a report of it in the *Picture Post* left behind on the boat. He read of the loss of the painting, the artist's collapse with influenza. But of anyone else in England he had no report, not for many years. The struggle to survive absorbed him, utterly, wholly: he had deserted his post, and was a wanted man who would be

423

court-martialled if he was discovered. Time passed but his longing for Liddy did not abate: he still missed her so very much but he knew he couldn't ever go back. He couldn't do it to her. He had to make the choice and, once made, stick with it.

Recasting himself as Frank Thorboys, a schoolteacher from Northamptonshire, a real person and not someone whose papers he'd stolen, and not giving way to the nightmares of battle, the shakes that overtook him, the attacks that were triggered by children's pop-guns in the market square, the scream of gulls high overhead, or the braying of horses, was a monumental struggle, one that threatened to overpower him for many years. To lose it all because one morning some young man he'd brought home the previous night, or someone he thought was a friend, came upon him staring intently at the most famous painting in the world: he couldn't risk it. He had, all things considered, made a life for himself out of the ruins of his former self. He loved his small, calm, ordered world in Dinard. He was loved.

And, gradually, as the decades passed, it came to be that the old familiar action of unrolling the painting and diving again into that world, imagining he was back in the garden with his big sister, their mother close by, believing that everything was golden, safe, happy once more, brought him no pleasure at all. And what would happen to the painting when he died? It hung, heavy on his heart. Over time, he saw he would have to leave the little town by the grey churning sea and return the painting to its rightful home once more.

'He caught a boat from Bristol to St Malo,' said Juliet's dad. 'He stayed there for a few weeks, and then he wandered again, and settled in Dinard. The war was over, many young men had not returned, the town was in a bad way. Frank Thorboys was welcomed most warmly. The Inspector of Sûreté himself came to express the hope that he would stay. They hoped he would work in the fields, marry one of the young ladies whose young men had been killed . . . John used to joke they'd never have welcomed him in had they known he was a fairy with one useless arm.'

'You *knew* him?' Juliet said. She sat facing her parents, leaning on the table, arms folded, staring at them. 'How? How on earth? And how strange he ended up in Dinard . . .'

'You don't see it yet?' said her mother, and she turned to Juliet's father. Both of them were pale; Juliet's mother had been crying as they outlined what they knew of John's story to her. 'She really doesn't remember it.'

'The Royal Wedding. Charles and Di,' Juliet said, suddenly.

'Exactly. You and Ev were already in the sitting room. We were getting ready to watch it. We had snacks, everything . . . And he simply walked up the drive.'

'Did he say who he was?'

'Afterwards. He introduced himself to us. He didn't know who was living in the house, whether the family had moved away. Until Frederic came here, and wrote to him about Stella, he didn't know Grandi had been born, you see. He knew Frederic from Dinard.'

'They were lovers.'

'Oh yes. Frederic's first in fact,' said her father. 'When Frederic was looking for a place outside London to open a shop, John told him about Godstow. Frederic wrote to him, telling him about the village, this lovely house, this strange woman he'd befriended called Stella Horner. Before that, John knew nothing.'

'He didn't know he had a sister?'

'No, and she didn't know he was still alive. Of course not; her mother never knew John had survived the war. Isn't it awful?' Juliet's father shook his head, his eyes swimming. 'It is all a great tragedy.'

Juliet could barely speak. 'I can't believe it. That's terrible, it's—'

'But no more than thousands of other families around the country,' said her mother, reaching across the wide table and patting her daughter's bare arm. Juliet looked down at her mother's hand on her skin. The old familiar fingers, long and tapered, the sapphire and diamond engagement ring. 'That's what war does. Uncle John wasn't a coward, he had shell-shock. He had it all his life. He'd sometimes have to leave the room, or his eyes would close and he wouldn't be there. He had nightmares about rats. Awful nightmares.'

'Yes. Rats.' Juliet's father opened his eyes wide. 'I'd forgotten. He wouldn't even kill a mosquito, but he was absolutely terrified of rats. There was one time we were staying with him, and we took a walk to the old harbour. We sat down, ordered a drink. It was dusk, you know. And a rat scuttled out from a wooden garage door and ran across the square. John screamed. I've never heard anything like it. He wouldn't stop. We had to help him all the way back home, he couldn't walk, he was shaking, sweat pouring down his face. It was horrible. He was an old man by then, almost ninety, but he was strong as anything, he'd spent half a century there, he loved the fresh air and the sea and the – other amusements, as it were. I think that night weakened him. He got the chest infection soon after.'

'Me too.' Juliet's mother had bowed her head but she looked up. 'Now, of course, one would instantly recognise he had PTSD. He should have had intensive psychotherapy. But of course he didn't. Oh, he was a lovely man, Juliet,' said Elvie, and she clasped her husband's hand.

'But why didn't he come back?' Juliet rubbed her eyes. 'Why didn't you bring me over to meet him? You went to visit him, is that how you ended up buying the house over there?'

'We had no idea of his existence until the day he turned up at the house. And what could we do? We felt very strongly . . . John needed protection. He needed a family, after all these years but he didn't want people to know he was Michael's uncle. He was terrified of being found out.'

Juliet's father nodded. 'But I couldn't just let him leave on his own.' He furrowed his brow.

'Of course, Stella was wonderful,' said Elvie, rather mechanically. She patted Michael's arm now. 'But she did rather start to lose the plot after that day. Any mention of John sent her off again. I think she'd worked *so* hard to build up this myth of her family, to have it utterly dismantled in one day . . . We felt awful about how she'd treated him. She really – I'd never seen her behave that way, before or since. As though he flipped a switch.'

'What did she do?'

426

Juliet's parents looked at each other.

'I still can't really explain it,' said Michael, after a pause. 'She wouldn't let him stay a moment longer. That's all.'

'Anyway, so that was how it happened. Daddy caught up with him – on the driveway—'

'He was walking away and he said, look, please don't upset your mother, I'm awfully sorry, I shouldn't have come back, and I said, we are coming to France next month, may we come and visit you if it's convenient? Where do you live?'

'And he said – I'm in Brittany. Your father was very clever, you see.'

'And I said – didn't I, Elvie? – my goodness, well we're coming to Brittany, isn't it a small world?' He blinked back something and Juliet, staring at him, wondered why she had never seen how kind he was before today. 'You see I couldn't let him walk away like that. Just couldn't. And I'm afraid I found it rather hard, the way Mum treated him then refused to discuss it ever again. But there you are. We go on.'

'Grandi used to say that. All the time.'

'Did she?'

'She did, Dad. I don't understand – did he tell you what he'd done with the painting? Didn't he ever mention it?'

'Well –' Juliet's father looked ashamed. 'You see, he mentioned something about it once or twice but I didn't think much of it. You know me. I wasn't really interested in Ned Horner. I know I should have been. You, my dear, made us so proud, understanding him and making your work all about his paintings. But I personally never got it. Never really got paintings at all. I like buildings. Mum was furious about me becoming a quantity surveyor. So cross. I think she wanted me to go to art college. Carry on the tradition.'

Juliet was thoughtful. 'But Dad – did he really tell you it was *The Garden of Lost and Found*? And you just didn't care?'

'He said he'd had one of his paintings once but he'd got rid of it. You know, when I was growing up, Ned Horner was terribly unfashionable. No one wanted them.'

'Do you remember one of your friends at Imperial found one in a junk shop, on the King's Road? And he wanted some of you to lend him the money to buy it?' said Elvie, amused.

'Yes. *The Artist's Wife and Her Dog*, or something. Old Jerry. He was rather into Victorian art and we used to rather laugh at him. We persuaded him not to buy it. Terrible waste of money.'

'Dear God,' said Juliet helplessly. 'Do you still see him?'

'No, lost touch with him years ago. He rather dropped us. Don't know why.'

'Can't imagine,' said Juliet. 'Poor Ned,' she said, thinking for a moment. 'He became the thing he most feared. A reactionary member of the bourgeoisie. And poor. He almost died rescuing Liddy and pulling himself out of poverty, and then working to give her this house and then he bought that damned painting back on some poetic whim and ruined himself. He'd have been declared bankrupt if he'd lived. Not the kind of legacy he wanted.'

'His son had all that, that's the irony.' Michael Horner stood up. 'When he died, the whole town turned out for him. Brass band, policemen in white gloves . . . They adored him. There's a water-colour of Frank's in the Hôtel de Ville, a view of the town, with a nice plaque to him. Very moving. We unveiled it, actually.' Juliet shook her head, marvelling at this. 'You can ask Frederic. And I think John was happy in his new life, my love. Not like Mum. She gradually lived more and more in the past . . .' He looked up, rather embarrassed at this confession. 'That's what I think, anyway.'

Juliet came round the table and embraced him, leaning in to her father's sturdy, broad frame. 'Oh, Dad. Yes, yes, of course. Poor Grandi. Poor John. Oh, Dad. Thank you for telling me. You too, Mum.'

'My dear one, I am so glad you know now,' he said, and Elvie stood up too, and the three of them hugged, tightly, silently.

Chapter Thirty-Nine

June 2015

Juliet sat in the car in the broiling heat for five minutes, not getting out, just watching the old street, window open, arm out of the window. The city smells of summer – tarmac, burning oil, petrol, pollution, barbecues, something indefinably primal – thudded through her.

She had been back to London a few times since she left, but this felt different. She was a visitor, not someone returning home. How packed the houses seemed together, how huge the cars, parked up on the pavements of her narrow road. It was early afternoon, and quiet. A knock on the car roof made her jump out of her skin and she looked out to see a face with a headscarf looming in at her.

'Zeina. You – gah. I nearly had a heart attack.'

'The year you've had and someone tapping your car gives you a heart attack? I'd say your priorities ain't quite right.' Juliet climbed out of the car and hugged her. 'What's this, hey? Hey . . .' Zeina patted her back as Juliet clung to her, burying her face in her shoulder.

'You said you'd come to visit.'

'You said you'd invite me. Oh, and your kid nearly died. Why are you here? Have you—' Zeina pulled herself away from Juliet, holding her by the shoulders, fake shock on her face. 'Oh my goodness, you've changed your mind, yes? Is that it? You're moving back?!'

'Yes! We're all moving in together! My three, me, Matt, and eight-months-pregnant Tess and her two children! . . . I'm picking up Bea. She's been staying for a week, her exams finished early.'

'But she's not there. She and Matt left an hour or so ago. I saw them coming back from the shops. Come inside, have a cuppa with me while you wait for them.'

Juliet looked at her watch. 'Sure. Or I could walk on the Heath . . .'

'You don't want to come to my house?' Zeina was smiling, head on one side. 'OK, babe. OK.'

'I do.' Juliet couldn't look at her. Standing here she felt a deep love for the simplicity of the life they'd had, where everyone lived on the same road or nearabouts, and life was easy, school was down the road, the Heath was metres away, the Tube, the corner shop, the pizza place and where everyone was from another place, was interesting, hardworking, hadn't made their mind up about stuff. 'But I don't want to sit in your kitchen. I think it might make me lose my shit. I miss you.' She felt fat tears, plopping from the corners of her eyes on to her sleeve. 'I really miss you.'

'You idiot.' Zeina put her arm round her and led her up the small path to her house. 'We speak all the time.'

'About solicitor things. Not normal things.'

'Stop being crazy and come inside. The kitchen's been painted. You won't recognise it and that'll make it easier.' Juliet nodded, wiping her eyes, and Zeina gave a half-sob, half-laugh. 'Oh, mate. I miss you too. I've flirted with other mums, but I don't like them as much.'

'Me too. Well, there's this nice woman, Jo, but I haven't seen her for ages. We chat at pick-up, and we've had coffee a few times, but now it's the holidays I'm too shy to take it further and ask her for a drink.'

'Oh good grief. Now,' said Zeina, when they were inside and the kettle was on. 'Now. Tell me quickly. What's happening with the painting.'

Zeina was acting as Juliet's lawyer and had already advised her on insurance. 'Sam might call today actually. He's meeting someone from the Tate.'

'Sam?'

'Hamilton. The museum director. I told you about him.'

'Ah. You like him.'

'What?'

'Your voice goes up when you talk about him. You like him. Or he likes you. Which one? Or both?'

'Neither. Both.' Juliet looked around the familiar kitchen, hers in reverse, the cork board, the word magnets on the fridge, the spider plant left on top of the kitchen cupboard that reproduced in looping brackets, hanging over boxes of tupperware – she had spent more time in this room than anyone else's. It was very strange to be back. She glanced into the garden, the Astroturf square that Nawal rode his digger around on, the swifts that circled overhead in the evenings, looping up and around the streets below.

We could just say it was a year off. I could sell Nightingale House, move back to London, buy my dream house on Dartmouth Park Avenue or somewhere in Highgate, pick our lives back up. Sandy wouldn't even remember it.

Then it hit her that Isla's playdate with Emily was tomorrow, and Sandy's coming home party was on Saturday, and Dr Mulligan was coming for lunch on Sunday, with her son who was Isla's age. And George and Frederic had found a chest of drawers they said would be perfect for the hallway, and two more pieces for the doll's house had turned up in a house clearance over in Walbrook, the recently deceased a long-forgotten schoolmate of Stella's who'd perhaps purloined them for herself, many years ago. The doll's house had not returned yet from the specialist who was repairing it at the Museum of Childhood but he promised it was fixable. So they were collecting new items for when it was back home again, this time probably to be kept in the hallway. Low down.

Honor had come several times to help with the garden, and had said she'd send her gardener over next week to give Juliet some advice. And, besides, the sweet peas needed cutting every day now, shoving into vases and giving out their cinnamon-sugar scent all over the house. The dahlias were just starting, and she couldn't bear to miss them – the first bursting out from the tight, dark buds into elaborate origami-puffs of blood red, fuchsia pink, bright orange, mixed in with blue cornflowers, the citrus-yellow-and-pale-pink snapdragons, the cool green of the leaves against the wall. She had to stake the sunflowers, and pick the camomile for tea, and sort out Sandy's room – he had a new big boy bed, with sides on it. Matt had said it was idiotic, buying a child who'd just suffered a head trauma a bed instead of keeping him in a cot, but Juliet felt the opposite – that he needed to be treated like a boy who was growing up, had things to look forward to, responsibility. He had been babied for three months, given his way on everything, and she had to give him freedom and teach him responsibility again.

All of that he could have in Nightingale House. Not here. Not any more. She had grown out of London, grown away from it. It was Matt's city, not hers. But more fundamental than any of that, it was that Juliet knew she couldn't leave the house. The pull she had always felt towards it throughout her life was, now that she lived there, stronger than ever. As if she and the house were entwined. It wasn't about Ned, or the painting, or Grandi. It was the house. It was her home. She wanted nothing else but that.

She looked down at her Converses, and saw with shame that they were caked in mud.

'What are you thinking about?' Zeina handed her the cup of tea.

'Just that it's so nice to see you. I miss you so much but I don't think I want to come back.'

'Well, you can afford to do whatever you want now.'

Juliet took a deep breath. 'That's partly what I wanted to discuss. I want to give away most of the money.' Zeina's mouth dropped open and she froze, teapot in hand. 'I said most of it, Zee, I'm not crazy. I want some for the house, and to live on, but I need to get rid of the rest before I get used to the idea. I don't want the children to be millionaires for no reason. It feels wrong, after what my family lost. That's not what the house is about. I had an idea for something and I wanted you to help me.'

432

'How much are you talking about?' Zeina reached for her lined pad and pen.

'I'm going to keep four million. Two hundred and fifty thousand in trust for each of the children, to help them buy somewhere, get them on their feet, they can't access it till they're twenty-one though. Can you do that? Another two hundred and fifty thousand in case we have to adapt parts of the house for Sandy or pay for physio or something.'

'Sure.' Zeina scribbled it down.

'Two million for me.' Juliet tried to make it sound casual, sitting in this kitchen talking about *millions* here and *trusts* there like it was normal. 'That house leaks money. A million for a new roof and kitchen and to keep me in new curtains and bulbs and fuel for the Aga, and so I've got a wodge of cash in case something bad happens.'

'Right. And the rest? You'll have a clear six or seven million if your mate Sam Ham is telling the truth.'

Juliet cleared her throat. 'I want to set up a trust for teaching art history in school. And fund school trips to art galleries and after that, further afield, to fund residential stays all over the UK to visit stately homes, the Yorkshire Sculpture Park, art galleries.' She tried not to sound nervous. She remembered what Sam had told her: *Everyone's bluffing. I got my job by bluffing. Just say what you want to do, you'll be amazed how many people listen to you.* 'So every child in this country has seen how beautiful a painting or a sculpture or a house can be. Not just children of National Trust members or people who take their kids to museums themselves, or can afford to go anywhere they want. Everyone has the right to have their mind enriched.'

'They should have the right to regular meals and not to have to go with Mum to a food bank every week, they should have parents who are paid a proper wage who aren't on a zero-hours contract,' said Zeina grimly.

'Well I know. And I'm sending you a list of donations I want to make too when the sale goes through, but I can't, like, *end* food banks, much as I'd like to. Is this possible, though? Can you set up some sort of charitable trust?'

'Yes, but you can't be the sole trustee. You need someone—'

'I've got someone. Sam.'

'Sam Ham again, eh?' Zeina scribbled some more. 'I remember you talking about him when he got that job. You couldn't stand him. Does he talk about you this much, too?'

'He's my boss.'

It was clear Zeina thought this was a shoddy answer, but she changed the subject. 'How is Bea?'

'I think she's OK. I am giving her a lot of space at the moment. To sort of find herself if that doesn't sound hokey.' Juliet hesitated. 'I have to remind myself not to yes to her too much though, just because I feel guilty about screwing everything up.'

Zeina put her hand on her arm. 'You still think that, do you?' Her eyes were wide with amazement.

'What?'

'That you screwed everything up.'

'God yes. Sandy – that wouldn't have happened if we'd been in London. Bea – she's been so unhappy. Isla's got no friends—'

And then she stopped. 'She has, actually. She had a playdate last week and a sleepover the week before. And Bea's not unhappy.' She was nodding. 'She's doing really well. They think she'll get some A*s for GCSEs. And Fin is nice. And – you know what? Frederic loves me. And George. And I love them.' She was counting on her fingers, and she could feel her face burning. 'What else? Mum and Dad have been terrific, and we barely spoke a year ago. And Honor is there if I need her, and I'm going to bloody well have that drink with Jo next week and I – well, I love going to work. And I planted some lupins from seed and they died, and it doesn't matter, because they're impossible to grow from seed. I should have just bought baby plants. But that's OK! I know that now and it's OK!' Zeina was shaking her head, lips curled inwards in a fond expression of bemusement. 'My point is a year ago . . . Wow, Zee, a year ago I was so unhappy, they all were, and it's not the house or the money that's made the difference.'

'Come on. It's helped.'

'It will help. It didn't then. It's that I made a change. And I wouldn't ever have had the courage to do it if that slimeball Henry Cudlip hadn't made me redundant or if that other slimeball Matt Taylor hadn't had an affair. Sorry, he's not a slimeball. But you know what I mean.'

Zeina tightened the pressure on her arm. 'Women! Why do we do this to ourselves! Matt is a slimeball. He had the affair and treated you like absolute shit, Ju. And the kids.'

'He did. But I'm saying I thought all these things were the worst things that could happen when they happened. But losing my job, finding out about Matt and Tess – they were the best things that could have happened. They forced me to make a change. You just get used to unhappiness, I think. I used to think of it like muscle memory. You forget how to be happy.' She rolled her head around her neck, feeling it click. 'Sandy is the exception. That wasn't a bad thing that turned out to be a great thing. That was on my watch.'

Zeina nodded, but she said, 'Listen, babe, accidents happen. That kid was always in everything. Remember the time he climbed on to your bedroom windowsill? Who's to say he wouldn't have had a worse accident if you'd stayed in London? You can't see that path cos you didn't take it. You took this one. You did the right thing. You've always done the right thing.'

Her voice was soft, and so kind. Juliet blinked, arms folded across her chest. 'Well—'

There was a knock on the door. 'That'll be Nawal or Yasmin.' Zeina got up, went down the hallway. 'Oh, hi there,' Juliet heard her say, in some surprise. 'Of course, babe. Come in.'

Bea entered, hands in her pockets and her backpack on, looking gingerly around, but when she saw Juliet she flung her arms round her. 'Mum! How's Sandy?'

'He's – yep, he's really good, darling. How's your week been?'

'It's been fab.' Bea nodded. 'Can Fin come down again next week?'

'Of course.' Juliet drained her mug. She looked up at Zeina, in the doorway. 'We should go and get Bea's stuff from across the road –'

'No need, I've got it,' said Bea. She patted the backpack. 'Let's go home.'

'Oh. Well. Don't you want to say bye to—'

'Don't ruin the symbolism of it, Mum. Anyway, Dad's taking Tess out to dinner tonight at some fancy Italian place in Hampstead so she's resting now. Her feet are killing her and she's hungry all the time and I heard her tell Dad she'd rather not see you.'

'Hey – well. So – did Dad say anything?'

'He said he'd try and come down for Sandy's thing on Saturday but he's not sure. Tess's kid has a kung-fu display.' Bea leaned against the wall, one foot up under her leg. Her fringe was getting long again – it was only a week or two since she'd cut it. Where did time go? Weeks, months, slipping away, and Bea was a young woman, sixteen in a couple of months.

Zeina opened the door. 'Car's still there, it hasn't been nicked in the crime cesspit of Zone 2. Is that it? Have you finished with me?'

Juliet stopped. 'There is one more thing. I want to buy another painting. It's in Geneva at the moment, in a vault. Don't laugh. It really is. Do I have to pay import tax on it?'

Zeina sighed, and folded her arms. 'Right. What painting is this?'

'Well, it's the sketch. The sketch of *The Garden of Lost and Found*.' Juliet scratched her nose. 'I know it sounds mad. It does sound mad. The guy who bought it won't loan it out. He doesn't want to bother with it any more, I think. He's been crucified for it. I offered him a bit above the market price and pointed out he'd look like a good guy if he sold it back to the great-granddaughter of the painter since she has somehow managed to acquire the other painting—'

'Which it turns out was in your own house all along anyway and your child had to suffer a severe head injury for you to find it—'

'Yes, well.' Juliet scratched her nose. 'I didn't go into that with him to be honest . . . he's not a details man.'

'Uh-uh.'

'But I think we have a deal. I want to take it back to the house

436

and hang it up again, in the study. So when I'm working and writing my biography of Horner I can stare at it. Can you check out the contract, when it comes?'

'All this work,' Zeina complained. 'Eid is coming up, I'm tired by about five and hungry, and you're giving me all this extra trouble.'

'Thanks, Zee. I loves ya.' Juliet kissed her again and headed down the front path, turning to say, 'Bea, do you need a—'

'Mum! I'm fifteen, for God's sake! I've had a pee, all right!'

'All right –' Juliet began and then stopped, and waved. 'Oh. Hi, Tess.'

Tess was standing in the doorway opposite, holding a bag of rubbish. She stared at Juliet without emotion. 'Let me help you with that,' said Juliet, and before she could think about it she was crossing the road towards her, taking the bag, slinging it into the bins by the front wall, not the nearest one, the second one.

'That bin leaks,' Juliet said, pointing. 'It's better—' She stopped, moving back, towards the gate, suddenly awkward.

'It's a new bin. But thanks.' Tess turned back to go. Juliet saw the deep, curved shadows under her eyes above her apple-like cheeks, the clear, waxy perfection of her slightly bloated, heavily-pregnant-woman's face and the dilated, slightly dead look in her eyes.

'How are you doing?' she said.

Tess turned slowly, and in obvious discomfort. She patted her large bump, snugly encased in Breton stripes. 'I'm OK. I have pelvic girdle pain. It's fucking agony.'

'I had that with Isla. It's awful. I'm so sorry. Matt will know what to do. He used to—' Juliet stopped, then said in a rush: 'I had a support belt I'd wear. He used to rub my hips, and my feet. Get him to do it.'

Tess gave a weary smile. 'I'm sure he'll remember. I'll ask him. When he's in a good mood.'

Matt's moods, the barometer of the house. Juliet felt a warm breeze on her face, liberty washing over her. Oh, how she must bring her girls up believing they never, ever needed to be with

437

someone for the sake of it. It was better to live contentedly alone than live like that. Far, far better.

'Anyway, I bet Matt's thrilled,' said Juliet. 'He's great with babies. I'm sure—'

She trailed off, remembering how very hard Isla had found being with Elise, Tess's first child. Juliet realised then her kids must visit their new half-brother or sister, must love them, but she'd have to make sure it wasn't for too long each time. This was a toxic situation, brewing right there. She thought for a moment.

'Matt really is great with babies.' She swallowed, and then went on. 'He sings them to sleep. And he's good at just having them around while he does stuff. Cooking, making tea. He used to empty the dishwasher with Isla strapped into the Baby Bjorn. He'd sing her Paul Weller. She loved it.' She nodded, brightly. 'He likes feeling useful. I stopped needing him, I suppose.' It was the truth, she saw it now. 'Listen, congratulations, Tess. I'm happy for you.' And that, she supposed, was also the truth. She was free, and she was out of here.

'I think the congratulations are all yours,' said Tess, thinly. 'Matt keeps saying how pleased he is for you.' She gave a short laugh. 'Just so you know. He's really pleased for you.'

'Oh – thanks.'

The dark shadows beneath Tess's eyes deepened as she looked down. 'It's bullshit, of course. But we have to say we believe it, don't we? Otherwise he's afraid he'll be a laughing stock.'

She gave a small, terrible twisted smile, hand still wrapped tentacle-like around her own bump. Juliet nodded, and looked at the bump but when she glanced up, Tess had shut the front door.

Juliet stared at her old house one last time: the evening sun on the neat cream and red brick frontage, the last of the honeysuckle clinging to the rotten trellis. She crossed the narrow road to her car.

'Righty-ho!' she said, brightly.

'She's weird,' said Zeina, under her breath.

'Zeina . . .' Juliet said warningly, nodding her head towards Bea, but Bea stuck her thumbs into her backpack straps.

'She is weird. But, then, so's Dad. I think they'll be good together.'

'Oh,' said Juliet. 'How?'

'They're both convinced there's a conspiracy against them. That everyone else is having a better time.' She shrugged. 'Money and better lives and stuff. She's got no money now she's divorced her husband and she loves money. So does Dad. She said you'd got loads, is that because you divorced Dad?'

'Sort of. I'll tell you about it on the way back home.' They smiled at each other and Juliet turned to Zeina. 'Look, I—'

'Don't,' said Zeina. 'Just go away. I love you and I miss you, and I'll be in touch about all that stuff. Give Sam my details.' She pulled her close to her. 'And give him your details.'

'Can we listen to your ABBA CD, Mum?' Bea said, as they got into the car.

'Why of course,' said Juliet, managing to hide her shock. 'Let's open with "Super Trouper" – it's a work of genius.'

'It is, Mum.' Bea made an awkward gesture, rubbing her silky head against Juliet's arm for a brief second then sitting back, half frowning, half smiling.

'So – wow. You think I'm right about something.'

'You are. You're right about a lot.'

Juliet glanced at Matt's house one last time as they drove away.

'Let's go home, darling,' she said, waving to Zeina as the car pulled away from the kerb.

Chapter Forty

One week later, and it was early July. As the last guest was leaving
– the Tolleys from Walbrook Farm, who had brought some of their
own pig pâté to Sandy's Welcome Home party and a load of frozen
sausages and two ready meals – 'We didn't want to bother you, now
he's home we thought you might be a bit swamped, what with
everything, and a few meals are good at a time like this,' Debs Tolley
had said, plonking them down almost defiantly in the little kitchen
– Juliet stood at the bottom of the stairs, listening out for Sandy.
It was just seven and he was already fast asleep, worn out by the
excitement of being at home and being with his siblings. He had
eaten too many sweets and bounced up and down on the sofa
cushions for a few seconds, then felt very dizzy and turned extremely
white. Juliet had tried not to freak out before reassuring herself it
was the bouncing, not anything more. She had taken him into the
dining room, and given him a proper, voice-raised, finger-wagging
talking-to, where she told him that if he bounced on things again
while he was recovering he'd have to go back to hospital.

'I don't care if that scares the crap out of you,' she'd added,
horrified at herself, but almost enjoying the thrill of the alarm on
his face. 'You are a very lucky little boy. And if you fall off anything
again before you're better, I will be furious with you.'

'No! You must come to my hospital and give my presents again,'
Sandy said, arms folded, and then he stalked out, yelling, 'Isla! Food!'

'His speech has really come on,' said Honor dryly in the background, nursing a glass of wine.

Juliet watched him fall asleep in his new bed, with his Peppa Pig
toys ranged against the wall and his new pop-up *Tiger Who Came to*

Tea book and his digger from Matt. She had resisted the urge to stay and check his breathing, his head position, the heat of the room . . . with huge force of will she had taken herself away, and down to the study, to have a little weep. For he seemed still so very small and vulnerable to her.

Honor appeared in the hallway now, draining her wine. 'I should be going,' she said. She put her glass on the hall table, and ruffled her hair in the mirror, tying her scarf around her neck again. 'Oh, by the way. My gardener's popping over this afternoon. Do you remember, I mentioned him? Is that OK?' Juliet looked blank. 'I've told him all about the place. He wants to see what he can do.'

As with many things over the last couple of months Juliet had no memory of this, but she nodded. 'That's great. Thank you so much for fixing me up with him.'

Honor laughed, then hugged her. Juliet smelled her delicious fragrance, so redolent of her childhood, and she felt her soft skin on her cheek as she kissed her. 'I'm so glad you're still here. All of you,' Honor said. 'Now, I'm leaving the car here. George is giving me a lift home, I've had too much wine.'

Juliet opened the french windows, and in a few moments heard the sound of George's car purring quietly up the drive. She smelled the fresh evening air, welcome in the stale, hot room.

On her desk lay the high-resolution photograph of *The Garden of Lost and Found* and a card from Sam, confirming the sale to the Tate. It had been waiting for her when she arrived back from London with Bea. He had dropped it round, but hadn't stayed.

The Tate will display the picture with The Nightingale *and* The Lilac Hours. *Twenty-five per cent of all proceeds from postcards, memorabilia, etc. will go to the Stella Horner Foundation for Art Education. They will be in touch with you separately about it. And, if I may, I'll call you soon.*

Thank you
S

It was coming back to the house for one night, at her request, before it went to the Tate for its unveiling. She would put the painting on the terrace, in front of the french windows, just above the rambling roses and Honor's newly planted foxgloves. She would see it in its rightful setting, once more before it left again.

What would Grandi make of it all? The absence of her huge spirit seemed particularly noticeable tonight, even if only to Juliet.

When she'd visited Grandi in hospital, after her stroke, an art therapist had come round the ward one day, with laminated reproductions of paintings, and shown them to the patients who greeted them with a mixture of total indifference or annoyance.

For three days in a row Juliet went to Walbrook hospital and sat with her, sweating because she was still breastfeeding and the heat of the ward and her winter clothes were too much. The nurses didn't like Grandi, she could tell – she was large, heavy to move around, and she moaned too much, and, besides, her drooping face and mouth were alarming, as though she'd been left out in the sun too long and melted. Her eyes swivelled, she kept the other patients awake – and she didn't seem to know Juliet, not at all. She ignored her, or stared past her.

On the third day the art therapist, a meek, small woman, younger than Juliet, had approached the bed. 'Here's some paintings for you to look at, Stella!' she'd said in a perky voice. 'Let's see, shall we? Van Gogh's *Sunflowers*. Look at the bright yellow, isn't it cheery? That's a David Hockney, of his parents. Look at the detail of his mother's hands. Very old and gnarled. Here's a lovely one. This is Edward Horner. *The Caged Nightingale*. Can you see the mechanical bird in her hand? And the girl is also – Oh. Oh dear.'

For Grandi had started writhing around, emitting wild, lowing groans, grinding against the sheets, her eyes bulging, her collapsed face immobile.

'She likes this painting,' said the art therapist, uncertainly. Juliet looked at her grandmother in alarm.

'It's OK,' she said. She grabbed Grandi's arm, stared into her

442

eyes, the dark-brown eyes that were like hers. 'Grandi, it's all right, I'm here.'

But Grandi was still tossing, almost screaming something. Juliet turned back to the art therapist, who was shuffling the laminated pages, awkwardly.

'It's called *The Nightingale*,' Juliet said.

'Yes, *The Caged Nightingale*.'

Grandi moaned, even louder. Other patients were staring at her; a nurse, in the corner, looked over. 'Awwwhohhh,' she was screaming. '*Awwwhooohhhhhhh.*'

'No,' said Juliet. 'It's just *The Nightingale*. No caging.'

'Well, it says "*The Caged Nightingale*" here,' said the young woman, slightly sharply. She scanned the label on the back. 'It's in the . . .' She peered. '. . . Tate Britain. "Purchased from Mrs Constance Whitty, nee Galveston, daughter of the famous art dealer Galveston whose purchase of this painting at the Royal Academy lifted the young artist out of poverty. The figure is his wife, Lydia Horner." Oh, I remember this painting. My grandmother used to take me to see it.' She stared at it as though for the first time. 'She loved the girl's face. And her hair. Isn't that funny.'

'Yes, that bit's right, but the title's still wrong,' said Juliet, and she turned back to her grandmother. One brown eye was fixed on her, filmy with tears. 'She wasn't caged. She wasn't ever caged. You see?'

But she didn't say any more – what was the point? The woman wasn't interested, good though her intentions were. Juliet closed her eyes in the heat, smelling hospital scent: antiseptic, urine, cloying sweetness, rancid cleaning products. When she opened them her grandmother was asleep, though the art therapist carried on. 'This is by Gainsborough, can you see the girls, their lovely dresses and their hair?'

'Yes,' said Juliet, staring at the picture, one of her favourites, of his two anxious little daughters, chasing a butterfly. 'I see them.'

'Lovely, isn't it? The patients always like this one. Pretty dresses.'

'She went mad.' Juliet pulled at her heavy clothes, sweat dripping down her spine.

'Sorry?' The art therapist was shuffling her pictures, and looked up.

'The one on the right. Mary. She went mad and had to go and live with her sister after her marriage broke down.'

'Really? Are you sure?' She didn't know what to do, and carried on putting the pictures away. 'Well, you obviously know more than I do.' She cast a dubious look down at Juliet's sleeping grandmother, her vast body not part of her any more. The bony, useless hands that staked plants and caught mice and brushed hair now heavy and lifeless at her side. 'Good luck, then. I'll be off to see some more patients.'

'Thank you,' Juliet called after her. She turned to her grandmother, and found her watching her, one eye half-open again, and jumped with shock.

They stared at each other, but Juliet knew she wasn't really seeing her. But, just in case, she squeezed one hand tightly, kissed the warm, smooth forehead.

'Thank you.'

Then Grandi gave a slight small sigh. She closed her eyes, and did not open them again, and after ten minutes or so, Juliet kissed her gently again and left her. She died a week later, and Juliet was not sorry. She knew Grandi would not be, either.

Now, standing looking out over the garden, she lifted out her grandmother's little exercise book, written just before the stroke. The close, beautifully looped italic hand, the careful underlining of each section, the letters . . . Poor Grandi, she thought. She'd pushed away the people who could have told her. She pushed away poor Dad, who left me to have the relationship with her. And then I was the only one left apart from dear, steady Frederic, and after a while she made sure she pushed me away too. And what difference would it have made, if she'd found the painting? If John had simply given it to her? Money wouldn't have made her happy. Looking at the original wouldn't have made her happy . . . those two children, the ones everyone remembered . . . the one she had sent away again . . .

Then Juliet could only remember the good times. How Grandi

444

had made corn dollies each August, and given them names, a whole world they'd created. How they'd slept in the Birdsnest one night every May half-term, to hear the nightingales singing. How her dark eyes gleamed as she read to her from the old children's books she'd pull at random down from the dusty shelves: *The Arabian Nights*, and *The Railway Children* and *Alice's Adventures in Wonderland*.

Footsteps sounded on the gravel outside – she looked up, still lost in thought.

'Hello?' she said to the silhouette in the doorway. 'Oh, you must be the . . .' She paused, feeling 'gardener' was a bit *Downton Abbey*. 'Are you the man who's coming to look at the garden?'

'The gardener, you mean?' a voice said, amused. 'Juliet?' The man in the doorway moved forward, out of shadow. A bulky figure, close-shaven, wellingtons caked in mud.

'Yes?' she said blankly.

'Don't you recognise me?'

She stared at him, shock flooding her veins. 'Ev?' She leaned forward. 'No. *Ev?*'

He had her hand, and was pressing it in his, and shaking it. 'Yes! I *knew* you didn't recognise me!'

His wild, curly Afro, which as a child he had refused to let his mother cut, was now trimmed down to the skull, so you could see the scar he'd got from jumping off the wall by the stream. His eyes were the same: liquid, alternately black and brown in the light. His skin, darker than hers when they used to hold their forearms next to each other. So many years . . . his hands – she held his hands in hers, laughing as she saw them because the nails were bitten to the quick, still packed with dirt in every line and crevice. And he was huge. He was *strapping*. He was almost unrecognisable from the small lithe boy who'd slipped out of streams and into trees and up on to roofs with her, all those summers ago.

'Look at you,' she said, shaking her head. 'Everett Adair! What happened to you!'

'Too many cakes and beers,' he said, patting his stomach.

'Rubbish! The height! The last time I saw you . . .'

Their last summer together had been a summer of firsts, losing their virginity to each other in the Dovecote, in the garden, up in the Birdsnest . . . He was eighteen, she was seventeen and he had gone to Birmingham in September and never come back, and at home in London she had been heartbroken for the whole autumn term, as rain dripped on to wet leaves and summer receded into memory. At Christmas she'd returned to Nightingale House yearning for him, but he wasn't there and then . . . She rubbed her forehead with one finger. She supposed she'd stopped missing him at some point. It was long ago . . . How long? Twenty, twenty-two –

'*Twenty-two years ago!* Is that right? Christ, we're old.' She looked down, still holding his hands. 'Were you this tall then?'

'I grew another three inches when I was eighteen. Or nineteen. And I found beer,' he said, and Juliet raised her eyebrows, and they both laughed.

'You never came back,' she said, after a while. 'You went away to university and you said you'd be back.'

'I didn't want to stay, Ju. I was the only black person for miles and miles.'

'Not *miles* and miles – there was – '

'My dad, Ju. There was me and my dad. And he loves living here still but . . . I wanted to try being unremarkable for once. You know, when you're in the city, no one thinks you're special. They don't stare, or speak in really nice bright voices to hide their white guilt. I liked that at first. I'd never had it before.'

'I never thought about it like that. I did afterwards but not . . . not then. I'm sorry.'

'We were kids. Why would you? Kids don't notice stuff like that.'

'But still, I wish I had. I thought everything was the same for us and it wasn't.' She nodded. 'Of course it wasn't. Come with me.' She drew him out on to the terrace, towards the evening sun, pouring him a glass of wine.

But Ev declined it, with a smile. 'I don't drink wine.'

'What?'

'My mother's most disappointed as you can imagine.' He was still jangling his car keys. 'Anyway, I'm back for a week or two and she suggested I come and look at the garden . . . is that OK?'

'It's wonderful,' she said, smiling into his face. 'It's just – glorious to see you. Where are you living now, then?'

'Nottingham at the moment. But I'm in Jamaica a lot, too. I like it there. Different roots, you know what I mean. Till I got this house and garden job I hadn't been back in the UK for eight years. Before then I was in Hatfield. Just outside London.'

'I didn't know that. You should have come into London. Said hi.'

'I can't face London any more. It does my head in.'

'Oh.' She knew him, the bones of him, inside and out, but she didn't know anything about what he liked or didn't like now. But then he scratched his scalp and said:

'Plus I was afraid . . . you know?'

'Afraid of what?'

'We'd meet and have . . . be different . . . nothing to say to each other. You know how it is.' He leaned against the table, looking at her.

'I do know. I've often wondered . . .' She smiled up at him, into his dark eyes, his boyish smile. 'You haven't really changed.'

'Oh, I have. *You* have.'

'Have I?'

'Oh yes. You wouldn't say boo to a goose, you were entirely in your own head. Or mine.'

'We were, weren't we?'

Ev folded his arms, his head on one side. 'I used to wonder about you, Ju. How you'd find real life.'

'Yep. Well, I've had some real life the last few years or so.' He looked a little blank. 'You know, three children, a divorce, hospitals, redundancy, moving house, family.' She shifted her weight, so she was staring at him properly, out of the sun. 'I'm happy now. Happy-ish. Sandy, that's the main thing, and the other two.'

'Who's Sandy?'

'Oh. My son. The one who had an accident, a couple of months ago. Fell from a ledge in the Dovecote.'

447

'Oh of course. That must have been . . . wow. Quite bad.'

'It was,' she said. 'He's back home today, that's why we're having a party.'

'Back from where?'

She stared at him, smiling to cover her surprise that he didn't get it. 'Hospital. He's been in hospital for two months.'

'Oh. Oh OK. Wow, Juliet, I guess Mum told me but I'd forgotten. I'm sorry.'

Something shifted, the mood changing. Juliet felt a lightness, a sense of release. 'How were you supposed to remember?'

'I suppose I let it slip my mind. So . . . I can't wait to see the garden, help you with it. I love being back here, this part of the world. Catching up, doing the sports stuff, seeing Mum and Dad.'

She blinked. Of course he didn't get it. He didn't have a kid who'd spent a couple of months in hospital. He didn't have kids! Why should he get it? And then a voice inside her head said: *Yes, but Frederic doesn't have kids, for God's sake, and he or George have been round every other day to see what they can do. I'd never met Fin before and the first time she came she brought round a card and she's a teenager! It's not that he doesn't have kids. It's just who he is.*

There was a short silence.

'You said sports stuff,' she said. 'What kind of thing do you do when you're back?'

'Off-roading. There's a place over the hill near my auntie. I've got an ATV. I go with a bunch of guys . . . Great guys. Fellow petrol-heads. It's my main thing there, back in Jamaica. We get together, roar round the countryside, feel the wind in our hair – or not . . .' He rubbed his shorn head. 'Causing mayhem . . . getting into trouble – nothing serious, more with our missuses, you know.'

'Oh. Yep. I know.'

'We're called "The Chaos Crew". We've got stickers for our bumpers. "Get out of our way, or get under our way."'

'Wow. How creepy.' said Juliet.

He put his head on one side. 'How? Oh – sorry. Are you easily offended?'

Juliet paused. 'Apparently so,' she said, laughing. 'Look –'

He moved before she did. 'So I'll have a nose around, if that's OK. You get back to them all. I'll stay out here. I'm not that person.'

'Not that person,' she echoed.

There was a slight pause, and she could hear wheels turning into the drive. 'And – yeah, we'll catch up after that. Whoa,' he said, as a car screeched down the drive. 'Someone's in a hurry.'

The sound of braking came behind them. Juliet turned, looking curiously. Sam was slamming the car door and almost running towards her.

'Juliet – look. Look what we found this morning—' He stopped. 'Sorry.'

'Nice Audi,' Ev was saying. 'Great, great wheels.'

'Thanks.' Sam turned back and looked at the car as if he'd never seen it before. 'I rented the wrong car by mistake, but I quite like it now. It's silver.'

'I'm Ev. Hi.' Ev held out his hand.

Still in something of a daze, Sam looked at him, and at Juliet, then at him again, but then his innate manners asserted themselves. 'Wow. Juliet talks about you all the time.' He was tall, but almost dwarfed by Ev. He shook Ev's hand. 'It's great to meet you. Well. I guess you and Juliet have a lot to catch up on but—' Juliet turned to look at him properly, and saw his eyes, the expression in them. 'But I need you just for a moment, Juliet.' His hand rested very lightly on her wrist. She nodded.

'Take your time,' she said to Ev.

'Hey – I can't stay long. Gotta thing with a thing. I'll check it out and then call you. I'll enjoy it. The old place hardly seems to have changed. Look – there's a starling nest, up in the elm.' His face creased into a smile. 'And the Japanese maple's still there. *Acer palmatum*. Let's see now . . .' He wandered off, between the borders of the Wilderness, down the path again.

'He always was slightly obsessive,' said Juliet, turning to Sam but, his eyes were fixed on hers.

'I'm sorry to drag you away from him,' he said. 'But it – this couldn't wait.'

It was just the two of them, on the terrace. She inhaled the smell of honeysuckle, of woodsmoke, of roses. She could hear the TV coming from the sitting room, and the evening call of the birds.

'I had to see you, you see,' he said. 'I—' He stopped. 'I don't know how to tell you this, Juliet.'

Juliet's heart started to thump, rather erratically, in her chest. 'Oh. Not – not today, maybe.'

'Why?'

'Oh, it's Sandy's welcome home from hospital party.'

'Of course. Damn. *Dammit.*' He smote his forehead, brushing his dark messy hair out of the way so it stuck up in different directions. 'I'd forgotten. I got the little guy a present, too. It's this disgusting animal, you hatch it out from an egg. It's awful, but the lady in the shop promised me he'd love it. Oh, I'm sorry, Juliet. I meant to bring it with me. You see—' The pressure on her wrist tightened. He looked at her, eyes urgently searching her face. 'You're looking at me like you know what I'm going to say already. Kate told you? You know?'

'Maybe – know what?'

'About the letter?'

'What letter?'

'The letter Kate the archivist found in Dalbeattie's travelling case—' He broke off. 'What did you think I was going to say?'

Juliet's face was aflame with instant mortification. 'Nothing.' She passed a hand over her forehead. 'Nothing at all!'

She'd never seen him other than calm and composed – it was rather funny, and perhaps it was the general tiredness of the last few weeks – or years – or the scent of honeysuckle, and the garden, so *alive*, or the fact he was there, in front of her, framed by red and purple salvias next to the steps dropping down to the Wilderness, but she saw him anew then. And she had always known this new person, somewhere in the back of her mind. *Yes. I know you. How did I not realise it?*

450

He took her hands in his then, both of them, and stared at her. 'Kate Nadin came in to see me today. She's been going through the last of Dalbeattie's papers, just before he died. He was travelling back to London, after the Ottawa commission, late in 1919. There was a letter in his small portable desk, the one he used to use to look at his plans on site. He didn't take it with him to London; the desk remained locked all these years; no one had thought to look inside it until Kate found the key in the box files of all his other papers. She opened it last week – there's a letter in there . . .'

'What does it say?'

'The truth,' he said, staring down at her. 'It – it changes everything.'

'How?'

He broke their grasp and reached into his breast pocket and pressed into her hands a thin paper envelope, covered in technical drawings and scrawled little towers of sums.

She took it, and he said:

'Not now – now you need to read it. But, later, I want you to know. That I will always, always be here for you. I will always look out for you. You don't need looking after. You don't!' he said, and the sweetest smile crossed his lips. 'Just know that people change.'

She thought of Ev, the ethereal sprite turned mile-high off-roading real-ale drinker. 'The Chaos Crew'. 'Course they do.' She looked down and saw his head, weaving in and out of the Wilderness.

'I'll be waiting, here,' he said. 'When you finish reading them. But you should go inside and sit down, I reckon.'

Just then, Isla appeared on the terrace, twisting the hem of her dress around her thumb. 'Hi, Mum. Hi, Mister . . .'

'Sam.'

'Well, hi, Mister Sam.'

He crouched down. 'Hi, Miss Isla. It's very nice to meet you. I've heard a lot about you.'

Isla nodded, complacently. 'Great. Mum, can I have a Hatchimal?'

'No. Isla, listen, darling, Mum's got to do something.'

'But, Mum, Sandy got one, from Nonna Luisa.'

451

'Still no. He has been ill.'

'It's not fair.' Isla turned to a stricken-looking Sam who was muttering '*Hatchimal* . . .' 'We came here a *year* ago and apart from Christmas I haven't had a single present, AND I have to play in this big stupid garden *all day*. And do you know it's all because Mum had an old, old, old man who was her old, old, old relative and he left her this old, old, old house and she wanted to let Dad live with Tess? And make a baby with her, which is not like an egg which is how Hatchimals do it and you have to hatch it yourself only she has two other children already and I don't. Like. Elise. So I have to go and stay with them, but really I'd rather be here. And,' she finished triumphantly, twisting the hem of her skirt around her finger and lifting it up so everyone could see her knickers. 'We are actually getting a puppy.'

'No we're actually not.'

'Yes we *actually* are.'

Sam glanced at Juliet. 'I have a spare Hatchimal,' he said. 'I bought one for your brother, but it's not right for him. She's looking for a new home. Would you be able to take her, next time I come to visit?'

'What? Yes! Yes, please!' said Isla, her slouching crossness transformed to ecstasy in a second. She stood up straight. 'Can I have him now?'

'Her. No – she's at home, she's not ready to – to hatch yet.'

'Why not?'

'Because, she hasn't incubated long enough,' said Sam, wildly.

'But it's a plastic toy,' said Isla, confused, and Sam laughed.

'I like you, Miss Isla.'

'I like you – can you bring the toy tomorrow?'

'Go away,' said Juliet, grasping her daughter's shoulders. 'I will come and see you later.'

She shoved her daughter gently towards the door. Sam turned towards her. 'Well, she is a card.'

'Yes, she is. A whole stationery shop of cards.' Juliet glanced towards the door and the house. Sam pointed at the envelope in her hands.

'Can't you just tell me what's in it?' said Juliet, her palms moist.

'Just read it.' He leaned forward then, and very gently, put his hand on her cheek, so the palm cupped her chin. His skin was warm, his touch firm. She knew he did it naturally. She caught his hand, holding it to her face. They stayed like that for a moment then he said, 'Wow. I'll go.'

Her cheek was warm where his fingers had pressed against her skin. She touched her hand to her face, slightly out of breath. He watched her, steadily.

'Juliet—'

'Why don't you walk in the garden? And you can stay for some food. A glass of something. Unless what's in it is so horrific I'll need to lie down. Unless you're telling me I don't own the house, and the painting isn't mine.'

He looked around to make sure there was no one about. 'I've taken the liberty of looking into that, and no, you're in the clear. It's all still yours, but it does change everything. And yes, I'd like to stay.'

'Great. That's really quite great.' They smiled at each other.

Alone at last, Juliet sat down on the stone settle outside the old house, and opened up the letters, the lichen-flecked stone pressing into her legs through her thin skirt, the warm sun bathing her shoulders, and she began to read. Behind her, the children yelped, and laughed, and called, in every room of the house. In front of her, in the wide garden, Sam walked amongst the last of the roses, waiting for her. And Juliet read.

Chapter Forty-One

29 July 1981

I have no plans now or at any time in the future to sell my father's sketch of The Garden of Lost and Found. *Thank you for your interest.*

Yours sincerely

She signed the letter with a flourish: *Stella Horner*. She had kept her name when she married, yes, even back then in 1943. The opprobrium! Someone had left a white feather on the doorstep of the house while Andrew was away fighting. Her mother had died by then: she knew they'd never have dared had Lydia Horner been alive. Creeping up to the house, at night? To pass judgement on one of the Horners? The very idea made Stella laugh.

Andrew's name was Yardley. I can't call myself Yardley with a straight face, it'll just make me think of toilet water, she'd declared when they became engaged. I make better lavender water than they do.

He hadn't smiled.

Stella stood up and stretched, the old pain in her hands, her knees, her back. Gardening injuries, her doctor called it. Though she had never met her father, she knew him: her mother had made sure of that. There were three pictures in the house: *The Meeting*, *The Death of a Nursemaid* and of course the sketch for *The Garden of Lost and Found*. Over the years, the first two had been sold, along with Ned's paint table, his easel, their finer pieces of furniture, the books – Stella grieved particularly for the Dickens editions, black and tooled in buttercup yellow gold. But Mum was there, always explaining: he bought back the painting, because he was driven slowly mad by the death of his other children, he burned it and the cost of it ruined them but they had to stay, because they had to save the house . . . So there were economies, all the time, very few new clothes and no holidays, and Stella went to school with other children who lived in far less grand houses but who had gleaming shoes and went to the seaside every summer.

It was hard to have any distance, living as an adult in the house you grew up in, but Stella Horner understood, even at the age of sixty-two, that her childhood was unusual, but also that it was very nearly perfect, and those two things could exist together. 'Mum' was everything to her, and she to Mum.

Liddy made sure her daughter was not cocooned away, either. There were trips to London, to see the Changing of the Guard, the Victoria and Albert Museum, where they would look at fragments of other houses, the Serpentine, the monkeys changing the lightbulbs on the glittering roof of Harrods department store. There was usually tea at an old friend of Mum's in a grand house in Kensington with other children, most of whom she liked: Stella was eminently capable of marching up to any child and befriending them. She was happy in the company of others, happy at school. She was brought up by Liddy to be strong, and kind, to look at the world with clear eyes and an open heart, to throw herself into things wholeheartedly. She grew like a young tree, strong and supple, striving towards the sun, welcoming the rain. She was Liddy's pride and joy.

Before the war, during the summer of 1936, her mother sold a couple of her father's sketches and Stella and Liddy were able to travel through France, into Germany, where they saw Hitler at a rally at Nuremberg, down to Austria, where they holidayed on the Grundlsee lake with a family from Vienna, old friends of her parents: the father, Richard Schoenberg, had been a painter and had known Ned. There was a month in Paris, learning French: but she had become too homesick for Nightingale House and her mother, and left after three weeks, weeping all the way back on the boat train towards London at her own foolishness. She was accepted and went up to Newnham College, Cambridge, where she studied hard, and made friends, went to dances, joined a choir, and where she stayed up late drinking cocoa and talking about the state of the world in her large room with the oval window that looked out over the formal gardens. Cambridge was where she first understood her love for Nightingale House was not merely homesickness, but something fundamental: she had to return there, it was a part of her.

She took a first-class degree, to her mother's joy. 'How proud Mother would be of you, dearest, girl,' she kept saying, over and over again. But Stella went straight back to Nightingale House afterwards, for war had broken out the previous year and she was needed there. She worked as a Land Girl, and she and Mum welcomed evacuees, six nice girls from Hornsey, and all thought of moving to London to train to be an architect went out of her head, and she was secretly glad, though she couldn't ever say it. She was glad to stay at Nightingale House and work the land during the day and provide for these girls in the evening. Glad to be useful. The Schoenbergs from Vienna were killed, every single one.

Then, in 1942, at a dance over in Walbrook, she met Andrew Yardley, who was handsome and teased her, and Stella liked being teased, being laughed at – she was often prone to savage introspection, and he was good at chivvying her out of it. But when he came to tea and she enthusiastically showed him around, she failed to notice his thin lips, tongue darting out between them now and then, as he took in the paintings, the garden her mother spent most of her time tending, the house, Dalbeattie's greatest achievement.

'No one's touched the place for years, have they?'

'No, silly, of course not. Why would you?'

'The windows are cracked – the casement's damp, there's rats, the front door sticks – don't you care?'

'The casement dries out every summer, so does the door. The rats are only cos our cat's had kittens, they'll be gone soon. And yes, we should replace some of the panes of glass. Don't frown, Andrew. You'll love it.'

Then came that awful time in his car, the time she didn't think about. She had said no, and he had hit her, and told her it was what he deserved, after putting up with all that nonsense, and besides, who else was there? Who else would she get? It never occurred to her no one else was an option.

She had put arnica on the dark-purple bruises between her thighs, and the green-yellow ones on her stomach. And so though she was brave, she was not brave enough to have him on her own, and so she had married him because she had to, but kept her name, *her own name*, as the last piece of defiance she had left in her. That is how it happened.

And when she told her mother, because she had thought they kept no secrets from each other, her mother had nodded, and said something she didn't understand.

'She was right, and I wish I could tell her she was right.'

'She? Who?'

Liddy was writing at her desk, the same desk that Stella used now, forty years later. She stopped, and folded the paper over. 'My sister. I loved her very much. Now, my bird, run along to the larder, and fetch some of that fruitcake from Mrs Beadle, and we'll have some for tea, and make some plans. You'll see, it'll all settle down.'

Stella had grown up thinking Liddy was magical, had powers she didn't really understand. The clearest example of this was that, a week after Mum's death, Stella lost her husband, shot by the strafing German guns during D-Day, before he'd even landed on French soil, his body sucked back into the sea. Bringing up Michael, who was merely one baby, after six malnourished, terrified, bedwetting evacuees, was a walk in the garden. After all, her mother had raised her entirely alone. She could easily do the same. And she did. Death had toughened her up. She knew how lucky she was. No point in complaining while the world was falling down around them all. So she got on with it.

Early one morning in late July 1981, Stella stood at her mother's grave, with a few of the last roses – Albertine, blowsy, watered pink-and-violet, delicious – in her hand. All was quiet, save for the odd sound of handbells, coming from the church tower – the bell-ringers practising for a celebratory peal after the Royal Wedding. Stella thought she was immune to weddings, but for some reason – the extreme youth, the curious passion and passivity of the bride, the Establishment's last gasp, its death throes? Perhaps her little granddaughter Juliet's extreme obsession with the whole day itself – Stella wasn't sure what, something fascinated her and she was caught up in the happy patriotism of it all. She bowed at her dead siblings and her dead father, whom she had never met, placing the roses gently at the foot of her mother's headstone. 'They're lovely this year.' She often talked to Liddy's grave. 'Delicious scent. I don't know why. The rain, perhaps.'

Lydia Dysart Horner 1874–1944
May is the fairest month for it is when the nightingales sing

She had had to fight to have that on the gravestone, too! Too secular, the vicar had said. But it was what she had wanted for her darling mother, who loved the garden best in May, when she said its greatest glories were yet to come.

Leaving the roses, and touching the grave with one slightly arthritic hand, Stella clambered down the churchyard to the worn iron gate and the darkness of the yew trees. She could hear birds singing. Little Ju and her friend Ev were in the garden, she singing something, he wandering off to examine things, peering down at beds, into tree stumps. Occasionally they would say something to each other, then go back to what they were doing. She could see his black head disappearing into bushes, her red-gold one spinning around, stopping, staring up at her surroundings. Stella stood watching. Warmth stole across her, the sun arching up into the sky. It had rained earlier, but it was going to be a lovely day.

She walked down towards the terrace, feet crunching on the gravel. Michael and Elvie were in the dining room, clearing up after breakfast and Stella hesitated before going in. She watched them too, saw her daughter-in-law methodically tidying and wiping the table, and her dear son, ambling around the room, picking up things at random, putting them away, obeying orders, in his own world.

He was so very different from her! It caught at her throat now as it did periodically: she'd pull him on to her knee, as a boy, to tell him the stories. Of how her parents came to the house – growing up in Highgate, the cemetery, dissolute Uncle Pertwee, awful Nurse Bryant, their hopeless father – of beloved Mary, Mum's sister, and Dalbeattie, her father's best friend, who had rebuilt the house with Ned. Of Liddy's mother, Helena, who'd grown up at Nightingale House before she had to marry their father. Of Liddy's children, and how they died, of Zipporah and Darling and all the other characters who made up her mother and father's rich story. 'Then they ran away and lived happily ever after, and her father couldn't catch her,' she'd tell Michael, but the child would slide off his chair and say, politely:

'Can I go and play, Mummy?'

'Of course.'

So when he and Elvie had produced a child Stella had made a rare journey into London to meet her, without much enthusiasm, it must be said, but then they had given her to Stella to hold and she had stared into her dark eyes.

My sun, my moon, my darling girl.

On her first visit to Nightingale House, when she was three months old, Juliet had opened her eyes again and stared at the nightingales on the pargeting in the sitting room, looked around her, taking everything in. Stella had never forgotten that look. As if she *knew* the place already. Juliet's eyes remained deep, dark blue, her nose small and round, but the thick, golden hair she was born with slowly became tinged with red. There was nothing of Elvie's suburban North London via Norfolk stock in her. She was a Pre-Raphaelite.

'Ev!' she called now. 'Ju? It's starting soon, do you want to come through to watch?'

'No, thanks,' Ev called back, just as Juliet said, 'Oh, yes please.'

Stella pulled at the stiff back door, which then swung open with a loud bang, and entered the kitchen.

'Shall I switch the TV on? Mrs B left some iced buns yesterday.'

'That's nice of her, isn't it? Very nice. I'll put the kettle on. Do turn on the TV.' Elvie gave a little sigh, and Stella found herself gazing at her curiously. 'It's going to be lovely, isn't it? They were saying on the radio thousands of people camped out in Hyde Park last night. They were given a jolly good time, by all accounts.'

Like her mother, though Stella was virulently allergic to patriotism in any form, her love for England and what she believed to be English values ran deep within her, deeper than anything else perhaps. 'Of course they were,' she said, swallowing a rude remark down and swinging a tray out from underneath the counter. 'I'll get the tea things. And, dare I say it, some crisps and peanuts. I think, for once, we could treat ourselves to some snacks in the sitting room.'

'Wonderful!' said Elvie and disappeared across to the sitting room. Stella heard her, calling to her son. 'Mike! Mike, love, come quickly! Not long now! Juliet! Everett! Let's gather, shall we?'

'Gather,' Stella muttered to herself, as she hunted in the terracotta bread bin for the buns. '*Gather.*' Juliet raced in, slamming the kitchen door shut.

'Grandi! Ev's chasing me!' she screamed with total delight. 'Argh!'

She dashed into the hallway, then off somewhere upstairs. Feet pattered overhead a few minutes later, then another scream as Juliet tried to hide herself somewhere. Stella smiled. It should be a house full of noise. She had done her best, all these years, to fill it with conversation – old Cambridge friends, villagers, evacuees, children and grandchildren of painters, family . . .

Searching for her stray tea mug, Stella wandered through to the dining room and out of the french windows back on to the terrace. Distracted, she began to deadhead the last remaining husks of lavender, rolling the heads between her fingers for the last scent. Liddy had always made bags of lavender each year, around this time. She must start it now, soon –

'Madam?'

A figure stood in front of her. She noticed idly that he had no shadow, for it was almost midday and the sun was high. He was tall, with a shock of white hair. Stella stared at him, blinking in the light.

'Yes? How can I help you?'

'Are you Stella – I'm sorry. I'm afraid I don't know your surname.'

Stella drew herself up. 'I'm Stella Horner.'

'Oh. I see.' He took a step back. 'Well, Stella Horner. Good morning.'

'How can I help you?' she repeated, in what she hoped was a polite tone.

Heat shimmered around her; he stepped closer, and something about him, some instinct made the hairs on her neck prickle. He lifted up his panama hat, and she peered into a pair of dark-blue eyes, shining as though through tears.

'Here I am,' he said, and she didn't understand what he meant. 'I'm – I am John. John Horner. I am your brother, my dear.'

Stella felt cold in the white-hot sun. She moved towards the porch, and put her hand on the stone chair Dalbeattie had carved for the weary traveller. Though the light was bright everything was strangely dark.

'I'm so sorry.' Politeness asserted itself. 'Forgive me, how can you be my brother?'

'It must be a shock, I know.'

'But your grave – I was there this morning.' She felt that curious lightheadedness she used to feel with Michael – as though she might just float away, into nothingness. 'You're dead.' She gave a small laugh. 'I know you're dead.'

'But I am not.' He took the hat off, now, blotting his forehead carefully with a neatly pressed linen square. She could see the wattle of skin under his chin, the purple shadows around his eyes. 'I – I deserted. I ran away from the war, you see.'

'Yes.' But she didn't see.

She offered him the old stone chair and he sank into it, gratefully,

461

kneading the fine straw of the panama between his bent fingers, eyes fixed on the distance.

'We'd fallen back towards the village. There was a great explosion – a shell, it took out the school, we'd been using it as cover. Four boys . . . thrown into the air . . . I heard someone shouting, "Horner's gone! We've lost him!" It's funny, I didn't think about it then. I've thought about it since. I didn't think at all. I simply ran. I ran away.' He looked up at her, and blinked in the sunlight. 'I've never said any of that before. I let the lie stand. I came back once, to see Dad – only . . . I – It's a very long story, as you might imagine, my dear, but now—'

He moved towards the door. 'Hang on,' she said, suddenly, not knowing why she said it, only that he wasn't coming into the house. 'How on earth do I know you're John Horner?'

'How do you know?' He turned around, away from the threshold. 'There's a bird, above the door, eating berries. A nightingale. *'Thy heart is warm when home th'art drawn.''* His voice was slow, and accented. 'There's four nightingale finials on the roof, and one of 'em has a chipped wing. Eliza threw a roof tile up there. It hit. She was my sister. She died of diphtheria. There were stars on the ceiling of the nursery, the Birdsnest, painted to look like the night sky. Hannah's sister had a puppy . . . He never had a name, they drowned him afterwards . . .' He stared at her again. 'So, Frederic wrote to me about you, but I still don't quite believe it. You're really Stella.'

'Frederic?' The name swam at her through time and space. 'Who – oh, the young man who's taken over the antiques shop? You know him?'

'I recommended he come here. I know him of old; he is from the town where I live, in France, in – ' His shoulders were slumped; he really didn't look well. Stella wished she could bring herself to sit down next to him, take him in her arms, hold his hand . . . But somehow she couldn't. 'It was he who let me know you were still here, that my mother had had another child.' He closed his eyes, the lids fluttering slowly in the bright sun. 'That is you, is it not?'

'Yes!' she said, almost angrily, and he said, gently:

'Really? It is you?'

She had long ago learned to shut out that which she didn't want to hear. There had been times before – you see – and she had closed her mind to it all. To bad things. Andrew, and Mum dying, and things she overheard. People talked. You kept on going. That's what you did. So Stella said in what she hoped was a tone of forgiveness:

'I don't know why you'd ask me that. Let us go on. You – you must want to see the place – it's so long, such a shocking time – but it's still standing as you see—' She felt she was falling, kaleidoscopic half-sentences of welcome and repulsion snagging in her mind. 'Is that why you are here?'

If she expected him to feel reproof he showed no sign of it. 'You must understand, I want nothing from you but I do want to lay the past to rest. Or to know I tried,' he said with a small, sad smile. 'I am old, and not well, and I have realised I had to return, one more time. I always thought I'd do it after the second war was over. But then in about 1950 I heard Mama had died, from two gossiping art critics who'd come on a motoring holiday to Dinard. They were sitting in the square, talking about my family . . . about the painting . . .' He looked up at her, sharply. Appraisingly. 'You know about the painting, of course?'

'Of course – how could I not?'

Mama. He called her Mama. Stella had often heard Mum speak of John. How he was her true companion for all those years, the child who was most like her. How he never wanted to marry anyone but her, his mother. How kind, beloved, funny, handsome he had been. Her face would light up. This was him, he was here.

And Stella knew some dreadful chasm had opened up now, one that could never be closed. The vanished years that she had grown up reliving with Mum over and over again in retelling were not past, they were here. She had always thought of their past as a completed circle, flat newspaper print, like the circles she used to cut out of the centre of Mum's old *Times* with the rusting twine scissors. It had been set as fact and now someone had cut it up

463

into pieces again. And she had always been so sure of herself, over every little thing.

John stood up, slowly, one hand on the seat.

'Frederic is coming to fetch me in half an hour or so. I would so very much like to see the old place again . . . I will not stay.' He took her hand, as though he might, just, understand what this cost her, and stared into her eyes. 'My . . . my sister. After all these years. Goodness . . .'

What could she do?

Wordlessly, she let him cross over the threshold of the house, and watched his face as he stared around him, at the light from the light well above the stairs, at the old coat rack. He gripped the squirrel newel post as if clinging on to it for dear life, then stared into its face. 'Hello, old friend,' he said. She could hear the droning tones of the television commentary from the sitting room. Once, her son called out to ask if she was all right.

'Just with a friend,' she called back.

A friend. He was well-dressed, a pressed fresh pink-and-white checked shirt, blue corduroy trousers, a light jacket whose breast pocket he kept patting. He was tall, but he stooped: with pain, she guessed. His white hair framed his tanned face, his blue eyes, bluer than any she'd seen. Once, only once did he let his emotion at the enormity of the homecoming escape him. They stood in Stella's own bedroom doorway, he leaning against the frame. She gestured him in, and was impatient when he did not go ahead; some chivalric notion, she assumed.

But he shook his head, and turned back, facing away.

'She died in here,' he said. 'She died, and Mama held her. I was watching, behind this door.'

And he wouldn't say any more, but turned, and leaned against the wall outside, and patted his heart. She worried then – he was so pale.

They sat together in the dining room, after she fetched him some elderflower cordial, the sound of hymns intercut with the droning

464

monotone of the wedding service reverberating through the other-wise quiet house. Stella didn't know what to say. She could not feel warmth towards him and she realised something in her must be wrong that she could not. A note hummed in her head.

'It's funny,' he said again. 'You – you were born when?'

She wished he wouldn't stare at her so much. There was a drawing of Mum on the stairs, Stella knew she looked like her. She didn't know why he'd try and cast aspersions on her, her role there, unless for some nefarious purpose. *But he's alive, and their child, and the house . . . he might want the house, or half of it . . .*

Thoughts, jostling, jabbing in her head, and she felt seasick. She cleared her throat.

'I was born in 1918. The year my father died.'

There was a long silence, and into it, John said:

'But he is not your father, my dear. You know that.'

He said it so quietly she took a moment to understand him.

'I think you are mistaken,' she said. The edges of the room were black. 'I must go and watch the rest of the wedding, my grand-daughter—'

'He can't be your father,' he said. 'You have brown eyes.'

'Very observant of you,' she said, and a breeze came from nowhere, slamming the front door shut with a huge bang. She jumped, and yet he did not. 'I have brown eyes, what of it?'

'But my mother had blue eyes, you see. The bluest eyes there were. And my father too, grey, really, stormy dark grey. You can't be their child. Perhaps one of them is your parent, but not both.' He said it slowly, patiently.

'That's rubbish.'

'It is scientific fact.'

'How dare you—'

John shook his head, sadly. 'I should not have said it. But you should have welcomed me.'

Stella felt something pop in her head. A light, little *pouf!* sound. She stood up, blinking. 'Get out.'

'What?'

465

She raised her hand and saw it was shaking, violently. 'I don't want you in the house any more.'

There was a heavy silence. 'Who are you?' he said, softly. 'This house was a place to welcome people. A refuge. You ask me to leave? Really? Did you – did you know my mother at all?'

Who are you? '*Get out!*' she said, her voice slightly louder. 'D-don't come here – d-d-d-don't ever come here again! Asking questions about Mum – about me . . . *me* . . . I'm their daughter!'

She blocked out the wave of sounds, of chatter, coming towards her, one exchange overheard at a London tea party, two women on a verandah, she inside playing with dolls, once at the vicarage after mulled wine for Advent Sunday, once, a young woman, strolling through the Royal Academy and pausing in front of her own father's painting *A Meeting*, as two old, old men talked in loud, pompous tones behind her. And once in a letter she had found soon after Mum's death that Stella had folded up into tiny pieces and hidden at the back of the bookshelf – folded it away as though that would make it another lost thing here.

She was so thin, a living skeleton. I heard she fooled them all. What could Liddy do?

They say she just appeared out of nowhere. A magic baby. Like she'd bought her from some place. It didn't make sense . . . still don't . . .

Died of a broken heart they said. Yes, I know. He was crossing back to meet her.

Dearest Liddy . . . will you call her Stella?

Loud cheering came from the room across the hall and they both turned around.

'What is that?' he said, wryly, almost amused.

'*And as the young couple make their way back down the aisle, the West Door of the cathedral is flung open and we can hear the roar of the crowd outside . . .*'

'Grandi! Come! Come *on*!!!!' Juliet, hair flying about her face, breathless, appeared in the doorway. 'Oh. Hello,' she said, blankly. 'Grandi, come and *watch it*!'

She saw John Horner stare at this little girl, saw him start, take in her features. He smiled, and patted the pocket over his heart again. 'Hello,' he said. 'I'm John, who are you?'

'This is Juliet,' said Stella. 'My granddaughter.' She passed a hand over her forehead and called low and quiet, under her breath: 'Please could you leave, leave now? I don't want you here.' She saw the confusion on her granddaughter's small face.

'Juliet,' said John, turning to her. 'Do you have a doll's house? Is it in the Dovecote?'

'Yes,' she said, smiling at him. 'I do. Do you know it?'

'I used to play with it when I was a child. I have something to go in the house that belongs to you. I have brought it back. Would you show me where the house is?'

Juliet plunged her hands into the pockets of her pinafore. 'Course,' she said. 'But you have to be very careful with it. It's very *old*.'

'Of course I will.' His eyes met Stella's. 'I am sorry. Sorry for it all. Goodbye, Stella,' he said, but she shook her head.

'I wish you would just go,' she said. 'I want you to go.'

'My dear – the past is not under our control. I am so sorry—'

'*I want you to go!*' Stella shouted, her voice cracking on the final word. Her son and his wife were standing inside, drinking their tea. She saw them, watching her with alarm, as the old man and the young girl walked down the drive towards the Dovecote, and a wave of pain and terror swept over her. Everything was gone, changed, ruined. Stella went into the study again, still watching them. The french windows were open, the garden at the height of its beauty. She went over to the bookshelves, to the furthest corner, and took out a worn, beautiful old hardback book – *The Arabian Nights* – and reached into the space where it had been, flat against the old grain of the wood. With clumsy, angry fingers she fumbled to unfold the hard wedge of paper in her hand. But when she did, she saw again how very fragile the paper was.

Dearest Liddy

Thank you for your letter. I have booked passage on the 'Valiant' next week. I will come to meet my daughter, and to bury my beloved. I cannot say more. But your kindness after these many years of silence overwhelms me.

When I made your house with Ned, I painted the gold stars on the ceiling of the nursery. Are they still there? I used to have a mobile of stars as a child, hanging from the ceiling – I remember it most particularly. I liked to lie on my back and watch the stars. I thought your children would like it too. Does my daughter sleep in that room? Will you call her Stella as her mother wished? I should like to think of her lying there looking at that ceiling. For her mother was a star, shining brightly, brighter than any other to me. She lied to me – she did what she thought was best – how on earth could she have believed it? How could I have failed to see it – oh Liddy – we two are left now and my heart is so heavy . . .

Dearest Liddy, thank you – I shall see you soon and this child, the miracle of all – oh my Mary, how she must have suffered, and how much she gave us.

I think only of you and the babe. I will be with you as soon as I may God speed.

Once more: in chestnuts and chicken,
LD

Tears fell from her eyes on to the thin, much-folded paper, dropping between the creases which had opened up into welts, on to the leather and gold-tooled blotter below, where Mum had sat that day Papa had painted her . . . Stella gripped the desk, as bells rang out. The wedding was over now, bells ringing on the television and then in real life, from the church behind her. A great, bellowing peal, loud, too loud.

As she looked out of the window Stella saw the old man walk up the drive. Her son and wife were waiting there for him.

Let them talk to him, she thought, her mind already unspooling. Let them discover him themselves. They don't know how Mum worked to save the place on her own, clearing the chimney, blocking out the draughts, sealing up the cracks herself, mending the curtains, the cushions, polishing the woodwork. They don't know what it was like here, woman's work, always woman's work, the upkeep of a house.

The sketch of *The Garden of Lost and Found* stood, as it always did, on the easel in the corner of the study, where Mum had set it long ago after Ned died. Stella picked up the paintbrush and gold paint from Juliet's paint set which she had bought her that summer for her arrival, and went over to the canvas. She hesitated – would she dare? She knew if she did she would be committing a sin. She could go out now to this man, apologise, invite him back in. She could undo the past, could look the truth squarely in the face, live freely. Sell the house, sell it and move away. Her hands hovered, over the canvas . . .

Then swiftly Stella added the falling star, golden sparks cascading to the ground. She stood back, and looked at the two children, and the new addition. 'That's me,' she said aloud. 'I'm in the painting. I'm there now, too.'

But then her frown darkened: it was only the sketch, after all.

She did not see that outside, in the Wilderness, Juliet and Ev played hide and seek, darting in and out of the tangled garden, sunshine flickering on their young bodies, like the shadow of birds' wings passing overhead.

*

469

When she had finished the letter from her great-grandmother to her great-grandfather, Juliet was still for a moment, and then she touched the metallic-edged black-ink markings with her fingertips. Feeling the words that had been written almost a hundred years ago, crossing an ocean. Everything had changed, and nothing, really. We keep on keeping on.

As the evening chorus sang in the trees behind her, she looked out through the french windows and down over the garden, studded with jewel-like coral, royal purple, peacock-blue, palest, gentlest pink. She was at the centre. She was the woman in the painting now. She saw the same view Liddy had seen that golden afternoon so long ago.

She folded up the letter, and put it back inside *The Arabian Nights*. Then Juliet got up and left the room, to look for Sam.

Empty again, the room was still, the view unchanged. We paint our own reality, after all.

Epilogue

February 1919

Dearest Dalbeattie

You have a daughter. Her name is Stella.

I lied when I sent you away to Ottawa. I know that, because of what has gone before, you and I cannot ever have the life we wanted for ourselves. Perhaps one day, in another time but not now and so I, like the heroine in a rather melodramatic novel, have sacrificed myself for your happiness.

I had the babe but I am afraid I am not well. To be short, something occurred during the birth, which was rather more taxing than I'd thought it would be, Dalbeattie – it requires considerably greater effort than marching for Women's Suffrage, I must tell you – I am lied to by doctors, always a bad sign. I have had six months with Stella – they have been everything to me. She is very like her father – her eyes are huge, she takes in everything. She makes juddering, peep-peep noises of great joy when I go to her in the morning. She loves her feet, and clutches them as she lies in her bed.

We are back in my little rooms in Hammersmith. I could not stay in the house alone without you, my darling. I know my end is not far away now. I cough most nights and keep Stella awake. Though till last week I was quite well but for some pain. I have made it very cosy, my dearest. I have sewn all Stella's clothes. The ring you gave me I sold and it has kept me and your child most comfortable these last few months. You left me ample but not enough for the cost of a babe! I have a nurse, a dear woman called Mrs leFay. She is a war widow. Before he died at Passchendaele her husband was a painter, and studied at the Academy, and we have conversations about painting, and art, and all of it. With *the water reflecting outside the window and the sound of boats and Stella's smiles and the care of Mrs leFay I am not unhappy. She has made it all very nice, as they say. She will be with me until the end. <u>You must not worry about me.</u>*

Next month I am giving Stella away. I am taking her to Nightingale House where I hope to prevail upon my sister to bring her up as her own. How will I persuade Liddy to do this, she who tore up my letters, who refuses to meet me these ten, twenty years, who rains curses down on my head? I shall dissemble. She already believes me to be a black-hearted wanton, lost to all sense of decency. I will put on a performance of such conviction she will gladly gather the child to her.

I reckon upon Liddy gazing into this little one's eyes and seeing what I see. For Stella is so like our mother it quite takes my breath away. Besides, she gives Liddy one more chance. She gives all of us one more chance, Dalbeattie. She can be, all of us, our last child; she can grow up at Nightingale House, free and wild, surrounded by birds, flowers, fresh, fresh air. She can have what Pertwee, and Liddy and I, and dearest John and Eliza, never had. A childhood free of sorrow, in the very house you yourself made into a home. I am telling you so you understand, you must not contact her, you – like I – must give up your claim on her so she can grow up not knowing what she is.

I am going soon – I am not sad. For I will see you again my dear love: in that great garden where we will all be together again, one day, you and I and our daughter – Goodbye, my dearest one – thank you for loving me.

M

All morning she had delayed going to the graveyard. She had a cold, and a terrible toothache somewhere at the back of her mouth; she had spent most of the week with her head wrapped in a scarf, a wad of gauze soaked in clove oil gingerly pressing against the tooth. The gum was tender, inflamed, and she could not swallow; it was the pain of it being in her head she found most alarming.

This was pain unseen, flooding you with sensation, making you wonder, self-pityingly she told herself, what life before it was like. But it was John's birthday, and she must go some time. Besides, they had finished Ned's gravestone a few weeks before and she still hadn't been. She wasn't sure why. The weather had been so bad, icy showers of sleet that turned the lanes into slides and flattened half the hopeful snowdrops on the lawn. But Liddy knew she must not put it off any longer, and so, at midday, when it was as light as it was going to get, she wrapped a moth-eaten shawl tightly round her head and gingerly set out.

She was careful all the time now; of walking, of lighting fires, of shutting doors, of pulling splinters. She was alone, the only one left, and she must live on, to remember them. So many regrets: the times she wished she'd gone to meet Mary, not burned her letters. That she had paid more attention to Ned, instead of ignoring him, and letting it happen. If she'd never gone to London that summer . . . if she'd urged John into a job away from the front . . . So many regrets that, on several occasions, she had thought about ending it all, but then no one would remember they were there, and the house would have to be sold – to a rich man who'd pull out the panelling and lay the entire garden to lawn, and – and *change* things. And *his* children would run about on the lawn – no, it was unthinkable.

The cold air was sharp, and smelled of wet earth, and something else – a fresh, metallic tang, of spring. As Liddy staggered up the lane towards the lych-gate she could see the lilac buds from the vicarage opposite, tiny, green-brown cracks on the black branch, but they were there. And the snowdrops, and the narcissi. Somewhere, in the trees behind her, a lone bird chirped.

Liddy loved spring. So had Ned, after they came here. The countryside had filled him with ideas, like water flowing from a tap into a jug. She pushed the lychgate open and crossed the frozen, crunching lawn of the graveyard, which in the summer swayed with orchids, meadow-grasses and fritillary butterflies. Liddy pulled her coat around her. It was Ned's coat, a military affair lined with bright, pillar-box red, which he had worn to paint in the Dovecote. Ned had bought it from Pertwee many years ago – she suspected it was a way of giving Pertwee money. It was a coat of excellent quality, a sign of her brother's taste for the finest things. Poor Pertwee. It had lasted over twenty years or more now.

There were catkins on the silver birch tree over past the church, where the Coote family vault stood set apart from the rest of the graves. Catkins . . . snowdrops . . . Liddy inhaled, trying to gauge the level of pain in her tooth, gingerly touching her cheek. It was all rather overwhelming and she tried to remember the last time she had left the grounds of the house. Weeks, probably. Since Christmas, but not for a long time. Days seemed to blur, really, now she was alone. She thought she felt better for being outside, in the fresh air.

'Liddy?'

A shapeless small figure in a brown cloak moved suddenly, below her elbow, and Liddy gave a cry of fright, and jammed her hand against her cheek. She looked down.

A tiny, white face stared up at her, caked in thick face powder. The eyes, those lovely brown eyes, were huge, almost half out of their sockets. Beneath the face, the cloak moved again, restless. 'Liddy?' it repeated.

'Mary?' Liddy whispered, the name catching in her throat.

Mary nodded. Her cheeks were red spots in the moon-like face. 'Sit down a while, Liddy, dearest,' she said, patting the bench. As if they were children again, in Liddy's room, and she, the youngest, was looking after her big sister. As she had for years. 'Are you in pain? Is it a tooth?'

Liddy nodded, and sat down. She noticed, with a twist of fear, the slow, careful way her sister moved along to accommodate her, the odd bulge of her cloak, the tendons in her white neck.

'Why are you here?' she said, finally.

'Aha, she senses the truth. Liddy, dearest.' She gave a faint laugh. 'I come on a mission of mercy. You wouldn't meet me.'

Liddy swallowed. 'I was worried about John. I did not want to—'

'I know, sister. But I needed to see you.' Mary patted her hand, reassuringly, and Liddy thrilled to her sister's touch. Her quiet, lilting voice! Her presence, the calm certainty of her, still – and then she turned and stared at Mary's white skin, stretched tight over the cheekbones, the forehead, the bones of skull visible underneath . . . the long, skeletal fingers, like bleached twigs. They were plucking at the rough brown hessian cloak, fumbling, parting it like curtains on a stage – her awful huge, white eyes, staring at Liddy, looked down between the folds of the parted cloak.

Liddy followed her gaze.

She found herself staring at a soft, downy head. She blinked. There was something moving next to it. Fingers, tiny fingers, part of a small arm, in scratchy raspberry-coloured wool. The fingers opened and closed. The nails were jagged, flimsy, they needed cutting; the knuckles indentations like little dashes in that plump small hand.

The child was pressed against Mary's chest. Mary wore a white cambric lace blouse; Liddy could see, underneath the thin fabric, her sister's heart, fluttering wildly, like a bird's wing. Mary covered the cloak again and said:

'It's a girl. She is six months old. I have stopped being able—'

She stopped, breathing heavily, as though overcoming some powerful sensation, then she looked up. 'I have stopped being able to look after her. I can't do it. I didn't ever want her. I tried to get rid of her. But you know – she clung on. She's here now and she needs milk, and I don't want to feed her any more. I'm not a mother. Not me.'

The times Mary had soothed Liddy's night terrors; the hours she had spent smoothing back her hair, secreting little items of food into her room, watching out for her impulsive sister at roads, guarding her from Bryant's notice . . . Not a mother.

'Were you able to feed her?' said Liddy, after a long pause.

'Oh, yes, for a while.' She was fiddling with the ribbon on her cloak; it fell around her, and Liddy saw the child properly for the first time, and her sister's wasted frame. She had to bite down on a nail she was chewing to keep from crying out in alarm. The child was held tightly, swaddled against Mary in a scarf tied to Mary's body. Mary undid the scarf, and handed her to Liddy, whose arms immediately adjusted to holding a baby, the old hold. She looked down into the dark-brown eyes then up at Mary, whose cheeks were even more flushed now, under the thick face powder.

'I am hot.'

'It is a freezing cold day, dearest – please, you must wrap up again.'

'No, don't make me.' She raised her hand, and Liddy followed her gaze, and saw a long, green car, waiting in the lane the other side of the church. 'Dymchurch waits for me, he's a great one.'

'Dymchurch?'

Mary began coughing, and swallowed it down. She smiled. 'Yes. He's a friend of – of Dalbeattie's. Now, listen to me, my dearest sister, for the boat leaves this evening. I ask a favour of you. Dalbeattie has written to me, now he is settled. He cannot have an illegitimate child with him in Canada you understand, it would not do. I am to join him there and this is why I have come. You must take her if she is not to go to an orphanage. She is called Stella.'

Liddy pressed a hand to her aching jaw, almost to steady herself, anchor herself back down in the reality of this pain. 'S-stella?'

'Yes, a little star.' Something convulsed her again, a whooping-cough wheeze that sounded like a sob. But she was grinning again, that manic, half-crazed grin. Liddy did not understand. She held more tightly on to the baby, who looked so very like Mary, so like Pertwee – the same dark expression around the eyes, and the thoughtfulness of their mother. She was snug in Liddy's arms, blinking slowly, up at the grey March sky.

'I cannot have a baby,' said Liddy, slowly. 'People will ask where she came from.'

'Why not?' Mary stood up suddenly, and gave a cry, which she muffled with her fist. 'I am fine, Liddy – it is merely cramp. You can do anything if you set your mind to it, my sister, of that I'm sure! Go to London tomorrow with her and stay at Galveston's. Lie about her age. She can be three months old, surely. Say she came as a surprise after Ned died. Say you are in town to buy her things. Stay with them for a month. Then come home and present her to the village. She is your child –' She put her hand on the baby's front, for a moment, moving her thumb up and down, and Stella opened her eyes. 'You are all alone, Liddy. You have no one. I want her to grow up with you. At the house.'

Liddy stared at her sister. 'How can you simply give her up, Mary?'

'You'll give her a good life, here, won't you? Better than she'd have with me on my own, in my rooms. There's barely room for me, let alone a baby. And I'm so tired of that life. I want to be with Dalbeattie. It's our turn now.' She gave another strange smile. Liddy could see her yellow teeth.

'Dearest,' said Liddy. 'Tell me honestly. What is wrong with you? You are so very thin.'

'Oh. I have had the influenza, and it has taken its toll. But the doctor advises sea air and rest, and Eno's Fruit Salts, and so I have spent the last of my money on this trip.' Her low, melodic voice washed over Liddy. *She is really here, I am with her, after all these years, and she lies, I know she lies.* 'Dalbeattie says he will make everything fine for me when I arrive. I am to have three new dresses, he said, and a hat trimmed with fur to keep me warm. And I am to cut my hair, for it is quite the fashion. They will all believe I am his wife after that.'

'Will you not send for her then?'

Mary cocked her head on one side, and glanced quickly at her child. 'No! Goodness, no, she'll be better off with you if you will have her.' She clasped Liddy's wrist in her bony grasp. 'Perhaps we'll have other children, but I am old, Liddy, I was forty-two when I delivered her.'

'And how will people—' Liddy blinked, overwhelmed at it all, struggling to stop her head from spinning. 'How will I explain it to people, that I am forty-four, nearly forty-five, and have suddenly produced a babe of my own?'

'You created Nightingale House. You made your own world, Liddy, dearest. Tell the story you decide to tell: people will believe what they want. Were you not at the centre of the painting?' She gave a careless shrug, and stuck her bottom lip out. Liddy almost believed her then.

A loud horn sounding made both sisters jump. Liddy clutched her burning tooth; the pain came back, with a jolt. Mary stood up now, slowly. 'I'll take her back, if you want. I'll find someone—' Her eyes were burning; she closed them, slowly, and drooped against the bench, and in a soft, desperate voice said, 'Oh my dearest Liddy . . . Please take her. Please make her your own, raise her here, give her a happy life. Give yourself some happiness. A fresh start. Hope. *Please.'*

And the two sisters gazed at each other and for one second Liddy saw Mary's expression shift, saw the dark eyes imploring, the gentle curve of the mouth press into an O. She saw her true sister as Liddy knew she really was: the kindest, the best of women, who fought for what she thought was right. Who had loved Liddy and Pertwee when no one else did. Who cared for them, when no one else could. Whom she had driven away after Eliza's death, who had been a stranger to her now for almost twenty years. And yet, as they stared at each other, the years rolled away – they were as nothing, nothing at all.

Liddy swallowed. Very quietly she said, 'I will take her – but you are not well and you must come back with me and have some beef tea, and rest—'

'No! I have not been well, it is true, and I am dreadfully thin – but Dalbeattie knows all, and will look after me!'

'Mary – you must come back with me,' said Liddy, steadily.

'I will run away if you make me. You know you cannot imprison me against my will.' There was the faintest hint of a smile in her eyes. 'Not after all these years. I will write to you – oh, yes.'

She bent over the child, and kissed the smooth forehead, her lips lingering for just a second too long. Hot tears fell down Liddy's cheeks: Mary had none. She straightened up, and looked around. 'Isn't it funny,' she said. 'We grew up next to a graveyard, too.'

Then she wrapped the cloak around herself, again, gritting her teeth for a second.

'No,' Liddy cried, unable to hide her desperation now. 'Please come back with me, my love. Come back—'

Mary had begun to try to run away, over the gravestones, as they had done as children, skipping over graves in Highgate Cemetery. Liddy chased after her, clutching Stella tightly. She thrust Mary's daughter at her one more time, whilst she removed Pertwee's thick coat, and then flung it around her sister's shoulders.

'It was—'

'Pertwee's. I know. I remember it.' Mary stood at the gate, wrapping the warm coat around her, swamped by its thickness, the red lining flashing bright in the dull light. The car engine rumbled and reverberated. 'God rest his soul. We – we three, we were not bad children, were we?'

'We were good children, and our mother loved us, as we have given love back,' said Liddy. Tears ran down her cheeks freely now. She took Stella from her mother.

'Must you really go?' she said softly, one more time. 'Can you not—'

'I cannot,' said Mary, her voice breaking. She tucked the paisley shawl around her daughter's shoulder, one last little gesture, her knuckles brushing her cheek. 'I must leave now. Dearest – dearest, Liddy—'

She hurried down the steps, a tiny, stumbling whirling cloud of dark navy, into the waiting car. A taxi cab. Liddy saw her face, once inside, collapse, the hunched way she leaned forward to speak to the driver, the strain in every movement as the car juddered into life, lurching off. Mary was flung backwards. She gathered her tiny hands into her lap – Mary's old, patient way – staring straight ahead as she was driven down the lane. And she did not once look up at her sister, holding the bundle in her arms.

Liddy stood at the edge of the churchyard staring at the child she held. Her hair was fair, silken like fur against the contours of her baby skull. Her cheeks were plump – she leaned forward, inhaling, feeling the satisfying peach-coolness of the skin.

Stella's unblinking eyes met Liddy's. The whites of her eyeballs had no veins, the hands had no scratches or scrapes, the face no freckles or wrinkles. She was unmarked by life.

The wind had stopped, and the birds were still singing. Liddy shivered though, in the cold, without her coat.

'Goodbye,' called Liddy, as loudly as she could. She did not know what else to do. 'I will love her. You must not worry, now.'

She turned, and walked very, very slowly back along the slippery path to the house. A cautious, metallic sun was beating through the pearl-streaked sky, turning the wet paving stones silver and gold.

'Your father built this house, and you will grow up here,' she told Stella, whose warmth, pressed against Liddy's aching heart, was like moving in front of a glowing fire after too long outside in the bitter cold. Pausing only for a second underneath the lintel with the nightingales, she crossed the threshold and, carefully this time, Lydia Dysart Horner closed the door on things known, and unknown.

Spring was coming. It was not here yet, but now she knew it was coming.

I am beginning to rub my eyes at the prospect of peace. I think it will require more courage than anything that has gone before. It isn't until one leaves off spinning round that one realises how giddy one is. One will have to teach one's wincing eyes to look at long vistas again instead of short ones – and one will at last fully recognise that the dead are not only dead for the duration of the war.

Cynthia Asquith's diary, 7 October 1918

Acknowledgements

Thanks to Mari Evans for being not just a brilliant editor and publisher and head of everything but making me believe I am a good writer. You are the best. Thank you for your hard work and for trusting me and encouraging me to be better every time.

Thanks to all the wonderful people at Headline: Yeti Lambregts, Viviane Basset, Frances Doyle, Becky Bader, Jess Whitlum-Cooper, Jenni Leech and Katie Sunley with extra thanks and love to Becky Hunter. Thanks to Georgina Moore for all of it and more.

Thanks to Jonathan Lloyd for his sage counsel and kindness and everyone at Curtis Brown especially Melissa Pimentel, Jodi Fabbri and Sabhbh Curran.

I wrote most of this book in the London Library and would like to thank the staff and trustees of this wonderful unique place which has made such a difference to my working life and the books I write.

Thank you to my Shannon France for looking after our children and bringing joy and order into the house. To Maria Colom for showing me her studio and her beautiful paintings, and explaining how she works. To Gill Evans for exploring Highgate Cemetery with me, to Ginny Walton for taking me around St Marylebone Church and to Martin Neild spreading the rug 'neath the tree, metaphorically and actually. Thanks to Bea McIntyre for gardening info and being my real life idol and David Roberts for auction and art world information. Sometimes writers need a stroke of luck and so I would particularly like to thank the God of fate (don't know her surname) for letting me bump into Natasha Mitchell one desperate morning, and to Nat for coffee and advice and for helping to make one of the most important characters finally slot into place. A special thank you to my old History of Art teacher, Catherine Grubb, who taught us Victorian Art and Architecture as part of our syllabus and made it so enthralling that years later the research I did for this book felt like an enormous pleasure not a chore.

I would like to remember Penny Vincenzi who died earlier this year and whom I miss very much. She made me try to be a better writer but also a better person and I think about her all the time. Floreat circum PV.

I have been so lucky to go to so many wonderful places all over the country to do festivals or talks. So almost finally, thank you to all the lovely readers who have bought my books over the past few years and those who let me know they enjoyed them. You have no idea how much easier it makes this strange job. Thank you to you and to the booksellers and librarians who understand the power of putting books into people's hands in a world of phones and fake news.

Finally thanks to my love Chris and to the little Bossa. Also to my favourite boys Jake and Sam O'Reilly and their parents. But this book is for Martha, who was very small when I started it, and who is now, as she often likes to tell me, A Big Girl.

November 2018

The Garden
of
Lost *and* Found

Reading group guide

1. The idea of Nightingale House is a vital part of the novel. What impact do you think it has on the family members who live there? How is the response to the house different for each character?

2. The themes of motherhood and childhood run throughout the story. Consider the mothers in the novel and how they cope with and respond to their children. Are there any common themes? Or are the differences predominantly societal and / or due to different attitudes towards motherhood at different periods of history?

3. Throughout the narrative, many of the characters keep secrets and even tell lies. Why do they do this? How much of their behaviour reflects real family life?

4. Why do you think the painting of *The Garden of Lost and Found* is so symbolically important to Ned and Liddy, and for what different reasons?

5. The idea of the ideal family home plays a crucial part in this story. Do you think that, in the end, it is essential to the characters' ability to find happiness, or only a small part of it?

6. *The Garden of Lost and Found* is the eponymous painting of the novel. Other titles the author considered were *Songs from Nightingale House* and *Hope House*. Why do you think she chose this one in the end? Do *you* think it is the right title for the book?

7. Juliet's actions – removing her children from the home and taking them into an entirely new setting where she will raise them alone – are bold, yet she is not particularly outgoing herself. Is the act of uprooting oneself from one's life and starting afresh treated as an impractical fantasy or a far-sighted solution in the novel?

8. *'Isn't it funny,'* she said. *'We grew up next to a graveyard, too.'* Mary and Liddy had a traumatic childhood. Do you think they manage to overcome it? Would they be proud of their descendants and of the present-day residents of Nightingale House?